WHAT THE HEART KNOWS

Tarrant bit his lip and moaned. "Woman, do you know what you're doing to me?" He hoped that she was fully aware of how she affected him. If she wasn't, if she had any doubts, she could end this torture right now.

"Do I know?" Meleah echoed. "I know it goes something like this." She slid her palms up and down his shirt. She massaged up to his shoulders, over his arms.

"And this?" he said huskily, massaging her in slow, concentric circles. He could feel her heartbeat quicken under his sensitive fingertips.

"Umm-hmm," Meleah nodded, closing her eyes.

"And this?" he continued, rubbing his thumb against her swollen nipple.

"Yes!" Her voice came out on a sigh. She arched her back, offering more of herself to him.

"Meleah, are you sure you want to do this?" He wasn't sure why he'd asked. A feeling maybe. Maybe it was something in her expression, so open and trusting. She'd held on to her virginity as a secret treasure. Now, she was offering herself to him freely.

"I don't want to do *this,*" she echoed. "I want *you.*"

BOOK YOUR PLACE ON OUR WEBSITE AND MAKE THE ARABESQUE ROMANCE CONNECTION!

We've created a customized website just for our very special Arabesque readers, where you can get the inside scoop on everything that's going on with Arabesque romance novels.

When you come online, you'll have the exciting opportunity to:

- View covers of upcoming books

- Learn about our future publishing schedule (listed by publication month and author)

- Find out when your favorite authors will be visiting a city near you

- Search for and order backlist books

- Check out author bios and background information

- Send e-mail to your favorite authors

- Join us in weekly chats with authors, readers and other guests

- Get writing guidelines

- AND MUCH MORE!

Visit our website at
http://www.arabesquebooks.com

WHAT THE HEART KNOWS

GERI GUILLAUME

ARABESQUE
BET
BOOKS

BET Publications, LLC
www.msbet.com
www.arabesquebooks.com

ARABESQUE BOOKS are published by

BET Publications, LLC
c/o BET BOOKS
1900 W Place NE
Washington, D.C. 20018-1211

BET Books is a trademark of Black Entertainment Television, Inc. ARABESQUE, the ARABESQUE logo and the BET BOOKS logo are trademarks and registered trademarks.

First Printing: June, 2000
10 9 8 7 6 5 4 3 2 1

Printed in the United States of America

PROLOGUE

"Go on, ask her."

"I'm not gonna ask her. You ask her."

"It was your idea."

"Yeah, but you're the one she's been giving the eye."

"Yeah, right. You mean rolling her eyes. That honey's throwing nothin' but attitude this way. You're not getting anywhere with her. Just finish your beer and let's get out of here."

It wasn't Tarrant Cole's first choice to come out to Papa Jack's tonight. Saturday night at one of the hottest sports bars on Galveston Island wasn't his idea of a good time. He'd made a conscious effort to avoid the place without a good reason why. Maybe because the place was so popular, he'd purposefully avoided it.

The noise and the smoke and the lackluster effort from Houston's baseball team, the Astros, were doing nothing to put him in a party mood. He clucked his tongue in silent commiseration. He was hoping that they'd have another shot at the division championship this year. Not the way they were missing balls. "Aw . . . c'mon, Bell. You can catch those pop flies in your sleep!" Tarrant gestured at the television.

"Calm down, man. It's just a game." Jackie D laughed at him.

"You didn't say that when you had twenty bucks riding on them last week," Momo reminded them. "You blubbered like a baby. Sad, sad case. Nothing is more pitiful than a man crying in his beer."

"Waste of a good drink," Brock muttered, then signaled for their server to refresh his.

After spending half the morning washing, waxing, and tuning up his refurbished, antique white 1969 Chevy, Tarrant had wanted to cruise up and down the seawall to show off the benefit of his hard work. The sound of a sweet, finely tuned engine revving up and down the strip couldn't compete with the sound of a put-down from the acerbic hostess who'd greeted them at the door tonight—no matter how incredibly fine she was.

But the brothas insisted—Momo, Jackie D, and Brock. They had been his best friends since junior high school. Tonight, they'd all ganged up on him. It had been a while since they'd been to Papa Jack's. It had been a while since they'd had a reason to celebrate. The completed truck that Tarrant had so lovingly, laboriously pieced together had to be taken out on its maiden voyage. So Tarrant had to go along. Besides, someone had to be the designated driver tonight. It might as well be him. Even if one of the others had volunteered to be designated tonight, Tarrant didn't want any one of them behind the wheel of his new toy.

Lucky for Tarrant, the brothas made the decision for him. The way they were knocking back the drafts, Tarrant had the feeling that he'd have to pour them into the bed of his truck to get them home again. They kept the pitchers coming, hoping that the hostess, Le-Le, would be impressed with their free flow of cash.

"How much money you got on you, Rant?" Momo asked, thumbing through his wallet.

"The same amount of money I'm going home with," Tarrant retorted.

"I'm running a little low and she's looking this way again. I think we can swing her if we put up for one more pitcher."

"Man, put that thing away. No woman is going to take a man seriously who carries a wallet with yellow smiley faces and a Velcro closure." Tarrant gave a small snort of disgust. He'd caught the look she'd tossed in their direction, and impressed wasn't it.

They might have had a chance with her if Jackie D hadn't tried to press the palm of his hand against her derriere as she'd led them to their booth. Tarrant snatched Jackie D back just as he'd come within millimeters of touching her. She'd spun around, pinning Jackie D with a stare so hard, Tarrant thought they'd all fall down like pins in a bowling alley.

She couldn't have known what they were doing behind her back. Maybe it was instinct. Maybe it was some reaction from the patrons who could see Jackie D that tipped her off. Or maybe she caught their reflection in some of the security mirrors. Tarrant felt like a school kid, caught in the vicinity of another who'd just made a rude noise at the rear of the class.

"Beth will be your server for the evening," she'd said, indicating a booth and making a quick getaway without offering them as much as a menu in retaliation. Things got steadily worse after that. Convinced that all she needed was a little attention, the brothas did everything in their power to win Le-Le back. They sent drinks to her hostess station. They sent messages by way of the server, Beth, including all of their phone numbers in hopes she might promise to call them. When that didn't seem to show signs of thawing her out, as Tarrant knew it wouldn't, they got bolder—and drunker—and shouted her name whenever she passed by them. Nothing. Not even a twitch of a smile in their direction. Even glaring at them became too much for her.

Too bad, Tarrant silently lamented, sipping at his bottled water. It might have made the evening slightly more bearable if the tall, auburn-haired woman with the husky voice and the diamond-cutting glare had been friendlier toward them. He'd seen her turn a dazzling smile to other patrons when she stopped by to chat and, for a brief flight of fancy, Tarrant wondered what it might be like to have some of that effortless sensuality spread their way.

Without meaning to, he found himself tracking her with his eyes—watching the way she worked the room like a queen holding court. The vibrant, two-piece red and purple outfit that clung to her hips and molded to her breasts added to her regal aura. The muted shimmer of the silky rayon cut through the haze of smoke and the cacophony of video game bleeps, chirps, and buzzes to telegraph a primal instinctual message to Tarrant that said, *Reach out and touch me!* No wonder Jackie D was so tempted. Her outfit seemed out of place among the sea of drably dressed servers and bartenders. Yet it suited her to a T.

After an hour of listening to his friends strike out with more frequency than his home team, Tarrant set his bottle down on the table with a definitive thud. Enough of this! He could sit back and fantasize about a woman he would probably never get to know or he could go out and wrap his hands around the warm, smooth curves of his custom-made, mahogany steering wheel. To some, it might be a poor substitute. But Tarrant was comforted by the fact that if he put forth the least bit of effort, his honey would respond to him the way he wanted.

"I'm out of here," he said, tossing a few bills on the table.

* * *

"Station five is clearing out. You want me to pick up your tip for you, Ms. Harmon?"

"What tip?" Meleah Harmon looked up from the podium that listed the seating chart for the restaurant section of Papa Jack's. She remembered seating the most obnoxious foursome she'd seen in a long time at station five. If she didn't have to, she didn't want to talk to them again. A simple nod as they were filing out the door was about all she could make herself give right now.

"Those guys over there said I could take half of what was there. The other half was for you. I think one guy said you ought to take it and buy yourself a new attitude."

"You keep all of it, Beth. You earned it tonight."

"Yes, ma'am!"

Meleah smiled. Beth was new to Papa Jack's. She'd been working there only a couple of weeks—just short-timer enough and needing to impress enough to refer to all of the "old-timers" as sir and ma'am.

Give her a little time, Meleah thought. Beth would soon start calling her Le-Le along with the rest of them. She kept her back to the dining area, her eyes trained on the front door. If she was lucky, a new set of better behaved customers would come in. She could busy herself with them, and forego the "Come again!" pleasantries that she didn't want to spare on the rowdy group filing out.

"To tell you the truth, Ms. Harmon, I'm kinda glad to see them go, too. I was afraid that if they couldn't get to you, they'd start hitting on me. Bunch of overgrown, horny teenagers. That's what they are. That's all they wanted to talk about—women, sex, and cars. All three at once if they could."

Meleah leaned close and said tightly, "None of them

tried to touch you, did they, Beth? Because if they did, we're not having any of that!"

"No, ma'am! Like I said, it was you they wanted. As long as I kept throwing food and beer at them, the animals stayed in their cages." Beth lowered her voice. "Speaking of which, here they come."

Meleah glanced over her shoulder and wished she hadn't. At that moment, the front doors opened again and a wave of new customers poured in. Meleah thanked goodness for small favors. Grabbing a stack of menus from underneath the podium, she ducked her head just as the foursome squeezed past. A few more seconds and they would be gone.

When she raised her head again to address her patrons, her eyes unwillingly strayed to the front entrance. She'd almost gotten away with making them think she'd wished them into oblivion. *Almost.*

She'd locked gazes with the biggest, burliest of them. Tall. Head shaved clean. Enough earrings studding the length of his ear to set off an airport metal detector. He'd paused in the entrance and glanced over his shoulder just as Meleah thought it was safe.

For a moment, their gazes locked. Silent communication passed between them. The open interest in his wide-set hazel eyes contrasted with the deep disdain reflecting in her ebony ones. For every unspoken curse she could think to telegraph to him, he responded with a visual caress. Dueling with the eyes, came to Meleah's mind. Somewhere between them, their eyebeams crossed. And Meleah thought she could smell the ozone burning in the atmosphere from the heat of his stare. All of this happened in the span of a couple of heartbeats. Just long enough for her patrons to remind her of their presence and his friends to call him outside.

ONE

"Last call, everybody! Last call . . . And I mean it this time. Come on, now. Let's go. Move it! That means you, too, short stuff." Charlotte Clark, the head server at Papa Jack's Sports Bar and Restaurant, grasped the rope handle of the brass bell hanging over the highly glossed, rectangular mahogany bar.

Despite the complaints from the last of the Tuesday-night stragglers, she pulled the rope handle with a vengeance and rang the bell once, then twice, to encourage the stragglers to settle their tabs. Tuesday night was Ladies' Night at Papa Jack's. If Charlotte had seen it once, she'd seen it a thousand times. If you hadn't hooked up with someone by closing time, chances were you weren't going to. It didn't do any good to try to make the night last any longer. That didn't stop some of the patrons from trying, however.

When one of her regulars threw her an irritated look and opened his mouth to protest the interruption, Charlotte held up her hand to stop him. "Crack open that wallet, pay up, and get your wannabe Will Smith-lookin' self outta here! Don't be giving me that look . . . like I really disturbed your tired mack. You know you didn't have a chance with that woman, anyway."

"Come on, Charlie," he cajoled. "Give me five more

minutes. Five more minutes and me and . . . what's your name again, sweet thing?" He turned back to the unimpressed woman just in time to see her slide off the barstool and saunter away from him. "See what you did, Charlie? You could have just cost me the one! We coulda been good together."

"Speaking of costs, your tab is up to seventy-five bucks, Marshon." With one hand, she stabbed at a key on the cash register, making the cash drawer slide open. The other hand was thrust under his nose. "Make good on that."

"Let me see." The man named Marshon licked his thumb and started to rifle through the crumpled bills in his wallet. "Thirty . . . forty . . . forty-one . . . forty-two fifty . . ."

With a bleary-eyed glare, Charlotte snatched the wallet from him, grabbed a handful of cash, then tossed the wallet back onto the bar. She'd had enough. For the past hour, she'd fought off what well could have been the mother of all migraine headaches. Her back ached from repeatedly lifting her serving tray. Her feet were on fire. Orthopedic shoes, her left eye. She had a good mind to take those overpriced clogs back to the store and throw them through the window. At that point, she didn't care if Marshon had enough to cover his bill for the night. If she had to, she'd make up the shortfall. Besides, he'd be back.

"Oh, no you don't! Get away from the jukebox. Save those quarters to call yourself a cab." She chased away another customer. That lovesick lothario had been dropping coins into the jukebox like music was going out of style. Charlotte knew that if she heard that same sappy selection one more time, she'd scream.

"What about you, Le-Le? Another cup of coffee before I shut everything down for the night?" Charlotte wearily leaned both elbows on the bar and called out to the auburn-haired woman in wire-rimmed glasses sitting on the last stool. "Le-Le? Yo, Meleah!"

The young woman didn't hear her. "Sugar, don't make me walk down there," Charlotte groaned. But she picked up a decanter of coffee and shuffled to the end of the bar despite her aching feet.

Meleah sat hunched over the bar with her elbows planted firmly on the smooth surface. Her heart-shaped face was propped on her fists. She was mouthing the text from an accounting textbook as she read silently to herself.

"How 'bout another cup to see you off?" Charlotte suggested.

"No thanks, Charlie. I'm good for the evening." Meleah leaned beside her to pick up a huge leather shoulder bag. She plopped the overstuffed bag onto the bar with a thud and started to rummage through it.

Charlotte cleared her throat loudly. "Looking for these, sugar?" She held a rumpled package of cigarettes just out of Meleah's reach.

"Hey! You went into my purse," Meleah accused her.

"Who me?" Charlotte lifted her eyebrows and pointed to herself with mock innocence. "Would I do that? They just fell out."

"Fell out, huh? Yeah, right after you kicked my purse over," she grumbled.

"Speaking of kicking, I thought you'd kicked these filthy things."

"I did!" Meleah protested. "And I was doing good, too. Until finals rolled around. Geez, these exams are whuppin' my behind. I didn't know going back to school could be so rough. I wish I'd never dropped out to go to work." Meleah let her head fall to the bar with a soft thud.

"Is that any reason to ruin your health?" Charlotte demanded.

"I promise I'll quit again next week. I just need something to get me through finals, Charlie," Meleah said in a muffled voice.

"What about those patches I picked up for you at the drugstore?"

"Patches-schmatches. I'm wearing enough of those things to bulletproof my arm. Come on, Charlie. Give me back the cigarettes. This is my last pack, I swear." Meleah raised her head and pleaded with two of the largest, most woeful ebony eyes Charlotte thought she would ever see. Charlotte chewed on her lower lip—wavering.

"Come on, Charlie. Just one. No on will know but you, me, and the ashtray."

"Nope. No can do." Charlotte smashed the crush-proof box between her hands and tossed the package into the trash, ignoring Meleah's groan of dismay as she let her head flop forward onto the bar again with a muffled, "Ouch!" Meleah reached up to massage her forehead, then moaned, "Shoot me. Somebody just shoot me and put me out of my misery."

"You wanna talk misery, sugar?" At the moment, Charlotte was not feeling very sympathetic. "I took over your shift tonight because you said you needed to study. I'm taking these cigarettes from you because I want to see you live long enough to enjoy the fruits of all of *my* hard work. No more sneaking out back to light up, Le-Le. I mean it."

"You've got no heart, Charlie," Meleah grumbled. She lifted a coffee mug to her lips, took a swig, then grimaced as the ice-cold, tarlike liquid slid down her throat. She held a coffee mug out to Charlotte. "Maybe you'd better top this off, after all. I've got four more chapters to go before I can knock off for the night."

"Then what are you doing here trying to study? You should be home or at least in the office."

"I know . . . I know . . . but it's too quiet at home. Every time I settle down to study, I get distracted. And Dad's taken over the office. He's stinking up the entire place with those foul-smelling cigars. But every time he lights up he makes me want to light up, too. That's not making it any easier to quit."

Charlotte chuckled softly. "I'll bet you'll be glad if Jack gets that loan to add on your own office."

"Dad promised me that when I hand him my diploma, he'll hand me the keys to my own office. That's why I gotta hit these books and kick butt on these exams."

Charlotte started to reach for the green-handled decanter that held decaffeinated coffee.

"Uh-uh. Are you kidding?" Meleah placed her hand over the lip of her coffee mug. "If you give me decaf now, I'll be asleep before I can turn the page." She pointed to an orange-handled coffee decanter. "Better make it the rough stuff. I need to stay awake."

"I'm just glad it was a slow night," Charlotte said, her tone indicating that it was anything but slow.

Meleah got the hint and gave an apologetic shrug. "Sorry I left you stuck out tonight, Charlie. I really did mean to keep a closer eye on my station. But I kept sneaking in the back to take a . . . uh . . . ."

"Study break?" Charlotte suggested, lifting a sardonic eyebrow at Meleah.

"Yeah, study break. Those breaks kept getting longer and longer and before I knew it, it was quitting time. I promise you this, just as soon as finals are over, I'll—"

"I know, I know . . . you'll make it up to me. But I gotta tell you, sugar, what'll mean more to me than your taking over my shift. I want to see you walk across that stage, diploma in hand."

"Deal!" Meleah raised her mug in salute to Charlotte, then lowered her head to her textbook again.

Charlotte glanced around her to see if anyone was watching, kicked off one shoe, then bent over to massage her cramping toes.

"What are your trying to do, woman? Bring a herd of health inspectors down on us?" Jack Harmon, Meleah's father crept up behind Charlotte and grasped her around her ample waist. Charlotte squawked, and hopped on one foot.

"Jack Harmon! What's the matter with you, sneaking up on me like that? You near about gave me a heart attack!"

"What kind of coronary did you think I had when I saw you tromping around a food service area without your shoes on those crusty size twelves?"

Charlotte put her hands on her hips. "Twelve!" She squawked. "I'm a size nine-and-a-half, if you must know."

"Nine-and-a-half," Jack mused, stroking his chin. "Just what is that in dog years, Charlie?" He grinned at her.

"You'll find out exactly how much nine-and-a-half is when I plant one against your backside." She waved the orthopedic shoe in a mock threat in front of him before sliding it back onto her foot.

Listening to the exchange, Meleah rolled her eyes. She didn't know who they thought they were fooling. As soon as they thought no one was around to see, Jack would have the offending feet in the palms of his hands, massaging Charlotte until her sighs of stolen pleasure drowned out the crack-and-pop of her aching feet.

"I don't know why you've got your briefs in a bunch, sugar. Nobody's around to see me with my shoes off, anyway," Charlotte said, shifting her weight from one foot to the other.

"Wrong. That's what I came to tell ya. We've still got a few stragglers up in the pool room," Jack corrected.

Charlotte groaned. She didn't feel like climbing a flight of stairs to chase them out. She wanted to go home. "I thought you closed down the pool area after you caught some of them sneaking in alcohol."

"Woman, have you lost your mind? Close the pool area on Ladies' Night? That's when I make the most money off those tables. I threw out the ones I caught sneaking in the booze but left the tables open."

"Out of the goodness of your heart for all the innocent pool players still lining up quarters on the table for a game or two. Right, Pops?" Meleah said sardonically.

"That's right. Gotta reward the decent folks out looking for a good time. I don't need a bunch of idiots trashing my place. Even worse, geeked up on booze they didn't even buy from me."

"Nobody can get a good buzz going with the way you water down the liquor." Charlotte tapped Jack in the chest with an empty beer bottle.

Jack grasped for the bottle, and in doing so, clasped his hand briefly over Charlotte's. She stepped closer to him, murmuring something about busting that bottle over his head if he tried any sexual harassment stuff on her.

"I'll just go and . . . clear out the pool room myself, in case anyone's listening . . . or cares," Meleah called loudly. She shook her head, seriously doubting if Jack or Charlotte had heard her.

"Play nice, you two," Meleah said over her shoulder as she left them.

She strode past rows of wall-mounted television sets

tuned to different sporting events, rounded the corner, and skipped up a short flight of stairs where several rooms contained pool, shuffleboard, and air hockey tables. The group that had been twenty strong over an hour ago had dwindled down to three. But it didn't seem to Meleah that it was any less quiet. The three who remained more than made up for those who had already left—either on their own or at her father's insistence.

Meleah stopped just before the doorway, mustering her strength. Though she hadn't performed her usual duties as hostess tonight, she was just as tired as Charlotte. She'd spent the past week pulling all-nighters to study for her final exams. She didn't feel like hassling with customers either. Somehow she had to get them out of there without offending them.

Galveston, despite its tourist attraction status, was still a small island. Word that a place was unfriendly toward its customers could kill business quicker than a revocation of a liquor license.

Meleah stepped through the door and waited for several seconds before speaking. She quickly sized up the group, determining if she should call for extra help to convince these stragglers to go. There were three of them—two men and a woman. One of the lingering customers, a tall, thin man with dirty-blond hair tied back into a rat tail braid, was in the middle of a shot. He paused and walked around the table several times to get the best angle. Pulling heavily from his long-necked beer, he wiped his mouth on the back of his sleeve and settled over the table. Meleah thought the least she could do was to let the man have his final shot. Based on the heated conversation she heard as she stood at the door, the winner of this game would take home a considerable amount of cash.

The fact that they were gambling should have been

reason enough to ask them to leave. But like it or not, there was nothing she could do to stop a friendly wager between friends. So she stood and waited for the opportunity to break up the game.

"Eight ball in the side." Rat Tail leaned over his shoulder and spoke to a stocky man with a prominent gold tooth.

"If you make that shot, I'll pay your mama fifty dollars," Gold Tooth retorted.

"Keep talkin' about my mama, son, and I'll send this cue stick up your corner pocket," Rat Tail threatened.

"Stop talking trash and make the shot, Durell," complained a young woman—wearing a leather halter and matching miniskirt showing plenty of torso and thigh—from the corner. "They're about to run us out of here." She gave a nod to Meleah standing patiently at the door.

Meleah's nose twitched. A long, slender cigarette was poised between the woman's ringed fingers.

Charlotte would kill me, Meleah thought, if she even sniffed the smoke from the girl's cigarette. She couldn't bum a cigarette from her. She couldn't . . .

"Hey," Meleah said, edging next to the girl.

"Hey," the girl responded, blowing a plume of smoke in Meleah's direction.

"You . . . uh . . . got a . . ." Meleah glanced over her shoulder to see if Charlotte was hovering nearby. She then gestured at the cigarette burning between the girl's fingers.

"Sure. Here you go."

She tossed Meleah a pack and a gold engraved lighter.

Rat Tail swiveled his neck around and gave a low whistle of appreciation. As Meleah raised the cigarette, Rat Tail zeroed in on her pursed lips. "Lookee here, lookee here. Come to see me run the table on junior here, sweet thing?"

Meleah gave what she hoped was a professional but disinterested smile. *Here we go again!* She wondered if Rat Tail was friends with the bunch who'd harassed her all evening.

"One more shot and the pot's mine. After I show junior here a thing or two, why don't you and me take the cash and find some private, up-close and personal ways to blow it, sweet thing."

"Take your shot," Meleah said coolly. "It's closing time."

Belly Button, standing in the corner, burst into open, derisive laughter. "Looks like the only action you're going to see tonight is on that table, Durell."

Rat Tail turned to Belly Button. "Shut your hole."

"Don't tell me to shut up!" Belly Button shot back.

Again Meleah considered getting someone up here with her. This looked like it was going to get ugly. Scenes like this weren't unusual to Papa Jack's. Whenever you mixed aggression and alcohol, it usually ended with a shouting match or two. Usually she could handle it. She'd perfected the no-nonsense tone and the frosty glare to help her deal with rowdy patrons. Tonight, however, she couldn't muster up the energy for it. She was too tired.

"Cool it," Gold Tooth warned, glancing skittishly over his shoulder at Meleah. He knew she was only a couple of steps away from calling the owner—the same man who'd asked their friends to leave with the aid of a baseball bat.

"I don't know who he is . . . telling me to shut up," Belly Button continued sullenly. "Mess with me, Durell, and you'll find your sorry tail walking home."

"I said shut your trap!" Rat Tail barked and raised the cue stick as if to strike Belly Button.

Fatigue dropped away from Meleah in a sudden surge of anger. Gambling was one thing, but she wasn't going to stand by and let a customer bully another. Not in her place. The lighter and the unlit cigarette dropped from her fingers.

Before Belly Button could cry out or Gold Tooth could scramble out of the way, Meleah strode up to Rat Tail and snatched the cue stick from his grasp. She slammed it against the green felt table, making sure that it scattered the billiards to ruin his last shot.

"That's enough. Settle your tabs and get out."

Rat Tail redirected his hostility at Meleah—calling her a crude name that brought heated patches of anger to her cheeks.

"You know what, lover boy? I've changed my mind. I'm gonna do you and your friends a favor. Why don't you just forget about the tab. Go on and get out."

"No woman tells me when and where I can go, sweet thing." Rat Tail advanced, making Meleah retreat against a far wall.

Meleah glanced over at Belly Button, a silent, desperate plea for help. She'd been able to make Rat Tail back down by threatening to leave him stranded. Now would be a perfect time to step in again. Not that Meleah thought the woman owed her any favors. The sharing of one cigarette didn't make them soul sisters. Yet would she stand there and let Rat Tail attack her? It seemed to Meleah that one oppressed woman should come to the defense of another.

Rat Tail raised his hands, palm outward, as if to shove her. Instinct made Meleah bring her arms up and redirect the force of Rat Tail's attack. He wound up slamming his palms against the wall instead.

"Leave her alone, Durell!" Belly Button spoke up.

"Yeah, D. Let's just go. She said we didn't have to pay up." Gold Tooth started for the door.

"Not yet," Rat Tail gritted. Meleah turned her head. It was more than just beer making his putrid breath reek. He reeked of hard liquor. Maybe he was one of the ones Pop didn't catch sneaking in alcohol. "Not until sweet thing says she'll come along for the ride."

"You don't need her, Durell," Belly Button said petulantly. "You've got me."

Rat Tail made a coughing, scornful laugh deep in his throat. "You?"

"Yeah, me! You're tellin' me that you're gonna pass this up for *that*?" Belly Button smoothed her hands over her outfit, pausing at the swell over her ample breasts. She continued over her flat stomach and rounded, full hips.

Rat Tail barely gave her a second glance. "Been there. Done that," he flung over his shoulder. He then turned his red-rimmed eyes to Meleah. "Now, how about that ride, sweet thing?"

"Maybe you can get some table action after all," Gold Tooth encouraged. He joined Rat Tail at the door and reached up to finger the soft auburn braids curling around Meleah's ear.

"Don't touch me!" Meleah slapped his hand away.

"What's the matter, sweet mama? We're not good enough for you? Do her, Durell! Do her now!" Gold Tooth grabbed one of Meleah's arms while Rat Tail grabbed the other, his free hand clamped over her mouth as they dragged her toward the pool table. Meleah's eyes widened in fear and disbelief. She tried to scream. Yet she knew the muffled sound would barely make it past the room. If Charlotte and Jack had sneaked off to the back office to be alone, there was no telling when they would notice she was missing.

"Do her, Durell!" Gold Tooth urged, his breath hot and putrid in Meleah's face. He helped to slam Meleah onto the pool table as Rat Tail pinned her down with his knee.

Meleah twisted her head. Gold Tooth's fingers were clamped on to her mouth, squeezing so tightly she winced. Her breath quickened as she heard, rather than saw, Rat Tail unzip his pants. She began to struggle in earnest now—summoning reserve strength to fight him. Meleah wrenched her head to the side, her teeth viciously clamping down on Gold Tooth's fingers.

He yowled and jerked his hand away.

"Pops!" Meleah called out, her voice strident. "Charlie!" She should have listened to her instincts. She should have had someone up here with her.

"Shut her up!" Rat Tail hissed, struggling to hold Meleah still while straddling her.

Gold Tooth drew back his fist to strike her.

"Touch me and so help me it'll be the last thing you ever do!" Meleah threatened.

"Let her go before they call the cops on us," Belly Button warned.

"Chill, Amber. Knowing D's skill with the ladies, this will only take a minute." Gold Tooth cackled. "Half a minute when he's really excited. Beer's not the only thing that flows through him quicker'n spit."

"Look, I'm outta here. Hang around if you want to, but I'm telling you that Rant won't bail us out again if we're picked up. Are you coming or not? Durell? Chico?"

If Belly Button's warning didn't sway them, perhaps it was the sight of Jack wielding a baseball bat. Leon, the six-foot-one, nearly three-hundred-pound cook for Papa Jack's, crashed like a stampeding bull through the door. Charlotte's screeching at them, hefting a broom, and giving the wall a solid *thwack* let Meleah know that her own private cavalry had come to her rescue.

Leon grabbed Gold Tooth by the scruff of the neck and flung him to the floor.

"*Yeow!* Take it easy, *vato!*" Gold Tooth complained.

"Take your hands off of her," Jack growled, waving the bat.

"Le-Le, are you all right, sugar?" Charlotte grabbed Meleah by the arm and hauled her off of the table. She wrapped her up in her arms and squeezed her until her ribs squeaked. Pressing Meleah's face into her bosom, she stroked her hair and made soothing noises.

Meleah didn't have to give the details of what had almost happened to her. The look on her face was enough for Jack. He swung the bat, barely missing the top of Rat Tail's head by the breadth of a blond strand. The whistle of the near miss was enough to make Rat Tail cringe.

"Hold up there, old man." Durell backed away.

"We don't want any trouble," Belly Button said quickly.

"If you mess with me, you're gonna get trouble." Jack tapped Rat Tail in the chest with the bat. "Now get the hell out of here and don't come back. You hear me?"

"Call the police," Leon insisted.

"Throw those animals under the jail," Charlotte encouraged.

"Go on and call them, old man. But she started it," Belly Button complained, glaring at Meleah.

"I started it?" Meleah echoed incredulously.

"Who are you calling old?" Jack countered with equal indignation, sucking in his belly and flaring his arms.

Belly Button slipped her purse strap across her shoulder and fished out her keys. "We're out of here." As she passed Meleah, she fixed her with a hard glare.

Meleah could only stare back in confusion. Why was Belly Button so mad at her? She'd tried to stop Rat Tail from smashing her face in with a cue stick.

"He didn't need you," Belly Button whispered tightly. "I'm his lady. You got that? I'm his lady."

"You can have him," Meleah flung after her.

"Go on, get your sorry tails out of my place," Jack urged, pushing Gold Tooth in the small of his back with the top of the bat.

"You're gonna let them go? After what they just tried to do to Le-Le?" Leon said. "Do it, Jack."

"We don't want any trouble," Belly Button insisted.

"Meleah, are you going to follow through with pressing charges?" Charlotte asked.

"They were crazy drunk," Meleah hedged.

"That's no excuse," Jack said. "Le-Le, say the word and I'll have 'em busted."

"I just want to go home and wash the stink of this whole night off of me. If you call the police, it'll just be a lot of he-saids and she-saids. Let them go, Pops. Just let them go!"

"Good riddance," Charlotte added, sweeping after them. She turned to Meleah. "Are you sure you're all right, sugar?"

"Now will you give me that cigarette?" Meleah gave a wan smile.

Charlotte clucked her tongue, partly in sympathy and partly in scolding.

"Stay with her, Charlie," Jack directed, "while we take out the trash."

Charlotte and Meleah watched from the upper window as Jack and Leon ushered the trio out to the parking lot. Meleah trembled with suppressed rage as Belly Button turned back, looked up, then gestured at Meleah with a middle finger.

"Don't you pay that little tramp no never-mind," Charlotte said, patting Meleah.

"Out of sight, out of mind," Meleah murmured as she watched Belly Button climb behind the wheel of her sports car. Arguing still with Rat Tail and Gold Tooth, she sped into the night in a squeal of tires.

TWO

As she started for home, Charlotte debated taking her normal route along the Galveston seawall. At this time of the morning, the sky was still dark and filled with stars. With her convertible top down, she could enjoy the feel of the stiff summer breeze blowing strong off of the Gulf of Mexico. The sound of the surf crashing against the shore was the perfect background noise she needed to drive from her head the crowd noise from Papa Jack's.

Then again, maybe she shouldn't take the seawall drive. This was the beginning of the summer tourist season. Traffic along that route would be heavier, trickier to navigate even though it was almost two o'clock in the morning. The seawall drive had more than its share of drag strip drivers in souped-up sports cars. Or sightseers looking for a place to park would pull each and every trick in the book to get the best spot along the seawall. You never knew when someone, out of the blue, would whip a fast U-turn to get to that perfect curbside view. During the summer season, even the people strolling along the seawall seemed crazier. The joggers, skaters, cyclists, and strollers all jostled for space. You just never knew when someone would dart into the road. Did she feel like braving that tonight? Was it worth it to take the shorter route to get to her bed ten minutes faster than she would if she took an alternate route?

Her train of thought was abruptly interrupted as the wail of an ambulance siren and flashing lights came up quickly behind her. Charlotte pulled over to the far right to let the emergency vehicle pass. When the ambulance and two beach patrol cars sped by her, she continued on. Within a mile ahead of her, a section of the road had been blocked off. Bright red flares sputtered in the road. Galveston police were also on the scene, cautioning drivers to move carefully around them.

Charlotte clucked her tongue in sympathy. She tried not to stare as she passed the scene of the three-car accident. Morbid curiosity caused her to sneak a peek. A small sports car had rear-ended another car, pushing it into the path of an oncoming vehicle.

"Oh . . . oh, no!" Charlotte cried out in sudden recognition. That sports car! It looked like . . . no . . . it couldn't be . . .

She tried not to look as she crept past. But she had to know. Was it *them?* She shook her head as a team of emergency medical technicians covered the face of one of the car's occupants, a tall, thin man with half a bloodied scalp dangling past his ear. The paramedics lifted him into the gaping rear of the ambulance. Charlotte would not have given it a second thought if she hadn't recognized the distinctive silver dollar ponytail clip that barely held Rat Tail's blond strands in place.

When the phone rang at four in the morning, it jarred Tarrant Cole from a sound sleep. He answered it with undisguised disorientation and more than a trace of mild irritation. Fumbling for the telephone and jamming it against his ear, he muttered, "Not this time, Amber. Forget it. I'm not coming to get you. Call a cab."

He slammed the phone back into the cradle, only to have it ring back immediately. Mild irritation turned quickly to open hostility. He hadn't long gone to bed; and to be awake so soon after he'd lain down was enough to try the patience of any man.

"Damn it, Amber. I mean it this time. It's your mess. You get out of it."

His sister, recently turned houseguest after their parents had washed their hands of her, had taken his car and a couple of twenties without his permission. As soon as he'd discovered that they were missing, he knew exactly what would happen. She'd go off cruising with those trifling friends of hers, wind up at some dive along the seawall, and drink until the money was gone. Or those so-called friends would start a fight and wind up escorted none-too-gently in the back of a police car.

That had been the routine from the time Amber Cole had turned fifteen.

For several years, their parents had tried everything, from cajoling to counseling, to get her to settle down. When those tactics failed, they tried a stint of tough love—turning Amber out on her nineteenth birthday and cutting her off from the free flow of funds that helped to fuel her rebellion.

Sympathizing with the rebel in her that, as the older, responsible brother, he was never allowed to develop, Tarrant took pity on his sister. Convinced that he could help her, he relented when she had come to him in contrite tears. He would allow her to move in with him on the condition that she seek professional help to stop drinking. When she complained about the lameness of the AA meetings, he found a special support group for her.

For almost six months, she'd faithfully adhered to the few, reasonable rules he'd laid out for her. No drinking. No drugs. And no associating with those who did them. He could get her to give up the booze, but those loser friends of hers were a different story. They continued to hang around her, pretending that they were helping her through her crisis. Tarrant knew better. He held his tongue because Amber seemed to be less of a handful when they were around.

He had to give her an ultimatum after he caught that thick-necked, gold-toothed cretin going through his things. Echoes of the argument rang in his head as insistently as the phone he'd slammed down again. He was *this* close to taking that sucker off the hook or at least turning the ringer off so he could still get messages. He squinted at the tiny liquid-crystal display attached to the phone—the caller ID box. He didn't recognize the number. But that didn't surprise him. She could be calling from any number of places.

Tarrant could prevent those loser friends from getting into his home, but he couldn't stop Amber from going out. Even when he stopped making car payments on the car their parents had bought for her and allowed it to be repossessed, she didn't get the message. She got around some kind of way—either by cab or by bus.

Some kind of way—hell. He didn't want to count the times an odd twenty wound up missing from his wallet. When he confronted her with it, she insisted that she did it only when her friends were in trouble and needed her help. They were her friends—the only ones who knew where she was coming from and accepted her without so many rules and restrictions. He supposed making her ride the bus was the final insult to her twisted sense of what was fair. It was just too uncool to be seen riding the bus. When Tarrant started keeping his wallet literally under lock and key, Amber took one of his cars instead, banking on the fact that he wouldn't report it stolen.

He picked up the phone again. "Call again one more time and you can—" Tarrant began, then stopped when a male voice broke in quickly.

"Is this Tarrant Cole? Owner of a 1999 Dodge Viper? Texas license plate number—"

Tarrant shot up in bed, fully alert now as a young male voice, trying hard to sound official and compassionate at the same time, repeated the license plate number of the car Amber took from him.

"Yes. That's my car," Tarrant croaked. He cleared his throat and demanded, "Who is this?"

"Mr. Cole, this is Officer Gil Rayford, Galveston PD. Sir, I'm calling to inform you that your vehicle has been involved in a multivehicle collision."

"A multivehicle collision?" Tarrant closed his eyes, fighting a wave of nauseating panic rising from the pit of his stomach. *Amber!*

"Yes, sir," Officer Rayford continued. "An accident."

"I know what a collision is, Officer," Tarrant snapped.

"Yes, sir. I'm sure you do, sir." Rayford's tone was conciliatory.

"How serious was it, Officer . . . Rayford did you say your name was?"

"Yes, sir. It's Rayford. One fatality."

"My sister, Amber Cole, was driving my car tonight. Was she the fatality?" Tarrant could barely bring himself to ask. He barely dared to hope that she'd somehow escaped harm.

It could happen. He almost found himself wishing that the officer was calling to report that she'd been a victim of a car-jacking instead. Yeah, maybe that was

it. Knowing the way Amber liked to dress to attract
attention, Tarrant could easily create the scenario in
his head. Some lowlifes at one of those sleazy clubs
would have been watching her. Maybe someone saw
the car she was driving and decided to take it. Maybe
at any moment, she would call—carless, moneyless,
ashamed. But alive!

"I see on the incident report that a woman identified as Amber Cole was transported by ambulance to
the University of Texas Medical Branch here in
Galveston."

"How was she identified?"

"We found a purse with her driver's license at the
scene of the accident."

Tarrant breathed a silent prayer of thanks. Maybe
she'd escaped serious harm after all. If they could iden-
tify her by photo, maybe it meant that she wasn't that
bad off. "And her condition?"

"She was alive when they took her to the hospital,
Mr. Cole."

"Oh, thank God!" Tarrant pressed the telephone to
his forehead, trying to reel in his careening emotions.

"Mr. Cole? Are you still there?" Rayford's tinny voice
came over the line.

"Yeah . . . yeah, I'm still here," Tarrant replied.

"You can pick up your car at the police impound
at—"

"You think I care about a car! That was my sister,
Officer Rayford," Tarrant snapped. He leaped up from
the bed and reached for his shirt and trousers. He had
to get to Amber. He had to let her know that even
though she'd broken curfew and who knew what other
rules, that he still loved her. He still believed in her.
Once she was released from the hospital, they would
begin again to reestablish bonds of trust. Maybe this

time they could build bonds stronger than the bond of family and obligation.

Tarrant stopped, his arm partially crammed into his sleeve as a thought suddenly occurred to him. "Officer, have our parents been notified?"

"Not yet, sir. Yours was the first number I called."

"Good. Don't call them. Let me do that after I find out more about Amber's condition."

"Yes, sir. And about your car?"

"Scrap it," Tarrant said tersely.

"Scrap it?" Rayford repeated incredulously. "A dream car like that?"

Tarrant heard the envy in the young man's voice. "You want it? You can have it, son. It's brought me nothing but trouble."

"Sounds tempting, sir. But I don't think it's allowed."

"Do what you want, Officer."

"Yes, sir. But you'll have to come down anyway and sign the release forms."

After getting directions to the police impound from the officer, Tarrant thanked the man, then slammed the phone back into the cradle. He forced his mind to work logically, methodically as he wrote down the information that the officer had given him. Only after he'd compiled a list of action items—contact the parents, contact the insurance agent, arrange for in-home care for his sister—did he allow his emotions to overcome reason. He buried his head in his hands and wept openly.

"Are you all right, Uncle Rant?"

Tarrant's head snapped up, the unchecked flood of emotion quickly blocked for the benefit of the tousled-haired urchin staring at him from his bedroom doorway.

"Squeak, what are you doing out of bed?"

"I'm . . . I'm thirsty, Uncle Rant. Can I have something to drink, please?"

"You know you're not supposed to have anything to drink after nine o'clock."

Alexa Cole wrinkled up her nose, and for a moment, Tarrant thought he was looking at his sister as she used to look at him nearly fifteen years ago. Amber's eight-year-old daughter Alexa was the spitting image of her.

"I promise I'll go right to the bathroom, Uncle Rant."

"Come on, you." Tarrant swung her up in his arms and tweaked her pigtail. Alexa giggled and rubbed her chubby hands over Tarrant's clean-shaven head. She wrinkled up her nose again and said, "When you said haircut, you really meant it, didn't ya, Uncle Chrome Dome?"

"We'll see about Uncle Chrome Dome if I have to do laundry for you before the end of the week, Squeak," he returned.

"I stopped wetting the bed when I was two years old, Uncle Rant."

"Then what was that all about when—"

"Oh that," Alexa said casually. "That was an accident."

"See? That's exactly what I meant."

"No! I meant I spilled my juice in the bed when I was reading under the covers."

"Oh . . ."

He carried her into the kitchen, set her on the counter next to the refrigerator, and pulled out a carton of juice. He pinched the opening and shook it several times before handling her the carton.

"Here. Take a hit of this: mango-orange-papaya juice. It'll put hair on your chest."

"When I fill out and get a chest," she retorted.

Alexa grabbed the carton with both hands, tilted it

to her lips, and drank straight from the carton. It was all right, her uncle told her often enough. Drinking right out of the juice carton or milk jug had its advantages, as long as she didn't spill any on her clothes to make more laundry for them to do. Besides that, it kept the glasses clean. When she was done, she handed the carton back to her uncle.

Tarrant gulped down several swallows before placing the near-empty carton back into the fridge. At the moment, he could have settled for something stronger— something about one hundred and eighty proof. But he had to keep a clear head. He started to wipe his mouth on the back of his sleeve but Alexa cleared her throat meaningfully.

"Get a napkin, Uncle Rant. Geez, what's the matter with you? We'll be washin' all day trying to get that juice stain out."

"Sorry, Squeak." He grinned at her. "I almost forgot myself." His smile quickly faded as he remembered what had gotten him out of bed in the first place. "Listen, Alexa . . ."

"Uh-oh. Am I in trouble? What did I do this time?" Her tone was long-suffering.

"Why do you say that?"

" 'Cause you called me Alexa. The only time you do that is when I'm about to be put on punishment."

"You're not in trouble," he said, smoothing over her hair. "I want you to get some things together. Some clothes, a few toys, crayons—whatever it is you little girls cram into your backpacks. I have some business to take care of. I want you to stay with Miss Julie."

"Miss Julie?" Alexa's voice was clearly disappointed. "Why I gotta stay with her?"

"Because I said so," Tarrant said bluntly.

"Why can't you just wait for Amber?" Alexa asked. "She can watch me."

Tarrant ground his jaw shut, on the verge of insisting that Alexa address her mother as such. It was a losing battle—one that even Amber didn't care to take up. It didn't bother Amber having the child nearly as much as it did when the child referred to her as mother.

"You're going to Miss Julie's," Tarrant insisted.

"You know she doesn't like me."

"That's not true, Squeak. She loves having you around."

"She only pretends to like me so you'll like her."

"Who told you that?"

"Nobody had to tell me. I knew it even before I heard her yakkin' on the phone to her girlfriends."

"You shouldn't eavesdrop, Squeak. It's not polite."

"It's kind of hard not to listen, Uncle Rant. As soon as you walk out the door she's on the phone." Alexa put her hand to her ear as if she was talking on the phone and gave her rendition of Tarrant's friend. " 'Yeah, girlfriend. That Tarrant Cole is the bomb! Just give me five minutes with him alone. Just five minutes. I'll jump start that engine of his, for sho!' That woman is a skeezer, Uncle Rant. She just wants to get into your pants."

"That's no way for a young lady to talk. You behave yourself while I'm gone, Squeak," he warned her. "I'll be back as soon as I can."

"You didn't say why we can't wait for Amber, Uncle Rant."

"That's right. I didn't. Now go on. Get your rear in gear."

He lifted her off the counter and sent her to her room with a swat on the behind. Alexa was a smart kid. Too smart. But she was still a child. There was no sense in worrying her with sketchy details until he knew more.

Tarrant went back into his bedroom to finish dressing. He picked up the notes he'd written to himself and crossed through the one about signing the papers to get his car back. The last thing on his mind was some bureaucratic release forms.

"And this one, and this one, and this one." The attendant on duty at the UTMB-Galveston emergency ward handed Tarrant a clipboard stacked with several hospital forms and indicated that he take a seat in the waiting area.

"All I want to know is—" Tarrant began.

She cut him off, pointing to the seat. "As soon as she's out of triage, you'll know what I know, Mr. Cole," she said crisply. She then turned her back on Tarrant, unimpressed and unintimidated by his resulting glower.

Raising both hands in acquiescence, Tarrant took a seat as she directed. He supposed he had to give this equivalent of a drill sergeant running the emergency room her due. How she managed to exude the essence of calm and control in the midst of what seemed like chaos to him, he'd never know. She'd stood up to him and made him back down when he'd been able to push himself to the front of the long line.

Tarrant was not a small man. He liked his meat and his potatoes. He worked out to keep on top of the bulk that could easily run away from him. His girth alone should have been enough to make the tiny emergency room attendant quake. Coupled with the full force of his scowl, Tarrant expected that she would give him the royal treatment.

But she didn't. He'd have to wait and worry with the rest of the emergency room occupants until the doctors working on Amber indicated that it was all right to see her.

"You're going to be all right. Do you hear me, Amber? You're going to be just fine." Tarrant sat by his sister's bedside, stroking her swollen face and trying to reach her through the fog of medication.

"I'm so sorry, Rant," Amber moaned, tears rolling down her cheeks over the laceration stitches. "I didn't mean to wreck your car. I didn't mean it . . ."

"Shh . . . don't worry about that now. The important thing is that you're safe. The doctors are going to fix you up just fine. They're gonna run some tests then get you fixed up."

"Not my fault," Amber struggled to say. "This time, I tried to do the right thing. I tried . . . didn't drink . . . I didn't . . . I didn't."

"I know it's not your fault, Amber. I'm not blaming you," Tarrant insisted.

"It was Durell. He snatched the wheel from me. He wanted to go back to that bar to wait for that girl."

"Durell." Tarrant muttered that name as a curse. He knew that scumbag would come to no good end. But did he have to drag his sister down with him when he went?

Amber shook her head. It wasn't Durell's fault either. If it weren't for that bitchy boss lady at that bar, throwing them out, setting those goons on them, Durell wouldn't have gotten so mad. He wouldn't have put up a fight when she got behind the wheel. No, it was that woman's fault. Who did she think she was eyeing her man, making him want her instead of Amber? Durell was her man. Hers!

"Not D's fault either, Rant. It was *hers*. All her fault."

Tarrant shook his head in confusion, wondering if

the medication and the trauma had affected Amber. She was the only woman in the car.

"Who's fault?" Tarrant leaned close. "Who, Amber? Who caused the accident?"

Amber Cole fought to remain conscious. What did that old man call that woman? Something with an *M*. Melanie? Melissa? No, something exotic sounding. Meleah! That was it! Amber mustered the last of her strength and croaked. "She caused it, Rant. The woman at the bar. Meleah."

"What bar? How did she cause the accident, Amber?" Tarrant pressed. "What did she do?"

But the effort was too much for her. Tarrant stood by helplessly as Amber closed her eyes and succumbed to the pain medication and the peace of mind it offered.

Tarrant sat in the chair beside her bed, staring at his sister. "No, Amber. This time, it's my fault," he muttered to the quiet room. No. Not so quiet. The buzz and hum of Amber's monitoring devices disturbed the silence. With each beep and bleep of her heart monitor, Tarrant thought he heard condemnation.

"My fault. My fault. My fault."

He couldn't blame anyone but himself. He was responsible for her well-being. He'd promised their parents that he'd watch out for her. Tarrant winced. He still hadn't called them. He was avoiding it, wanting to talk more with the doctor about Amber's condition before telling them. At least that's what he told himself. He knew the truth. He simply didn't want to face them now.

Some big watchdog brother he turned out to be. He should have known he couldn't handle her. What made him think he could this time? History had already proven that he didn't have what it took to be big brother protector.

Tarrant rubbed his tired eyes, but he couldn't wipe away the image of his sister lying there in the hospital. A bittersweet wave of déjà vu swept over him. This wasn't the first time he had to stand vigil over her. This wasn't the first time he had sat in silent condemnation of his abilities as big brother.

They were kids—only kids. He was fourteen and Amber was seven. Their parents were going to be gone only a couple of hours. He could handle watching her for a couple of hours, couldn't he? No sweat. He had it all under control. All he had to do was sit her out in the front yard with her dolls and her crayons, then he could do pretty much what he wanted.

When a group of teenagers from the high school he would be attending next year drove by in what Tarrant considered his dream car, a 1965 candy-apple-red Mustang, Tarrant didn't think twice about leaving the front yard. He was only going to chat them up a little bit; find out where they got it. Maybe he would put the word out that he was looking to own one someday, too.

When they offered him a ride to the end of the block and back, there was no doubt that he wouldn't go. Even then, Momo, Jackie D, and Brock had their brotherly hold over him. What was it they had told him? Zero to light speed in sixty seconds? He took one look at his sister and hopped in. He'd be gone only sixty seconds. Just up the block. Another sixty seconds and he would be back. Nothing could happen in two minutes. Amber would never even notice that he was gone.

Two minutes somehow stretched for ten. Ten minutes! God, how he wished he could get those ten minutes back. He would have given anything. Anything!

The sight of his sister, lying in the road after being struck by a car . . .

Tarrant cursed, driving out the memory, dulling the sounds of the ambulance that took her away, the rage and disappointment in their parents' voices echoing off the waiting room walls, and the heavy weight of distrust and recrimination that followed him for years to come.

When Amber had come to him, begging to be allowed to live with him until she could get her act together, Tarrant snatched at the chance like a drowning man to a life preserver. Maybe that's why he'd gone so easy on her. He didn't force the issue when he knew she wasn't making her AA meetings. He ignored the money that somehow disappeared from his wallet. He closed his eyes to her party binges. If he'd really been trying to help her, he wouldn't have left his car keys easily accessible to her.

What was he trying to prove? That he could be a supportive brother? That he trusted her? He should have made her earn his trust. And now she was lying here, asking him to believe in her once more.

"Where do we go from here, Amber?" he murmured aloud. "What am I supposed to do now?"

Tarrant knew she could not answer him, and probably would not be able to for another twenty-four hours. She would be stable enough to withstand the surgery. It would take at least that long for the medicine to work through her system, for him to believe that her senses weren't impaired. But she'd been so sure this time—so convinced of her innocence.

"There's only one way to find out what happened last night, darlin'," he murmured, stroking her hair. "You rest easy now. Big brother is on the case."

* * *

Just get off my case!

Tarrant squeezed his lips together to keep from shouting at his parents. He stood in the waiting room, his arms folded stubbornly across his chest. The only indication that he was listening to the tirade was the spasmodic tic in his jaw caused by the superhuman effort to keep his mouth shut.

He didn't want to call them. He avoided it as long as he could. When he finally made the call, he sat in the waiting room—dreading the arrival of his parents as much as he did the report of Amber's progress from the doctor.

When his parents finally arrived at the hospital, Tarrant was sitting in the waiting room, with his head hung low. A Styrofoam cup of coffee—the coffee long since gone cold—rolled back and forth between his hands. His expression was bleak as he stared at some invisible spot through the cup, beyond the floor.

His mother, Beryl Cole, reached him first. She placed her multiringed hand on his shoulder and squeezed. Tarrant reached up and squeezed back before actually looking into his mother's concerned face.

"Rant? What in God's name happened to her? What happened to my little baby?"

"God had nothing to do with this!" Tarrant's father, Ashton, bellowed. "Somebody tell me how the hell you managed to let Amber wind up in the hospital again?"

Tarrant shot up, spilling the contents of the cup on the waiting room floor. The abruptness of his movement startled his mother. The fury on his face frightened her. Tarrant's father reacted to the implied threat by swelling up and bumping Tarrant's shoulder with his own. "Answer me, boy."

"Ash, please!" Beryl edged between them. "Not here. Not now."

"I asked you a simple question, boy." Ashton lowered his voice but didn't back away.

"I told you all I know over the phone. I got a call in the middle of the night from the police. Amber must have gotten a set of my keys and gone drinking."

"Oh, Rant," Beryl moaned. "My poor baby."

"We sent her to you so you could watch her." Ashton stabbed his finger into Tarrant's chest.

"Wrong as usual, old man." Tarrant slapped his father's hand away. "You didn't send her to me. She came to me after you threw her out. She didn't have anywhere else to go. Amber's wild but she's not crazy. She knew if she tried to shack up with those friends of hers, she'd have been dead long before now."

"She's not . . . she's not dead?" The bluster blew out of Ashton. He sank into the vinyl covered seat.

Tarrant shook his head no. "She's in surgery. Head trauma is all they'll tell me."

"How long has she been in there?" Beryl asked.

"An hour. Maybe more. Maybe less. I don't know. I don't know anything anymore."

"What about . . . the little girl?" The disgust in Ashton's voice was undisguised.

"Her name is Alexa, old man. And she's your grand-daughter. What's the matter with you? Why can't you accept that?"

"Where is she, Rant?" Beryl echoed.

"I left her with a friend, Mama."

"You shoulda left her with her daddy . . . if we knew who the cradle-robbing son of a bitch was."

"Ash, watch your language," Beryl said automatically. "You go and get that child, Rant. Get her some things together and bring her home to me. She shouldn't be left with strangers at a time like this. She should be with family."

"She's a stranger to me," Ashton grumbled.

"But she doesn't have to be," Beryl insisted. "Will you do that for me, Rant? Bring her home."

"I'll do it, Mama. Squeak will get a real kick out of it. She talks about Granny and Grandpa all of the time."

Beryl's eyes misted. "You call her Squeak. I suppose that's about right. What was it you used to call Amber?"

"You mean, the little snot?" Tarrant suggested.

"Nice try." Beryl's mouth twisted into a wry smile. "I know it was a four-letter word that started with *s* and ended with *t.*"

"I'm surprised you remember that." Tarrant looked sheepish.

"Your mother has a very long memory. In fact, I'm still paying for things I did back in nineteen thirty-two," Ashton complained.

"Speaking of long, I suppose it's a good sign that she's been in so long, isn't it? I mean, if there was no hope for her, we'd have found out by now, wouldn't we?"

Again Tarrant squeezed his mother's hand. "Keep praying, Mama. Just keep praying."

"If my baby pulls through this, I'm gonna—"

"What?" Tarrant interjected, resenting that his father always turned the conversation to himself. "What are you going to do for her, old man, that you couldn't do six or seven years ago when she started getting into trouble? Huh, old man? You tell me that."

"What could I do? Obviously more than you could do for her. Maybe I was wrong to put her out. All of that talk show psychobabble about tough love . . . I fell for it and I screwed up. So sue me. I'm an old man. What's your excuse, big brother? Huh? You let her trick you into thinking that she'd change, that she was even capable of changing. Truth is, she punked

you, boy. She took your money, your keys, your car.
She and those friends took you as easily as if you'd
bent over for them and said—"

Tarrant reached out and jerked his father to him by
the collar. No small feat since, even at sixty-eight,
Ashton Cole still had considerable girth.

"That's enough!" Beryl's voice cut in sharply. She
edged between them once again. "I said stop it, and
I mean it. Tarrant, let go of your father."

Tarrant wished he could. He wished he could let go
of his father. He carried the weight of his father's disappointed expectations in him like he imagined that
Santa Claus carried around the sack of misfit toys.
Didn't ask for it. Didn't need it. But he couldn't let
go.

Beryl tried a different tactic. "Rant, I could use some
coffee. Could you get me some coffee, son? Please?
Please!" She had to pry Tarrant's fingers from his father's shirt by force, one by one. "Go on, son. Go on."

Once he was out of earshot, Beryl whirled on her
husband. "You have *got* to ease up on him, Ash. You're
going to drive him too hard. You'll lose him for good."

Ashton grumbled in his throat, rattling phlegm as
if he had the urge to spit. His nostrils flared as he
struggled to breathe. "That boy . . ."

"That boy is a man, Ashton. A grown man. He was
a boy when he let Amber get hurt the first time. And
that was so long ago. You can't keep punishing him
for that."

"That was my baby, Beryl."

"She was my baby, too, Ashton Cole."

"But look how she turned out. She wouldn't be
so . . . so . . . I don't know." He struggled for the
right words. "She hasn't been right since the accident."

"Amber is who she is," Beryl insisted. "You can't

heap all of that guilt and blame for how she turned out on Tarrant."

"I wouldn't be so hard on him if he showed the least bit of remorse for leaving her like that. She was just a baby. We trusted him to watch out for her. But then, just like now, he sits there, his head full of all of that macho man crap . . . too much of a big man even to apologize. And where does he get off? Bucking up against me like that? I can still turn him over my knee, you know. He's not too big for me to take a strap to."

"You know where he gets it from, don't you?" Beryl folded her arms across her chest and regarded her husband with a mixture of annoyance and adoration. "He gets it from his papa. You know you don't mean all of that bluster, Ash. You've never laid a hand on those kids. I wouldn't let you. You're just shooting off at the mouth. But does that mean you don't love him? Of course not. And Tarrant wouldn't be here if he didn't care about his sister. As for remorse, there isn't a day that goes by that he doesn't suffer the pain of poor judgment. When he was a boy, we treated him like a man. Maybe too soon. But now that he's a man, Ash, you've got to stop treating him like a child. It's tearing you both apart. Is that what you want? You want your son to become a stranger to you?"

"No." Ashton blew out his breath. "You know that. It's the last thing that I want."

THREE

Papa Jack's on a Saturday night was the last place Tarrant wanted to be. He fought back the wave of déjà vu that threatened to overwhelm him. He was here just a week ago. He didn't enjoy it then; he certainly wasn't looking forward to being here tonight. Not alone. Not without the brothas. The only reason he'd been resigned to come back here was to get some of the answers that Amber could not provide.

Until he and the police had all the facts, Tarrant knew that not having those answers was the only thing keeping them from charging his sister with manslaughter—voluntary, involuntary, or vehicular. Tarrant ground his teeth together. The distinction of how they charged his sister didn't make a bit of difference to him. She'd still be rotting in a jail cell. If there was any chance at all that she wasn't at fault—any chance at all—he had to grab at it.

He had Officer Rayford fax him a copy of the accident report. The report said that his car had swerved into the path of oncoming traffic. Eyewitness reports corroborated the report. However, no one could give a reason for the swerve. No crazy tourists darting in the road. No spills on the causeway—not even a stray bird flying into the windshield.

The investigator's initial suspicion had been that this

was an alcohol-related incident. But Amber had not
been drinking that night. She'd been adamant about
that. She'd even demanded on the scene to be allowed
to take a Breathalyzer test. No problem with the police
complying with that request. When it came back negative, Tarrant insisted that the doctors at the hospital
perform other tests to disprove she'd been under the
influence of drugs. If they also came back negative, he
could turn his big brother instincts elsewhere. No alcohol. No drugs. Yet the accident had occurred. No
disproving that. All Tarrant had was a name uttered
by his sister and that crumpled cocktail napkin. It was
all he had to go on, since every time Tarrant tried to
bring that night up to Amber she closed up tight. She
refused to talk or she suddenly became very woozy.
Maybe he pressed to her too hard. The next thing he
knew, they were calling him back to the hospital. Amber was now in a coma. He became more determined
than ever to find out who had done this to her. So
Tarrant went back to Papa Jack's, grasping at the last
chance to prove that he could be big brother protector.

The place looked harmless enough. Nothing to dis-
tinguish it from the scores of other holes-in-the-wall
dotting the island. But it was close enough to the
seawall, with just the right amount of garish, glowing
neon lights to attract a steady stream of Saturday night
cruisers looking for a good time. There was enough
traffic moving around Papa Jack's to make driving in
his newly refurbished '69 Chevy a nightmare. If one
more hotshot peeled out of that parking lot, sending
up thick clouds of gravel and dust to nick the antique
white finish on his truck, he'd have to step out and
have words. It had taken him a long time to find all
the parts to restore that baby. He already had a buyer
lined up for it. He didn't want to dicker over the price

because some knucklehead with a heavy foot couldn't slow down enough to keep the gravel from flying.

He circled the parking lot several times before finally making his own parking spot near the side entrance of the restaurant. Checking for any tow trucks eager to make an easy haul of the illegally parked vehicle, Tarrant fell into step behind a group about to enter. When one of the male members of his adopted party grew suspicious of the open, interested glances his female companion tossed in Tarrant's direction, Tarrant slowed to hang back a little more.

Once through the entrance, Tarrant's eyes immediately zeroed in on the hostess station, expecting the one named Le-Le to greet him with a double dose of sensuality and scorn. She wasn't here tonight. At least, at the moment, a young man with a scraggly looking goatee occupied that position. Tarrant almost grinned. He wouldn't be checking out that action tonight—not like he did when Le-Le held the spot a week ago.

The crowd he'd walked in with split left to head for the bar. Tarrant moved right to stand in front of the podium.

"How many in your party tonight, sir?" the host greeted him.

"Flying solo tonight," Tarrant replied, looking around just in case Le-Le was in hearing distance. It had been only a week. Not long enough for her to forget their rowdy behavior but maybe long enough for her to forgive.

"Smoking or nonsmoking?"

"Non."

"Right this way, sir." He led Tarrant to a small table that overlooked the main floor. Rectangular bar to the left, stairs leading to another level to the right of him. The smell of fried food hung heavily in the air. A blaring jukebox competed with the sounds of enthusiastic sports fans cheering their favorite teams from wall-mounted television sets.

It was pretty much as he'd remembered it the night he and the brothas were here. Tarrant closed his eyes, trying to picture Amber here the night of the accident. He knew his sister, knew her tastes. He tried to reconcile what he knew about his sister with what he was witnessing here tonight. This wasn't exactly a place to host the kiddie hour. Tarrant didn't like to think that Amber would be hanging out in a place like this. Maybe it was a case of holding her to a higher standard. After all, he and his friends were hanging out at Papa Jack's. Yet it didn't surprise him that Amber would pick this spot to chill with her friends, too. If Papa Jack's was as jumping on Tuesday as it was here tonight, it would have attracted his sister here.

Still, he wasn't sure that this was the right place. He had only a name to go on—the name she'd whispered before slipping into sedative-induced sleep. That and a crumpled cocktail napkin he'd found in her purse were literal straws he'd grasped to help clear his sister of any involvement in the accident.

Moments later a young man dressed in a striped referee uniform and dark pants whizzed past his table. "Be right with you, sir!"

"Take your time." Tarrant waved him off. He was in no hurry. As far as everyone else in the restaurant was concerned, he was here to kick back, take in a game or two, maybe polish off a few beers. Nice and relaxed. Just like everyone else. In the meantime, he'd wait and watch for the woman named Meleah.

"Back in a sec." The kid whooshed by him again, hefting a tantalizing platter of sizzling beef fajitas, grilled peppers, and onions.

"Still here," Tarrant murmured, scanning the crowd. Full house tonight. Papa Jack's was doing pretty well for itself. Maybe it wasn't as much of a dive as he had suspected.

By the third time the kid passed him, Tarrant was starting to get a little edgy. Enough was enough. He was doing fine until he smelled those grilled onions. He raised his hand to get the young man's attention.

"Say, Trae. Isn't that your station?" Charlotte jerked her thumb at Tarrant's table.

Trae twisted. "Oh, yeah, I almost forgot about him."

"What's the matter with you?" Charlotte slapped her hand against the back of Trae's head. The resounding slap sounded worse than it actually felt. "I thought I warned you about that. You've got to hit each and every station at least three times if you want a decent tip."

"I did hit the table!" Trae protested, rubbing his head. "I just didn't stop and he didn't make me."

"What do you mean, he didn't make you?" Charlotte snapped. "What does he have to do? Stick out his foot and trip you?"

"I'm telling you, Charlotte, that he never said a word to me about an order. Not even a drink."

"That means he's not here for the food. And he's not watching the game. I wonder what he is here for?"

"I think he's a narc," Trae muttered out of the corner of his mouth. "After the trouble Jack and Le-Le had on Tuesday, I wouldn't be surprised if the entire Galveston PD started crawling around the place."

"Nah! He's no undercover cop. Too conspicuous." Charlotte quickly dismissed the idea. Kind of hard to miss him. Big guy—at least six-three or six-four. He had the physique of a professional athlete. Dressed plainly enough in a black T-shirt, well-worn jeans, and loafers without socks, giving Charlotte the impression that he was no slave to fashion. But she could spot the genuine leather band of his Rolex watch from across the room. Charlotte's eyes narrowed. Those ratty jeans didn't fool her for a minute. He was dressing down on purpose.

"Just to be sure, Trae, why don't you let me take that station. You weren't here that night. If he is a cop, you wouldn't be able to tell him anything and you don't need to get involved."

"Fine by me. If you're gonna take him, can I go on my break now?"

"Yeah, sure," Charlotte said distractedly. As he filed past him she muttered, "Last break for you tonight, junior. You've hardly broken a sweat as it is."

She grabbed a menu, filled two baskets—one with pretzels, the other with peanuts—and filled a frosted mug with a cold, frothy draft. Plastering a pleasant smile on her face, she set the peace offering on the table in front of Tarrant.

"Welcome to Papa Jack's, sugar. I'm Charlotte, I'll be your server for the evening."

"What happened to the rocket man?" Tarrant meant the kid who'd left him sitting at the table without as much as a pack of crackers to munch on.

"Well, since you're a first-timer to Papa Jack's, I thought you'd like the royal treatment. What will it be?"

Tarrant almost smiled. Technically it wasn't his first time. It had just been a while. The Saturday he and the brothas wound up here felt like his first time. Did he receive the royal treatment? Yeah, the royal cold shoulder from the ice princess. Well, no sense in beating around the bush. He might as well get what he'd come for. But before that . . .

"The fajitas look good," Tarrant murmured.

"Grilled onions melt in your mouth," Charlotte said

promptly and noted that he hadn't even looked at the menu. No, he definitely wasn't here for the food, and he'd shown no interest in the baseball game playing out on the television above his head.

"Anything else?"

"Yeah . . . I'm looking for someone. I don't know if she works here or not."

"I've been with Papa Jack's since the doors opened. I know all of the regulars. Why don't you tell me who you're looking for and *maybe* I can help," Charlotte said amiably. But she was certain to stress the word *maybe*. No promises, implied or otherwise. If he was a cop, she wasn't about to turn anyone in if they were part of Papa Jack's family. And if he wasn't, if he was trouble, she definitely wasn't going to talk.

Tarrant leaned forward in his chair, regarding Charlotte suspiciously. He didn't buy that honey-sweet, hometown amiability. She had no reason to help him. Why would she offer? Then again, what could he lose by asking. If she lied and claimed she didn't know this Meleah person, it would all come out if this case went to trial anyway.

"Her name is Meleah," Tarrant said simply.

Charlotte lifted an eyebrow. "No last name?" A cop would have a first name, last name, and maybe even a photo to flash around. She'd seen enough police dramas on TV. They always had at least a mug shot when they were searching for someone. This man wasn't a cop. That worried her even more, now that she'd eliminated that possibility. What was he? He was still trouble, but he was trouble of a different breed.

This time Tarrant did smile. It wasn't as if the name was very common. She either knew the woman or she didn't.

"Maybe she's a professional," Tarrant replied. "You know, the kind who goes by only one name." When he caught a flicker of something in Charlotte's eyes, he had his answer. She knew her all right. And she hadn't liked his inference.

"Why are you looking for her?" Charlotte asked bluntly.

"I just need to ask her a few questions."

"About?" Charlotte pressed.

"Are you going to bring my order or not?" Tarrant deliberately evaded the question.

"Yes, sir. Be back in a sec," Charlotte gritted.

"Yeah, that's what rocket man said," Tarrant retorted, and leaned back in this chair to mollify himself with the beer and pretzels until his order came.

Fifteen minutes later, Charlotte returned to his table and set down the order without a word. She whisked the near-empty mug on top of her serving tray and replaced it with a full one. Tarrant accepted the food with a wordless nod of thanks. He bent his head to his food, then looked up again when he noted Charlotte still standing over him.

"Thank you," he said, intending to dismiss her. He jerked his head in the direction of her station at the bar for emphasis. Charlotte hesitated, opened her mouth as if she wanted to say something, and thought better of it. When Meleah came on for the evening, she'd tell her that this man was looking for her. And if Meleah decided to go over to him, Charlotte would make darn sure that she hung around to find out what he wanted. She had an uneasy feeling about him.

If it hadn't been for that incident, Charlotte would have just shrugged this man off as one of the many who found Meleah worth a second look. Just as he hadn't struck her as the law enforcement type, he hadn't given her the impression that he was there to try to flirt with her either. So what did he want?

"That's him, sugar," Charlotte said, as soon as Meleah tapped her on the shoulder to let her know that she'd arrived. "That's the one who's been asking for you."

"Did he say what he wanted?"

"Nope, pretty close-mouthed about it."

Meleah smiled. "Thank goodness for small favors. As long as he isn't complaining about the service." She'd come in from the rear of the restaurant, pausing only to swing by her father's office to throw on a bright red blazer over the simple cotton T-shirt and jeans she wore. She made a cursory check of the bar's inventory, using business as a buffer between herself and the hulk sitting across the room.

"Don't you think you'd better go see what he wants?" Charlotte prompted gently.

"He's waited this long," Meleah said with forced nonchalance in her voice. She didn't like the vibes she was getting from that man either. She was already jittery from her ordeal Tuesday night. She didn't need to rush right into a situation that, even without much information, was starting to make her feel even worse. "Besides, if he didn't leave on account of Trae's sloppy service, he's not going anywhere soon."

"How did you know . . ." Charlotte began, then clamped her mouth shut.

"Because he should have been back from his break twenty minutes ago." Meleah noted the time he left on the log. "I've been pretty loose about folks covering around here because I'm the main culprit," Meleah said. "But finals are about over. So's the sloppy service. It stops tonight."

"Yes, ma'am! I'll pass the word," Charlotte said smartly. As she'd told that man, she'd been with Papa Jack's a long time. She was the senior server. But no one was more senior than Jack and his daughter Meleah. When it came down to business, Charlotte knew when to drop the familiarity. "Now that we've been warned, you can quit stalling. Go over there and see what he wants before he burns a hole in this bar with that laser beam glare. Do you want me to go with you? I can hang around, acting like I'm actually working."

"Uh-uh. I'll take care of this," Meleah said crisply.

Charlotte leaned close and said, "Nothin's gonna happen to you again, Le-Le. Not like . . . you know . . . what almost happened up there in the pool room. He wouldn't dare try anything. Not with so many people around."

Meleah took a deep breath. "You ought to take that mind-reading act on the road, Charlie." She tugged her jacket smooth and stepped from the bar. A couple of patrons, waiting their turn for her attention, started to move toward her. She murmured a polite but no-nonsense rebuff, then continued across the room.

When their gazes locked across the room, Meleah almost a missed a step. Him again! She remembered him. He and his friends had been a pain in her butt all night. She thought she'd pretty much given him the brush-off when he left. She didn't expect to see him back. But now he was.

Meleah quickly scanned the area. Where were his sidekicks? She expected at any moment for them to bum's rush her from every corner, force her to sit down and listen to their tired old lines about how they could rock her world.

She swallowed convulsively against the deep frown lines carved into the recesses of the man's wide, hard mouth. The open, interested looks he had given her

last Saturday night were in total contrast to the look
he was giving her now. She couldn't even begin to describe the look. It was a look of fury mingled with con-
tempt and, if she wasn't mistaken, she thought she
sensed a kind of disappointment.

He sat with his palms resting lightly on the tabletop.
But there was nothing easy or relaxed in his stance.
She could almost feel the tension tightening across his
shoulders. She saw the involuntary flex of his arms as
he stood to greet her.

At five seven-and-a-half, Meleah was used to looking
most men directly in the eyes when she approached.
She found this an asset when rejecting their advances.
She wouldn't be able to do so with this one—wouldn't
be able to dismiss him, wouldn't be able to reject his
offer to join him at the table.

"Charlotte tells me that you were asking about me."

"Are you Meleah?" Tarrant asked, though he already knew the answer.

"I am."

"Then I was."

"What do you want?" Meleah asked. The gruffness
in the man's voice, the no-nonsense attitude was
enough to make her want to dispense with the pleasantries.

"Have a seat," he said, again more of a command
than a request.

Meleah's spine stiffened. She wasn't used to being
ordered around in her own place. She folded her arms
across her chest. "No, I think I'll stand."

Tarrant paused, recognizing a brick wall when he
saw one. He'd better rethink his strategy if he wanted
to get anything out of this woman. Hell, he'd better
develop a strategy, or Amber was as good as convicted.

"Please," he gritted, gesturing toward the empty seat
facing him. "Can I get you anything?"

Meleah bit the inside of her cheek to keep from
smiling. Something told her that even that little bit of
effort to be pleasant was as painful for him as a root
canal. "Don't tell me you don't like eating alone," Meleah said, her eyes flicking to the nearly demolished
platter of fajitas. A few stray grilled onions and one
tortilla was all that remained of the full order. *He can
really put it away,* Meleah thought. A full order was usually enough to satisfy at least two. Her gaze flicked over
him. She found herself wondering how often he
worked out. He had to work out. A man who could
put away food like that couldn't remain in good physical condition for very long. And he was in very good
condition. She quickly shut off the part of her that
could have appreciated looking at him a little bit
longer. He was trouble. No second thoughts about it.

He pushed the plate away. It was a subtle message,
but one that told Meleah that he was ready to focus
on her now. She eased into the seat across from him,
folding her hands on top of the table. "What can I do
for you, Mr. . . ." She raised her eyebrows, indicating
for him to fill in the blank.

"Cole," he supplied.

"Mr. Cole," she echoed. She didn't question
whether or not it was his real name. A tiny voice in
the back of her mind bothered her. It made her question why she would be willing to give him even the
tiniest bit of her trust.

Tarrant reached into his back pocket and pulled out
his wallet. He pulled out two items—a credit card and
a photograph. He made sure that Meleah had a clear
view of both. If she had any doubts that he was who
he said he was, the credit card should prove it. He was
sure that she must have caught a glimpse of his driver's
license, too. The other item was a picture of Amber
in one of her rare moments, smiling, happy, and sober.

"Do you recognize the woman in this picture?" He pushed the photo across the table to her. Tarrant watched Meleah pick up the photo and raise it closer to her.

Even in the reduced lighting of the sports bar, Meleah had no trouble remembering the girl. It was Belly Button! Instantly the horror of that night flooded back to her. To keep herself from crumpling the picture in her hand, she placed it deliberately on the table and pushed it back across to Tarrant.

"I've seen her in here," Meleah said quietly. "She came in last Tuesday. It was Ladies' Night. I haven't seen her since." If he was a disgruntled husband or boyfriend looking for her, she wasn't about to tell him what kind of trash the girl was hanging out with. If he was a private detective, looking to track her down, Meleah had told him enough of the truth to send him on his way to pick up some other thread to find the little ungrateful tramp.

Tarrant read her body language as easily as he would a billboard. Seeing Amber's picture rattled her. Maybe even scared her. She was biting down on her lower lip—whether to stop it from trembling or to stop it from talking, he couldn't be sure.

"Who is she?" Meleah asked. "Some kind of runaway?"

"Did you serve her any alcohol while she was here?"

"You answer my questions and I'll answer yours," Meleah countered.

"All right," Tarrant acquiesced. "She's my little sister."

"Ohhh . . ." Meleah let out a breath of understanding. That partially answered why he was being such a hard case. He was worried about his baby sister. "Is she missing?"

"She's in the hospital," Tarrant ground out.

"The . . . the hospital?" Meleah stammered. Her mind flashed back to Rat Tail's animosity that night. He was pretty worked up. Could he have turned that back on Belly Button?

"That's right. In the hospital. She said you put her there."

"Excuse me?" Incredulity hit Meleah like a punch to the stomach. "She said what?" What was the matter with that girl? She misplaced blame like most folks did their car keys. "With all due respect to your injured sister, Mr. Cole, what is she? Some kind of nutcase?"

"Her name is Amber," Tarrant snapped. "And she's in trouble."

"She's very troubled," Meleah said acerbically, then wished she could have recalled the reply. The man was obviously upset. The muscles worked in his cheeks as if he were literally biting down on rage. She took a deep breath, put on the mask of the adept business-woman and said, "According to your sister . . . Amber, is it? . . . how exactly did I accomplish putting her in the hospital?"

"She's in a coma. She didn't give me all of the de-tails. But before she went under she mentioned you."

"So she could have been hallucinating."

"It's possible. That's why I'm here. To get to the heart of the matter."

"What are you? Some kind of cop?"

"Nope. Just a concerned brother."

As well you should be. Meleah kept the thought to herself. That girl had some major issues.

"I didn't hurt your sister, Mr. Cole. No one at Papa Jack's did, if that's what you're here to find out."

"You'll have to excuse me if I don't just jump and take a perfect stranger's word for it." It was Tarrant's turn to be sarcastic.

"If you'll excuse me, this conversation has gone on way too long." Meleah stood up.

"I'm not leaving until I find out the truth," Tarrant warned her.

"You can stay as long as you want until closing time. Come back as often as you'd like." Her tone was anything but welcoming—flashes of Le-Le the scorn queen from last Saturday. She leaned on the table until her face was within inches of his. "But if you hassle me or any of my customers in your little investigation, I'll have the real cops on you so fast, it'll make a drug bust look like a kiddie party. Have I made myself clear, Mr. Cole?"

"As glass," Tarrant replied, lifting his empty mug to her in salute.

FOUR

Tarrant took his usual seat and gave the usual suspects at the bar a jaunty wave. Le-Le, Charlotte, and Trae, the rocket man, acknowledged him with the barest of nods, then went about their business. The other man, presumably the manager, an older guy with a potbelly and a loud mouth, hadn't made it in yet. At least, Tarrant hadn't seen him yet. He could be in the back office. He usually came out once or twice before closing time, double-checking Meleah's checks and causing enough of a stir to remind everyone that he had enough pull around the place to shake things up. Boss man. Cock of the walk. King of the hill. He was Papa Jack.

"Look at him." Charlotte shook her head as she watched Tarrant from across the room. "Look at the poor, deluded fool. Somebody ought to tell him that his sister is trash and put him out of his misery."

"It won't be me," Meleah said, shaking her head.

"Why not?" Trae wanted to know. "Why don't you just tell him what happened so you can get rid of him."

"I don't want to talk about it," Meleah said tightly. "He's not hurting anyone or anything. He'll get bored and go away."

Charlotte and Trae exchanged glances. Maybe they should have told Meleah about the accident Charlotte had witnessed the night of Meleah's attack. They thought they were doing her a favor by helping her to put the whole ugly incident out of her mind. Now that incident was back to haunt them in the form of big bad brother. Charlotte shook her head as she hefted a tray and moved away from them. Her voice wafted back as she sang, "I don't think so, sugar."

Four nights in a row, Tarrant returned to Papa Jack's. Sometimes he ordered dinner. Sometimes he didn't. He didn't bother becoming interested in any of the games picked up by satellite dish and broadcast for the rest of the paying customers. Right now the trials and triumphs of some soccer team in Brazil didn't concern him one bit. He was here to find out what led to his sister being in that accident.

Now, more than ever, Tarrant was convinced that a string of events, beyond Amber's control, had led to that accident. She wasn't at fault. She couldn't have been. Every conceivable drug test had come back. They'd all been negative. When Amber was driving that night, she had not been high. That much he could prove. But she had been upset. Upset enough to get caught up in a stupid argument. That much he had to piece together without solid facts.

The chain of events started here. Something happened here that night that was the catalyst for the tragedy. The fact that Amber was still out of it was the thin thread that kept his sister from hanging. He had the feeling that he didn't have much time. His sister was out of surgery. But it was only a matter of time before the police investigators began to press the issue. They'd want answers. He was determined to get them before they did. Anything he could do to make them believe he and his family would fully cooperate could only help Amber's case.

His first plan of attack was to gather the details of

what happened to Amber after she left the restaurant.
He'd wormed some of it out of Charlotte—Papa Jack's
self-appointed head of the grapevine. Trying to figure
out what happened that night would take days of sift-
ing through gossip and third-hand he-said she-saids.

As protective as she'd been of Meleah the night he'd
shown up alone, she was even more so in the following
nights. Meleah must have told her what he'd wanted.
Charlotte flew quickly to the girl's defense, making
sure that no one served Tarrant's table but herself.
She was going to limit Tarrant's exposure to anyone
who might be able to give him a clue as to what happened. Once she'd figured out who he was, she'd given
out slips of information that definitely put Amber here
that night. When Tarrant tried to press for details of
Meleah's involvement, she closed up tighter than her
much-bemoaned orthopedic shoes.

By the fourth night, Tarrant though he had a handle
on the atmosphere of Papa Jack's. The clientele was a
mixed bag of tourists and locals, surfers and surgeons,
bikers and bankers. But the core keeping the place
going was the small group of regulars. They stuck to
each other and by each other like family. They _were_ a
family. And they weren't about to let him, an outsider,
come in there and stir up trouble. The only way he
was going to get anything out of any of them was to
become a part of them.

Becoming a valued customer wasn't going to work.
He didn't think he could spend enough time, sitting
in his chair, to ever make him earn their trust. But
that didn't stop him from showing up night after night.
Not bothering anybody. Minding his own business. Oc-
casionally he'd let a comment out. Slip a question in.
Cool. Natural. He was just watching the flow of things,
waiting for his opportunity to insinuate himself into
the tightly knit group.

When Le-Le passed him no less than twenty times without giving him as much as a sniff of disdain, Tarrant smiled into his beer. He was wearing her down. It was just a matter of time.

"Give it up! You don't have a prayer!" someone shouted from the crowd, startling Tarrant out of his solitary brooding. It was a few beats before Tarrant realized that they weren't talking to him. He turned his attention across the room. Boss man had arrived on the scene, stirring things up with his usual gusto. Jack Harmon shushed the heckler into silence. "Quiet! They're about to announce my lucky numbers!" His shout reached every corner of Papa Jack's. As if caught in a time warp, rattling glasses on the trays of table attendants stilled. Pool cues ceased to find their marks on green felt tables. Even the discord of chirps, groans, and sirens from the video arcade seemed to freeze in midaction at Jack's command. Almost every eye turned toward a television monitor to see the Wednesday night lottery number announced. Several patrons pulled out their own tickets and waited expectantly with Jack.

"Go on and turn it up, Le-Le," Jack directed to Meleah, as she sat with her chin propped on her fist. In front of her was a stack, several inches thick, of invoices. She flipped through them, systematically entering numbers by touch into a calculator. Pencils rested behind both ears and were tucked into her hair.

"I'm telling you, Pops, if you let me buy a decent computer, I can have these statements straightened out like that!" She snapped her fingers for emphasis. "The three-eighty-six you've got back in your office is so slow. I've upgraded its memory and disk space. I can't keep pushing that old thing like I've been. I swear the thing groans every time I turn it on."

"Ooh, baby, I love it when you talk dirty like that, Le-Le," Jack's heckler teased her.

Without looking up from her work, she held up her hand, palm facing the heckler's face. "Talk to the hand, Marshon. Talk to the hand." She pushed her wire-rimmed glasses up on her nose and shifted through another stack of multicolored receipts. "Pops, there are some very slick accounting software packages on the market. I can't even look at them. That old dinosaur of a computer back there couldn't take it."

"Yeah, yeah, sure, sure. Software . . . market . . . slick," Jack said impatiently and indicated that she hurry. "As soon as I win this lottery, you can buy a hundred computers. Now turn up the TV so I can hear them call my lucky numbers."

"That's where half of our profits are going—to that stupid lottery," Meleah complained. "It's worse than gambling."

"It's not gambling. It's fate."

"It's fatal," Meleah retorted. "It's killing us. Bleeding us to death in nickels and dimes."

"Well, four million will buy a lot of bandages. That's what the pot is now, you know. And it's all mine. You'll see," Jack predicted as he pulled out a paper ticket with the combination of numbers he'd selected. "I'm gonna win this time, Meleah. I can feel it in my bones."

"What you're feeling, Pops, is that extra five pounds you've put on. I told you to stop sneaking that fried cheese."

"When I win, I'll hire somebody to go on a diet for me. And I don't sneak half as much fried cheese as you do those cancer sticks you've been sucking on."

"Hey! I haven't had a smoke in eight days, ten hours, twenty-two minutes and counting," Meleah complained. She looked to Charlotte for confirmation. But Charlotte was busy arranging her own lottery tickets on the bar to check against tonight's numbers. Meleah shook her head in resignation, and reached for the remote control. The announcer had finished the perquisite speech on security and verification for the lottery, and was wishing all of the ticket holders luck.

"Ten dollars every week, and for what? All he has to show for it is a trash can full of losing tickets, and a lifetime full of wasted dreams," she muttered to herself.

"You leave your old daddy alone, sugar. It does him good to dream. Lord knows I've had enough dreams of my own of what I'd do with all of that dough."

"He's wasting money, Charlotte," she complained. "And then he wonders why we're barely squeaking by every month."

"It's his money, sugar. Let him do what he wants. You're just the accountant, remember?"

"What do you mean *just* the accountant?!" Meleah bristled. "I busted my butt to double-major in school, Charlotte—accounting and business management! I jumped through hoops to get that MBA. Do you know how many hours I put in studying and still put my hours in at the restaurant? How many tests I had to take? How many bullets I had to sweat? How many all-nighters I pulled? I think I have more of a say in where the money goes than just the accountant. Besides, I'm also his—"

"I said shush!" Jack waved her into silence.

"Quiet, sugar, they're gonna announce now!" Charlotte echoed.

". . . only child, as if anybody's listening," Meleah finished under her breath.

She watched as Jack gripped his ticket tightly with the same expectant expression on his face that she had come to recognize since the Texas state lottery began. Meleah sighed, then buried her head in her work. She didn't want to see the same look of disappointment that was to come when Jack lost again. It hurt her too much to see his face crumple when he realized that his dreams would not come to him quickly in a lucky rush. Instead he would have to continue to do what he'd done for the last twenty years—work for his dream by the sweat of his two hands.

When the last number was called, Meleah automatically reached for the remote control to turn down the volume. She knew what to expect. It was the same thing every week, twice a week. Now that her father had lost, he'd rip the ticket into several pieces. He'd accuse the lottery officials of rigging the game and exclaim loudly how the honest folks who worked hard for their money never had a fair chance. Charlotte would console him in her honey-sweet, southern drawl. And Meleah would be forced to step in as the voice of reason to try to convince him not to waste his time and money.

Meleah waited for the sound of ripping paper, for the bitter comments from Jack, and for Charlotte's consolation. She waited for several seconds. When neither came, she looked up in mild curiosity. Jack stood behind the bar, his face turned toward the television that now showed the somber faces of the local news broadcasters.

Between Jack's large, shaking hands was the ticket. Charlotte stood on the opposite side of the bar, leaning over to grasp him by the shoulders. She was screeching something, but Meleah was too concerned by the stunned expression on Jack's broad face to pay attention to what Charlotte was saying.

"Pops?" Meleah stood up. "Pops, what is it?"

Jack turned slowly toward Meleah. The blank look in his deep-set eyes frightened her. Charlotte was still clutching Jack's shoulders, shaking him, and screaming. Jack blinked once—ever so slowly. Then, as if he were suddenly pushed, he fell backward, dragging Charlotte over the bar with him.

Bottles tipped and spilled their contents. Glasses crashed to the floor, scattering shards in every direction. Meleah stood up, with her hands pressed to her mouth, as she watched Charlotte's stocking-clad legs and orthopedic shoes flailing as she hung precariously onto the lip of the bar.

Meleah skirted the edge of the bar, and knelt down beside her father. "Pops, are you all right? What's the matter with you?" She patted his cheeks, and smoothed her hands over his salt-and-pepper hair.

"Never mind about me, girl," he croaked. "Is the ticket all right? Did I tear it? Did I get it wet?"

"The ticket? What are you talking about?"

"The ticket!" Charlotte cried out. "There it is!" She pointed to the slip of paper lying underneath a broken tumbler. "Get it, Jack!"

Charlotte and Jack dove for the ticket at the same time. Jack reached it first. He snatched it from the floor, then tossed it aside in disgust. "That ain't it, Charlie!"

"What about that one?" Charlotte scooped up several of the duds. "Or that one? Or this one?"

Jack went through several, his face getting more and more panicstricken as he said, "No . . . No . . . No! Where is it?!"

"Has everyone suddenly lost their minds? What's going on?" Meleah entreated.

"Here it is! Oh, my precious! My sweet precious!" Jack brushed a glass away, ignoring the tiny cuts and scratches on his hands. "Oh, my beauty! It's a winner, Meleah, girl! We've won! We've won!" Jack crowed. He rocked back and forth as if he cradled a small child.

"You . . . you won?" Meleah stammered. "You mean the lottery? The four-million-dollar lottery? You're not serious, Pops!"

"Does this look like a joke?" Jack retorted. He held the ticket out to her to let her verify the numbers.

"You won?" Meleah repeated. "I can't believe you won!" Meleah fell limply against one of the cabinets, and handed the ticket back to him. "How could you win? You can't win!"

"I won! I won! I won!" Jack stood up and shouted in a hoarse whisper. When he received no response from the Wednesday night crowd, he cleared his throat, and shouted: "Just don't stand there, let's get this party started! From now until closing, everything is on the house!"

As several patrons converged around the bar, Jack amended, "Except the alcohol. You folks know the rules. No booze bingeing in my place." He endured some good-natured teasing, some well-wishes, then made a dash for his office.

"I gotta call the Pastor. I know the church could use a new roof. And I'm so far behind in my tithes that Saint Peter himself is going to audit me. And then I gotta call the garage, and tell them to go ahead and replace that transmission on my truck. Scratch that! Forget the transmission. I'll buy a new truck—a whole fleet of 'em! And I gotta call our distributors, and tell them to deposit those checks I wrote last week and I gotta call . . ."

He left Meleah sitting in the middle of the floor. "Pops? Pops!" Meleah called out after him. "I can't believe he won. There's got to be a mistake."

"He's only been playing the same numbers for five years, sugar," Charlotte answered for Jack. "He plays a combination of your birthday, his birthday, wedding anniversary, and a few other secret numbers that are special to him for heaven only knows why."

"This will have to be verified," Meleah said quickly. "Isn't there a number you're supposed to call?"

"Oh, so you *have* been listening to those lottery drawings. And all this time I thought you'd been keeping that brainy head of yours buried in your accounting books," Charlotte teased. She looked down at her uniform to adjust it, then tsked-tsked at the stain of crushed pretzels, peanut shells, and seltzer water splattered across her shirt.

"After all of these years, something sank in," Meleah admitted.

"On the back of the ticket," Charlotte supplied, "there's a hotline number. Ain't that a fitting term? That ticket your daddy's holding is about as hot as they come!"

Both Meleah and Charlotte pivoted as the door to Jack's office was flung open. He burst back into the bar, flung open his arms, and bellowed, "I won! Good Lord, I'm a millionaire!"

Charlotte turned to Meleah as she picked up her tray and said, "Looks like I'm gonna be hopping for the rest of the night. If I were you, Le-Le, I'd go out and buy that computer you wanted so badly before Jack's generous heart gives away the whole four mil."

"Four million dollars," Meleah moaned as she sank to the floor. "How in the world are we going to manage four million dollars?"

"Now we see if all of that education crammed in that head of yours will do us all some good."

"Oh no . . . this is beyond my little MBA," Meleah quickly declared. "Something like this needs a professional. Someone should call a lawyer, an investment counselor."

"An exorcist," Charlotte retorted. "Your daddy's

gonna be spending cash like a man possessed if you don't do something quick."

Meleah started to pick up two halves of a broken mug and absently fit the pieces together. With a little glue, she thought, she could make the mug as good as new. She then tossed the mug into the trash. Time to readjust her attitude! Now that they were millionaires, they wouldn't have to scrimp, save, and recycle every piece of chipped crockery that made its way back to the kitchen.

On second thought, she removed the mug, wrapped it in a napkin, and placed it carefully under the bar to be repaired later. There was no sense in letting the money go completely to their heads. She grabbed a fresh glass, filled it with her favorite white wine, and held it aloft in a silent toast to Pops and his faith in numbers.

Tarrant didn't believe it. He couldn't believe it. It had to be some kind of act, some sort of publicity stunt to get the crowd going. He thought back to the last few nights he'd staked out Papa Jack's. Last night, Tuesday, had been Ladies' Night. Monday night had been All You Can Eat shrimp night. On Sunday the place was closed. And Saturday night was your normal, run-of-the-mill pack 'em in and sauce 'em night. There was a little something for everyone to get the crowd in a drinking, money-spending mood. But this—this was something different. Tarrant couldn't figure how faking a lottery win would make folks want to spend money.

The longer he watched the activity going back and forth between the bar, the hostess station, and the back office, Tarrant started to believe that maybe this wasn't a stunt. The ripple of excitement that spread through the staff couldn't be faked. And the look on Meleah's face as she tried to keep up the appearance of business-as-usual was enough to convince him that the Harmon family really had hit the jackpot. She was distracted and incredulous and giddy all at the same time.

On impulse Tarrant hailed a passing server. "Say, rocket man, what's going on over there?" he asked, nodding at the bar where a couple of bartenders fought over the honor of sweeping up the mess that Charlotte and Jack had made. Tarrant figured that service was going to be five star around here for a while. There was nothing like the smell of money to make the hourly workers shape up.

"Didn't you hear? The old man won the big one."

"The lottery? You don't say?"

"Yeah. Four million bucks. Can you believe it?"

"Lucky him," Tarrant replied.

"Lucky us, I'm hoping," the rocket man confessed.

"Look, do me a favor, son. What does the boss lady drink?"

"Sir?"

"Meleah Harmon. What's she partial to?"

"White wine, I think."

"Why don't you pour one up and take it over to her. Tell her it's from me."

The rocket man grinned. "If you're planning to get lucky, too, that probably won't do it. She doesn't usually accept drinks from the customers."

"Maybe the thought of four mil has put her in a friendlier mood. You never know. Do it anyway. If you get her to take it, there's a twenty waiting for you." Tarrant waved a crisp bill under the server's nose.

"Yes, sir!"

"Thanks," Tarrant said, settling back in his chair. A few minutes later, the rocket man set a glass of white wine and a large, tropical flower in front of Meleah with a flourish. He performed a short bow, then pointed at Tarrant's table. Tarrant smiled. He had to admire the young man's style. The flower was a nice touch. He couldn't remember seeing any flower stands on the road. It had to come from someone's private garden. The small trail of mud left on the floor when he'd approached Meleah confirmed it. The boy had gone foraging. Ah! The temptation of the twenty.

Tarrant waited expectantly as the rocket man and Meleah exchanged a few words. She glanced over her shoulder at Tarrant. He saw her hesitate, could almost hear the inner debate going on inside of her head. He gestured at the empty seat. *Come on, Le-Le,* he silently implored her. *Come to papa.*

He'd been very careful to keep that seat empty. Even on Ladies' Night. He wanted no doubt in her mind why he was there. He was there for her. Though it would have been more to his liking if she would have come to him because she was interested. In fact, when he found out that the focus of his investigation was the elusive Le-Le, he'd been very disappointed. He hadn't wanted to come back to Papa Jack's after his sister's accident. Thinking that he might have another chance to meet Le-Le was the only saving grace that kept him excited about going back.

"Guess who's back and up to his junior sleuthing," Meleah said to Charlotte in passing.

"Oh, yeah? What does he want?"

"He wants me to go over and talk to him. He sent these over." Meleah pointed to the offerings.

Charlotte raised her eyebrows. "Not the most original I've seen to get a girl's attention; but it's still pretty effective."

Meleah lowered her voice "Do you think I should go?"

"He's just trying to find someone to blame for his sister being so messed up. That ain't your problem, Le-Le. Like you said, maybe if you ignore him, he'll get tired of hanging around here and he'll go away."

"I feel so sorry for him," Meleah whispered. "I mean, she's in the hospital."

Charlotte put her hand on Meleah's shoulder and said, "I didn't want to tell you, Le-Le. I didn't want to dredge up any more bad feelings."

"Tell me what, Charlie?"

"I saw the accident. That is . . . I saw the result of it. It was pretty bad. Somebody died. I guess that's why he's hanging around here so much."

"He's just looking for answers," Meleah rationalized.

"Well . . . there's no harm in talking to him. You've got nothing to hide or be afraid of."

"Who's afraid?" Meleah said, with an air of false bravado. "Just because his sister sat on her behind and did nothing while her friends almost raped me."

"He may be trying to help his sister, Le-Le, but something tells me that he's nothing like her. I don't know why. Call it instinct. He won't hurt you . . . but I could be wrong. This lottery business has got me so shaken up, I wouldn't trust myself to remember my own name. You go on and talk to the man if you want to, sugar. If he makes one sneaky move, you sing out. We've got your back, girlfriend."

"Thanks, Charlie," Meleah said. "Maybe I should talk to him. He may hear a few things that he doesn't want to about his sister . . . but at least he'll know the truth." She picked up the wineglass and the flower and moved across the floor.

Tarrant rose as she approached and pulled out the chair for her. By now the restaurant noise had reached a fevered pitch. For her to hear him, he'd either have to shout or speak very softly, almost directly in her ear. He opted for the latter.

Sliding his chair within inches of hers, Tarrant placed both elbows on the table, resting his chin on clasped hands. "So what made you change your mind?"

"The iris," Meleah said honestly, as she gently traced the fragile petals with her fingertip. "This shade of purple happens to be my favorite."

Tarrant wasn't sure what to make of the admission. This was the most personal piece of information he'd gotten directly from her. Everything else he'd learned about her was either by ferreting it out from the staff or from sheer observation.

"Looks good on you, too," Tarrant admitted. His eyes flicked over her. Tonight the splashes of purple were intermingled with traces of pale green and royal blue. "It has for the past few nights you've worn it."

"You would know. You've been parked right there in that spot."

"I told you that I would."

"Why are you here, Mr. Cole? What do you want? I told you that I had nothing to do with your sister's accident."

"Amber says that you did. I have to believe her."

"Why—because she's your sister?" Meleah said with more than a hint of sarcasm. "What if I told you that you can't believe everything she says?"

"That's more than what you've told me over the past few days. You haven't said more than three words to me. . . . No . . . No, I take it back. I believe the other night you said to me, 'Trae will be your server to-night.' "

"Certainly not enough to keep you coming back night after night."

"You mean, why am I subjecting myself to this sort of nontreatment? Any rational man wouldn't do it. You've got that right."

"Mr. Cole, you're either stubborn or stupid. Which is it?" Meleah mimicked Tarrant's stance, resting her chin on her hands.

The simple motion of her leaning forward to address him assaulted his senses from all angles. The scent of her perfume was light. Yet it cut through the restaurant's free-floating aromas of fried food, draft beer, and the press of human bodies. His eyes were immediately drawn to the shimmer of a string of gold and amethyst beads around her neck. A single tear-shaped stone hung at the opening of her blouse, catching the light and sending off sparks that disappeared into the deep tones of her skin. He timed her breathing with the rise and fall of that stone. Slow. Easy. Relaxed. If she was nervous or agitated about being here with him, he couldn't tell by her breathing.

Underneath the table, she'd crossed her feet at the ankles. Demure. But the movement caused her to lean even closer—if only for a second while she righted herself. For a fraction, Tarrant thought he felt the warmth of her thigh press against his. Subtle. Yeah, right. About as subtle as the thought of a freight train bearing down on him to make his pulse pound at his temples. What was she doing to him? What was he doing to himself? He had to get his equilibrium back.

"You really expect me to answer a question like that?" He didn't have to reach hard to put the edge in his voice. He was definitely on edge.

"No, of course not." Meleah paused, took a sip of the wine, then asked, "Now that you've got me over here, what do you want?"

"I want you to tell me how you know my sister."

"I don't know her."

"What happened the night of the accident? She was here. That much I know."

"She was here with some of her . . . friends."

Tarrant didn't miss the hesitation. Probably the same scummy crew that she'd been hanging out with—the ones he had forbidden her to see.

"And?" he pressed.

"They got too rowdy so we threw them out."

"And that's all."

"That's all that matters," Meleah murmured. She lowered her eyes, toyed nervously with the flower. She didn't want to go into the details. She didn't want to dredge up the memory. It was best forgotten.

"There has to be more," Tarrant insisted. The rise and fall of the stone quickened. She was bothered.

Meleah chewed on her bottom lip. Of course there was more. But she didn't want to tell this man what kind of people his sister hung out with. She didn't want to be the one to break the news.

"Go home, Mr. Cole. You already know all you need to know about your sister."

Whatever fantasies he'd built into his mind about his sister's innocence, she didn't want to be the one to tear them down. Let him park at Papa Jack's every night if he had to. It wasn't going to come from her. Whatever problems that family had, they were none of her business.

FIVE

To say that winning the lottery was a boost for Jack Harmon's business was an understatement. Jack knew the jolt would happen. In fact, he counted on it. He elected to have his name and establishment printed in the newspaper when they announced the winning lottery numbers. He was the first to call the local television stations to invite their news coverage.

He posted flyers in every establishment that would let him. "Stop by Papa Jack's!" he would greet the shop owners and their patrons. "The only restaurant on the seawall where every customer is treated like a millionaire."

Because of Jack's aggressive advertising, Papa Jack's stayed packed with customers from opening to closing. Everyone wanted to meet the local celebrity. They came to prove, or disprove, their personal theories about how money affected people. Jack played the part of grand host to the hilt. He tried to make a personal appearance at every table, every booth. "Try this. You'll love this," he would say, pointing to a dish on the updated menu. Or "Play that. You'll have a blast!" He would draw the customer's attention to a newly installed arcade game. He couldn't figure it out, but the young ones loved any game that allowed them to blow monsters or aliens to bits. Jack couldn't understand the attraction. He was a pinball man himself. But that didn't stop him from hyping the new games anyway.

Meleah should have been overjoyed that, for the first time she could remember since taking over the books, their profit column outbalanced the loss. Cash receipts more than tripled the first night after Jack appeared on television during his acceptance of the first lottery check installment. She should have looked forward to dealing with their creditors—knowing that she didn't have to beg for more time to pay the restaurant's debts. She should have been thrilled to deposit their daily profits, instead of going to the bank to request extensions on their loans.

She should have been. But she wasn't. Meleah was miserable. She thought she was busy before her father won the lottery. Now she was absolutely swamped with work. There were days, she thought ruefully, that she wished she were *just* the accountant. Now, in addition to being an accountant, she became a part-time cook to help keep up with the meal orders. She assisted Charlotte with covering the additional tables Jack added to make room for more customers. She became Papa Jack's media consultant, letter and telephone call screener, financial advisor, social calendar keeper, inventory manager, and did many more tasks, which she lumped into the general category of "too much work."

After three weeks of such exhausting work, Meleah and the other employees were ready to revolt. Backed by Charlotte, Leon, and Trae, Meleah stormed into Jack's office.

"That's it. We have had it, Pops," Meleah declared. "We can't go on like this."

"What do you mean?" Jack growled. He peeked over a pile of papers. Several similar stacks sprouted like mushrooms all over his office. Requests for charitable donations, offers from companies to extend credit to him, and out-and-out junk mail—people trying to get him to buy things he wouldn't buy even if he had four *zillion* dollars. He was going through them as fast as he could at Meleah's insistence. They were a fire hazard. Besides, she couldn't sit in her own cramped corner for the stacks.

"You know exactly what we mean, sugar," Charlotte put in, stabbing a finger at him. "I like making money as much as the next person, but these hours are killing me. I can't remember the last time I had a night off."

"I know, I know," Jack soothed. "I'm doing everything I can to help the situation."

"Like what?" Leon wanted to know.

"I put ads in all the papers from *Kemah* to *Cut-N-Shoot*. We should be getting responses any day now."

"Oh, we've been getting responses, all right," Meleah said, crossing her arms across her chest. "All of them more worried about how much over the minimum wage they'll be getting instead of how well they can do the job."

"We've had some likely candidates," Charlotte said in Jack's defense.

"But as soon as they saw how crazy it is around here, they backed out," Trae retorted. "I had one guy go on break. When I went out to check on him, I found his jersey and his serving tray in the trash."

"In the meantime, how about cutting back some of the business hours," Charlotte suggested.

"Woman, have you lost your mind? And miss the opportunity to make some real money?"

"You just won the lottery, you greedy old buzzard. How much more do you need?" Leon folded his brawny arms across his chest and demanded.

"It's not just for me, you hash slinger," Jack retorted. "It's for you, too. It's because I won that I've been staying open for so long. What happens when my celebrity status wears off and we go back to normal operations? You can't tell me that you haven't enjoyed the padding of your paychecks since we've been famous."

Leon mumbled a reluctant agreement, but Charlotte said, "So what happens when you hire these new people and we go back to normal operations? Will we have to go back to the days of late paychecks? Or will you have the heart to lay them off again?"

"Over my dead body!" Meleah declared. "I didn't take all of those business courses to let a windfall make us lose our minds now."

"That's my Le-Le," Jack said proudly. "We'll do this right, or we won't do it at all. With Meleah helping me plan things out, we'll get the people we need, you'll get the work time and the play time you deserve, and we'll all be able to retire happy."

"I know *you're* not talking about retiring, sugar," Charlotte said. "Everybody else had bets that with your first lottery installment, you'd be on the first boat to Cancún, or some other exotic place, to spend the rest of your twilight years. Unless I miss my guess, you haven't begun to slow down."

"I don't know how to slow down," Jack complained.

"How do you know until you've tried?" Meleah asked. "You need to take it easy. Remember what the doctor told you. Lay off the fat and the salt and stay off of your feet."

"What would I look like, a dried-up old prune, sitting on some beach, in one of those teensy-weensy little bathing trunks?"

"Now there's a thought that will give a gal nightmares," Charlotte mused. She leaned over the desk and patted Jack's paunch.

Jack sucked in his stomach. "What are you talking about, woman? This is nothing but solid muscle."

"Between your ears," Charlotte retorted.

"Between my l—"

"Let's not go there, Pops," Meleah quickly interjected.

"Seriously now, Jack, what about a trip back home? Didn't you say you always wanted to go back to Beaumont as a big shot?" For all of Leon's gruffness, he sounded genuinely concerned about Jack.

"If I weren't here to watch over you, I don't know what would happen. Leon, I couldn't trust you not to give all of my customers food poisoning," Jack teased. "And you, Charlotte, would wind up setting the place on fire with your flaming concoctions. Now get out of here, all of you, and let me get back to doing what I do best."

"All right, we'll go, but if something doesn't change soon, we'll be back," Leon promised.

Meleah kissed her father on the forehead and said, "Speaking of getting back soon, if I'm going to make it back before the dinner crowd, I'd better head out now. I've got a few errands to run. When I get back, we can talk about that stack of mail that I've labeled 'top priority' for you."

Jack groaned in anticipation of the work. "Which stack would that be now?"

Meleah's arms swept the room. "That would be all of them, of course. Look at this place. This room is a firetrap, Pops. I want this place cleaned up before I get back. And I'll be back soon," Meleah promised.

"See that you do. You're not leaving me here all alone to wade through all of this," Jack warned, as he started to rifle through his stack of paperwork. It seemed to Jack that the harder he worked to get through the stack, the bigger the stack became. He didn't like being tied to the desk. He much preferred to be out greeting the customers. But with all the changes he had made to improve Papa Jack's, this seemed to be part of the package.

Jack had built Papa Jack's from the ground up. Twenty years of his life was built into every inch. The people he hired to help run it were friends as well as employees.

"Some friends," he muttered. "They want me to slow down. They're not fooling me. They just want to get rid of me so they can they can take over the place. Well, I'm not going!"

Jack often grumbled that they couldn't do without him. It was closer to the truth to say that he couldn't bear the thought of deserting them. They'd seen him through the lean times. Now it was his turn to make sure they would never have to see them again.

Two hours later, he was still sitting at his desk trying to weed out the multiple requests for donations from various local charities.

"How did you slip past my Meleah's eagle eyes?" he murmured, surprised that Meleah had not marked this one package for him as high, medium, or low priority mail. The envelope was simply addressed *Jack* in neat, printed letters. He scanned the contents, then crumpled the paper convulsively in his hand. "Great. Another one," he muttered as he stood and strode quickly to the door. He flung it open and shouted, "Meleah!"

"She's not here, sugar," Charlotte called back. She swabbed at a table with one hand and lifted several items of litter with her other hand. "She should be back in a little bit. What's the matter?"

"Let me know as soon as she gets back, will you, Charlie?"

"Sure thing."

Jack turned to go back into his office, then faced Charlotte again.

"Charlie, do me a favor, will ya? Call the bank, and make sure Meleah's made it. She usually goes into the lobby instead of the drive-through, doesn't she? Call that teller that you're always sweet-talking."

"I'll call him," Charlotte said, frowning. "What's the matter, Jack?"

"Nothing. Just call for me, won't you?"

Charlotte tossed the bottles and napkins into the appropriate recycling bins, then dialed from behind the bar.

"I know you, Jack. Something's wrong. Tell me what it is."

"Just a feeling."

"Would that feeling have anything to do with that piece of paper you've got smashed in your hands?" Charlotte asked, lifting an eyebrow at Jack.

Jack nodded tightly and passed it to Charlotte. "Crank letter number four hundred and seventy-five," he said in disgust.

Charlotte scanned it while she waited for the bank to locate her favorite teller. "Oh, Jack. What's the matter with folks these days? They ain't got nothin' better to do than to send us trash like this?" she lamented, then directed her next comments into the phone. "Hey, Donny, sugar! This is Charlotte over at Papa Jack's. Fine, fine. Thanks for asking. Listen, I called you because I need a favor. Not that one. You know I don't have to beg for that anymore." She giggled in response to the teller's next comments, making Jack roll his eyes and press her to get on with the reason for the call.

"I just want to know if Ms. Harmon has made it to

the bank yet? She did? Is she still there? Oh, well."
Charlotte covered the mouthpiece with her hand and
said, "We missed her by about twenty minutes."

When Jack muttered something about giving Meleah
an electronic ankle bracelet to track her movements,
Charlotte snickered. "Good luck trying to get her to
wear it." Then she turned her attention back to the
telephone. "Yes . . . yes . . . things are going just fine.
Business couldn't be better. You ought to stop on by
sometime. Weekends are especially busy, but I think I
could find the time to swing by your table."

Jack stood by impatiently while Charlotte continued
to make small talk. Finally, he snatched the phone
from Charlotte and said hastily into the mouthpiece,
"Stop by Papa Jack's when you get the chance, Donny.
Bye." He slammed the phone into the cradle.

"Now that was rude," Charlotte complained. "That's
no way to treat the guy who saved our butts when it
came to adding up those bounced check fees."

"So I'll give him a free meal," Jack conceded. "If
she left the bank about half an hour ago, where the
devil is she?"

Charlotte shrugged. "She said she had some shopping to do. A woman with four mil to play with can't
get it all done in a couple of hours, sugar."

"She doesn't need to be traipsing all over this island.
Not now. She's an easy mark for every money-hungry
no-account."

"What are you going to do about that?" She pointed
to the paper still clutched in Jack's hand.

"What can I do?"

"Certainly not put another roughneck on Le-Le's
heels to watch over her. You tried hiring a bodyguard
before and it nearly made her go ballistic."

"How was I supposed to know the cat was going to

spend more time watching her behind than watching her back?" Jack grumbled.

"You meant well, sugar," Charlotte soothed. "It's just that Le-Le never was the type to have somebody hovering around her."

"I don't like getting those notes every week."

"So far they've just been cranks. Nothing to get too worked up about."

"Promise me you won't tell Meleah about this. She's got enough on her mind without worrying herself about something like this," he said, and shook the letter at her.

"Then you aren't taking this one too seriously?"

"I am . . . and I'm not," Jack said dubiously. "It's probably the work of some crackpot. I'll just keep my eyes open, and see what happens."

"Then again, sugar, this may be something we should be worrying about."

"We?" Jack said, raising his eyebrows, teasing her. He knew fully well the lengths Charlotte had gone to show Meleah her love.

"Well, Meleah's my girl, too! I practically helped to raise her."

"Yes, you did." Jack smiled softly. "And I never thanked you properly for all those days off you gave up to baby-sit when no one else could."

"Seeing her grow up so smart and sexy is all the thanks I need, sugar."

"Sexy?" Jack's eyebrows raised. "My baby girl isn't sexy."

"You've been behind the bar too long," Charlotte said. "Meleah's a grown woman now, Jack. Every man with well-developed hormones knows it. Why don't you?"

"I know I've been busy, but I haven't been that busy,

have I? How come I didn't know my little girl isn't so little anymore?"

"Poor, poor Papa Jack," Charlotte soothed as she patted his cheek condescendingly. "Go on back to your paperwork. Maybe by the time you come out again, you will have painlessly become a grandpa."

Jack chuckled and covered her hand with his. "Forget being a grandpa. I wouldn't mind trying to become a daddy again. Any takers?"

"The only daddy you can be for me is my sugar daddy." Charlotte glanced around to make sure no one was watching—openly—then blew a soft kiss into his ear. "Any takers?"

"Come on back to my office, Charlie, and let's see what we can do to ink out a deal."

Trae suddenly clinked a pair of beer mugs together. He clinked a little too loudly just to announce himself. The mugs shattered across the mahogany bar.

"Sorry, Mr. H."

"No matter. I'll just take it out of your scrawny hide," Jack said pleasantly enough, not taking his eyes off the sway of Charlotte's rounded bottom as she switched toward the back office.

"Yes, sir. I just wanted to let you know that while you and Miss Charlotte were . . . uh . . . talking, I took a phone call for you. Some guy calling about the ad in the newspaper for evening work. I told him you'd see him around four. Good enough?"

Jack waved his hand to acknowledge he'd heard him, then retreated into his office. The door closed behind them, but not before Charlotte's playful giggle escaped.

By late afternoon, Meleah still had not returned from the bank. Jack prowled his office like a caged tiger, his fists clenching and unclenching in nervous tension.

"Where is she?" he demanded more than once. "Charlotte, somebody better find out where that girl is or I'm calling the police."

"You're overreacting, sugar. Give her some time. She probably went shopping or met with some of her friends. Calm down, Jack. You said yourself that note was probably a crank. Now get your questions ready for that guy. He'll be here any minute."

"What guy?"

"Trae told you about him. He's applying for a job to help take some of the load off of us poor, over-worked, minimum-wage menials."

"Oh, right. I forgot."

"I swear, Jack Harmon! If Meleah leaves you alone for a couple of hours, you're ready to fall to pieces. Now go comb your hair. And for mercy's sake, put on a tie! What kind of image are you trying to give? You're supposed to be a savvy business tycoon. You look a mess."

"There's nothing wrong with the way I look," Jack said, self-consciously running his fingers through the sides of his remaining hair. "You're one who should talk. You'd better go fix your lipstick."

"What's the point. You're just going to kiss it off again," Charlotte said coyly. She blew him a kiss.

Jack smacked his lips. "Can't help it. This shade looks better on me than it does on you."

"You pervert!" Charlotte laughed out loud.

"Shh!" Jack shushed her when a discrete knock sounded on the door.

"Mr. H. Your applicant's here. He looks like a keeper, too."

"Be out in a minute, Trae!" Jack called to keep the

curious young server from poking his head in the door. "Go on out and stall him, Charlie, while I, uh . . ."

"Spruce up the office?" she suggested with raised eyebrows toward a can of air freshener. "Good idea. I don't want the first decent applicant we've had in days to catch you looking like this. We're supposed to be a four star joint, remember?"

Charlotte tugged her uniform back into some semblance of order, smoothed her hand over her hair, then opened the door.

"So," she said too casually to Trae. "You think we might not have to throw this one back?"

"Yeah. He's . . ." Trae began.

Charlotte came to a screeching halt when she saw Trae's "keeper" applicant.

"You?" Charlotte swallowed back a small cry of disappointment. Oh, no! Meleah would never go for it. Never in a million years. She didn't care if had credentials out the *wazoo*. It was bad enough that he'd practically stalked them for several nights. After Meleah had given him the brush-off, Charlotte didn't think she'd ever see him around here again. And now he was back—after three weeks.

Charlotte then moved quickly to greet him with an outstretched hand. "Sorry. I didn't mean to gawk at you, Mr. Cole. It's just that I didn't expect to see you here applying for a position at Papa Jack's."

"Why not? The offer is open to everyone, isn't it? I mean, I don't remember reading the lines 'position to be filled by everyone but Tarrant Cole.' " Tarrant smiled to assure her that he was teasing. Deep down inside, both knew that he wasn't. Unless they could come up with a legitimate reason, they would at least have to grant him the interview.

Charlotte grimaced. She hated it when people got all legal on her. She quickly masked her annoyance and smiled. "It's just that you don't look like our typical bartender."

"I don't?" He sounded amused by her assessment.

"Uh-uh." She shook her head vigorously. "You look more like you should be posing on the cover of some magazine. You know, like *GQ*. That doesn't spell hurtin' for money to me, Mr. Cole. This job isn't exactly one you could retire on, sugar." Charlotte thought back to the first night she remembered seeing him at Papa Jack's—all dressed down but still smelling like money. What was he doing here? He'd be working for peanuts here. It seemed to her that he had enough money to buy the whole danged peanut farm.

Tarrant shrugged, drawing attention to his broad expanse of shoulders clad in a dark blue jacket. "Maybe I'd look more the part standing behind a bar, mixing drinks," he replied.

Despite her annoyance, Charlotte found herself reassessing Tarrant. She thought that he was perfectly dressed for the interview—not too corporate, not too casual. She knew that Jack would be watching that kind of subtle clue very carefully. Potential candidates who had come in dressed to the nines were almost immediately crossed off the list. Jack had figured that if they could afford those kinds of threads, they wouldn't be happy working for tips at the bar.

On the other hand, if they came in dressed in casual clothes, it told him that if they didn't care how they looked to interview for the job, they wouldn't care about the job itself. Jack knew that sometimes he may have been too quick to judge by appearances alone. With Meleah constantly warning him against potential discrimination suits, he made sure he talked long enough with each candidate to confirm his original impression.

This one ought to make a deep impression, Charlotte

thought. She circled around him, making soft noises of approval under her breath.

Dark blue jacket, starched white shirt, tailored gray pants—very traditional. The bold-pattern tie that he wore was just brash enough to let Charlotte know that he had a flair for fashion as well. She tilted her head, checking out his left ear. He'd meticulously removed each of the earrings that had studded his ear the nights he'd staked out Papa Jack's.

"Do I open my mouth and let you check my teeth, too?" Tarrant asked, twisting around to follow her progress.

"Don't put it past me. What makes you want to work here of all places, Mr. Cole?" Charlotte asked bluntly.

Tarrant gambled that Charlotte was just being nosy and wasn't actually going to conduct the interview. When he'd decided to answer the ad in the paper, he'd had a plan, a strategy for getting this job. He was going to work on the old man first. He would appeal to his sense of the entrepreneur. And if Meleah herself had conducted the interview, he'd mix in just enough charm to remind her that having him around might not be so bad. He'd hadn't counted on Charlotte, however. He hadn't worked her into the equation. If he had to, he would. But he had to know how to adjust his thinking in order to get to her. "Are you phase one of the interview or are you just screening the applicants?"

His question was an honest one, but risky in light of the fact that if she had any pull with Jack Harmon, he'd just ruined his chances of getting this job. Not that it was such a plum, as Charlotte had hinted. But he had to get it. He had to be hired on here at Papa Jack's.

"Both. Neither," Charlotte said, lifting her chin to glare up at him. She didn't miss the implication of his question. His tone said plainly to her that since she was just the head server, he wasn't going to waste his time answering any of her questions, especially if she wasn't the one with the say-so. It was time to set Mr. *GQ* straight. "You can rest assured that if I don't like your answer, you won't be getting through to Jack Harmon. You know that, don't you, sugar?"

"I do now," Tarrant said with exaggerated politeness.

"So," Charlotte said, folding her arms across her chest and thrusting out her dimpled chin. "Let's start from the top. What makes you want to work at Papa Jack's?"

"Nice setup you have here," Tarrant remarked, looking around the restaurant. Without the haze of food and smoke, without the noise and the crowds and the general hustle of Galveston nightlife, Tarrant thought that the place actually didn't seem that bad. Whatever Charlotte must have seen in his eyes or heard in his voice, it touched a nerve with her. "You've made some improvements since I've been here."

"We started out back in seventy-two as a little hole in the wall with a twelve-inch black-and-white TV with a coat hanger for an antenna and only two things on the menu—beer and pretzels. And sometimes we ran out of pretzels."

"But not beer?"

"Are you kidding? What's a sports bar without beer? Jack would have set up his own still before he let that happen. But you're not here because you like draft. You've hardly drunk anything at all while you were here."

"You remember all of that?"

"I've got a memory like a steel trap," Charlotte bragged. "In fact, a lot of folks are interested in this place since Jack won the lottery. You did hear about that, didn't you, Mr. Cole?"

"I think I may have read something about it."

"Sure you did," Charlotte prattled on. "In fact, you were here that night, weren't you?" Charlotte touched him lightly on the chest with her index finger.

"Sure was."

"That's what I thought." Her tone changed to something slightly disgusted. She wondered if he was one of the ones sniffing around here after Jack's money. It wouldn't surprise her. After all, he must have had one disappointing evening when Meleah told him that his sister's accident was just an accident. No one at Papa Jack's was to blame. Charlotte hadn't believed that this Tarrant Cole would give up so easily. But it had been three weeks since he'd last shown his face around here. Maybe he'd accepted that. Then again, maybe not. Here he was, figurative hat in hand, begging for a piece of the pie. At least he was doing it the old-fashioned way, asking for a job to give the appearance of earning any money that Jack doled out.

"If you'll wait just a moment, I'll go and get Jack. He'll be the one conducting the interview."

Tarrant nodded. He'd gotten past round one.

"Trae should have given you an application to fill out."

"He did."

"Do you have your paperwork all ready?"

Tarrant tapped a leather portfolio holding his resume. "Right here."

"Somehow I knew you'd have everything all together, sugar."

At that moment, Jack Harmon opened the door to his office and began, "Charlie, has that girl—"

He'd hardly gotten the words out before Meleah opened the front door, her arms filled with packages from various stores. She could barely see over the top of them. She twisted her head to direct something to a barrel-chested, bow-legged young man trailing behind her. "Do me a favor, Elliot, and grab that box on the front seat, will you?"

"I told you that you should have picked up that little luggage carrier cart," the young man muttered, brushing away an invisible spec of lint from his tailored slacks.

"What do I need a cart for, Ell? I've got you," Meleah said sweetly.

"Cute. Real cute," Elliot returned. "I'll be back in a bit."

"Where on God's green earth have you been!" Jack bellowed. Meleah jumped, making several packages slip from her arms to the floor.

"Pops!" Meleah cried in dismay, kneeling down to gather them again. "Look what you made me do."

Tarrant started forward to help Meleah. Even after her cold brush-off and several weeks to cool off, he still felt an undeniable tug—a tightening in his abdomen that rippled all the way to his groin. He'd barely taken a step when Charlotte grasped him by the arm, squeezed, and said, "Trust me, sugar. If you stick your nose in it now, you'll only make your potential employer mad at you."

Tarrant turned a puzzled gaze to Charlotte, but remained where he stood.

"I asked you a question, Meleah. Where have you been?" Jack exclaimed, pushing through Charlotte and Tarrant.

"Hey, hey. Uncle J. What's the word?" The young man pushed himself past Tarrant with a muttered, " 'Scuse me, cuz." He made a fist and held it out to Jack to give him a little *dap*.

Jack slapped the boy's hand away. "I ain't got time for your foolishness, Elliot."

"Aw, Uncle J. Don't lose your cool. If you have to blame anyone, blame me. I'm the one who kept Le-Le out, dragging her around town. We had some shopping to do."

"I told you I was going to run errands. I even left you a note. Didn't you get it?" Meleah reminded her father.

All of the bluster blew out of Jack. "Maybe I did. I just forgot."

"I wrote it in the desk organizer I bought you. If you used it for something other than to prop up the corner of that rickety old desk, you wouldn't forget so much, Pops. If I have to move your desk one more time to pry it loose . . ." Her voice trailed off with quiet warning.

"Never mind about my desk. And sorry I yelled at you. I've had a long, hard day."

"It's only three o'clock." Meleah twisted her arm to glance at her watch.

"But it started at four in the morning—" Jack returned.

"You think your day was hard, try haggling with the salespersons on commission," Elliot cut in.

Jack started to rummage through Meleah's packages. "What did you do? Buy up half of the island?"

"Oh, Pops, wait until you check this out!" Meleah said excitedly. "There's more stuff out in the car. Come on, Ell. Let's show Pops what we got!"

Charlotte cleared her throat loudly, and gestured in Tarrant's direction. "Something else you're forgetting?"

"You? What are you doing here?" Meleah asked bluntly. "I thought I told you that there was nothing here for you at Papa Jack's."

Again Tarrant reassessed his mode of approach. He wasn't going to work much magic on Meleah with an irate father and a nosy—whatever he was—eyeing him from head to foot. He slammed on the mental brakes. The man eyeing him with a mixture of suspicion and curiosity, if not a favorite of Jack's, was close to Meleah. From what he'd observed, the woman had a very small circle of friends and family. This worked best when he didn't have an audience.

"Nothing but a J-O-B," Tarrant returned. "I'm here for an interview."

"You've got to be kidding."

"Serious as a heart attack."

"Pops?" Meleah then turned to her father in question. "You offering this man a job?"

"You're that fellow come to apply for that bartending job?" Jack asked.

"Yes, sir. I'm Tarrant Cole," Tarrant said, introducing himself. He extended his hand.

"I'm Jack Harmon. This is my daughter, Meleah." Jack followed suit, clasping hands and pumping vigorously.

"He knows who we are, Pops. I'm surprised that you don't you know who he is," Meleah said.

"What a minute . . . you're that guy, aren't you?" Jack said, squinting at Tarrant and shaking his index finger at him.

"Well, that certainly narrows it down," Charlotte quipped.

"Ohhhh. You mean *that* guy," Elliot said. "Le-Le told me all about him, Uncle J. Sorry about your sister, dawg." Elliot drawled. "Bad news." He made a fist and pumped it against his chest a couple of times over his heart. "I feel for you. If you need a good doctor, let me know. I know folks all over this island. I can get you a hook-up."

Tarrant ignored him, thinking, *Clown. You don't know the first thing about what I'm feeling.* He turned his attention back to Meleah. "Talking about me behind my back, Ms. Harmon?"

"Nothing you haven't heard before. Nothing I won't say again to your face," Meleah said in a chilling mix of sugar and venom.

"So are you gonna interview him or what?" Charlotte demanded. "It's not as if we don't need the extra help, Jack."

Meleah made a small sound in the back of her throat, then resumed her seat at her favorite spot at the end of the bar. She and her cousin Elliot began to rummage through the bags.

"Come on, Mr. Cole"—Jack motioned—"let's get the preliminaries over with."

Tarrant took a mental deep breath to prepare for the interview. He'd been in business for himself for a while. It had been a long time since had to put on a performance. Already he'd been thrown more curves than he cared for in one afternoon. Speaking of curves . . .

As Tarrant passed Meleah, he stole a glance at her. He wondered if she would participate in the interview. At the moment, he didn't know if he wanted her in the room or not. She was definitely a distraction. He didn't know if he could bounce back and forth between the persona he intended to display for Jack Harmon and the one he held in reserve for Jack's daughter. If Jack was as bulldog protective as he appeared, he wouldn't approve of Tarrant coming on to his daughter—not even a hint of flirtation.

The big man passed her, as watchful as ever. But Meleah ignored him, pretending to be too absorbed in peeling the cellophane wrapper from a computer software accounting package to notice him. Yet as he walked away, she followed him with her eyes without turning her head. She would have continued to watch him if her cousin Elliot hadn't popped in front of her saying, "Whatcha got to drink in this joint, Le-Le? I'm parched."

"You'd better stick to orange juice. And don't doctor it," Charlotte warned. Over her shoulder, she said to Tarrant. "Good luck, Mr. Cole."

"Thanks." Tarrant turned his smile on Charlotte, then followed Jack into his office.

Charlotte hopped onto the stool next to Meleah. "Well? What do you think?"

"About what?" Meleah asked.

"Don't act like you don't know. What do you think about Mr. Cole, sugar? Do you think he's server material?"

"How should I know?"

"Do you think we should hire him?"

"We? Leave me out of it. That will be up to Pops to decide."

"I thought you'd want a piece of that interview action yourself," Elliot said, grabbing a gin bottle and holding it over his orange juice.

Charlotte snatched it from him. "It's only three o'clock in the afternoon, Ell. Why don't you cool it on the alcohol."

"If my folks can start at ten o'clock in the morning, I think I'm doing pretty good by waiting until after the sun has made tracks across the sky. What about it, Le-Le?"

"I'm not drinking," Meleah said distractedly. She then looked up at Elliot. "What makes you say that? Why would you think I'd be interested in him?" She sounded defensive.

"I saw you checking him out," Elliot teased.

"That oh-so-sexy voice," Charlotte put in.

"What has a sexy voice got to do with how well he mixes cocktails?" Meleah asked. "If I were interested in him at all, that would be the only reason."

"You don't have to tell me how well a star-quality personality will pack 'em in, Le-Le," Elliot told her. "That's the only reason some of those jokers keep coming back, night after night. They're all waiting for their star—that would be you—to fall for one of them."

"I don't know about you, but with these long hours we've been keeping, I'd rather look at Tarrant for most of the evening than some skinny kid. Sugar, if I were a few years younger . . ."

"You'd still be old enough to be his—"

"Older sister," Charlotte cut in.

"Yeah, right. You can get yourself worked up over him if you want, Charlotte. I'm staying out of it. Pops said he would handle that end of the business for the time being. Let him. The more excuses he has not to go through those papers, the better. I've got more than enough to do without wasting my time chatting with Mr. Ultra-Brite Smile."

Charlotte cleared her throat and hoped that Meleah wouldn't find out about the evil notes that Jack was receiving.

"My . . . my! Is it just me or did a cold front just breeze through here in the middle of June?" Elliot teased her.

"Well, I hope he gets the job," Charlotte said.

"Why? What if he's lousy with the customers?"

"I dunno. There's something about him—something I like. Call it instinct, if you will."

"Call it hormones," Meleah retorted. "I think you like him because he turned that pretty-boy smile on you."

"He does have a nice smile."

"Too practiced." Meleah dismissed it. "Too fake."

Elliot tsked in mock sympathy. "I didn't figure you to be a player hater, Le-Le."

"He has a pleasant voice," Charlotte continued. "It should work out well as he's chatting up the customers. A good bartender knows how to work the crowd. And I don't have to mention his great body."

"If you didn't have to, why did you?"

"What's the matter with you, sugar? Have you been playing accountant so long that you've forgotten what a good figure is?" Charlotte laughed aloud at her own pun. She and Elliot slapped high-fives.

"You're right about one thing, Charlotte," Meleah said in a deceptive, acquiescent voice. Charlotte recognized the tone Meleah used when she was about to become her most cutting.

"And what's that?"

"There is something about him. I think it's trouble. I can't put my finger on it . . ."

"Maybe that's your trouble."

"What do you mean?"

"You're playing it too cool with only trying to put a finger on him. Why not go whole hog and use both hands? I know if I get the chance, I will."

"Charlotte, I don't think you should be making comments like that. That kinda comment might be considered sexual harassment if overheard by the wrong people."

"Oh, pooh-pooh!" Charlotte said derisively. "Who's talking about harassing? I'm talking about two adults trying out some very adult—"

"I think that's enough, Charlotte," Meleah said sharply. "I don't want to talk about Mr. Cole anymore."

"Fine, if that's the way you feel about it. But if he gets the job, you'd better get used to the sound of his name."

SIX

"How about a drink, Mr. Cole? Name your poison," Jack offered, as he closed the office door behind him.

"No, thanks. Not while I'm working." Tarrant waved the offer aside.

"I haven't offered you the job yet, son." Jack raised his eyebrows in surprise. It was pretty presumptuous to assume that he could just walk in off the street and get the job.

"Pounding the pavement is very hard work, Mr. Harmon."

"You don't look none the worse for wear. How long have you been out of work?"

"I'm not exactly out of work."

"You mean you have another job? I don't know if it was clear enough in the ad in the paper, but I'm looking for full-time help, not a moonlighter, son."

"That wasn't my intention. I can give you all the hours you need."

"You're not working?"

"I am."

"But you said—"

"I know what I said. And I told you, I can give you all the hours you need. I set my own hours. I guess you can say I'm a little like you, Mr. Harmon. I'm a businessman."

"Business not going too good? Is that why you're willing to work for peanuts?"

"Business is as good as it gets. I just need a little extra to put me over the edge. I have uh . . . extra expenses."

"Meleah told me that your sister was recently in an accident."

"She's in a coma," Tarrant said, and hoped that his tone didn't convey all of the bitterness he felt at having to ask the ones he thought responsible for her condition to help her out of it.

Jack cursed softly under his breath. "I'm sorry to hear that, Mr. Cole. It's all coming back to me now. She was here about a month ago . . . with some real losers."

Tarrant stiffened, then shifted uneasily. Jack seemed a little callous to him. That was his sister, for goodness' sake. "Loser or not, Mr. Harmon, she's my sister and I have to help her."

Loyal, Jack thought, and filed away that piece of information for future reference. He scanned Tarrant's application, paying special attention to what he'd listed as his strengths.

"You restore cars for a living? Been making a living at it for about six years now," Jack read aloud. "It's obviously been doing fine by you."

"I do all right."

"More than all right," Jack said crisply. He compared Tarrant's well-tailored look with his own. If Jack had to give a name to his own appearance, he'd label it geriatric grunge. "Son, I don't think you'd fit in here at Papa Jack's. I'll probably bring a herd of lawyers and EEOC people down on me, but I gotta be straight with you. You're way overqualified for what we'd have you do here. You wouldn't be happy emptying ashtrays and chasing down dirty glasses. That's grunt work. College kid material. They're so desperate for cash, they'd haul trash on their backs if I asked them to. But you . . . I don't think you'd bend that far for me."

"I'm willing to work, Mr. Harmon." Tarrant leaned forward, trying to impress Jack with his sincerity. "I told you. I need the next extra money just as badly as some snot-nosed kid. I don't want to play the sympathy card but I'll be just as straight with you. My sister's medical bills are mounting into the thousands every day. She's not covered on my insurance or my parents'. That means that money comes out of my pocket. Unlike some folks, I don't think I'm going to hit the lottery."

When Jack grunted, Tarrant wasn't sure if it was in irritation at his jab at Jack's sudden accumulation of wealth or not. So far his plan had been working according to his predictions. He knew that Jack Harmon was a tough old bird. Tarrant figured that he had exactly five minutes to prove why he should be given a job here. Maybe less than five minutes. After Meleah's hatchet job, reminding her father that he'd quietly harassed them for a time, he figured that the clock was ticking on him. He'd gotten past that Charlotte, and now he was in the interview chair—secretly sweating bullets and hoping that fortune was with him.

"What happened to your sister was a tragedy and I'm sorry for that . . . but I don't owe you any favors."

"I'm not asking for any. I'm asking for a job."

"The trouble is, you've come asking here. Knowing how you feel about your sister, that puts me in an uncomfortable position." Jack paused. "Then again, that's what you were banking on, isn't it?"

Tarrant didn't respond. When he didn't, Jack pushed him a little more. "I have just one more question for you." He leaned back in his chair and propped his feet on his desk, and puffed alight an expensive cigar. When he saw Tarrant's face show an interest, he pushed the box across the desk and said, "Help yourself."

"What would you like to know?" Tarrant asked, sniffing the thickly rolled cigar appreciatively. He slipped it inside of his jacket pocket. "Pleasure later. This is business."

"Speaking of business . . . what do you think about my daughter?"

"Your daughter?" Tarrant asked, taken off guard by the abrupt shift in the conversation.

"Meleah," Jack elaborated. "You remember her, don't you?" he teased, knowing fully well that Tarrant did remember her. "Tell me what you think about her."

Tarrant paused noticeably before answering. He wanted to be very careful not to offend Mr. Harmon. He also took his time because he wasn't quite certain what his first impression was. He didn't want to count the night that he and the brothas wound up at Papa Jack's. That wasn't a fair assessment of her. Or was it?

For the pressure she'd been under, she'd handled herself very well. It was busy that night. Yet she ran the place without signs of strain or slowing down. When Jackie D had threatened to give her a swat on her behind, she could have thrown them out. But she hadn't. Tarrant didn't want to think it was because she didn't want to lose a paying customer. For every one that slipped out the door, a dozen more clamored to get inside.

In the nights that followed, when he'd become a permanent, nightly resident—silently but steadily watching her—she had remained even. Not knowing his intentions, she could have called the cops on him to escort him from the premises. Or worse, she could have had the countless number of island roughnecks who buzzed around her, vying for her attention, forcibly remove him. More than once, Tarrant found himself locked in a staring match with some steroid-enhanced goon across the room. If it weren't so disturbing, Tarrant would almost laugh out loud. He knew he didn't stand a chance with her. Why would they consider him a competitor for Meleah's attention?

Each night when he left, he kept a close watch over his shoulder, expecting at any moment to find himself dragged into a dark alley and beaten into an unrecognizable pulp. Such was the power this woman seemed to have. She ruled the restaurant. Her subjects were unquestioningly loyal to her. Why he wasn't tracked down, he didn't know. Maybe she was a more benevolent ruler than she let on with her ice princess routine.

When she'd finally agreed to meet him at his table, Tarrant thought he'd seen true sympathy in her eyes. Her attractive physical appearance on top of a caring soul could be his undoing. If it weren't for the fact that he was on a mission, Tarrant could see himself falling into the rank-and-file of those waiting for their moment to serve in her court.

"I think your daughter is very . . . nice," Tarrant said cautiously, then looked up in surprise when Jack exploded into laughter. Jack had watched Tarrant thinking for several seconds, knowing he would probably come up with something diplomatic to keep from ruining his chance with this job. But the look on Tarrant's face when he thought he was keeping a neutral expression was enough for Jack to know that "nice" wasn't what Tarrant was really thinking.

"Come on now, Mr. Cole. I know you can do better than that," Jack said with a derisive snort. "I thought we were talking straight here—man to man."

Despite what Charlotte said about him, he wasn't

completely clueless when it came to his own daughter. Jack knew the effect Meleah had on men. Too many times Jack had watched them approach her where she sat at her favorite stool. They were intent on breaking through her ice princess defenses, only to be gently but firmly turned away by her rebuffs. Night after night, sometimes the same men within the same night would try to engage her in conversation. Watching them, Jack would shake his head in silent commiseration. Poor idiots. Why didn't they ever learn?

Sometimes his little girl remained tight-lipped and unresponsive. Sometimes she would cut them down with a well-timed, tart-tongued remark. Other nights she laughed just as easily, and flirted just as outrageously. Yet the end to Meleah's laughter and flirting always coincided with the bar's last call. From then on, she became all business.

More than one of the men chasing her would then turn to Jack for consolation and advice. They all wanted to know the same thing. Why would a woman like her be content to remain alone when they obviously had so much to offer her?

Jack couldn't blame them for risking rejection night after night. The qualities they saw in Meleah were the same ones that had attracted Jack to Meleah's mother. Marian Harmon was one striking woman. It had taken Jack over two years to win Marian's affection. To this day, he still insisted that the reason why he wound up with her was not because of his persistence, but her pity.

Meleah had inherited Marian's same thick auburn hair, snapping ebony eyes, and flawless skin. Unfortunately she had also inherited Jack's stubborn streak. When Marian was killed in a boating accident, Meleah was only six years old. Even at six, Jack could see how strong willed she would become. She refused to believe her mother was gone. She demanded to be taken to the marina every day for a month where she could watch the ships come in and wait for her mother.

Jack cleared his throat gruffly to cover the sudden choking sensation of unshed tears.

"Well?" he demanded of Tarrant. "What do you have to say for yourself, son?"

"What do you want me to say, sir?"

"You can start off by speaking your mind," Jack encouraged. "No one holds their tongue around here. If you're going to hold your own, you'd better be prepared to do the same."

"I hardly know your daughter. How can I make a snap judgment?"

"And still get the job?" Jack teased. "Let me clue you in on something. Meleah is a lot of things. She's smart as a whip, with a tongue to match. Pretty as a picture, loyal, stubborn, and sentimental. There's no room on that list for 'nice.'"

"Tell me, Mr. Harmon, how was I supposed to know all of that? The last few times I was out here, your daughter didn't give me much play."

"Everyone has a first impression. What's yours?"

"Before I answer that, what does this have to do with my getting the job?"

"How badly do you want it?"

"You already know the answer to that. What I don't know is why you're asking."

"All right, Mr. Cole, I'll tell you why I asked you what you thought of Meleah. I wanted to know what you thought because you'll be spending a lot of time with her. Her hand is in every phase of this business. You don't have anything against women bosses, do you, Cole?"

"A boss is a boss is a boss." Tarrant shrugged noncommittally. "I just want to do my job, and collect my paycheck."

"Since you've been running your own business, how do you think you'll adjust to having someone telling you what to do? Not just telling you, but telling you often?"

"Everyone who comes to my restoration shop for a special-request vehicle makes me their boss. At any given time, I have as many as ten bosses. I don't think one more is going to break me."

Jack raised his eyebrows but remained silent. The man had a point.

"So do I get the job?"

"I'm going to say yes. But I'm giving you six weeks probation. If it looks like you mesh, then you're on for as long as you want to stay. Deal?"

"Deal," Tarrant said, extending his hand for a shake to seal the agreement. Jack nodded in approval. There was something to be said for a man who still believed in the bond of a firm handshake.

"Let me get you a W-2 form for you to fill out and see about getting you a uniform."

"Uniform?"

"It's a sports bar, Mr. Cole. We have to keep a certain image. You'll be wearing a striped referee jersey. Wear it with dark pants and comfortable shoes. On a good night, you're going to start to feel like a ref."

"What do you mean?"

"Since you're new to Papa Jack's, I can't just start you out behind the bar . . . not until I know you know how to mix a couple of drinks without poisoning somebody."

"I've got a little experience behind the bar," Tarrant said.

"You do? Where? It didn't say so on your application."

"It was a temporary job. It lasted for only a couple of weeks." When he first started his own restoration business, times were rough. He took whatever odd job he could find to keep from going bankrupt. His stint as a bartender wasn't a temporary job because of the nature of the work, but because of the nature of his sister. When Amber showed up a couple of times on his shift at the local club, begging him to give her freebies, he knew it couldn't last. He moved on.

"I can mix your standards—Seven-and-Sevens, Blue Hawaiians, daiquiris from any fruit on God's green earth. I know just the right balance of alcohol and mixer to keep your patrons coming back without breaking your liquor budget. You want flashy, I can do flashy . . . behind the back stuff. I can put on a show for you. But if that's not what you want, if you want sympathetic and silent, I can do that, too," Tarrant assured him. "I'm not much of a drinker so you won't have to worry about your stock coming up short."

"I don't doubt it," Jack said. Nothing in this man's assertion said ego trip or fraud. He knew what he was doing. But he couldn't just start him out behind the bar—not without making sure that those who'd been there, those who had seniority, trusted him.

"You, son, are going to start out as a rookie. A bar back. Your job is to keep the bartenders happy. Keep them stocked with whatever they need. On busy nights, I may have as many as five tenders serving the customers. You've got to keep all five happy. It won't be easy. Some of them get kind of testy when their supply runs low. Most likely you'll find yourself pulled in five different directions at once. Can you handle that?"

"We'll see, won't we?" Tarrant answered with just enough confidence to give Jack the impression that Tarrant had an idea what he was getting himself into. He did know. At least he thought he did. He'd seen how the servers and the bartenders literally had Trae, the rocket man, shooting around like someone had lit a fire under him. Tarrant didn't expect to be treated as head lackey for long. He intended to make himself so valuable at Papa Jack's that they wouldn't dare waste his talents on chasing after dirty glasses.

"You won't regret this, Mr. Harmon," Tarrant said.

"I'd better not. By the way, my friends call me Jack," Jack said. "Welcome to Papa Jack's, Tarrant." He lifted his glass in a toast to him. "Here's to days and nights of thirsty, armchair athletes."

Charlotte and Elliot stood at Jack's door, with their ears placed against it.

"Sounds like a go."

"Big man scored a big hit with Jack," Elliot whispered loudly to Meleah.

"What are you doing? Get away from that door!"

"Hush, Le-Le. I can't hear what's going on inside when you're flapping your lips," Elliot shushed her.

"If Pops knew you were eavesdropping . . ." Meleah let her voice trail off threateningly.

Charlotte threw Meleah a disgusted look over her shoulder. "How do you ever expect to learn anything important that goes on around here if you don't listen every now and then?"

"I'm the business manager, Charlotte," Meleah said, in a mock indignant voice. "If I don't know what's going on around here, then it shouldn't be happening."

"Meleah, will you get over here!" Charlotte said with more urgency.

"Me?" Meleah asked, pointing to herself. "You're not going to get me in trouble with you."

"You don't want to know what Pops is saying about you to Tarrant Cole?"

"Don't know. Don't want to know," Meleah said, opening a box containing the computer manuals.

"All right. If you say so," Charlotte said in a voice designed to pique Meleah's curiosity. "But if I were you . . ." Her voice trailed off ominously.

Meleah slid off her stool, and tiptoed to the door. "Get out of the way. Give a girl some room," she whispered, elbowing both Charlotte and Elliot out of the way. "What's so important that you feel like you had to drag me into this?"

As soon as Meleah placed her ear to the door, she heard two chairs sliding back across the wooden floor. She could also hear voices. The words were muffled but started to grow louder as Jack and Tarrant approached the door. Charlotte and Meleah stifled their guilty giggles, and scurried over to the bar. Meleah hastily picked up a manual, and started speaking rapidly to Charlotte as Jack opened the door.

"And with the extra five-point-two gigabyte hard drive, I can increase my storage capacity," Meleah said breathlessly.

"You don't say, five-point-two whatcha-ma-jiggers," Charlotte replied in her most interested voice.

Jack and Tarrant exchanged amused glances. Who did they think they were fooling?

"Well, ladies," Jack hailed them. "Say hello to our new employee."

"That was fast," Meleah muttered under her breath to Charlotte.

"Oh, what a surprise!" Charlotte said loudly to cover Meleah's comment.

"You can cut the innocent act, folks," Jack said, planting his hands on his hips. "Charlotte, I know you're not trying to make me believe you weren't listening in at the door. I can see the makeup stains you left all up and down the woodwork."

"I told y'all you shouldn't be listening in on other folks' conversations," Elliot said snidely.

Meleah turned and punched him on the arm.

"Don't be mad at me because your butt got caught."

"So," Meleah said, clearing her throat. "When do you start, Mr. Cole?" She congratulated herself on sounding professional when in truth, every sense in her body was gathering for one collective yell: *No!*

"Tonight," Tarrant said. He wished that she were wearing the amethyst necklace today. He wanted to know how the news affected her.

"Charlotte will show you where the uniforms are. Oh, and make sure he gets a policy manual, too, would you?" Meleah said, then turned back to her computer manual, and turned several more pages as if completely engrossed.

"There'll be a quiz on our policies tomorrow," Charlotte teased Tarrant.

"Don't worry. I don't have any trouble reading between the lines," Tarrant said, commenting directly on Meleah's cool reception.

"Right this way, Mr. Cole," Charlotte said, crooking her finger at him. She turned on her heel, and walked past Meleah, winking as she did so. As Tarrant followed behind Charlotte, he paused at Meleah's stool.

"A Pentium three." He nodded appreciatively at the computer box. "A lot of power at your fingertips."

"You know about computers?" Charlotte asked.

"Maybe you could help Meleah set it up later." Jack suggested to test both Meleah and Tarrant. If he was going to work here, he'd better learn how to play nice with the lady boss.

"Oh, no, you don't have to do that," Meleah said quickly. "I can do it myself."

Tarrant then reached over her shoulder, and grasped her book.

"Hey! What do you think you're . . ." she sputtered.

"You may get more out of the manual, Ms. Harmon, if you stop reading it upside down," he remarked just loud enough for everyone to hear.

Meleah felt her face burn hot. Charlotte's snicker at her expense didn't help matters either. She flashed her a look that said "traitor!" Meleah then squared her shoulders, and said with mock awe, "Thanks for the advice, Mr. Cole. But if I need help, I'll be sure to come to you to draw on your expansive expertise."

As Charlotte led him toward the storeroom, Tarrant said, "Now why do I get the feeling that she'll see me and the computer burn in hell before she calls me?"

"Go on, call him in here," Jack encouraged. "Tarrant said he knows about these things."

Jack helped Meleah lift the new computer out of its Styrofoam packing and placed it on her desk.

"Charlotte is giving him a tour of Papa Jack's, Pops," Meleah said, her voice tinged with exasperation. "Besides, I don't need his help. The salesclerk told me that all I really had to do was plug it in, and I could get right to work."

"Uh-huh," Jack said, unconvinced. "And did the clerk tell you where this little do-hickey goes?" Jack held up a rectangular object with a wide slit in the front, and several cables dangling from the back. He shook it several times.

"No, Pops, she didn't," Meleah said, carefully taking the object from him. "But I don't need Mr. Cole to tell me what to do with this and where it goes. It's obvious that this is—"

"An external high-density disk drive," Tarrant offered from the entrance of Jack's office.

Jack looked up quickly. How long had Tarrant been standing there? And what had he heard? Not that they were saying anything that he shouldn't hear. It was the fact that he'd come up so quietly that bothered him. A man that big shouldn't be that stealthy. It made Jack edgy.

"Right," Meleah said promptly. "I'm going to use the two-fifty megabyte disks to back up the hard drive. I learned the hard way from that old clunker over there that crashes happen." She frowned at the old three-eighty-six computer with a monochromatic monitor as if she were looking at an old, sickly, suffering family pet that should be put out of its misery.

"All done with the tour?" Jack called, removing yet another item from Meleah's stack of boxes. When he shook the box to check its contents, Meleah promptly relieved him of that, too. "You touch one more thing, old man, and I'm going to put you over in the corner. You will not be allowed to touch any of my things."

"Aw . . . you never let me have any fun," Jack complained. He made a comic show of sitting on his hands.

Watching the exchange between Meleah and Jack, Tarrant experienced a brief, intense moment of jealousy. He had often called his father old man. But it was never with the obvious affection Meleah showed for her father. He wondered if he and his father ever shared a light moment like the one he'd just witnessed.

"The tour . . ." Tarrant said, clearing his throat and bringing their attention back to him. "Charlotte seems to think I'm ready to start. She said the true test of my memory skills will come tonight during the peak hours."

"You've got that right. There's a big basketball game

on tonight," Jack said, rubbing his hands briskly. "That always packs 'em in."

"Basketball is out of season," Tarrant said knowingly. "What is this? Some sort of satellite pick from some, obscure foreign country where all of the has-beens and never was's go to play? Why all of the interest in this one game?"

"This isn't your regular basketball game. It's a charity game," Jack said.

Meleah tsked at Jack. "There's nothing charitable about this match. This is a grudge match between the San Antonio Spurs and the Houston Rockets. I guess the teams want bragging rights as the best team in Texas."

"The game is a complete sell-out. There's not a seat left, so a lot of armchair athletes will pack it in to get seats in front of all of our televisions before the game starts. Orders will be flying so hot and heavy that you won't have time to remember, just react."

"I'm ready," Tarrant said with calm assurance.

"We'll see," Meleah muttered.

"See? Meleah's pulling out her new toy, and I thought you might help her get it set up if you have the time," Jack said quickly, to cover Meleah's comment.

"This is not a toy, Pops. It's very state-of-the-art equipment."

"Where's your printer?" Tarrant asked, glancing at the boxes scattered around the room.

"Printer?" Meleah asked.

"Didn't the person who sold you all of this talk to you about peripherals?"

"Well, *duh!* Of course she did. Why do you think I picked up that external storage drive? I thought for now I'd keep everything on disk," Meleah said defensively. "It's the best course of action. We save space and save a tree at the same time." What did this Cole person think she was—an idiot? She'd done her research before she bought the computer. She frowned at him to let him know that she didn't appreciate having her judgment questioned by a new employee.

"Is she going to need a printer?" Jack wanted to know.

"It's a handy piece of equipment to have. But I'm sure Ms. Harmon is very well aware of that," Tarrant placated, showing that he understood her frown of disapproval.

"That settles it. Meleah, take the checkbook and go right out and buy you one of those printer things," Jack said, waving his hand toward the door.

"I don't think that's a good idea, Pops."

"Why not? Tarrant says you need one."

"He gave a suggestion, Pops, not an order," she retorted.

"Now, Meleah, don't get upset. The man was only trying to help."

Meleah's husky voice dropped another octave, indicating that she was about to get nasty. "Did I ask for his help?"

"It wouldn't hurt you to be a little friendly toward the man. You were the one who asked for him, begged me to get him, in fact."

"I didn't ask for *him!*" Meleah said, jerking her thumb in Tarrant's direction.

"Oh, you don't remember storming into my office, threatening my life, if we didn't get more help? You asked for him, I got him. Now you're stuck with him. Now deal with that!" Jack said triumphantly.

"You didn't even screen him properly. You didn't even test him at the bar. If he turns out to be no good, you'll be stuck. So deal with that!"

"Don't try to hide your feelings. Say what you really

mean. I'll just pretend that I'm not here. And it's only six weeks worth of stuck." Again, Meleah and Jack were behaving as if Tarrant wasn't around. Tarrant reminded them of his presence.

"Besides," Meleah continued on a calmer note, "the stores will be closing in about an hour, and I want to do more comparison shopping before picking up the first thing that comes along."

"You'll be more pleased with the quality if you go with a laser printer," Tarrant contributed.

"I'll be sure to keep that in mind when I go," Meleah said in dismissal, reaching into another box to pull out her monitor.

"Why don't you take Tarrant with you," Jack suggested.

"Pops," Meleah said, with a hint of warning.

Jack then raised his hand in surrender. "I'm only trying to help." He cleared his throat and said, "Your shift starts in a couple of hours, Tarrant. Maybe you want to grab something to eat before the first of the crowd roars in."

"I've got my uniform and no place I need to be. Why don't I grab a bite here to sample more of Leon's fine cuisine."

"C'mon, then. Our club sandwich is the best in the city."

"I prefer the beef fajitas," Tarrant said.

"That'll work." Jack nodded in agreement. "Coming, Meleah?"

"No thanks, Pops," Meleah said, her voice muffled as she leaned deep into a large box to pull out another piece of equipment. "I'll grab something later."

As she leaned forward, Tarrant found his eyes roving along the long line of her legs, over the smooth curve of her denim-clad derriere, to her trim waist all the way up to her hair—that mass of silk and spirals! He felt his fingers twitch, as an irrepressible impulse to touch her passed rapidly from his brain to his hand. For a moment, Tarrant put himself in Jackie D's shoes. He understood what his friend must have been going through when he'd almost swatted Meleah on her behind. Though it was only six weeks, it seemed like ages ago. He felt just that tied to this Harmon family.

"You guys go on ahead." She waved them away as she continued to rummage. "I'll be along later."

"Come on, Tarrant. My stomach's complaining loud enough for the both of us. A man could die of hunger waiting for her. How about those fajitas?"

Jack could have been offering him a piece of his multimillion-dollar winnings, for all Tarrant heard. He blinked, forcing his mind back where he was, what he was supposed to be doing. Tarrant had been staring at her as if he and Meleah were the only ones in the room. He was going to have to stop that. He was going to have to stop blanking out every time that woman enticed him. No, not enticed. That didn't come near what he was starting to experience whenever she came around. It was full-blown arousal. And if he didn't do something fast, everyone would know it.

Before, when he'd had that reaction, he'd been sitting at his table, under the cover of the semidark restaurant. This was still broad daylight, in the small, cramped office space. It would be pretty obvious to everyone what he was thinking if he didn't do something quickly. He shifted his arms so that the uniform shirt draped over his arm covered his groin.

"I . . . I think I'll take a rain check on that, Mr. Harmon. Now that I think about it, there is something I need to take care of before tonight." He had to do something to get his perspective back. And he knew just the thing to do it. A simple visit to Amber's bedside in the hospital would remind him quick, fast, and in a hurry why he was taking this low-paying, high-stress, no-gratitude job where the boss was a beautiful but all-business enchantress. "Let me know what time I need to be here."

Jack looked askance at him. He wondered if Tarrant had backed out because Meleah decided not to join them.

"All right then. I'll see you at five-thirty sharp."

"I'll be here," Tarrant promised. He shook Jack's hand briefly once again.

SEVEN

"Hang on to my hand while we're crossing the street, Squeak." Tarrant looked down at his niece. She looked so small standing beside him. Her eyes were large and frightened. Mentally he cursed himself for putting that look on her face. He should have been straight from the start with her. Alexa was a sharp kid. She could have handled the news of her mother's accident if they'd kept her informed all along. It had been five weeks since Amber's accident. In all of that time, he and his parents had tried to shield Alexa from the truth. Instead of calming her, hitting her with the truth all at once was having the opposite effect.

Now all of those details would be revealed to her. She would see Amber lying in the hospital, with all of her frailties and her failings exposed. Alexa didn't have any illusions about her mother. She knew Amber wasn't perfect. She'd heard the talk. She'd seen the men come and go. She'd heard Uncle Rant and Amber arguing—yelling in a whisper when they thought she might be asleep. Though it made her sad to hear them argue, because she'd seen it so much, she'd taken it as normal. This was the way things were. This was the way things were supposed to be. Their job was to fight, make up, then pretend everything was okay. Her job was to be the kid. Her job was to pretend that she believed that everything was going to be okay when they told her. Her job was to play with the presents they bought to placate her, go willingly to the homes where they left her. She could do that, as long as she knew that sooner or later, things would get back to normal—whatever that was.

Going to the hospital, however, was something different. This was something out of her realm of normality. She knew that sometimes people went into the hospital and never came back. It had happened to her best friend's dad. He went into the hospital and he didn't come back. He had something on the brain. A tuber, or something like that. Everyone kept telling her friend that everything was going to be okay. And it wasn't.

Despite all else that Amber did, she always came back. And no matter how many times Uncle Rant shuffled her from friend to friend, he always came back to get her when he said he would.

But now he was taking her to a place where there were no guarantees. Alexa wasn't sure how to handle that. So when Uncle Rant told her to hang on to his hand, she did so without arguing, without trying to convince him what a big kid she was. She was going to hang on for dear life because that's exactly what he was to her—dear life. She didn't know what she would have done without him. He was the one who read her stories at night, made her school lunches in the day. He attended the parent-teacher meetings, drove her to the dance recital practices. He slapped the bandages on her knees when she fell down and fixed her hair when those little twigs kept sticking up. Somewhere in the back of her mind, she knew that it was the mothers who did that for the other girls in her school. But there was nothing that said that an uncle couldn't be a mother, too. She knew. She'd asked.

"Remember, Squeak, you can still talk to your mom even though she may not seem like she can hear you. It's like she's asleep. But the doctors say she may know you. She may still hear you. So when we get inside her room, say what's on your mind. Say what's in your heart. Do you want a little privacy?"

Alexa nodded. She already knew what she wanted to say. She'd been thinking about it since her uncle told her what had happened to Amber. They entered the hospital and walked down the long corridor lined with doctors and nurses in their crisp white or rumpled mint-green scrubs. She saw patients in hospital gowns or personal robes ambling along, dragging their cold metal poles with clear liquids drip-drip-dripping into bandage-covered arms. She closed her ears to the sound of pages coming over the public address system. She didn't want to hear if one of those pages was for the doctors who were treating her mother. She didn't want to know. She knew too much already.

"Here we are, Squeak."

Alexa squeezed her uncle's hand as he stopped in front of a door. She watched him rap once, then twice on the door with his knuckles and poke his head in the doorway. It was a private room, so he didn't have to worry about intruding on anyone else's private moment with their loved one.

"Don't be afraid. It's all right," he encouraged her with a small nudge toward her mother's bed.

"She's all wired," Alexa murmured, indicating the monitors that tracked Amber's heart rate, breathing, and brain activity.

"I know. That's so the doctors know when to give your mommy medicine, and how much to give her."

Alexa took a step toward the bed, then stopped. She whirled around and buried her face in Tarrant's pants leg.

"Take me back, Uncle Rant. I don't want to be here!"

"Are you sure, Squeak? I know this isn't the best situation, but it's been a while since you've seen your mom. Don't you even want to tell her that you're here?" Tarrant didn't want to push her. The only thing he'd ever made Alexa do was finish her homework and eat her vegetables. She could usually get out of any one of those if she made a good enough case to him. This time he couldn't let her talk him out of it. This was something important. This was her mother! As screwy as it was, Amber had given Alexa her life. If the unspeakable ever happened, if Amber's condition deteriorated, he would never forgive himself if hadn't given Alexa the chance to say good-bye or I love you. As painful as it was to watch, he would make her go through with this. She would have to hate him now and seek therapy later. This was something that had to be.

Alexa pouted. Amber never seemed to care that she was around before. Why should it matter now?

"Go on, Alexa," Tarrant said firmly. She knew by his tone that this was something he really wanted her to do. When she dragged her feet, Tarrant's expression softened. "Do you want me to stay with you?" It was a softening, not a total relenting. She would have to go forward.

Alexa shook her head no. "Uh-huh. I'm all right now. I'll go."

"I'll be right outside if you need me. Okay?"

She nodded, but her gaze was focused on the figure of her mother lying in the hospital bed. Alexa approached her slowly, her hands jammed into the pockets of her pink and purple floral romper.

"Hi, Mama," Alexa whispered, then shook her head. That didn't even sound right. She never called Amber

"Mama." She'd always said that she hated to be reminded that she was the mother of an nine-year-old.

"Uh . . . hello, Amber," Alexa corrected. "Are you in there? Can you hear me?"

Alexa moved closer to the bed until she was within touching distance of her mother. She reached out her hand tentatively, shakily. She placed it on Alexa's hand on top of the covers. Alexa jerked her hand back. Her mother's hand was glacier cold to the touch. She jammed her hands back into her pockets.

"Uncle Rant said I should talk to you. He says that even though you're sleeping, you know what I'm saying. I wish it was true, Amber. I wanna tell you something. I've been waiting to tell you for a long time now. But you're always so busy. You're never home. . . ." Alexa paused, feeling a lump form in her throat the size of the pillow her mother was sleeping on. She wiped her nose on her sleeve when the first signs of a crybaby drip started to tickle her nose. "But I'm gonna do this anyway. Uncle Rant says you can hear me and that you should know what's in my heart."

Alexa leaned closer, her lips just inches away from her mother's cheek. She then turned her head slightly so that her words would be directed in her mother's ear. "I wanted you to know this, Alexa . . . Mama . . . and I mean this with all of my heart."

Furtively she looked over her shoulder at the nurse who'd unexpectedly entered the room. Alexa paused. This was her moment, a private moment meant for her and her mom. She didn't want an audience.

"I'm talkin' to my mom," Alexa told the nurse. "My uncle Rant said I could."

The nurse smiled at the image of mother and daughter, and hesitated just a moment before approaching the bed. "It's all right, sweetie. Go on and talk to her."

She busied herself with minor tasks across the room to give the little girl the moment she needed.

Alexa smiled angelically then turned back to Amber. "Mama," she whispered. "If you're in there, if you can hear me, I want you to stay in there. I hope you die in there. I hope you never come back. You hear me? You ain't never been nothing but heartache for everyone you ever touched. Do us all a favor and die in that bed! I pray to God that you die so hard, a whole team of doctors and nurses couldn't bring you back."

With that said, Alexa leaned as close as she could, pretended to plant a kiss on her mother's cheek, and wheeled out of the room. She burst into the hallway, chest heaving, fists clenched tight.

Tarrant stopped her flight by clamping his hand on her shoulder. "You all right, Squeak?"

"Yeah," Alexa said, swiping at her cheek and nose. "I'm all right. Everything's going to be all right. I prayed to God."

Tarrant smiled. "Come on then. Granny and Grandpa are waiting."

Next to taking care of a little girl, busing tables had to be the hardest job Tarrant ever had. Like Alexa's questions, it never stopped. He barely had time to catch his breath before someone was sending him off on another errand.

"Two seltzer waters, one light beer, three fuzzy navels, and one sex on the beach!" Charlotte called out an order as she breezed up to the bar. "Pool room could use a sweep," she indicated to Tarrant. "And I'm not talking about with a broom either. Let's save that pleasure for after hours."

"I'm on it," Tarrant said, trying to match her enthusiasm. But after four hours, he was starting to feel as flat as the near-empty beer mugs Charlotte was leaving for him to clean.

"Four margaritas, two more light beers." Trae the rocket man added to the pile of dirty glasses when he set his order in the queue to be filled.

At that moment, several patrons chose to let out vocal cries of dismay as Houston's basketball team, the closest Galveston would come to calling a home team, lost to a longtime Texas rival.

"So much for home court advantage," Trae muttered in disgust. "I had thirty bucks riding on that game."

Charlotte turned back to Tarrant and blew out an exaggerated sigh of relief. "Things should slow down now."

"What do you mean, slow down?" Tarrant winked at her. "I was just starting to get into the swing of things."

"Nice try." She wagged her finger at him. "But you must be exhausted. I know I am. Cheering for the local boys makes a crowd very thirsty. Since we've lost, everyone will sit back, nurse their drinks for a while, and then go home." Charlotte made sure her orders were strategically placed on her tray, then disappeared into the crowd.

Tarrant made a mental calculation of how many drinks had been served tonight. He knew he might be off—way off. He could judge only by the number of glasses he'd collected tonight. That didn't take into account refills or the other bar backs working against him to gather as many glasses as they could for their bartenders. Since he was in the fact-finding mode, he had to do something to try to get a better feel of just how much money Papa Jack's was making off of getting people drunk.

He adjusted his numbers by chatting up the bartenders. By stroking their egos a little, he could get them to brag. Again he found himself having to mentally adjust their numbers. Whether the bartenders were under-reporting, to keep from giving it all away to the IRS, or over-reporting, to keep from being outdone by the bartender's friendly competition, between the two extremes, Tarrant figured he'd come pretty close to figuring it out.

"Hey, big guy, don't clock out on us yet." One of the bartenders snapped his fingers in front of Tarrant when he noticed Tarrant staring off into space. "We could use another case of tequila."

"Put the request on the requisition slip, and I'll have Ms. Harmon okay it," Tarrant said.

"Do yourself a favor and don't comment on the game. Ms. Harmon gets a little testy when the Rockets lose. She doesn't care if it is just exhibition play." The bartender nodded across the room. Meleah was gesturing in disgust at the television and complaining to anyone who would listen. When the postgame commentators filled the screen, she reached for a remote control and switched to another sports station. She then entered the office, slamming the door so hard it rattled the glasses on the surrounding tables.

"Thanks, I'll remember that." Tarrant acknowledged the tip, completed the requisition form to restock the bar, and headed for the Harmon office.

"Game over already?" Jack looked up from his paperwork to ask Meleah.

"One lousy free throw. They couldn't make one lousy free throw? What are we paying those overinflated salaries for? Million-dollar contracts, and they can't make a lousy free throw! Next time I'm rooting for the Spurs!" Meleah threw herself into a chair, folded her arms across her chest, and propped up her feet on her father's desk.

Jack grasped her by the ankles, lifted, and removed several invoices from underneath her feet. He let her feet fall back onto the desk with a heavy thud. "Don't defect yet. We still have a chance. The women's team, the Comets, looks pretty promising. They're looking pretty strong in the preseason. Maybe they can capture a fourth championship and bring some glory back to this city of bridesmaids."

Meleah's face brightened. "Yeah. The women. Leave it to the women to save the day!"

"Hey now, it's not always the women who save the day. Look at how our friend Cole stepped up to the plate."

"Your friend," Meleah reminded her father. "You're the one who hired him right off the street."

"You don't think he'll work out?"

"I don't know, Pops." Meleah shrugged. "We'll see."

"But you're not happy with my decision."

"I don't trust him," she responded bluntly. "It's not healthy for him hanging around here."

"I know. Leon's fried cheese is going to kill us all." Jack made a weak attempt at humor.

"That's not what I'm talking about, Pops, and you know it. Somewhere behind that pretty-boy smile shows the teeth behind. You mark my words."

"You thinking that he's going to try to get some twisted sense of revenge for what happened to his sister? I'm not having any of that, Le-Le. I told him that we don't owe him anything for what that little tramp did."

"How do we know the whole darn family isn't dysfunctional?" Meleah said tightly. "What if he's a psycho? What if he's waiting for his chance to strike at us when we least expect it? Or even when we most expect it? Pops, we could have let a homicidal murderer on the premises . . . paying him to be here, in fact. Didn't you think about that when you hired him?"

Jack's eyes cut to his bottom drawer of his desk. That's where he'd been keeping all of the threatening notes he'd received since winning the lottery. He kept the drawer under lock and key to keep Meleah from knowing the full extent of someone's sick twistedness. Well, he thought in resignation, if Tarrant was going to try to get back at them, he'd rather have the man close at hand where he could keep an eye on him.

Yet even with all of Meleah's reservations, even with the tragic cloud that seemed to follow Tarrant, Jack couldn't make himself believe that Tarrant was responsible for the demented outpourings that seemed to find Jack no matter how hard he tried to shield his family and his friends from it. If he could have called it women's intuition without making himself seem nutty, he would have. Something about that Tarrant made him want to trust him. It made him want to help him. Maybe he was a little hasty for giving Tarrant that job. But he didn't think so. Maybe it was the way Tarrant looked him straight in the eye during the interview. Maybe it was the way he exhibited a kind of quiet confidence and control that said to Jack this wasn't the type of man prone to irrational acts.

"Yeah. I thought about it," was all Jack said to convey the mixed feelings he had inside. He knew he had to hire somebody quickly to help take that load off of his regular staff. He expected to hire more people as the weeks went by. Some would go. Some would stay. Papa Jack's would be a revolving door of new hires until things settled down. But something in Jack's gut told him that Tarrant Cole would be around for a while.

"I hope you know what you're doing, Pops," Meleah

said as an ending to their conversation. "I'm staying out of it."

Tarrant wasn't an eavesdropper. That is, he didn't used to be. His parents had always told him that it was wrong to listen to other people's conversations. But he couldn't help it. The office door was as thin as the ice he seemed to be skating on—if the tone of Meleah's voice was any indication. When he caught a bartender waving at him from across the room to hurry, he rapped his knuckles on the door.

He stuck his head in the office. "Ms. Harmon?"

"Yes, Mr. Cole. What is it?" Meleah sat up straighter. She shot her father an "I told you so" glance. The man was always around.

"Joey at the bar told me that you had to sign this requisition. It's for tequila."

"There's been a run on margaritas tonight, eh?" Jack chuckled. "Nothing makes a bad game better than a perfectly prepared margarita or if it's a really bad game—shooters." He placed extra emphasis on the last word for Meleah's benefit. She propped her cheek on her fist and glared at Jack from underneath her lashes.

"That's a very thirsty crowd out there tonight." Tarrant kept his tone light, conversational. He knew they were suspicious of him, or at least wary. He had to keep cool. He had to get them relaxed around him. That was the only way he was going to get what he'd come after.

"Yeah? Well, since the Rockets lost, I have the feeling that their thirst will be miraculously quenched," Meleah grumbled.

"I didn't know you were a basketball fan, Ms. Harmon." He wasn't going to call her Le-Le like other employees did. It was too soon. It would probably alienate her if he did.

"Well, with running a sports bar, you tend to get attached to the home teams."

"Too bad about that last free throw, huh?" Jack couldn't help teasing Meleah.

"You're pushing my buttons, old man," she said, as she handed the requisition back to Tarrant.

As he pocketed the requisition and headed for the door, Meleah and Jack were still arguing the skills of their hometown basketball team. Meleah was vocal, expressive. She waved her arms in the air to emphasize her point while Jack countered just as loudly. Tarrant grinned and shook his head. Suddenly something hit him. It wasn't an idea, but a piece of wadded paper that Meleah had tried to sail across the room to land in the wastepaper basket by the door. He bent down to retrieve the paper and held it up.

"This belong to you?"

"Sorry, Mr. Cole," Meleah said in chagrin. "It would have been a three-pointer if Pops hadn't jostled my elbow with that flagrant foul."

"Don't look at me. I was nowhere near you."

Tarrant saw an opportunity to get past some of her defenses. He didn't have much time. If he wanted to get information, he had to get close to the source. "It's not as easy as it looks, you know."

"What isn't as easy as it looks?" Meleah asked, wadding up another piece of paper.

"Making a free throw under all of that pressure."

"Don't tell me they can't make the shot. They're supposed to be professionals. That's their job."

"They're human," Tarrant countered. "They make mistakes."

"They're overpaid," she retorted. "We pay them too much money to make those kinds of mistakes. If we don't make allowances for other professionals, we shouldn't make allowances for them—"

"You've got that right," Jack broke in. "Take heart surgeons, for instance. No one says, 'Oh, I'm sorry you lost the patient, doctor. But that's okay, you were under a lot of pressure.' They get paid the big bucks to make the big plays."

Tarrant shrugged, and said, "Everyone criticizes when a player makes a mistake. But they keep forgetting that they're only human. Aren't they allowed to make mistakes?"

"Not when decent seats to the playoff games are going for over a hundred bucks," Meleah said in derision. "Not when you have to pay the cable companies to view games that should have been shown on local television. For that kind of money, I want to see a perfect game. I want to see a score on every drive up the court. I want to see every free throw made."

"You think free throws are easy?"

"How hard can it be to stand in one spot and throw a ball?"

"Why don't you find out?" Tarrant suggested. "You have basketball nets out there. Why don't you find out for yourself how hard it is? Have you ever tried to make a clutch free throw, with crowds yelling around you, after you've spent an hour running up and down the court, with the pressure of your self-esteem on the line."

"I smell a challenge!" Jack roared.

Tarrant canted his head in the direction of the door. "I've got a break coming to me. I would give all of my tips for tonight to see you make just one free throw under those conditions."

"But I haven't been running up and down the court, as you say. There are no fans yelling and screaming at me," Meleah hedged. "We can't prove anything."

Jack tucked his palms under his armpits and flapped. "Chicken!" he cackled.

"Oh, why don't you go on and lay that egg." Meleah turned on her father.

"You gonna let him come up in here and chicken you out of your own sports bar, Le-Le?" Jack goaded.

"I am *not* running around this sports bar," Meleah said emphatically. "You can just get that right out of your heads." She pointed to both Jack and Tarrant.

"Okay, forget about the running part. You let me worry about getting a crowd together for you," Tarrant encouraged.

"You're really serious about this, aren't you?"

"A true fan will do anything to support the team. If you make that free throw under the conditions I set up, then I'll be convinced that you know what you're talking about."

"Why should I have to prove anything to you?"

"You don't have to prove anything to me. But if you don't accept my challenge, will you be able to look me in the eye tomorrow?"

"Go set up your conditions, Mr. Cole. I'll be out in five minutes. If I make the free throw, I get your tips for the entire week."

"Hey!" Tarrant started to protest.

"Don't start whining now." Jack switched sides. "My Le-Le's gonna teach you three of life's little lessons. First, never make sucker bets with the owner of the sports bar. Second, never doubt the conviction of a true fan."

"And third?"

"Never, ever tick off the boss," Meleah added, putting her hands on her hips and leaning into his face.

"You're on. Five minutes and it's courtside," he reminded her. Tarrant closed the door behind him. He took a deep breath. *Whew!* The look that Meleah was giving him and the way Jack was laughing, he'd prob-ably just lost his tips for a week. For a moment, Tarrant considered that he might have been hustled. It was a little too convenient for him—Meleah missing that free throw. In the back of his mind, he reminded himself to ask some of the other employees if they'd ever found themselves in this situation.

He hated to see the money go. It was the tips that brought a bar back from below the poverty line to just barely struggling. But that was okay. He could deal with that. What he hoped to gain was worth more than a few hundred dollars.

While Tarrant was setting up for the bet, Meleah wadded several pieces of paper, and practiced making free throws into a wastepaper basket.

"Not bad," she muttered. She attempted twenty-five shots, and made seventeen of them.

"Stop stalling, chicken. Your pigeon is waiting." Jack shooed her toward the door. Meleah checked her watch, took a deep breath, then headed for the bas-ketball cages. Each cage was set up with the basketball goal at regulation height. Painted on the floor was the regulation-length free throw line, as well as the three-point line. When she got there, Tarrant had just fin-ished putting fifteen basketballs around the free throw line. He'd rounded up several patrons to stand around the cage. He had them cheering and chanting. Some of them had been instructed to cheer for Meleah. Oth-ers had been urged to boo and hiss as if they were part of the opposing team. Meleah bit the inside of her cheek to keep from smiling. If she could say one thing for the man, he was resourceful.

Meleah saw Charlotte slip behind the crowd. She looked as if she could barely suppress her laughter. She waved over Jack, who let out a raucous laugh.

"Go get 'em, Meleah, girl!"

"Sissy girl!" another patron countered.

"Ah, go home to your mama, girlie!"

"You can do it, Meleah!" Charlotte urged.

"Five bucks says she won't make it," someone shouted.

"No bettin' in my place," Jack said sternly. "But if you care to make a generous donation to the Meleah Harmon school of basketball free throws, I'd be more than happy to take your money."

"How's that for pressure?" Tarrant sauntered past Meleah and whispered for her ears only.

"No sweat," she countered with false bravado to cover the shiver that suddenly rolled unexpectedly down her spine. Something about his tone, the intimacy of it, brought a warmth to her face that had nothing to do with how she was about to expose her talent—or lack of—to everyone at Papa Jack's. With slow, deliberate steps, she moved into the basketball cage.

"Since I'm putting so much on the line," Tarrant said, "I thought I would make the bet a bit sweeter. I've set a timer. If you make ten free throws in twenty seconds, you win the bet."

"But those players have to make only two free throws, and there's no time limit for them," Meleah objected.

"I've combined the pressure of the game with the fatigue factor. It's only fair. Want to back out?"

"Of course not. You just say when. But I want you to know that I hate to lose."

"Will I lose my job if you lose?" Tarrant asked.

"Why, Mr. Cole," Meleah said with exaggerated sweetness. "That would make me a sore loser. Are you sure *you* want to go through with this?"

Tarrant considered her statement. After hearing how she attacked the home team after claiming she was a fan, he wasn't so sure anymore. But he'd set this up. He had to go through with it or lose face. "All right. Let's do this."

He made a signal to the crowd. The cheering and jeering began in earnest now. Meleah flexed her fingers, shook out her arms, and blew out several deep breaths. Tarrant raised his hand to warn Meleah that he was starting the time. When his hand came down sharply, Meleah bent for the first ball. For a moment, there was complete silence. The crowd was expectantly holding their breaths, waiting to see what would happen next. When the first ball sailed through the air and fell through the net with a sibilant *whoosh!* a cheer came up for Meleah's side.

Meleah didn't stop to admire her handiwork. She bent for another ball and another and another. The second and third balls were off the mark. She gritted her teeth, and bent for the fourth, fifth, and sixth. *Follow through,* she reminded herself. *Make sure the wrist bends far enough to put a good arch on the ball. Whoosh! Bang-whoosh! Kerboing!* Another miss. The fourth went through. The fifth collided with the backboard, and went in. The sixth collided with the rim, and sailed away.

"Fifteen seconds!" Tarrant warned.

Meleah reached for the seventh ball. It fell through. She slid over, and scooped up the eighth one. Smooth and even, the shot arched upward, and fell through the net. The ninth ball went in. And the tenth.

"Ten seconds," Tarrant warned.

"She'll never make it!"

"In your eye!" Jack snorted.

"Like hell she won't. Go get 'em, sugar!" Charlotte cheered. "Shoot the lights out!"

The eleventh was a miss. The twelfth was dead center. Thirteen followed twelve down.

"Five seconds, four, three . . ." Tarrant counted down.

The fourteenth ball hit the rim, and ricocheted around the cage.

"Two . . ."

Ball number fifteen flew from Meleah's fingertips.

"One! I win, Ms. Harmon," Tarrant shouted, just as the ball hit the rim. It bounced once, twice, then plopped through the net.

"Guess again, Mr. Cole," Meleah said breathlessly. She pulled her hair away from her face, and fanned her flushed cheeks to cool herself off. "I made that last shot."

"You ran out of time," Tarrant countered.

"Hold on a minute. This is a regulation-size half court, right?"

"Yeah."

"And the balls are regulation size? The goal is regulation height?"

"So?" He was beginning to get suspicious. But it was too late. Meleah had already backed him into a corner. She turned to face the crowd as she said, "So even in regulation play, if the ball leaves the player's hand before the buzzer and goes in, the point counts. The ball was in the air when time ran out. I win, Mr. Cole!"

Tarrant opened his mouth to protest, then closed it quickly.

"Pay up, pretty boy!" someone in the crowd shouted. Meleah definitely had the home court advantage tonight.

"You win," Tarrant conceded.

"I told you I don't like to lose, Mr. Cole," Meleah said smugly.

"Nobody likes a sore winner, Ms. Harmon," Tarrant teased.

"Now, Mr. Cole, don't get your briefs in a bunch. I won fair and square."

"The game was rigged!" someone from the crowd shouted.

"I smell a setup!"

Meleah cocked an eyebrow at Tarrant. "Do you believe that?"

"How could the game be rigged? I set it up. Why would I set myself up to lose?" Indeed, why would he set himself up to lose? Why would he sit in that restaurant, night after night, knowing that Meleah would ignore him? Why would he give up his own lucrative automobile restoration business to work for peanuts at a bar where he knew the patrons would be hostile toward him? Why? For Amber. He was doing it for Amber. The closer he got to Meleah, the closer he got to finding out what happened the night of the accident. The more he could learn about Papa Jack's policy on serving alcohol, the more he could shift the blame for that accident where it rightfully belonged.

"Then no hard feelings?" Meleah held out her hand to demonstrate her good sportsmanship. Tarrant regarded it for a moment. No. No hard feelings. Nothing hard about revenge. It was all sweet.

"None." He clasped his large hand over hers. As soon as his hand touched hers, he knew that sooner or later, he would give in to the impulse that had plagued him since first laying eyes on Meleah. Her hand was warm, smooth, and felt as natural in his as if it belonged there. He felt foolish for standing there well past the time when he should have released her, but he couldn't bring himself to do it. Not yet. He just wanted to stand there, feeling the warm pulse of Meleah's hand pound in sync with his. He wanted to savor for a moment longer the glow of her flushed cheeks

and the sparkle in her eyes, and pretend that thoughts
of him brought that look of pleasure to her face.

"Make way for the trophy!" Charlotte suddenly
called, as she stepped between them. Charlotte's intru-
sion forced Tarrant to break contact. She held aloft
on her tray the brandy snifter Tarrant used to collect
tips.

"I believe this belongs to you, sugar," Charlotte said,
and handed the glass stuffed with bills to Meleah. Tarrant moaned softly—as much in dismay for the loss of
Meleah's touch as he was for the loss of his hard-
earned tips.

"Good grief, sugar, I think there's almost two hundred dollars in that glass!" Charlotte said, adding to
his grief.

"Cheer up, Mr. Cole," Meleah gloated. "You
couldn't possibly lose this much again."

EIGHT

"Hah! Pay up, Pops. You've lost again! When are you going to learn not to challenge me? I kick butt at basketball and I take no prisoners at pool." Meleah stood with a cue stick in her hand, gloating over her latest victory.

"You're still harping on the bet you made with Tarrant, Le-Le? That was two weeks ago."

"Victory tastes so much sweeter when the odds are against you. And the taste only gets better with time."

"You wouldn't have won this time if I hadn't scratched on the eight ball," Jack said, wagging a finger at Meleah. He picked up a cube of chalk, and rubbed it absently against the top of his cue stick.

"I tried to tell you that you were putting too much spin on the cue ball," Meleah said.

"I couldn't help it. My hand slipped."

"You weren't concentrating on the game," Meleah accused him. "Come to think about it, your mind's been in outer space lately. What's been on your mind, Pops? Anything I can do to help?"

Jack considered telling Meleah about the notes. They were coming with regular frequency now, though he couldn't quite figure out how. He must have been desperate. When Elliot, otherwise known as Mr. Hook Up, said he could get him a security system installed for a fraction of the cost, Jack actually considered it. He more than considered it. He had Elliot bring his friend over and they worked out a deal to put in an intruder alarm. The reason it was so cheap was because it was nonmonitored. Noise only. But that was better than nothing at all. After a couple of times of forgetting to enter the code within sixty seconds of entering the building, Jack was pretty convinced that what he had put in place was a good deterrent for the money. He was frugal, yes. But not when it came to his daughter. As soon as Elliot could find his security friend again, Jack planned to put in more security devices, cameras, direct connections to law enforcement, the works.

"Don't you worry about what's worrying me," Jack admonished her. "Now that we're loaded, we should have no more worries."

"Sometimes having money brings more troubles that you've bargained for."

"Yeah? And who told you that?" Jack scoffed.

"I saw it on a talk show. The host had this panel of folks who'd recently come into a whole lot of money."

"What show was that? I should have been on that show."

"Well, it wasn't 'Lifestyles of the Rich and Stingy,' " Meleah joked. She gathered the billiards again to rack for a new game.

"Hah. Hah. Hah. You're funny. You need to take that act on the road. Maybe Montel could do a show on 'Lifestyles of the Recently Disinherited.' "

"Anyway," Meleah continued. "The panel sat around complaining about how terrible it was being rich."

"Did they now? Well, now it's our turn to bellyache about having too much money. Lord knows, we've had our share of complaining because of the lack of it."

"We won't ever have to worry about the lack of money again if . . ." Meleah let her voice trail off dramatically.

"If what?"

"If you call that investment counselor I researched for you. Have you done it?"

"I said I'll get around to it."

"Pops," Meleah said, with a hint of warning. "Don't put this off like you have the other things I've asked you to do."

"What other things?" Jack said indignantly. "I've been good. Didn't I hire that extra help you and Charlotte have been ragging me about?"

"One thing. You did one little thing and you expect me to get off of your back? No, sir. You're not getting off that easy. You haven't looked into upgrading the employee benefits plan with better insurance, profit sharing, and retirement accounts." Meleah ticked off on her fingers.

"Oh, that . . ."

"And putting in a real alarm system and extra lights in the parking lot." She held up two more fingers. "Not that rigging that Elliot had his friend slap together for us. I want that so-called security system ripped out and a real one put in."

"I'm on it, Meleah. Really I am. I'm gathering estimates," he assured her.

"How many have you gathered so far?"

"Oh, it's kind of hard to say," Jack hedged. "There's so much paper on my desk. I can't really say for sure."

"Take a wild stab at it."

"One?" he said querulously.

"What do you mean, one? What have you been doing all of this time? I put that task in your organizer to have done by the end of last week and I put a reminder on your calendar on the computer."

"You know I don't go near that contraption if I don't have to. I don't trust anything that thinks it's smarter than I am."

"Pathetic," Meleah muttered, shaking her head. "Pops, if we're going to have more and more customers coming through here, I want a real security system. I want cameras watching the parking lot and back alleys. I want emergency assistance at our beck and call. Besides that, we're still shorthanded. We need another cook. Leon can barely keep up with the orders. And now that we've added new rest rooms, I was thinking a rest room attendant would be a nice touch."

"In a sports bar?" Jack sputtered. "Le-Le, this is a working-class place. People come here to be rowdy, not intimidated by a bunch of snobs watching how much soap they use, or whether or not they use up an entire roll of bathroom tissue before asking for another. I won't have my place turned into a magnet for snobs!"

"Then dress the attendant in a football helmet, and stick a golf club in his hands, if it's atmosphere you're worried about. But there's nothing wrong with making the customers feel appreciated. Let someone greet them at the door to make them feel welcome."

"You're our official greeter, my dear."

"I can't be everywhere at once," Meleah complained. "Let someone offer to get their tokens for the video games. Let somebody offer to wait on them hand and foot. The working class wants to feel just as pampered as the filthy rich."

"As long as we hire really friendly people. No snobs," Jack grumbled.

"No snobs," Meleah agreed. "But that comes back to my reason for bringing all of this up."

"All right, all right," Jack relented. "I'll talk to your investment contact. What's his name again?"

"Loren Gauthier," Meleah supplied. "You won't be sorry, Pops. He's very good at what he does."

"I take it you've investigated him thoroughly?"

"He comes highly recommended."

"Just because he's your friend doesn't mean he knows what he's doing. You told me the same thing when Elliot brought a bozo through here to help set up at that security system."

"You know me better than that, Pops. I don't mix friendship with business. And I certainly don't deal with bozos."

Jack paused. His expression was disturbed, almost fearful when he asked, "We can't help mixing friendship and business sometimes, Le-Le. Sometimes it just happens."

"Not if you watch yourself."

"You mean, you don't think of Charlotte as a friend?"

"That's different, Pops," Meleah said, laying a hand against Jack's cheek. "Charlotte is my family."

"She is like family, isn't she?" Jack chuckled. "She loves you, you know. She thinks the world of us."

"And I care about her, too." Meleah grinned at her father. "What do you mean 'us'?" It was the first time he'd ever openly expressed to Meleah how he felt about Charlotte. Meleah used that slip to press home her point. "That's why I want to make sure that if she ever decides to leave Papa Jack's, she'll be set for life."

"Has Charlotte said anything about leaving?" Jack said in alarm. "I know I've been working her pretty hard, but . . ."

"No, of course she hasn't said anything."

"Then what makes you think she wants to leave?"

"Pops, she can't work here forever. And everybody has to leave sooner or later. I'm just saying that if she leaves . . ."

"All right, all right, I get your message. I'll call him first thing tomorrow."

"I thought you'd say that," Meleah retorted. "And I know you well enough to know that if it's something you don't want to do, tomorrow will never come. So I took matters into my own hands."

"Typical," Jack muttered. "You called him yourself, didn't you."

"You'd better believe it."

"Why am I not surprised?"

"Don't be mad, Pops. I'm not trying to get into your business. I'm trying to do what's best for our business. You struggled to send me to school. Let me do what I'm supposed to do to pay you back for all of the support everyone at Papa Jack's has given me. I want to earn my keep now. I want to do what I know is right to make Papa Jack's successful. Isn't that what you put me through school for? So I can run Papa Jack's for you?"

Jack felt proud and melancholy all at the same time. He was so proud of Meleah. She was everything an old geezer like him could ever hope for in a daughter. When most of his friends complained about their children, their wastrel ways, he couldn't say enough to lift her up in their eyes. He just wished with all of his heart that his wife Marian had been alive to see the kind of woman Meleah had turned out to be. Whenever the moments came on him when he was missing his first love, he had only to look at Meleah to satisfy his yearning to connect with his wife again. He felt the bittersweet mixture of love and pain swell his heart beyond its capacity. Some of what he was feeling surged up, spilled over into his eyes. It made them water.

Jack was in the middle of taking a shot when his eyes blurred. He turned his head to the side and swiped his face on his sleeve. He missed his shot and used reaching for a different cue stick to hide his sudden descent into emotion from his daughter. "Damn sunlight," he grumbled. "In my eyes."

Meleah's throat constricted. This was a side of her father that she seldom got to see, though she knew he loved her beyond measure. The face that Jack presented to the world was the face of a man of the public. He was a shrewd businessman. When he played the part of Papa Jack's to the hilt, he was loud, brassy, and some folks said a bit crude. He knew many people but had few close friends. Yet Meleah knew that for his small circle of friends and family his feelings ran deep. She imagined that lately Charlotte had gotten to see more of Jack's private side. If she hadn't known her father's capacity for love, she could have been jealous of the attention that Jack showered on Charlotte.

She supposed that's why she threw herself so deeply into the business, to keep from thinking about the time Jack shared with someone else. For a while, she was trying to prove that she could run this business to gain her father's pride and his attention. *Look, Pops. Look what I can do. Don't you love me more now that I can help you?* Going for her master's in business was the ultimate bid for attention.

As she grew to know Charlotte, and to accept Charlotte's feelings for her father, Meleah realized that the more people Jack let into his life, the more his love for his daughter materialized. It sounded strange, like the opposite should be true. But the more Jack loved, the more love he had to give—the miracle of love.

"Mr. Harmon, phone call!" Tarrant hailed from the entrance of the billiard room and broke into Meleah's reverie.

"That should be Loren." Meleah had to clear her throat to ease the lump of emotion that had settled there.

"I'll talk to him. But just that. No promises," Jack said to her. "If I think he's trying to hustle me, I'm out of there."

"You'll thank me when your four million blossoms into eight," she said, turning back to finish the game.

"We'll finish the conversation and the game later," Jack promised. "Get all the practice you can, Le-Le. You're gonna need it."

"Keep talking, old man. One of these days, you might convince yourself," Meleah teased in turn.

Tarrant allowed Jack to pass. "Didn't mean to disturb your game, sir. But Charlotte sent me up here after you." He stood with a broom in one hand and a long-handled dustpan in the other. Jack smiled and wondered if there really was a phone call, or was Charlotte feeling a little lonely and neglected. "No problem, Cole. Handle your business."

Handle your business. Jack's comment echoed in Tarrant's head. He was sure that Jack meant sweep up the trash left behind by last night's crowd. There was a lot of it, too. Another night of free-flowing booze and bucks. Jack must have raked in thousands. From his vantage point, Tarrant could watch the patrons all over the place drink themselves into a near stupor. Another few weeks, and he figured he'd have enough evidence to prove that Papa Jack's consistently continued to serve drinks long past when some patrons should have been cut off. And a few more weeks, by mid-August, his probation period should be up anyway.

As he started to sweep up the outskirts of the pool room, careful not to disturb Meleah, he sighed softly. It wasn't going to be easy bringing this place down. Not from the standpoint of evidence. That was covered. He meant not easy in the respect that he really did like these people. He didn't want to hurt them. They were a quirky bunch. They were funny and devoted and generous. But they had hurt his sister. What kind of big brother would he be if he let that go? Worthless.

Meleah heard Tarrant moving around the room. She could feel his eyes on her but she kept playing. If she concentrated on the game in front of her, she didn't have to think about the game Tarrant Cole must be playing. She couldn't quite figure it out yet. On the surface, he appeared respectful, hardworking, and amiable. But he wasn't fooling anyone. He was after something. It had to be something connected with his sister. Until she could figure out exactly what he wanted, she would play it cool. She would keep her distance and let him trip himself up.

As she concentrated, she took her lower lip between her teeth, then released it. She drew the cue stick back, prepared to strike the cue ball. The cue stick connected solidly with the ivory cue ball. *Clack!* It seemed loud in the stillness of the room.

Tarrant didn't try to engage her in conversation. He told himself that he didn't want to break her concentration. He really wanted the opportunity to observe her without the barriers she tossed up each time he came near her. Ever since the night of the free-throw fiasco, Meleah had been careful to keep a certain, cool distance from him. Tarrant was puzzled. Maybe she didn't feel the same spark he did when he held her hand. But she should have at least felt comfortable enough around him not to avoid him. He'd shown her he was a good sport as well as a good worker.

Tarrant had done everything he could think of to get her to relax around him. Casual conversation hadn't worked. Whenever he tried to strike up one, she quickly redirected the conversation to topics related to work at Papa Jack's. Charlotte overheard him on several occasions trying to get Meleah to talk to him. When Meleah sharply rebuked him, Charlotte winced in sympathy for Tarrant. Under the pretense of tidying up around the bar, Charlotte had edged closer to Tarrant.

"You'll never get to her at the rate you're going, sugar," she once remarked. "You're going about it all wrong."

In response, Tarrant had pretended that he didn't know what she was talking about.

"Hey, I may have only my GED, but I ain't stupid," Charlotte said. "You get any more puppy dog around Le-Le and I'll have to put a collar on you."

"She's dogging me pretty bad," Tarrant admitted. "What do you think I should do?"

"First of all, stop trying to come on to her. She gets enough of that every night."

"But I wasn't—" Tarrant began to deny.

"Sure you were, sugar. Every man does. They have to. I think it's in their genes. Or maybe I should say, in their *jeans,*" Charlotte said, clueing him in to her meaning by hooking her finger in the belt loop of his pants.

"Charlotte, you didn't come over to make a slam on every man, did you? Because if it's man-bashing you want—"

"I'm trying to give you some advice, Tarrant. Now shut up and listen. Meleah is very dedicated to her work. Why don't you try asking her about it sometime?"

"That's all she ever talks about is work. How to improve this, or how to change that."

"That's just a way to get her going. Start off talking about work, and maybe she'll relax, and change the subject herself."

"I doubt it."

"You could always challenge her to another contest.

That ought to really put her at ease," Charlotte teased, and moved away again.

Standing behind Meleah now, watching her play pool, was as close as he'd come to seeing her at ease. His gaze swept over the pool room. Not a bad place to start, Tarrant mused. This was a room designed to encourage people to relax. It was large, filled with over a dozen green felt tables. Tiffany-style lamps hung from chains on the ceiling. The walls were lined with the racks to hold the billiards equipment and vintage photographs of pool tournaments that had taken place at Papa Jack's. Tall wooden stools covered with plump leather cushions were placed randomly in the corners, inviting spectators. Since it was early afternoon, the room held only two occupants—Meleah and Tarrant.

The afternoon sun slanted through the miniblinds, casting odd shadows over the room. Tarrant remained in the shadows, keeping as quiet as possible. Meleah, on the other hand, seemed to attract the light to her. One sunbeam glanced across her face, drawing attention to her high cheekbones and wide, luminous eyes. He watched her circle around to another side, assessing the best shot. As she pursed her mouth in concentration, Tarrant's eyes were drawn to her full, moist lips. He imagined how her mouth would feel in a deep, all-consuming kiss.

Meleah nodded her head, acknowledging the table for the shot she wanted. She drew her arm back, rocking back slightly. Tarrant's attention was redirected to her profile. Her knees were slightly bent, drawing her denim shorts tighter against her thighs and bottom. The soft cotton blouse, partially open at the throat, slipped to one side to reveal a portion of her breast. She reached up, tucked an errant strand of hair behind her ear, and murmured aloud to herself, "Six in the corner."

"Nine in the side pocket is a better shot," Tarrant commented.

Meleah's head snapped up. She applied a fresh coat of blue chalk to the edge of her cue stick. She banked the cue ball off the edge of the table to sink both the six ball she had called and the nine ball Tarrant had suggested.

"Seven, off of the two, into the side pocket," Meleah said in response, and successfully sank the number seven billiard ball, too.

"You're very good, Ms. Harmon." Tarrant gave Meleah a genuine compliment.

"I've been playing since I could see over a table," she said. "I should have picked up a few skills by now."

She's got skills, all right—Tarrant thought ruefully. But the skills he was thinking about had nothing to do with her abilities as a pool shark. He didn't know if it was practiced or innate, but she was very skilled at making him feel like he was walking on land mines. He knew he shouldn't walk across that field. He would be better off he if turned around and went back the way he came. Sometimes he was almost convinced that she gave him beckoning looks. Sometimes he was almost certain that if he could navigate through the explosions, he would eventually come to rest in the safe haven of her arms. Maybe he was imagining it. Maybe he was just seeing what he wanted to see. He'd convinced himself that someone at Papa Jack's was responsible for Amber's condition. It wouldn't be a stretch to believe that he'd also convinced himself that Meleah was feeling some of the same conflict.

"You're very good," he continued, "but I'm better."

Meleah raised an eyebrow at the obvious challenge. She started for another billiard, then straightened. "All right, Mr. Cole, here's a chance to put your money where your mouth is—again."

"Why don't we turn a cliché into cash, Ms. Harmon."

"What do you suggest?"

"A little wager . . . say, my one-week salary against yours?"

Meleah gave a mock sigh. "I thought you had enough of handing your money over to me, Mr. Cole."

"I guess you can say I'm a glutton for punishment."

"I didn't figure you for that type, Mr. Cole."

"What type is that, Ms. Harmon? A gambler?"

"A sucker," she corrected.

Tarrant chuckled softly as he reached for his own cue stick. "How many?" he asked.

"How many what?"

"How many games will I have to beat you before you're ready to eat those words?"

"We can play until closing time," she said. "Or we can play just one game. It doesn't matter. You aren't going to beat me. I don't like losing."

"Famous last words," Tarrant taunted.

"I'll rack 'em up. You break," Meleah said, gesturing toward the table. "Like Charlotte likes to say, 'I'm gonna beat you like you stole something.' "

Tarrant inclined his head graciously as Meleah stepped back to observe him. He must be some kind of glutton for punishment, she thought in bemusement. Night after night, he came back so they could work him like a dog. And for what? What did he hope to gain? Certainly not her sympathy. What then? Her forgiveness? She might be able to forget what his sister had done to her. The fact that she could come up here to this pool room without breaking into a cold sweat was proof enough of that. Not total forgetfulness. Not like oblivion. But she could forget enough to make her function.

But forgiveness. It wasn't in her. Not for that. Not

now. When it came to forgiving Amber Cole, she had a cold, hard stone in her heart. Instead of supporting her against a lowlife like that Rat Tail, Amber Cole had blamed her.

Convulsively Meleah's hands clenched. They had almost taken something from her, something very precious. They had almost taken her security, her sense of well-being. If she couldn't feel safe in a place where she'd practically grown up, where could she feel safe? Papa Jack's was more home to her than her actual house. When Amber stood by while her friends tried to rape her, Meleah felt a little piece of her naivete die away. She knew nightlife could be tough, but somehow she'd always been shielded from the worst part of that. Her family at Papa Jack's had always been careful to keep her out of the mess that sometimes broke out there. This time she was in the thick of it. She was even the source of it. It made her sick to think about it.

What made her even sicker was to think what would have happened if Amber and her friends had succeeded. What if they'd gone through with it? She would have lost something much more precious to her, something she'd carefully guarded for almost thirty years. Not even Charlotte knew that she was still a virgin. It was none of their business—a private thing that she'd worked out in her own mind. She didn't want her sexuality to be a topic of conversation. Her choice didn't affect her ability to run the business. So why should it matter? She didn't think about it. That is, once she'd made the decision to remain celibate, she didn't really think about it again until forced to confront it that night.

Having Tarrant around was a constant reminder of that night and her life choice. Every day she faced him, she faced her choice. What unsettled her most was that he was making her reevaluate her choice. Of all of the people who'd come through Papa Jack's, he was the only one who could make her waver.

Meleah sighed. In another place and time, she might have liked Tarrant Cole. She might have even considered dating him. It took a lot to admit that to herself. When Pops agreed to hire him, she'd made up her mind not to like him. She noted with a wry smile that their women patrons liked him enough for all of them. The first nights after he'd started, she'd watched how he handled the attention from some of them. They were stuffing money with their phone numbers written on the bills into his tip jar, approaching him directly with requests for his phone number, even trying to hang out after closing to follow him to his car. If he took any of them up on their offers, he didn't do it in front of her.

Maybe he was trying to be professional; Meleah gave him the benefit of the doubt. But how long could he withstand night after night the onslaught of free and easy sex? It was enough to test the resolve of a saint, and saintly he wasn't. When the crowds had gone and the only ones left were the closing crew, Meleah had heard him going line-for-line with Jack when he was at his raunchiest. She knew that she shouldn't have laughed at some of those jokes. They were dirty—but oh, so funny! Too many times to count, Meleah had to slip on the mask of disapproving manager to keep her face from cracking into laughter. Sometimes he caught her gaze over the heads of others. At those times, she knew that she wasn't fooling him. With the veneer of respectability stripped away, with the humor peeled aside, the raw emotion was left exposed. They had both fought off unwanted attention all night long. At the end of the night, they were too tired to fight anymore. She sat at her favorite stool at the end of the bar, with her elbows on the bar. Her face rested in the palms of her hands. Her expression was drowsy.

Tarrant kept her company while Jack wrapped up his duties—or whatever it was that he and Charlotte did together in the back office. He would stand behind the bar, polishing what he could. He didn't speak to Meleah unless she spoke first. Sometimes long minutes, even an hour would pass without them saying a word—simply being there. As tired as he was, he didn't want the nights to end. He looked forward to those moments when he could forget about what he had done tonight. Each night he worked at Papa Jack's was one more night he would use to destroy them.

"I hate to be the one to defeat you, Ms. Harmon," Tarrant remarked, partially in reference to the pool game. "It doesn't look good for a new employee to embarrass the boss."

The sound of billiard after billiard falling into a pocket raised Meleah's competitive spirit.

"What are they offering at the banks these days?" Tarrant asked.

"I think it's up to seven percent. Why do you want to know?"

"I just wanted to know how much money your check will be making in my bank account."

"I wouldn't count your pennies just yet, Mr. Cole."

Tarrant laughed softly. "Oh? I think I've got this game wrapped up. Eight ball in the side pocket." The cue ball connected solidly, sending the intended ball into the pocket Tarrant indicated. He leaned on the cue stick, regarding her smugly.

"Do I collect my money now, or at the end of the week?"

"Mr. Cole, there's something I didn't tell you."

"And that is?"

"You don't get to collect on your bet."

"Why not?" Tarrant asked. He was getting that oh-so-familiar feeling of being suckered by her once again.

"I'm not salaried at Papa Jack's. I don't collect a paycheck."

"I guess you wouldn't have to, with your father winning that lottery."

"You think I get to see any of that money?" she scoffed. "Most of it is being invested, Mr. Cole."

"Back into the business?"

"That's the only reason why I haven't made a stink about his being so stingy. I want to turn this place into the first-class, family-oriented business that I always imagined it could be."

"So Mr. Harmon isn't shooting you any extra cash. You don't seem to be walking around in rags. What is the source of your income, if you don't mind my asking? Don't tell me you've got a sugar daddy," Tarrant asked partially in teasing. Another part of him didn't want to know. Meleah Harmon was so much her own woman. He didn't want to think that she owed her look of success to some sleazy soul who asked her to do who-knew-what to get a few extra dollars from him.

"That's not really any of your business," Meleah rebuked him.

"You know, Ms. Harmon, sometimes I have to wonder about your unsportsmanlike conduct."

"What do you mean?"

"You knew you didn't have a salary to lose."

"I told you that I didn't like to lose."

"Why did you bet me, if you had no intention of playing fair?"

"Call it curiosity. When I accepted your challenge, I thought, this is a chance to see how good you really are."

"And what conclusion did you come to, Ms. Harmon?"

"Oh, you're good all right."

"But not good enough."

Meleah glanced up at him sharply. "Why would you say something like that?"

"I don't know," he said and shrugged. "Maybe it's the way you seem to look down on me."

"I don't!" Meleah vehemently denied. "I've never done that. When have you ever seen me do that?"

"Then why don't you treat me like you do the other employees? Why don't you joke around with me like you do with Charlotte and Leon?"

"I've known them longer. Almost all my life."

"And what if . . . what if I said I want to get to know you better, too?" His eyes swept over her, pausing at the top buttons of her blouse.

Meleah felt her skin flush warmly under his gaze. The warmth spread from her cheeks, down her neck, and settled as a fluttering in the pit of her stomach. There he went again, making her think. Part of her was flattered. He didn't look at other women like that. Only her. Or should she be insulted? She was his boss, after all. What did it say for her professionalism if she allowed the employees to ogle her like so much eye candy?

"I'd say I think you're handing me a line of B.S.," Meleah retorted, opting for a token show of indignation. "Maybe I am a sore loser," she conceded. "But I'm a fair boss. I'm not taking your money, Tarrant."

"Not the kind of response I was hoping to get. The money part, I'll keep. You thinking that I'm just handing you a line, I don't want you to think like that at all."

Meleah popped her fingers and sang a few lines from a Rolling Stones song. "You can't . . ." *snap* ". . . always get . . ." *snap* ". . . what you want!" *Snap! Snap! Snap!*

She'd sung to him to try to ease the sting of his losing to her again. She'd meant it as a joke. But Tarrant wasn't laughing anymore. He wasn't kidding.

"Sure you can," he said, stepping closer to her. He plucked the cue stick from her hands and tossed his cue stick and hers onto the table—where they rolled from one end of the table to the other.

Meleah was distracted by the sight of the pale wood against the bright green table. The whispery slide of the wood rolling against the smooth green felt sounded suspiciously like hands running over bare skin—magnified one thousand times. A thousand was a good number. It was the number of times she'd wondered if she would ever let him touch her. It was the number of reasons she could think of why she shouldn't. It was the number of reasons she could think of why she should. As Tarrant grasped her chin in his hand, and gently turned her head to face him, Meleah placed her hands against his shoulders. She applied ambiguous pressure—not sure if she wanted to push him away or draw him closer.

She opened her mouth to form some sort of retort. But reason was failing her. Eloquence or witty repartee had no place here. This was an incoherent moment. If she tried to speak now, it would only come out as gibberish. Somewhere in the back of her mind, she thought that she didn't have to wonder anymore if she would ever let him touch her. She already had her answer. He was doing it—and she was letting him.

Tarrant wrapped his arms around her waist, and gripped the pool table behind them. Flexing his arms, he pulled himself toward the table. Meleah backed up, trying to escape from the directness of his approach. There was nowhere for her to go. The table pressed against her bottom; Tarrant's firm thighs were pressed against the length of hers.

When Tarrant touched his lips to the pulse point below her ear, she found her voice again.

"Um . . . what do you . . . uh . . ."

"Shh . . ." He laid his finger against her lips. "It's bad enough you had to sing to me, missing the key and the beat by a country mile," Tarrant teased her. "Don't ruin the mood by talking, too."

Meleah wrinkled her nose. "Come on. I wasn't that bad, was I?"

"Woman, you must be tone deaf."

"Not being able to hear came in handy when I had to tune out those weak lines you and your buddies threw my way." She reminded him of the brothas' behavior the night they came in to Papa Jack's to celebrate the maiden voyage of his '69 Chevy.

"Let me see if I can make up for that," Tarrant said suggestively. He nipped at her ear, and traced the tiny indentation of her skin with his tongue.

Meleah caught her lower lip between her teeth and hummed softly, deep in her throat, indicating her pleasure. "Ummm . . . not a bad start." She made an effort to sound unimpressed.

"That was just the warm-up. You know, like practicing the scales."

Let's hear it for do-re-mi, Meleah thought as she closed her eyes and considered what she was allowing to happen. She'd heard a lot of negative talk from the ladies who'd come to the restaurant to participate in Ladies' Night. They stood around in packs, singling out men they wanted to get a chance to know from those they'd never give a chance in hell. They were all fearful of the same thing—getting played. That is, they were afraid of being treated like a fool. They were afraid of being taken advantage of.

As she stood there, trading touches with Tarrant, she didn't feel any of that apprehension. She *wanted* to be played—but in a completely difference sense. The playing those women were talking about would, indeed, strike a sour chord with her. There was no harmony when one gave without getting anything in return. She didn't get the impression that this was the case here. Tarrant was playing her, but with all of the tender care a skilled musician would treat his instrument. She wanted to be strummed and thrummed. She wanted him to touch her in all the places that would cause her pitch to rise, her tone to deepen. If he thought her voluntary singing was bad!

Tarrant grasped her hips. When he shifted slightly, his knee gently but insistently nudging her thighs apart, Meleah experienced a moment of hesitation. There was no mistaking the intention of the gesture. No word games, no sly looks could disguise the blatant precursor to the act she'd avoided for so long. Heat and hardness pressed in on her. For a moment, flashes of the night of Rat Tail's attack flooded in on her. She had the same sense of events spinning out of control. She had to do something. And that something, she was sure, didn't involve calling Pops to her rescue.

"Wait . . . wait a minute. Hold up!" Meleah said, edging her forearms between them to break the contact.

Tarrant didn't press his obvious height and weight advantage. But he didn't back away either.

"What's wrong, boss lady?" he asked, his voice husky.

"I am not about to let things go down like that," Meleah said, trying to squirm free of his grasp. It only made matters worse. They seemed to be sealed at the hips. Her movement only intensified the sensation.

"What things, Meleah?" Tarrant continued.

Meleah almost moaned in despair. This was the first time he'd ever called her by her first name. The sound

of her name coming from him, the look of his mouth
when he formed the word unsettled her. She couldn't
organize her thoughts. Everything was so much easier
when she was boss lady and he was the lackey.

"Don't play dumb. You know what things. Your . . .
your thingy and mine . . . doing that thing they're not
supposed to be doing."

Tarrant laughed out loud. She could feel his laughter through her arms as it rumbled in his chest.

"My thingy?" he teased her.

"That." She lowered her lashes and indicated his
groin.

"Oh, that!" Tarrant said, as if understanding suddenly dawned on him. "Don't mind that. That's just
his way of saying that he likes you. He likes you a lot,
boss lady."

"We haven't even been formally introduced." Meleah tried to sound prim. She'd never thought much
about her own body in terms of what anyone else
would consider desirable, or even adequate. It never
really mattered what anyone else thought because she
had every intention of letting her one-and-only see her
this exposed, this intimate. That's why she was able to
ignore the catcalls from other men.

But here she was, letting Tarrant touch her. The
thought that he might find her lacking crossed her
mind. She knew what the glamour magazines set as
the standard for a desirable woman. She knew what
the women who came through the restaurant tried to
imitate. Meleah had always done what felt right to her
in terms of choosing her clothes. She wasn't a fitness
fanatic. But she wasn't a slouch either. This was the
first time she'd ever really cared what someone
thought of her physically.

"Well," Tarrant drawled. A wicked gleam appeared
in his hazel eyes. "I could have suggested that you two

shake hands, but I didn't feel like getting my face slapped."

"You just might still," Meleah said, with none of the conviction she should have for such an awkward, yet compelling situation. Here she was. And whether she wanted to admit it to herself or not, here is where she wanted to stay.

Tarrant sensed this. "If it's formal introductions you need, how about this for starters?" Tarrant said suggestively. He traced the ball of his thumb over the curve of Meleah's bottom lip. Meleah tried to turn her head aside. The calloused roughness of his palms grazed her cheek. He turned her face back to him, searching her clouded questioning eyes for any indication of relenting. As much as he wanted to, he would not kiss her without her permission. Tarrant lowered his face to within inches of hers. A soft sigh escaped her lips. His nostrils flared, taking in the sweet smell of her breath. She smelled faintly of honey. Sweet. Enticing. His tongue flicked out and touched her lower lip. This time Meleah moaned audibly. She murmured his name and closed her eyes. She never saw him complete the distance between them. But she felt him bend her head back with the force of his kiss. He grasped the back of her neck, supporting her, and drawing her into him. He did so slowly, with building intensity. Inch by inch, moment by moment, he drew her into his circle of passion. Skillfully his lips moved over her. He took any evidence of her resistance, and smoothed it away with the slow, circular motion of his head as he kissed her.

Meleah opened her lips to him and allowed him full access to all of the hidden corners of her mouth. She'd never been kissed like this before. Each sensation was a small revelation to her—from the firmness of his lips to the warm roughness of his tongue. Her mind imag-

ined how her body would feel if she allowed his mo-
bile, conquering mouth to explore points beyond her
mouth.

Pressure to explore further built within her, urging
her to deepen the kiss. Her senses flared to life, con-
suming her, driving her. She grasped the back of his
head, drawing him closer and closer. She felt her body,
of its own accord, molding into him. Slowly, deliberately grinding her pelvis into his. It was the closest
she'd ever come to expecting—no, demanding—anyone to take charge of her body.

"Ahem!" Charlotte's delicate cough from the entrance of the billiards room broke the spell, and gave
Meleah the impetus she needed to sever contact. She
shoved against Tarrant's arm, and circled around to
the opposite end of the table.

"Sorry to interrupt your . . . game," Charlotte said,
trying and failing to sound as if everything was business
as usual. Her quick eyes took in Meleah's look of embarrassment as she scrambled to rearrange her cloth-
ing. Tarrant's look of frustration was equally telling.
He stood with his back to Charlotte, one hand placed
on his hip. The other gripped the pool table.

"Tarrant," Charlotte continued, "you have a phone
call."

"Could you take a message, Charlotte?" He was in
no mood to take a call from one of those relentless
Ladies' Night regulars. In his state of mind, he might
be tempted to cave in.

"I think you want to take this call. It's UTMB."

Tarrant's head snapped around to face her. "Amber?"

"There's been a change in her condition," Charlotte
said, then went on quickly to allay his fears. "For the
better. She's awake and asking for you."

He then glanced at Meleah. She nodded at his unspoken request. "You'd better go to her."

"I'll be back."

"Take all the time that you need."

NINE

By the time Tarrant reached the hospital, his parents had already arrived. He saw Alexa drinking juice by the nurses' station.

"Hey, Squeak." He came up to her and tugged on her pigtail. He couldn't help noticing that since Alexa had been living with his parents, her hair was combed a little neater. Her clothes seemed to match a little better. He felt a little twinge of guilt. He'd done the best that he could with her since Amber was absent so much. Tarrant toyed with the possibility that maybe there were things that some women were better at handling than men. He shook his head, grinning and imagining Meleah's or Charlotte's response to that supposition. They'd probably respond by challenging him to a boxing match and whipping the tar out of him.

"Granny and Grandpa are in there, Uncle Rant," Alexa said, indicating the room with the jerk of her thumb.

"Then what are you doing out here?"

"She didn't ask for me." Alexa's voice caught in her throat. She looked away, blinking fast before she could start to cry. She told herself she wouldn't cry. Not this time. Amber Cole would never make her cry again.

"Awww . . . Squeak." Tarrant fumbled for the right words. He laid his hand on top of her head. "She's just . . . well . . . she's just sick. She's not feeling so good, so . . . it's not like she doesn't love you or anything."

"It's all right, Uncle Rant. I don't need to be in there. I've already said what I wanted to say to her." Alexa patted his hand. She looked up at him, her expression understanding. It quickly changed to one of puzzlement.

"What? What's wrong?" Tarrant noted her knitted eyebrows.

"You switching teams on me, Uncle Rant?"

"What is that supposed to mean?"

"When did you start wearing lipstick?"

"Huh?" He touched his hand to his mouth. Still sensitive lips quivered at the thought of Meleah's kiss. "Oh! Well, that's just . . . uh . . ." His voice trailed off. Sins of omission, he could justify. But to flat out lie to her? The kid trusted him. He would never do anything to betray that.

"If you try to tell me it's Kool-Aid, I'll make Grandma wash out your mouth with soap."

"It's not Kool-Aid, Squeak."

"And please don't tell me you've been locking lips with your friend Miss Julie. You know I can't stand that skeezer."

"Watch your language," Tarrant said automatically. "No, it's not Miss Julie either."

"Good. I knew you wouldn't fall for somebody like that."

Tarrant started to protest. He wouldn't exactly call what he was doing falling for Meleah. He was attracted to her . . . yes. There was no denying that. And maybe she'd been on his mind a little more than usual. But that was to be expected. He was seeing her in action every night. He was spending an inordinate amount of time with her, especially after closing hours. Maybe that kiss they shared pushed the bounds of an employee-employer relationship. But that shouldn't be considered falling for someone, should it? Especially when he fully intended to use any information he got from associating with her to help clear his sister's name.

Tarrant looked up when Amber's door swung open and his parents stepped out. His father gave him a tight-lipped nod of acknowledgment. At least that was something, Tarrant thought. A few weeks ago, his father would have jumped on him, possibly blaming him for the fact that Amber hadn't made more progress by now.

"I'm glad you could get away from work." Beryl clasped her son to her and squeezed. "She's been calling for you."

"How does she look?"

"Like a wreck," Ashton grumbled. Beryl shot him a warning look. "But the doctor says her vital signs look strong. It looks really good for her. Thank God for that."

"Can I see her now?"

"Go on, son. It'll do her a world of good to see you."

"Speaking of good, Squeak looks good. What have you been feeding her?"

"Some of my stick-to-the-ribs cookin'," Beryl said proudly. "I swear, if she didn't eat three helpings of red beans and rice when I brought her home, she didn't eat one."

"You mean, you didn't have to spread sugar over everything for her to eat it?"

"She tried to pull that on me," Beryl admitted. "But your father threatened to make her eat his cookin'. After she saw how it stuck to the bottom of the pot and peeled away with that oh-so-blackened aroma, she decided to take her chances with me."

"I should have brought her to you sooner, Mama," Tarrant lamented. He thought about all of the days he muddled through in helping to raise Amber. He'd asked his female friends for advice when he was truly stumped, gently but firmly turning aside their offers to share the raising duties. They were just thinly veiled offers to share his bed.

"It wouldn't have been the right time. All things in their due time, Rant."

"She's with us now," Ashton said firmly and met Tarrant's gaze head-on. "And with us she'll stay until . . ." He didn't finish the sentence. He couldn't imagine not having his little granddaughter around him now.

"Maybe, when Amber gets out of here, she'll take more of an interest in . . . her life," Tarrant said, glancing down at Alexa.

Ashton and Beryl exchanged concerned looks. Tarrant read the look perfectly. They doubted it. In fact, they had had several discussions about what should happen to Alexa. If Amber had not and would not change her ways, it would be unfair to send Alexa back into that environment. And with the late hours that Tarrant was now keeping, she couldn't go back to him either. So what was to be done with her?

"I'm going in now," Tarrant murmured, needing to break the uncomfortable silence.

"Just remember that she looks worse than she actually is," Beryl said. Tarrant gave a wry smile. It was the same thing he'd said to Alexa when he'd first brought her in to see Amber.

He pushed the door open slowly. Amber was lying on her back, staring up at the ceiling. If she'd heard him enter, she gave no indication of it.

"Amber?" Tarrant called softly.

She lowered her head and managed a weak smile. "Hey, big brother," she croaked.

"Here. Let me get you something." He poured a cup of water from the pitcher at her bedside and raised the cup and straw to her lips. "How are you feelin', kiddo?"

"Like I got a full body makeover by a mack truck," she said.

"You're lookin' good, Amber."

"Liar. But thanks anyway. They tell me that I can look forward to at least a year of physical therapy to get back the use of my legs."

"Yeah? That's good news."

Amber shrugged. "I suppose. It could have been worse. I could have been Durell. And with the crack on the head that Chico got, he may have the mental capacity of a potato for the rest of his life."

"That's an improvement over that gold-toothed cretin."

"Don't start on them, Rant."

"Sorry, kiddo. I didn't come in here to argue with you. I came in here to—"

"Give me a pep talk? Tell me how much you support me? I'm really not much in the mood to hear it, big brother. All day long I listen to the blah-blah of all of the quack doctors telling me how good my chances are."

"They're the experts. They should know."

"You think I want to hear my chances of recovery are good? You think I want to hear that as soon as I get up and walk, they're going to walk my black butt to the execution chamber? Durell's a stiff. Chico's a vegetable. I'm the only one they've got to pin that accident on. Yeah. I'm really looking forward to hearing about that."

"Amber . . ." Tarrant sighed. "I just wish . . ."

"Well, it's too late for that. All of that wishing isn't going to do me a bit of good. It just pisses me off that the one time I did good, the one time I didn't drink, I got busted. God, you want to talk about wishes? I wish I'd never heard of Papa Jack's. I wish I'd never gone within a hundred miles of that place. Durell was doing some pretty heavy drinking. He's a mean drunk, you know, Rant? But I could have handled him if it hadn't been for that Rasta-braid-wearin' wannabe."

Meleah! She was talking about Meleah. She had to be. Now that Amber was more lucid, she could answer the questions that Meleah wouldn't.

"You want to tell me what happened that night, Amber? Anything I can take back to the D.A. will help clear you."

"I don't want to talk about it," Amber said, sullenly turning her head aside.

Again Tarrant felt a mounting wall of frustration. What was it about these women? If Meleah and Amber would just open their mouths and give him a full picture of the events that night, he wouldn't have to sneak around, pretending to be something he wasn't. He wasn't a bartender. He was a big brother. He wasn't a junior sleuth. He was just a car jock. All he wanted to do was rebuild engines, piece together power trains.

Amber was right about one thing. If he didn't discover something fast, she would be charged.

"I'm trying to help you, kiddo. But you've got to help me. You said it was Meleah's fault that you were in the accident. How was it her fault? Why? I gotta know. No district attorney is going to believe that anyone else was to blame unless you give me proof. I'm doing the best that I can."

"Mama says you've been spending a lot of time out there. What are you doing?" She sounded suspicious.

She'd hoped that he hadn't gone out there and fallen under that Meleah person's spell, too.

"I'm a bartender," he admitted.

"You're working there? You're serving drinks, Rant? How is that going to help me?"

"It's weak, but it's a chance, Amber. Maybe we can get Papa Jack's to shoulder some of the blame for the accident. Maybe we can show that they weren't being responsible servers. If your friends were drunk out of their minds, maybe we can prove that they had a hand in it. Durell has a rap sheet of violent offenses as long as the bandages wrapped around your head. Between that and Papa Jack's serving policy, I think we can clear you. That's why I'm there, trying to establish a history. But you're the only one who can give us the details of that night, Amber. You're the only one who can help me seal it. So you'd better start talking."

"You're awfully quiet tonight, Le-Le," Charlotte said, edging close to Meleah, sitting at the end of the bar. She'd watched her nursing the same drink for over an hour. Meleah had swirled her swizzle stick around the fruit-laden drink so many times that Charlotte thought she'd stir up a small hurricane in the glass. But, Charlotte knew that was only a poor imitation of the turmoil that must be going inside of Meleah's thoughts.

"A lot on my mind, I guess." Meleah shrugged, taking a small sip of her daiquiri.

"Yeah, that Tarrant is quite a handful." Charlotte winked broadly at her.

Meleah's face flushed warm. "Oh . . . he wasn't— that is, I . . ."

"Save it. I know he's been on your mind tonight. As soon as he called and said he wouldn't be in tonight, you went into mental meltdown. I can't say that I blame you, sugar. The way you two were pawing each other this afternoon, I wouldn't be surprised if he didn't give you enough to brood about for the next three weeks."

"Shh! Keep it down, will you, Charlie? Like I really need Pops to hear about my complete lapse in professionalism."

"A little lapse in professionalism is good for the soul," Charlotte said. "I try to have at least two or three lapses a week," Charlotte said as she sailed away.

"You mean a day," Meleah muttered under her breath.

"I heard that!" Charlotte called out to her.

"Heard what?" Elliot Caudle bellied up to the bar next to Meleah. He dragged a seat next to her and tapped the bar twice to indicate to Charlotte to set him up.

"Say, Le-Le, where's the big guy tonight?" He looked around for Tarrant.

"How should I know?" Meleah said testily. "It's not as if I'm keeping special tabs on the guy."

"Speaking of tabs, Charlie, you gonna hook me up or not. I'm thirstier than a big dog."

"You haven't cleared your last tab, sugar."

"Can a fella help it if he stays broke? It's not as if I won the lottery, you know."

"Other folks in here didn't win the lottery and they can pay up just fine. Just because you're Jack's nephew doesn't mean you can milk him," Charlotte said as she turned away to draw a draft for Elliot.

"Spoken like a true cow," Elliot whispered to Meleah.

"I heard that," Charlotte said, without turning around. She set the beer on the bar and slid it down to him.

"Tarrant took a little time off to take care of some

personal business," Charlotte supplied. "Why do you want to know?"

Elliot shrugged. "Just curious. It's just strange not to see him around. He's been sticking close to Papa Jack's like white on rice the past few weeks."

"Maybe he got what he wanted," Meleah said. "Maybe he'll leave now."

"Sounds like you want him gone." Charlotte didn't expect that to come from Meleah.

Meleah looked up and shook her head. *Not now, Charlie!* She pleaded with her eyes. She wanted her to keep quiet for just a little while longer. She didn't want Elliot to get one whiff of what had happened between Tarrant and her. He wouldn't be able to keep it to himself. That motor mouth would let it slip to Jack. And then she would have to take back all of those things she'd said about not mixing business and friendship. She hated being proved wrong almost as much as she hated losing.

"Why would I want that? He's such a good worker," Meleah said, with all of the professionalism she could muster.

"So does this mean that you don't mind that I asked him to tend bar at Jack's party next Saturday?" Charlotte asked, partly in teasing and partly in all seriousness. No matter what else Tarrant might be, he was a hard worker.

Meleah cleared her throat and said in a voice too squeaky to be her own, "Mind? Who me? No, I don't mind. Why should I mind? Let the man earn a few extra bucks. He's doing it to help his sister. I'm more than willing to—"

"You got that right, sugar!" Charlotte interrupted, making a sound between a snort and a laugh.

"Don't you have some customers to go hassle?" Meleah demanded, glaring at her.

As Charlotte passed Meleah, she patted her cheek. "You keep telling yourself those fairy tales, sugar."

"Party? What kind of a party?" Elliot wanted to know.

"Nothing fancy," Meleah said. "Just a little I-won-four-million-and-I-want-to-gloat-to-my-family-and-friends kind of a party. It's being held at our new house."

"House, my left eye. Jack's bought himself a near-mansion. Uncle's living large since he won that lottery. The way he's spending his cash, it's a miracle he has any of it left," Elliot mused.

"Don't you think for a minute that I'm going to let him blow it all." Meleah thought she'd set the record straight. "I know it seems a little much because we've been scraping by for so long. But he hasn't gone completely insane with spending. I won't let him."

"You need a financial advisor?"

"Are you volunteering?"

"You've got to be kidding. That's too much like work. But I know some folks who can help you set up a portfolio."

"No thanks, Ell, I've got it covered."

"Well, what about this party? You got a caterer? I know some folks who can burn, Le-Le. You say the word and I can have tables, decorations, the works set up just like that!" Elliot snapped his fingers.

"For somebody who doesn't have a job, Elliot, you sure do know a lot of hardworking people. Ever thought of hitting them up for some work of your own?"

"Getting folks together is a full-time job, cuz. Do you know how long it took me to find that guy who set up your alarm?"

"Let me guess. You're about to send your itty-bitty dialing finger on vacation?" Meleah said, waving her index finger under his nose.

"You're testier than usual tonight, Le-Le. What's got your panties in a pinch?"

"Stay out of my panties, Ell," Meleah said automatically. She ignored the snickers from some of the patrons hovering around them.

"Come on, cuz. You can tell me. I know you think I'm just a shiftless no-account. But if it's one thing you learn when you're trying to avoid work, it's how to keep your ears open and your mouth shut."

"I guess I'm just a little nervous about this whole Tarrant and Amber thing."

"Amber? Who's Amber?"

"His sister. Don't you remember? She's the one who got into that accident a month or so ago. Tarrant got a call from the hospital today."

"She isn't . . . she didn't croak on him, did she?"

"I don't think so. I think she's out of her coma . . . or at least, her condition took a turn for the better."

"That's good news, right? That's what you wanted to hear. Didn't you say that big guy was hanging around only to pick up some extra dollars to help his sister? If she's getting out soon, that means he can stop hanging around here."

"Yeah. Every dark cloud has a silver lining," Meleah said, but she didn't sound or look convinced. She planted her elbows on the bar, balled up her fists, and rested her cheeks on them.

"Don't do that. It makes you look like a chipmunk," Elliot advised. "That's not the face of a woman who wants to get rid of a pest."

"He hasn't been a pest. Not really," Meleah admitted reluctantly. "I mean, he's been working his butt off. You can't find good help like that these days."

"Been watching his butt, have you?" Elliot teased.

"That's not funny, Ell."

"I'm serious. Have you been checking him out?"

"Like an overdue library book," Meleah sighed. "He really is a nice guy. How he wound up with such a loser for a sister, I'll never know. If she's awake, there's no telling what kind of lies she's telling on me at the hospital."

"Why don't you go and find out?"

"What do you mean? I can't go there!"

"Why not?"

"Because."

"A more convincing argument, I've never heard," Elliot retorted.

"I don't think it's appropriate. I don't have a reason for being there."

"Sure you do. You just told me that you wanted to know what she's been saying about you."

"But I can't tell *him* that. What if he sees me at the hospital?"

"All the better, cuz. Tell him that as a concerned, considerate boss, you were worried about him and his family. Take some flowers to the girl, if you want to. Do whatever you have to do to get into that room."

"I don't think I can. I mean, it's bad enough that he thinks Papa Jack's is responsible for his sister's accident."

"How do you know that?"

"Before he started working here, he told me that Amber blamed me."

Elliot clucked his tongue. "I'd say that all of that money has made y'all lose your minds, but all of this happened before Jack won the lottery. So what other crazy idea made him decide to hire the man."

Meleah shrugged. "I don't know. I just know that he's here, he's been here, and now . . ."

"You may lose him," Elliot ended for her.

Glumly Meleah nodded her head.

"You need to go, Meleah," Elliot insisted.

"I can't go. I can't leave Charlotte stuck out here to close," Meleah made an excuse.

"I can help her out," Elliot offered. "Show me where the cash register is."

"Don't even try it."

"Give me the key to the liquor cabinet. I can serve. Or the key to your office. I can sign those liquor requisition slips just as fast as you can."

"That's too much like work, Ell," Meleah teased him. "Heaven forbid I put you in the path of manual labor."

"Very funny. See, here I am, trying to help you out by covering for you. And what do you do? You dog me out. See if I try to offer you any more favors."

"Do you really think I should go, Ell?" Meleah chewed on her lower lip in indecision.

"Don't do that. You're eating off all of your lipstick," Elliot cautioned. "See? Now you've got it all over your teeth. Yeah, girl. Go to him."

"Okay. I'm going. But if they run me out of there, I'm going to tell them that you told me I should."

"Since when did you need my permission to do something you want to do anyway? If you go now, you'll be back before anyone ever notices you're gone. You know you want to go. Le-Le, you won't rest easy in your mind until you can defend yourself in front of that Amber. What's that my mama always said? Tell the truth and shame the devil. As long as that witch is dropping poison in the big guy's ear, things will never be right between the two of you."

"Things were wrong between us from the start," Meleah said. "What makes you think they ought to be right now?"

"We'll be right back, Amber," Beryl promised her daughter. "We're going to grab a bite to eat." She leaned forward and kissed Amber on the forehead, then wiped away the faint lipstick trace she left there. The wipe became a caress as Amber pouted.

"You just got here, Mama," Amber complained.

"That's not true. We've been here practically all day," Tarrant contradicted. He checked his watch. By now activity at Papa Jack's would be in full swing. He imagined Charlotte and Meleah and Trae, flying from one section of the restaurant to the other, trying to keep up with the demands of a hot night, and cursing him under their breaths for his not being there. He didn't want to call in to say that he wouldn't be there. But Amber had been so insistent. Having their parents there didn't make her any better. In fact, the more attention she got, the more she seemed to need.

"You know how grouchy your father gets when he doesn't get his daily allowance of salt, grease, and empty calories," Beryl continued.

As if on cue, Ashton grabbed his stomach to muffle the rumble and gurgle. "I'm not eating down in the cafeteria again. The last time I tried their meatloaf, it almost put me in the hospital."

"It's closed by now anyway," Tarrant said, glancing at his watch again.

"You act like there's someplace else you'd rather be," Amber said. "I thought you'd be glad to see me alert and awake."

"I am glad, Amber," Tarrant said patiently. "It's just that . . ."

"Maybe he's tired of listening to you whine and complain," Alexa muttered from over in the corner. "Everybody knows you're hurting."

Everyone turned to stare at her. She'd been so quiet, they'd almost forgotten that she was there. Amber certainly had. She had not asked for Alexa—not even once.

"Squeak," Tarrant began.

"Save it, Uncle Rant," she said sullenly, and shot up out of the chair.

"Where are you going?" Beryl asked.

"As if anyone cares."

"Watch your tone, little girl," Ashton chastised.

"I'm going to wait outside." She thrust her hands into her pockets and stomped outside.

Tarrant's gaze swung from Amber's to Alexa's. At that moment, he couldn't tell whose expression was the most petulant. "Don't let her leave like that, Amber. Say something to her. Call her back."

Amber shook her head. "She won't listen to me. I don't know what's the matter with that girl."

If it weren't for the little girl crying right in front of where she wanted to go, Meleah was certain that she would have turned around and pretended that she'd never let Elliot talk her into this foolishness. What did she think she was going to accomplish by visiting Amber in the hospital? If anything, she would probably make the girl take a turn for the worse. She would have turned around, except for the little girl. She happened to look up. Her expression was so woeful that Meleah could not ignore it. She couldn't pretend that she didn't see her. Their gazes locked and some sort of silent communication passed between them. Whatever had caused the little girl pain and the pain of Meleah's fear and uncertainty met in midair.

Meleah got a grip on her nerves by clinging tight to the sympathy plant she'd brought along. The girl wiped her nose on her sleeve.

"Hi," Meleah said simply, walking up to her.

"Hey," the girl responded.

"I'm looking for Amber Cole's room. Is this it?" Meleah asked, though she already knew. The nurse on duty at the floor station had told her.

"Yeah."

"Is it . . . is it all right if I go in?"

The girl shrugged listlessly. "She's already got some people in there. I left because four's a crowd."

"Oh, I don't believe that," Meleah said, shaking her head. "When you're hurt, there's nothing like friends and family to make you feel better."

"Nice try, lady. But I don't think you know what you're talking about."

Meleah gave a half smile. "It wouldn't be the first time." She shifted the plant to one hand and held out the other hand. "My name's Meleah."

The girl stared at Meleah's offered hand for a moment, then started to hold out her own. "Wait a minute. I gotta get the snot off first." She wiped her hand on her pants leg, then tried again. "Okay. Now it's clean. I'm Alexa."

"Pleasure to meet you, Alexa," Meleah said and gave what she hoped was a reassuring smile. The business with the mucus on the hand threw her for a moment. But the girl's expression was sincere, so she was careful to accept the greeting in the spirit that it was given.

"Are you a friend of Amber's?" Alexa asked.

"No, not really. Actually I'm a little closer to her brother, Tarrant Cole."

"You know my uncle Rant?" The girl's expression seemed to brighten.

"Tarrant is your uncle?"

Alexa nodded vigorously. "He's in there now with my grandpa and grandma. You want me to go get him and tell him that you're out here?"

"Well . . ." Meleah hesitated. It was bad enough that she had expected to run into Tarrant here. She hadn't counted on participating in an entire family reunion. "Maybe you shouldn't disturb their private time. I can wait." She started to back away.

"You won't. Things were busting up anyway. My grandfolks were going to leave to get something to eat and I think Uncle Rant was starting to wish he was somewhere else."

Meleah's curiosity was piqued. She didn't want to press the girl for information. It wasn't really her business. Where Tarrant Cole went and what he did on his own time was nobody's business but his own. Yet that didn't stop her from wanting to know.

Alexa didn't miss the hesitation. She canted her head, looking at Meleah with a puzzled expression on her face. The woman was chewing on her lower lip nervously, systematically removing the deep berry-colored lipstick she'd reapplied before leaving the parking lot.

Alexa's face suddenly broke into a wide grin. She'd bet this was the woman that her uncle Rant had been kissing right before he came to the hospital or she'd trade in all her crayons. It was a perfect color match— the hue on this woman's lips and the traces left on his.

"Come on, Meleah" Alexa said, grabbing Meleah by the sleeve. She tugged her toward the door before Meleah could protest.

"No, wait." The words died on her lips as Alexa pushed open the door and called out.

"Look, everybody. Look who I brought!" Alexa announced.

When four pairs of eyes swung to focus on her, Meleah froze where she stood. She'd worked up a scenario in her mind about what she'd say, once she'd come face to face with Amber Cole. After all of this time, all of her repressed animosity, Meleah was certain that her indictment of the girl would be scathing. She would tell her exactly what she thought of her and her lowlife friends. She'd berate her for her trashy clothes and her willingness to flaunt her body. She'd tear into her for hanging out with people who didn't respect her—in fact, they'd abused her. Most of all, she'd let Amber Cole know how much she hated her for making her a victim. She'd curse her for dragging her from her safe, secure world of Papa Jack's into the dark, disgusting place that people went who had no love for themselves, let alone anybody else.

Seeing her now, with the tubes and monitors and bandages surrounding her, the words wouldn't come. The hate, which had burned like a slow, steady flame, slowly fizzled, then died. She had nothing to say to her. It no longer mattered to her what Amber had told Tarrant. Meleah knew the truth. And knowing that, she could hold up her head and walk away victorious without ever having uttered a word.

"Meleah, what are you doing here?" Tarrant asked.

"What is she doing here? Get her out of here!" Amber screeched. She tried to sit up. Her arms flailed, as if she were trying to reach Meleah to strangle her with her bare hands.

Meleah took a startled step backward. Though she didn't know why she should be so surprised. What made her think a near-death experience would give the girl any sense? For as much compassion as Meleah suddenly had for Amber, Amber still had just as much venom.

"I came to see if you were all right," Meleah found her voice to say.

"Get her out of here!" Amber said. "Get that witch away from me."

"Amber, sweetheart, calm down!" Beryl entreated, trying to press Amber back into the pillows. She was afraid that Amber would rip the IV drip administering antibiotics out of her arm.

"Lady, I don't know who you are, but I think you'd better leave." Ashton interposed himself between Amber and Meleah.

"Get her out of here, Daddy!" Amber cried out. "Don't let her hurt me like she did Chico and Durell. Daddy! Don't let her hurt me again. Please, Daddy!"

Meleah went from compassionate to irate. She let the planter drop to the floor in a crash as she said, "You deluded little liar. I never hurt you. I never even touched you."

"Come on, Meleah." Tarrant grasped her by the shoulders and tried to hustle her out of the door. Meleah pointed at Amber as she allowed herself to be backed out of the door. "You'd better get your life right, little girl, before you're called to account in heaven. God can't abide a liar!"

"Daddy!" Amber's wail was in her ears as Tarrant took Meleah into the corridor. He could feel her trembling beneath his fingertips.

"I can't believe she's telling everybody that I hurt her! Where does she get off with that daddy nonsense. She wasn't calling for her daddy when she was sitting by and watching her friends trying to rape me!"

"What . . . what did you say?" Tarrant's fingers convulsed and dug into the soft flesh of her shoulders.

Meleah winced, then looked up in horror. She'd sworn that she would never reveal to Tarrant what had happened that night. At first, she'd told herself that she kept silent to keep from getting involved. She didn't want to have anything to do with Amber or her friends. She just wanted to forget that night. Then as Tarrant continued to hang around and she grew to know him, even develop feelings for him, she had kept her peace to keep from hurting him. She didn't know how much he knew about his sister—but Meleah didn't want to be the one to hurt him more. So she kept her mouth shut and instructed everyone else to do the same. It wasn't too hard to expect everyone else's loyalty. They had accepted Tarrant into Papa Jack's circle of family—and family protected their own.

She jerked away from him, pressing her lips closely together.

"It doesn't matter," she whispered. "I knew I shouldn't have come here."

"Now will you tell me what happened that night, Meleah. Be straight with me."

"Why don't you ask your precious Amber," she flung at him.

"I'm asking you," Tarrant ground out.

"All right," Meleah said, spinning around to face him. She gripped her elbows tightly and began in a low, flat voice. "You want to hear it? This is the way it happened. All of the truth. No embellishments. Amber and her friends came to Papa Jack's. We think they were already drunk when they got there. Some of the others who were hanging out in the pool room with them were sneaking in alcohol. Pops caught some of them and threw them out. But since he couldn't prove that Amber and her friends were part of them, he let them stay. They stayed until closing. I went upstairs to close down the pool room. They didn't want to leave right away so I let them finish their game. One of them hit on me pretty heavy. When I turned him down, he got ugly. Really ugly. There's nothing worse than an ugly drunk, Tarrant."

Meleah paused, hoping that was enough for Tarrant. She hoped he knew enough about the type that Amber hung out with to paint the sordid picture that Meleah was doing her best to erase.

"Go on," he pressed her.

Meleah closed her eyes. "When I refused him, he . . . they . . . they pinned me against a wall. At first, I think they were trying to scare me. But it didn't stop there. They pushed me down on the pool table. Durell started to open his pants and . . . and . . ."

Her voice grew ragged as details she thought she'd forgotten, or at least successfully suppressed, crowded in on her. The sound of a zipper jerking down, the creak of a leather jacket, the hiss of Durell's breath in her face. "I can still see him. I can still smell him leaning over me. Stinking!" Her stomach churned at the memory. "And all that time, all she did was stand there. Your sister, so quick to pin the blame on somebody else, just stood there. If it hadn't been for Pops and Charlie and Leon, that animal would have gone through with it."

Tarrant also closed his eyes, trying to imagine that night in as much vivid detail. His fists clenched. He was certain that if he had been there, they would not have been able to drive away from Papa Jack's. The fact that Jack showed that much restraint was a testimony to the man's character. "Why didn't you just tell me this before?" Tarrant demanded.

"Do you think I wanted to dredge up that memory? I just wanted to forget about it and get on with my life! I can count myself lucky that they didn't actually finish what they started. But that doesn't make me any less scared, any less violated in my thoughts."

Tarrant sank down in a nearby chair. Shame for his sister's actions, or rather nonaction, was not nearly as overwhelming as his own shame for feeling that he had to get some kind of revenge against the Harmons. For seven weeks, since he'd learned of Amber's accident, he had been skulking around. Once he'd gotten a job at Papa Jack's, he had spent his time plotting and planning. He'd abused their good will and their trust. He turned to her, his eyes haunted.

"So why is Amber blaming you for the accident?" he asked, his voice hollow.

Meleah sat next to him. She was quiet for several seconds before answering. She could see that he was hurt by what she'd just told him. This was the moment she'd hoped to avoid. Now that it had come, she didn't want to drive the proverbial knife any deeper.

"I don't know, Tarrant. I don't know."

"God, I can't believe she put you through this. You should have come to me, Meleah. You should have told me something." He reached out and touched a single braid that had fallen across her forehead. Tenderly he tucked it back behind her ear. No wonder she'd panicked in the pool room when he kissed her. With the way his luck was going, it might have been the same damned pool table, for all he knew.

She pressed her palm against his hand so that he cupped her cheek. Closing her eyes, she nuzzled her cheek against his palm. At that moment, all of the fighting, protective spirit that had made him want to rush to Amber's defense transferred to Meleah. If he had been there, there was no telling what he would have done. If he'd seen those animals putting their hands on her . . .

He jerked his hand back before it could convulse into the fist that reflected the anger and revulsion he had inside of him.

Meleah sensed him withdraw from her in more than just physical distance. Maybe she should have been more open with him from the beginning. But it was too late to think about should-have's and might-have-been's. It didn't matter. He knew now. She smoothed her hand over his brow and kissed him gently on the forehead. "What could I have said, Tarrant? Except for the facts as I knew them, I couldn't tell you how her mind was working. In some twisted way, she blamed me for Durell wanting me and not her. She told me that night that he was her man. She was out of her mind with jealousy. She still is. She can't, or won't, see the truth. Instead of taking responsibility for her own actions, she just has to have someone to blame."

"You gotta do right by me, Rant," Amber had pleaded. It was the last thing she'd said to her brother before he left her at the hospital. "You gotta make sure that I don't go to jail for something that wasn't even my fault."

When he'd countered by asking her about Durell, Chico, and Meleah, Amber had volleyed with, "Yeah, they were a little drunk. I never denied that. But someone should have cut them off. I'm not taking this fall by myself, big brother. I may be in jail, but that shouldn't stop us from getting some payback, huh? Sue 'em. Sue the pants off of 'em. Hit them where it hurts."

Lawsuits. Those were the last words of his father, threatening to bring them down on everyone at Papa Jack's for putting his baby girl in that hospital. It was enough to make Tarrant want to curse. Amber crying on one hand, Ashton was threatening on the other. What was he going to do? He knew one thing. He knew he wasn't going back to Papa Jack's. He couldn't. Not knowing what he knew now. How could he show his face there now? Meleah must think he was some kind of a punk, letting his sister trick him into thinking that Papa Jack's was responsible for her screw-up. No, sir. He wasn't going back there. All the horsepower in his '69 Chevy couldn't drag him back.

TEN

"Right on time, Tarrant, my boy!" Jack clapped the younger man on the back, and ushered him into the house. "You're even a little early."

"I wanted to be sure that everything was set up before your guests arrived. I don't like scrambling around at the last minute. It makes me kinda crazy." Tarrant made an excuse.

He hadn't intended to come back at all. If it weren't for Alexa, accusing him of being a coward, he would not have come back. She called him every day from his parents' house, sometimes twice a day, urging him to go back and clear the air with Meleah. He didn't know how she figured out they were a little more than employee and employer. The fact was, she knew and she wasn't going to get off his case until he acknowledged it, too.

To counter Alexa's matchmaking efforts, his father badgered him to get back into Papa Jack's fold. He'd clamped down on the idea of a lawsuit like a fighting pit bull clamped down on the jugular of his unlucky opponent. Amber had told him of Tarrant's plan to infiltrate the bar, gather evidence of their serving policy, and then use the information against him. During the week of Tarrant's defection from the bar, Ashton had called just as many times as Alexa. He badgered, pleaded, and threatened until Tarrant agreed to go back. Tarrant agreed; but in his mind, it was only to put some closure between himself and Meleah. It had been fun for a while, but this was business.

"You sound like Le-Le," Jack complained, breaking into Tarrant's thoughts. "She's always pushing me to be at one place or another. Tonight I'm not rushing for anybody. I'm ready to get my party on! Why don't we start this off with a little preparty drink, eh, Tarrant?"

"Jack, I think you've been sampling the merchandise already," Tarrant accused him.

"You do your job, son, and I'll do mine. I've got to make sure I'm serving only the finest quality, don't I?" Jack's dark eyes were red-rimmed. He hid a tiny belch behind his hand. "Besides, I wanted to get my share before those buzzards guzzle it all down for themselves."

"Buzzards?" Tarrant asked, confused by the statement. He didn't think Jack was the kind of person who would surround himself with people he didn't like or respect. He wondered whether or not Jack was referring to the flood of people who were drawn to his instant wealth.

"My dearest family and friends," Jack said promptly. "I'd give my life's blood for any one of them. But I wouldn't trust them with the keys to my liquor cabinet. No, sir!"

"Speaking of liquor, where do you want me to set up?" Tarrant asked briskly.

Jack steered Tarrant toward the rear of the house. "This way, Tarrant. The weather looks like it's going to cooperate, so we'll have the party outside. By the way, glad to have you back, son. I have to say that I hated getting that resignation letter from you. You're one hell of a bartender. Didn't a night go by that half the ladies in the place weren't asking for you."

"I don't plan to stay, Jack," Tarrant said. "I promised Charlotte I'd be here tonight. After that, I'm through."

"That business with your sister . . . we should have told you sooner. I'm sorry, Tarrant."

"I understand why you didn't," Tarrant said tightly. "If I were in your place, I don't think I would have come straight out with it myself. It wasn't a very pleasant scene."

"Can we put it behind us?" Jack stuck out his hand.

"Consider the matter closed."

They stepped through the sliding glass doors of the patio, and onto the cobbled concrete surrounding an Olympic-sized swimming pool. The serving bar was at one end of the pool; a table filled with hors d'oeuvres, entrees, and desserts sat at the end closest to the patio doors.

"Why'd you separate the serving tables?" Tarrant wanted to know.

"Simple mathematics. The food is twice as easy to get to. Maybe if my guests have to do a stint around the pool to get to the liquor, they'll think twice about going for refills." Jack laughed, then poked Tarrant in the ribs. "An old trick I learned from my dad, God rest his soul. Only he used to hide his liquor in the library. None of his friends finished school past the sixth or seventh grade, you see. He figured his stash was as safe in there as in any place."

Jack tittered again. He glanced at his watch. "What's keeping Meleah? She knows the guests will be here soon. No reason why you can't start your duties now, Tarrant. Why don't we see about topping off this glass?"

Tarrant ducked behind the bar to make a quick in-

ventory. With a fresh drink in his hand, Jack started
for the house.

"Hurry up, Meleah! The guests will be here at any
moment now, girl!" he bellowed. He then muttered
loud enough for Tarrant to hear: "Women! They'd be
late for their own funeral if they thought their outfit
wasn't right."

Meleah paused in the middle of sliding into her
dress, and stuck her head out of her bedroom window
overlooking the pool. "I'm coming! I'm coming!" Meleah yelled back. She locked gazes with Tarrant for just
a moment. It was a fifty-fifty split whether he would
show up here tonight. She'd hadn't heard from him
since their conversation a week ago in the hospital—
except for that resignation letter he'd faxed to them.
She'd gone through the rest of the work week, relieved
that the whole story was finally out and resentful that
he hadn't wanted to face her in person to quit. Had
she been that much of an ogre that he couldn't face
her? She couldn't have been that bad of a boss, could
she? When she remarked on this to Charlotte, Charlotte had hit her in the back of her head.

"Yeow! What did you do that for?" Meleah said,
glancing around to see if other employees had seen
her being treated like a child.

"I'm trying to shake some sense loose in that head
of yours. Whatever crap you've crowded in there to
convince yourself that this is just about business, you'd
better shake it out of there. This has nothing to do
with your abilities as a boss."

Meleah shook her head. "You're wrong, Charlotte."

"Am I? I don't think so, sugar. That's just another
one of those fairy tales you're telling yourself. Both of
you are telling yourselves fairy tales. He's trying just as

hard to tell himself that he's not in love with you as you're telling yourself that this is just business as usual. If you're going to tell yourselves stories, I just wish you two would get on the same page."

"You know so much. You tell me why he isn't here," Meleah had demanded. "Maybe it's just good riddance to bad rubbish. The whole lot of them."

She'd sounded belligerent to Charlotte. But Charlotte had watched Meleah grow up. She knew all of her looks, all of her expressions. Her ultra-professionalism was a mask for insecurity. Scorn was a mask for vulnerability. She knew what Meleah meant by the mere quality of her voice. She could read the tones within tones masked by subtler tones. She knew that Meleah was more hurt than mad, more afraid than scornful. She wanted him back and no amount of posturing would disguise that."

"Don't worry, sugar. He'll be back. He will."

With Charlotte's assertion echoing in her ears, Meleah had approached tonight's party daring to hope that he would be. She'd picked up her outfit for tonight's affair with Tarrant in mind. He was a man of quiet, classic tastes. Her outfit was a simple, two-piece silk ensemble that Meleah thought accented her finest features. The sales assistant who sold it to her might as well have saved his sales pitch for someone with a little more indecision, and a lot less resolve. Meleah was drawn to the outfit when she saw it on a mannequin who looked so much like her, she had to do a double-take. The mannequin was not petite. It was tall, with a generous amount of hips. Looking at it also made Meleah pull open the neck of her T-shirt and compare the cup size of her brassiere with the mannequin's. Yep. Whoever had molded this life-sized mixture of paint and plastic had also managed to mimic her less than generous bust line.

It didn't matter, Meleah told herself. The dress would accent her other features. No one would even notice that she wished she had been given a little more in the breast department. No one would care. It would just be her father's friends at the party tonight. They wouldn't care if she came dressed in a sheet of aluminum foil. She would be dressing to please only herself tonight. Right?

Meleah walked up to the sales assistant without waiting to be accosted as she entered the boutique. She pointed to the dress and expressed her preference of color. She didn't even blink when the assistant hesitantly told her the price. The assistant tried to interest Meleah in another, less expensive ensemble. Meleah assumed that because she'd walked into the boutique with her favorite faded jeans and T-shirt, that the assistant had doubts about her ability to afford such simple elegance.

"You bring me *that* dress in the size and color I asked for," Meleah commanded, "or bring me someone who will."

Fifteen minutes later, Meleah was in another store, searching for accessories to accompany the dress the sales assistant scrambled to bring her. Now, as she stood in front of her mirror, she held the skirt up to her, and congratulated herself on her purchase.

The cream-colored, mock wrap skirt fell just above her knees. The blouse, a matching tank top, dipped softly at the neck into a vee, and dropped dramatically in the back almost to the waistline of the skirt. The color vaguely reminded Meleah of that old truck that Tarrant was so proud of.

She slid the blouse over her head, reveling in the delicious sensation of silk sliding over her bare skin. She'd chosen an ornate copper necklace, pressed into ingots, with matching earrings. A wide copper band clamped over her wrist.

Meleah swept up her hair, and allowed a few tendrils to dangle at ears, bangs, and down her back.

"Not bad, Le-Le, my girl," she said in her best imitation of her father. She dabbed perfume behind her ears, at her wrists, then as an afterthought, trailed a line of the fragrance down her back, and behind her knees. She wasn't quite sure why she added perfume where she did—something she remembered reading about pulse points, and the lasting power of certain scents. Even the perfume she wore tonight was a departure from her usual, understated floral scent.

Tonight Meleah felt she needed something special, different—even exotic. She'd purchased a musk oil that promised her that with the magic of the oil, she could conquer the world and beyond. Meleah remembered chuckling at the advertising claim. The world beyond? What should she expect by using it? Would she be wooed by Martians? Or maybe the inhabitants of the planet Venus, who were supposedly skilled in the arts of love. Would someone swoop down, carry her away, and make her their queen? Meleah had bought the scent despite her skepticism, intrigued by the idea of her own body chemistry shaping the way the scent was perceived by others.

As Meleah closed the door behind her, she wondered why she'd gone through the trouble. Who was she trying to impress? The people coming tonight were mostly her father's friends. These longtime friends were more like family to her.

"There'd better be a Martian or two," she murmured. "Or this ensemble will be a very expensive lesson in vanity."

She paused, listening as she heard her father tromping to answer the doorbell. A burst of laughter, some well-meaning teasing, and the first of her father's guests arrived. Bill and Hannah Caudle were hustled through the house, preceded by Jack bellowing for Meleah to come down.

"You don't have to shout, Pops. I'm right here," Meleah called from the stairs.

Bill Caudle's head snapped up. "Goodness, Meleah! Is that you? Jack, tell me. Is that the same little Meleah who just a short while ago was in braids and braces? Come here, girl. Give your old uncle Bill a kiss!"

"Not so old that you've forgotten how to flirt with the ladies," Hannah said. She turned to Meleah, her dark eyes twinkling. "I always said you'd grow up to be a beauty."

"It's in the genes," Jack said proudly, taking credit for all of Meleah's careful preparations.

"Not in yours, you grizzled old barkeep. That beauty is pure Marian," Hannah retorted. "Can't you see the resemblance?" Hannah turned her head this way and that. She was Meleah's aunt. Her mother's sister.

Meleah smiled, but her gaze darted automatically to the wall on which hung the portrait of her mother, Marian.

Jack saw the look, and felt his heart constrict. It wasn't fair! Though he'd had twelve wonderful years with his Marian, it wasn't nearly enough. He felt robbed of an opportunity of a lifetime to spend the rest of it with the love of his life. He could only imagine how paltry Meleah's six years with Marian must have seemed to her. Thank God for Charlotte coming into their lives when she did. Taming a room full of hungry drunks, he could handle. A child, a preteen, a teenager and then a young woman? He was good, but he wasn't that good.

"Both of you keep quiet. Give Meleah a little credit

for knowing how to turn a head or two." Hannah silenced them both.

"Let's go out to the bar," Jack said gruffly. "We can lift a toast to the memory of Marian."

Hannah looked around at all of the grandeur of Jack and Meleah's new home. It was a far cry from the three-bedroom house they'd come from. Though Marian had been proud of it, being the first home she and Jack bought together, the little crackerbox could have fit three times into the house Jack and Meleah were living in now.

"Marian would have loved this," Hannah murmured. "She would have had a decorating orgy getting this place together."

"I swear, Marian could work miracles with a swath of cloth and some scissors," Jack said fondly. "She loved mirrored panels. She could make a room look twice its size. And don't get me started with her slipcovers and throw pillows."

"She made do because she had to," Hannah said, turning to face Jack. Her tone was pleasant enough. But Meleah read between the lines.

"I'm sure she's looking down on us now, so proud of what we've been able to accomplish."

"Of course she is." Hannah patted her hand.

"Those drinks won't drink themselves," Jack continued. "Let's get this party started."

"Best idea I'm sure you'll have all evening." Bill guffawed, slapped Jack on the back, and propelled him forward. Hannah linked arms with Meleah and said, "How are you doing, Meleah? It's been so long since I've seen you."

"I know. We're so close yet we still don't get a chance to see each other. You should come to Galveston more often, Hannah. I see Elliot more often than enough for the both of us."

"I can't," Hannah said softly. "Too many memories. Too many ghosts. Every time I come here and hear the pounding of the surf, I can't help thinking that maybe I could have done something to help her—"

"Hannah," Meleah interrupted. "It wasn't your fault. It was no one's fault. Mom was her own woman. She did what she wanted, when she wanted. She would have gone boating even if you had been here."

"I should have been here to stop her. I should have been here to warn her about the weather."

"She knew to check the weather reports just as much as the next person."

"That's your father talking, Meleah," Hannah cautioned. "You couldn't know what your mother knew or didn't know. You were only six."

"Come on," Meleah said briskly to cover the unshed tears threatening to make her voice crack. "Let's get to the refreshment tables before those two eat and drink it all. Speaking of eating and drinking, where is that son of yours?"

"He said something about seeing to some business. He'll be here a little later," Hannah said distractedly. Her eyes were greedily roving over the refreshments table and the servers tending them.

"Set 'em up, Tarrant, my boy!" Jack hailed from the far end of the pool.

Tarrant turned from his conversation with one of the caterers. He began to acknowledge Jack's order with a dutiful "Yes, sir." But as Meleah stepped into view, his voice froze in mid s. His eyes swept over her, more than once. For a moment, he almost forgot that he was supposed to be working. He started around the bar. During the week of his absence, if he'd convinced himself that he could walk out of her life, he was just as convincing when he told himself that he could walk back into it by going to her now.

"Tarrant?" Jack snapped his fingers.

"Yes, sir . . . uh . . . I'm sorry, Jack. What can I get for you?"

"Your full attention, for one thing." Jack snickered.

"Yes, sir." Tarrant cleared his throat, and forced himself to focus his eyes, and his attention, on Jack.

"Get me the usual, Tarrant," Jack continued.

"And you, sir?" Tarrant directed at Bill Caudle.

"I'll take a scotch."

"No double?" Jack raised his eyebrows in surprise. He figured Bill would be the main person he'd had have to watch to protect his liquor stock.

"I'm pacing myself," Bill said amiably. He turned, and called over his shoulder, "Can I get you ladies anything?"

"I'll take him," Hannah whispered to Meleah, in reference to Tarrant.

"That was our new bartender," Meleah supplied.

"Ohhhh. So that's the big guy," Hannah said, using the nickname that her son Elliot had dubbed him.

"That's him." Meleah forced herself to sound cavalier.

"You said was?" Hannah picked up on the implication immediately. "Has he been eighty-sixed?"

"He quit on his own," Meleah said softly. As she approached the bar, she spoke up. She congratulated herself on sounding neutral as she ordered, "Ginger ale for me, please, Mr. Cole."

"Coming right up."

Hannah joined Meleah and said, "So, Mr. Cole, Meleah tells me that you're a new addition to Papa Jack's."

"Very new," Tarrant supplied.

"Still got that new-penny shine to you." She smiled up at him. "What made you quit? From what my son tells me, you haven't been around long enough for that old goat Jack to run you off."

"This is my aunt Hannah. Elliot's mother." Meleah made introductions.

"Oh . . ." Tarrant said, as if everything was now evident to him. He could see the resemblance between mother and son. That explained the rather pointed questions from her. The most striking resemblance between Hannah and Elliot was the mouth. Always running. "Can I get a ginger ale for you, too, ma'am?" Tarrant asked.

Hannah wrinkled her nose. "I suppose I should set an example for our young, impressionable Meleah. Go on, give me a ginger ale, too. But after this one, I want nothing but sparkling white wine."

Tarrant whisked out another napkin and an ice-filled glass for Hannah.

She raised her glass to him in thanks. As she did so, Tarrant watched Meleah in the reflection of Hannah's glass as she sipped at her own drink.

Man! he thought to himself. *I must be losing my mind.* He couldn't take his eyes off of her—not even when he couldn't get a full glimpse of her. Had he fallen for her so hard that he had to resort to stealing glances of her to satisfy himself?

When Meleah heard more voices greeting her father, she said, "Excuse me, Hannah. I've got to play hostess."

"You don't have to baby-sit me, Meleah. Something tells me that this will be my place to perch for the evening."

"I'll be back as soon as I can then." She set her glass aside, and moved away. This time Tarrant did not try to hide his interest in her. Something about the rustle of silk as she moved, the suggestive sway of her hips, and the tantalizing glimpses of her bare skin, drew his eyes so that he couldn't look away.

"Amazing, isn't she?" Hannah said casually. "At first, I couldn't understand what she was doing hanging around these old geezers tonight. I mean, why wasn't she out with friends her own age? Now I think I understand."

Tarrant didn't respond, but he didn't move away either.

Hannah gulped down her drink, and asked for an immediate refill. She reminded him to skip the ginger ale. After her third glass, she peered closely at Tarrant and said, "You like her, don't you."

"Who, ma'am?"

"You know who I'm talking about. I saw you checking her out. I'm talking about Meleah. You like her, don't you? You think she's sexy?"

"Ms. Harmon is a very competent boss," Tarrant replied.

Hannah burst out laughing. "If that isn't the most diplomatic answer I've ever heard. I'm not talking about work! I'm asking you whether or not you'd like to jump her bones. Oh, that was a little crude, wasn't it? I meant to say, wouldn't you like to make love to her. Don't be shy, big guy. You can tell me."

"I thought the patrons were supposed to confide in the bartender—not the other way around," Tarrant said evasively.

"I won't tell," Hannah leaned close, whispered to him.

Tarrant said nothing. He kept his face neutral, even though the overpowering smell of alcohol and Hannah's perfume made his head swim. For a moment, he imagined himself as trapped as Meleah must have felt when Chico and Durell attacked her.

"That's all right. You don't have to say anything. I

already know. You can't help yourself. It was the same way with her mother. You would have liked Marian. She had the same fire; the same brains hidden by a body that just wouldn't quit. Men just flocked to her like . . . like . . . buzzards. Forgive me if I'm too direct, Mr. Cole. The wine makes my tongue a little loose."

"Yes, ma'am," Tarrant said automatically.

Hannah sighed, and propped her hands on her fists. "Marian was my sister. God, how I miss her! It isn't fair! She still had so much living to do. Why'd you have to leave us, Marian? Why?"

Hannah sobbed, then hiccuped. She held out her glass to Tarrant again.

"You don't know," she said in a conspiratory whisper. "But I do."

She turned a baleful gaze to Jack Harmon. He was in the middle of yet another telling of his reaction to winning the lottery. "The lucky bastard," she muttered. "Marian was the best thing that ever happened to him. Better than Papa Jack's or the lottery, or anything that God sees fit to throw his way."

"He does seem to have his share of treasures," Tarrant responded, his eyes still glued to Meleah as she performed her duties as co-host of the party.

"I just hope that Jack has the sense God gave him not to squander his windfall this time! With Meleah managing his money, I know he'll do a lot better by her than he did by Marian. I'm the one who introduced them, you know."

"Jack and Marian?"

"It's all my fault. I should have kept my mouth shut the first time I saw Jack. I saw him first. He . . . Meleah . . . his money. All of it should have been mine. All mine." She hiccuped again and put her head down on the bar. She made a soft, mewling sound. And Tar-

rant could see her fleshy shoulders trembling. For a
moment, he thought she might be weeping. But when
she raised her head, her mouth was drawn back into
a wide grin. Laughter, loud and raucous, bubbled from
her lips. It was barely silenced when she raised a glass
to her mouth and drained the rest of the contents of
her glass.

Instead of comforting him, or even amusing him,
Hannah's laughter chilled his blood as deeply as the
wine he poured. The smile never once reached Hannah's eyes.

ELEVEN

"Now . . . now . . . now see here, Uncle Dub!" Meleah said loudly, as she fended off the advance of another, old-time family friend. "Why don't you just head over to the buffet table, and put something solid in your stomach."

"What? And ruin the perfectly good beer buzz I've got sloshing inside of me now? Meleah, you're trying to distract me."

"Distract, nothing!" Meleah gasped, as Dub made a lunge for her. "I'm telling you that I don't want to go for a swim. I'm not dressed for it."

"Aw, don't be a wet rag, Meleah." Dub snorted. He managed to grasp a protesting Meleah around the waist.

"Now cut that out, Uncle Dub! Pops!" She appealed to her father, hoping that he was listening to her half-joking, half-concerned plea for help.

"Stop wiggling, Meleah, and show your uncle Dub your form."

"Pops!" Meleah called out with more urgency as she saw that the besotted old friend of the family intended to toss her into the pool. He wasn't her uncle. And the last thing she wanted was for him to see or touch her form. Several of the attendees laughed good-naturedly, and egged Dub on.

"No! Stop it! Let me go!" Meleah began to struggle in earnest. She didn't want to look foolish in front of the guests if Dub was only teasing. Yet she didn't want to be dunked into the water if he wasn't.

"Dub, don't!" Meleah clung to his arms. He swept a hand under her knees, and lifted her off her feet. Her cries drew Tarrant's attention from the far side of the pool. He paused in mid-shake of a martini. He looked around him, gauging the reaction of Jack's guests. Most weren't even paying attention. The few that were paying attention seemed to find Meleah's predicament hilarious.

"I don't doubt it," Tarrant muttered to himself in disgust. Hannah's guzzling of the wine was barely an indicator of how most of the guests responded to the free food and alcohol. They had all consumed enough alcohol to make their judgment impaired. Tarrant shook his head. He didn't consider himself to be a stick in the mud. He liked having a good time as much as the next person. And even though, more often than not, he elected himself to be the designated driver when he and the brothas hung out, this seemed to him a little excessive. He'd never seen an orgy. He'd never expect to find himself at one. But this, according to his limited vision of one, had to fit the bill. He experienced a moment of doubt. Maybe there was something to Amber's story, after all.

For a moment, the voice of Ashton Cole's reasoning drowned out the party noise from Tarrant's ears. Desperate to prove that he would now support Amber where he had failed in the past, Ashton had been the loudest to cry for Tarrant to return to Papa Jack's. Amber was so adamant. Where there was smoke, there had to be a fire. There had to be some substance to her claims. Where there was alcohol, there would be abusers. Where there were abusers, there were those who were willing to take advantage. Jack had booted out the ones sneaking in booze and had kept serving those who had stayed, the ones who had paid. Was he concerned about Meleah's safety when he had been counting the cash receipts for the night?

"My drink," an impatient guest encouraged.

"Sorry," Tarrant said in distraction, his attention still on Meleah and Dub.

"You can't be serious!" was the last thing he heard Meleah snap followed by a resounding splash. Someone squealed as others scrambled to get out of the way. A wave washed onto the redwood deck.

"Cannonball!" Dub shouted, and jumped into the pool in the wake of Meleah's splash. Meleah had barely managed to bob to the surface for air before Dub's coiled body landed on top of her. She felt the air whoosh out of her lungs as Dub's body blotted out all light.

"Tag!" Dub shouted as he bobbed to the surface. "You're it, Le-Le! Come on out and get me, girl! Le-Le? Meleah . . . come on out, now. Stop kidding around!"

"Meleah!" Tarrant called out, setting aside a bottle of seltzer. "Hey! What about my drink!" someone shouted as Tarrant shrugged out of his uniform jacket and kicked off his shoes. He reached the edge of the pool in three long strides, and dove into the water. It took only a few powerful strokes to bring him to where Meleah was limply floating to the surface.

"Meleah?" a bewildered Dub called. He began to dog paddle toward her, too.

"Get away from her!" Tarrant snarled. Maybe Amber could stand by and watch Meleah get hurt. But he couldn't. He wouldn't. Longtime family friend or Amber's loser friends, it didn't matter to him. Meleah was the only one that mattered.

He flipped Meleah onto her back, grasped her under her chin, and towed her to the edge of the pool. With Dub's help, Tarrant managed to haul her to the deck.

"Is she going to be all right?" Dub moaned.

Tarrant felt for a pulse. "Thank God," he breathed, finding one, strong and steady, just under her jaw. He then rolled her over onto her stomach, and pressed on her back to force the water from her lungs. Guests gathered around them, buzzing with questions. Meleah coughed several times, and tried to sit up.

"Take it easy," Tarrant directed, holding her back.

"Where is he?" was the first thing she demanded, swiping her hair from her eyes. "I'll kill him. I'm gonna wrap my bare hands around his neck and squeeze the very life out of him!"

"You mean Uncle Dub?" Tarrant sat back on his heels and grinned at her.

"I mean Pops for inviting him!"

"I'm sorry, Meleah," Dub said, honestly contrite. "I didn't know—"

"That I couldn't swim?" she replied. "Like I'm really going to broadcast that I'm the only one living by the beach that can't swim."

"I thought living around the beach all your life that you'd know."

Meleah lowered her eyes, and said belligerently, "Well, I don't know."

Tarrant stood, and without waiting for permission, lifted Meleah into his arms. He held her tightly to him, and with a look of thinly disguised disgust, forced the crowd to part for him. He carried her without protest into the house. "Get me out of here," she whispered to him.

"Where to?"

"In there." Meleah nodded toward a closed door. "It's the library."

Placing Meleah carefully on the couch, he asked, "Are you all right?"

"I'm fine. Nothing bruised but my pride."

"And your chin," Tarrant remarked, lifting her face toward him. Dub must have struck her hard enough to knock her temporarily unconscious. A mottled bruise was starting to form on her cheek and chin.

He eased next to her. "Sit up," Tarrant directed and placed a pillow behind her back. "What were you doing horsing around the pool, Meleah, if you can't swim. You could have drowned."

"You don't have to tell me that!" she said vehemently.

"Why can't you swim?"

"Because I never learned." Meleah shrugged.

"Why not?"

"What is this? Twenty questions? Because I didn't want to." She pressed her lips together to avoid the subject. Tarrant continued to stare expectantly.

"Don't look at me like that."

"Like what?"

"Like *that!*" She raised her eyebrows at him.

"If you don't want to talk about it, I'll understand. It wouldn't be the first time you haven't exactly been square with me."

"This has nothing to do with you, Tarrant. This is personal to me."

"You don't understand by now that you are personal to me, boss lady?" he asked softly.

Meleah sighed and closed her eyes. She took a breath and began slowly. "It's not something I like to talk about. Don't take it personally, Tarrant. I don't talk about it to anyone. When I was a little girl, just barely six years old, my mother was killed in a boating accident. She was on one of the wind-surfer things and it capsized. She got caught in an undertow and she drowned. I haven't had the heart, or the courage, to go near the water. I don't know why Pops insisted on putting in that pool. Maybe he thought I would eventually get tired of looking at it and would agree to learn. I never did."

"Stubborn," he murmured, shaking his head. "That is . . . that's what your father told me about you."

"Not stubborn. I'm prudent," she corrected. "I have no intention of dying like she did! All I have to do is stay away from Dub and the pool, and I'll be just fine, thank you!" Meleah then looked down at her outfit, and groaned in dismay. "Will you look at this! Look at my dress! Do you know how much this ensemble cost me! And now it's ruined!"

Tarrant glanced at Meleah, then quickly averted his eyes. He didn't want to see how the pale material became translucent against her skin. He didn't want to know how the soft silk folds molded to her breasts. Her undignified dip into the cold water made her nipples pert and prominent. The skirt adhered to her hips, and shifted to reveal more than a hint of her thighs. When Meleah drew her soaking hair away from her neck and face, she drew Tarrant's attention to her shoulders—still glittering from the iridescent powder she'd dusted on before the party. His hands clenched involuntarily, as if to prevent themselves from reaching out to touch her. He couldn't afford to have another episode like they had in the pool room—not when he was still so unsure. Was he planning to bring them down or wasn't he? Which pulled him harder? The desire to finally be able to gain his father's acceptance or respect? Or was it desire for this vulnerable—and very dripping wet—woman.

"Do Jack's bashes always end like this?" Tarrant

forced himself to sound gruff. He stood abruptly, and strode to the far side of the room. If he didn't have to look at her, he could clear his thoughts. As clinging as his own clothes were, if he didn't get a grip on his emotions, it would be pretty evident what he'd been thinking. He grasped the front of his trousers and tried to pull them away from his soaking skin. Any extra room he could give himself would buy him that much more time to stop thinking like a lover and start thinking like a lawyer.

"What do you mean, do they always end like this?" Meleah asked. "Pops and I don't give very many parties. We've always worked so hard trying to pay the bills."

"Everyone is stinking drunk. No wonder they thought it was funny when you went in."

"You were the one mixing and serving the drinks. Why didn't you limit them?" Meleah flared.

"I'm only the hired help. I don't make the decisions," Tarrant retorted. "Jack was the one hounding me to keep the glasses full. I'm just doing my job, boss lady, for however long I have it."

"Well, at least we don't have to worry about anyone hurting anyone else or themselves when they leave here."

"What are you talking about?"

"No one leaves tonight in the state they're in," Meleah declared. "By ten o'clock tonight, Pops will have gotten every cab in Galveston County, Texas City, even as far as Kemah, if he has to, to escort his guests away from here. We're going to have one mother of a slumber party tonight, Tarrant. Every sofa or soft spot on the rug will be taken up by Pops and his friends."

"Cabs?" Tarrant asked.

"You didn't think he'd let someone that wasted drive home, did you?" she gasped.

"I didn't know."

"You should have known," Meleah said. "Did you think that policy manual we gave you was just for pleasure reading? It's clearly stated in the policy manual that it's the responsibility of each of Papa Jack's employees to see that the patrons, when they leave, are not a danger to themselves or anyone else," Meleah quoted verbatim from the book.

"Yeah . . . yeah, I think I remember reading something about that," Tarrant said vaguely.

Meleah turned her head as she heard Dub threaten once again to toss another guest into the pool.

"At least my near-drowning hasn't dampened the spirit of the party," she said with a wry smile. She heard another splash, followed by another. Someone started to laugh as more people dove into the pool. Meleah drew up her legs and hugged her knees. She buried her face in her knees, her shoulders trembling.

"Are you cold?" Tarrant asked solicitously. "Maybe you ought to go up and change." He suggested it as much for his own sanity as for her well-being.

"I'm not cold," Meleah said distractedly.

Tarrant crossed the room and sat next to her again. "Come here, boss lady," he said, wrapping his arms around her.

Meleah settled against him. "It's just . . ." She looked up at him with haunted eyes

"What is it, Meleah? What's wrong?" Tarrant was concerned by the distant look in her eyes, and by her effort to keep herself from trembling. She bit her lower lip, and said in a small whisper, "It just came to me what it must have been like for her."

"You mean your mother?"

"I wonder, was she conscious when she fell off the catamaran? Did she know what was happening to her? Was she afraid? Angry? What was she feeling in the last few seconds before the water filled her lungs? Did she cry out? Did she fight for her life? Did she give up hope, knowing that there was no one there to help her?"

Huge tears welled in her eyes. She blinked rapidly, trying to force them back.

"Maybe she didn't suffer," Tarrant suggested.

"Oh yeah, that makes me feel a whole lot better!" Meleah said harshly.

Not knowing how to comfort her, Tarrant remained silent. He did what came instinctually to him. He reached out gingerly, and placed his large palm against the back of her head. Meleah flinched, resisting his touch. With subtle insistence, he drew her to him until her head rested against his shoulder. When her trembling increased, he began to rock her as he would a small child. He made soft, soothing noises to comfort her. He smoothed her hair, and caressed her back. Meleah grasped his arms, and squeezed. Her nails dug into his flesh, but he didn't let go.

"He should have been there!" she declared. "Why wasn't he there?"

Tarrant assumed that she was referring to Jack. He couldn't answer her questions about her mother's death. He hoped that she wouldn't start to wonder about Jack's whereabouts at her own near-drowning. Telling her that he'd seen Jack and Charlotte sneak off when they thought no one was watching wouldn't do her any good now. Or maybe they didn't care if anyone was watching. Since he had no response to her question, he allowed prudent silence to be his answer.

"If he loved her, he would have known she was in danger!" Meleah sobbed. "He should have known! He should have felt it. If he loved her as much as he said he did, he would have felt it in his heart." Her tears flowed freely now. She made no effort to control them.

Tarrant drew her closer to him. He could feel her heart thudding in her chest. Tremors wracked her whole body now. Tarrant was starting to get worried. He wrapped his arms around her, his cheek pressed against hers. He murmured in her ear. Words weren't important. He wanted her to know that she could lean him. She could draw strength from him. Meleah clung to him, almost in desperation. Tarrant had been right. She could have died in that pool. Because of a moment of foolishness, her life could have ended. The fact that he'd given her life back to her sobered her.

As her tears subsided, she released her grip on him, and raised her arms to rest comfortably around his neck. She started to pull away, her cheek sliding against his. Tarrant was reluctant to let go. He ran his fingers across her hair, twisting the auburn mass into a single long cord. He smoothed over her bruised chin, pausing to gently hold her captive until he could meet her eyes.

"I'm sure your father loved your mother, Meleah," he soothed. "If he could have, he would have moved heaven and earth to save her."

"Don't get me wrong, Tarrant. I love my father. But I . . . I've always had this nagging doubt in the back of my mind. I was only a child when she died. People don't go away forever when you're that young. They just don't. And my father . . . when you're six years old, your father is a superman. He couldn't do any wrong in my eyes. And suddenly both of those truths became lies for me. Mother wasn't coming back and my father . . . he . . . he . . . he didn't save her. I'm a grown woman now and I still can't get over that. If I still have my doubts, knowing what I know, how can you be sure of what he would have done?" she whispered.

"Because it's what I would have done," he declared.

Of that, he had no doubt. He would have swum through the entire Gulf of Mexico to save Meleah from a thousand killer Dubs, if he had to.

"You would?" Meleah asked, on a slowly exhaled breath. The warmth of her sigh blew across him. He focused his gaze on the tender, full lips that allowed the sigh to escape. With tentative, exploring fingers, Tarrant touched his index finger to Meleah's mouth and traced the outline. When she didn't pull away, he leaned close to her. "Heaven and earth?" she echoed. The advertisement for the perfume she'd purchased flashed through her mind. For a moment, Meleah wondered if she really did have power over both.

"Meleah!" Jack burst into the library. His face wrinkled with concern.

Tarrant wanted to curse whatever powers that be that destroyed such a perfect moment.

"Sugar, are you all right?" Charlotte was close behind him.

"Meleah, tell me you're okay!" Jack continued.

Tarrant stood quickly, and backed away from the couch to allow Jack and Charlotte to place themselves one on either side of Meleah.

"I, uh . . ." He cleared his throat, then continued. "I guess I had better get back to the bar." Yet he made no movement to leave. It didn't matter. No one seemed to notice that he was there.

"I'm fine," Meleah tried to assure him.

"That idiot Dub! I ought to wring his neck," Jack threatened.

"What could he have been thinking?" Charlotte wanted to know.

"He wasn't thinking. He was drinking," Meleah retorted. "But Tarrant kept a cool head and pulled me out." She looked up at Tarrant, and said, "Thank you."

"I'm just glad that you're all right, Meleah," Tarrant said quietly.

Charlotte raised her eyebrows but said nothing. In all of this time, this was the first time she'd ever heard Tarrant call Meleah by her first name. This was a breakthrough if she'd ever heard one.

"That makes two of us."

"I'll kill that idiot Dub!" Jack declared.

"Take a number," Meleah said, her acerbic tongue returning. "He's mine. You can have what's left."

"Now you won't do any such thing," Charlotte chastised. "Just settle down. Thank goodness that no one was really hurt."

"Promise me something, Meleah," Tarrant called from the door.

"If I can," Meleah said cautiously.

"I don't want something like this to happen again."

"That's easy enough to fix. You limit Dub's alcohol, and I'll put a cover on that pool. Problem solved."

"And in the meantime, I think you should enroll in swimming classes," Charlotte suggested.

"I second that!" Jack declared, patting her hand.

"Swimming classes!" Meleah exclaimed. "I've avoided them for over twenty years. Why would I start now?"

"Because you never know when a good lesson or two will come in handy."

"I . . . I don't know if I can," Meleah faltered.

"The YMCA has classes every summer for all skill levels—from beginner to advanced. I suggest you sign up," Tarrant said. "If you don't, I'll sign you up myself."

Tarrant closed the door behind him. He could hear Jack's excited voice and Meleah's low response to him. A moment later, Jack flung the door open, and hurried to catch up to Tarrant.

"Tarrant," he began. Tarrant read the depth of emotion in his eyes. "You saved my little girl. I won't forget that. I owe you one."

"Do you think she's going to be all right?"

"I think so. I'll have our doctor look her over."

"I was serious about the lessons, Jack," Tarrant reminded him.

"I know you were. We'll both have to work on her to get her to go. She's a little stubborn, you know."

"Noooo," Tarrant said in a voice that let Jack know he meant just the opposite.

"And another thing, Tarrant . . . I know you weren't planning on coming back. But, for obvious reasons, I'm glad that you did. And to show you how grateful I am for your looking out for my little girl, there'll be bonus in your next paycheck, son."

"I don't want money for—" Tarrant began to protest.

"How else can I repay you?" Jack cut him off.

Tarrant opened his mouth to reply. He didn't want their stinking money. Look what it got them, so-called friends who seemed more interested in what they could guzzle than human life. Meleah almost drowned and the party played on. He didn't want Jack's money. He wanted Jack's most valued treasure. He wanted Meleah.

"I wish you would reconsider your resignation, Tarrant. I want you around for what you've been doing for Meleah."

"I'm not sure what you mean," Tarrant hedged.

"Sure you do," Jack contradicted. "Whether she wants to admit or not, I think she has a thing for you."

Tarrant wondered if Charlotte had mentioned to Jack catching them in an embrace.

"I know you've been trying to help your sister out. And I've been trying to schedule as much time as I could for you to make the dollars. Maybe we can think of a way to get you some more cash." Jack started talking fast, seeing a look coming over Tarrant that reminded him of Meleah when she was at her most stubborn. He knew he would probably insult Tarrant for what he was about to suggest. But he was thinking purely selfishly now. He had received another note. This time it threatened all of them. He wanted to tell him about it. He had not even shared the information with Charlotte. He didn't want her to worry.

Tarrant had already proven that he was watching out for Meleah. Jack thought that if he could grease the man's palm with some extra cash, he could get a built-in bodyguard for Meleah. She had outright rejected the men that he had hired to watch over her.

"What did you have in mind?" Tarrant asked, skepticism replacing scorn. Jack didn't get a chance to go into detail. He became distracted as his guests started to get restless.

"Say, Jack! You're out of vodka! What kind of party are you throwing here anyway?"

"Awww . . . keep your shirt on!" Jack yelled back. "You lushes aren't going to drink me out of house and home."

"Back to work?" Tarrant suggested, gesturing toward the door. He hoped that he could keep his professionalism for the rest of the evening.

"You can't go out like that, son. You want to run home and get a change of clothes?"

"I've got a change in my gym bag out in my car," Tarrant told him. "Give me a minute and I'll have your friends guzzling in no time."

"Yeah. You'd better get going before they tear the place apart. I'll be there in a moment," Jack promised.

"I just want to make certain that Meleah's all right. We'll talk more about my idea later."

"Sure thing, Jack." Tarrant nodded once, and returned to his station at the bar. When Jack returned to the library, Meleah was resting her head on Charlotte's shoulder. Charlotte placed her finger lightly against her lips to warn him to be still. He nodded once, then backed out.

He couldn't back out now. He was in too deep. He didn't mean for things to go this far. But they had. Now there was nothing left for him to do but go forward with his plan. If they'd just been straight with him from the start, he could have handled it. But they weren't. They weren't forthcoming at all. They'd left him with no choice. No one could blame him for feeling the way that he did. It wasn't his fault. Did they think they could treat his family like trash and get away with it? No way in hell was he going to stand by now. Let them laugh it up. Let them drink until their stupid livers rotted in their bodies. Celebration party, his butt. He knew what the real deal was. They were just flaunting it in his face. He knew the truth now. He knew what they really thought about him now. No amount of money in the world was going to soothe the ills they'd heaped on him. Let them think that they'd gotten away with murder. Soon everyone would know.

"I know it's in here somewhere," Meleah muttered to herself. She'd spent half the morning rooting through the storeroom looking for a box of odds and ends she'd stored once she'd moved into her new office. Maybe she was wasting her time, but she felt a nagging compulsion to find that box and rifle through the contents. She knew that her obsession was spurred on by the events this weekend. Specifically she replayed in her head the party Pops had given and her near-drowning. She couldn't forget the look of disgust Tarrant had on his face. She imagined that it was quite a difficult position he was in. All of this time, he'd been convinced that Papa Jack's serving policy was the cause of his sister's accident. Her confession at the hospital might have redeemed them. The fact that he was willing to quit, in her mind give up trying to pin the blame on them, was enough to let her know that maybe he finally believed them. Then, there was the party.

True to Meleah's word, everyone was either forced into a cab or allowed to crash at their house until the effects of the party could be flushed from their system with plenty of hot coffee and a decent after-party breakfast. But the damage had been done. What little headway she had gained by opening up to him was lost in a moment of horseplay.

That idiot Dub and his cannonball routine had left an impression on him that wouldn't go away. The best Meleah figured she could do was strengthen the section in the policy manual. In order to do that, she had to update the thing. She was certain that the text hadn't been reviewed in years. The original electronic copy was stored on disk somewhere, at the bottom of some box, buried in the bowels of their storeroom. First thing Monday, she had resolved to dig it out, update it, and redistribute it. That was why she was rummaging through boxes when she should have been helping the staff prepare for the evening crowd. It was a perfectly legitimate task. But to hear Charlotte talk, she was just hiding from Tarrant. She knew that he would be in, sometime today, to collect his last paycheck, turn in his uniform. When Charlotte had said something about making him go through an exit interview, Meleah had suddenly found it necessary to be elsewhere. She wasn't avoiding him. Not really. But if she happened not to be around when he arrived, she didn't think it would be a big deal.

"Wouldn't have worked out anyway," she muttered. "I never really trusted him. He was too good."

She started through the storeroom, then paused when a movement out of the corner of her eye caught her attention.

"Hello?" she called out, a little embarrassed that someone might have overheard her tantrum. "Is anybody there?" When nobody answered, she shrugged, and continued forward. As soon as she did, she heard a definite creak.

"Whiskers?" she called out. "Trae? I hope you didn't let that cat loose in here again." She thought their youngest employee had learned his lesson about bringing that cat to work after she caught the animal doing his business in the bottom drawer of her desk. She liked animals as much as the next person. And she knew that Trae sometimes cut extra time off of his errand-running by going straight from the vet, when he had to, to work. But Meleah thought she'd carefully explained that she simply couldn't allow the animal around the food service area. They had a hard enough time keeping the six-legged pests out. The excuse that his cat was a good huntress and thought of cockroaches as a delicacy was no consolation to her when she reached for a file and wound up with her hand in a pile instead. If Whiskers were running loose in the storeroom, she'd have known it by now. She would have heard her. No, it wasn't her.

"Is someone hiding in here?" Meleah suddenly demanded. She pivoted to reach for the second light switch to illuminate the back half of the storeroom, and was suddenly shoved from behind. Meleah cried out, as her face scraped the rough brick wall. A gloved hand held her head tightly against the wall.

"I got your whiskers right here," a voice, low and harsh, grated in her ear.

Meleah squirmed, trying to turn her head.

"You want me to snap your neck? Don't turn around."

"Who are you? What do you want?"

A hand clamped over her mouth. "Shut up!"

Meleah was afraid, but more than that, she was angry. When was this invasion of her security going to stop? First it was Amber and her cronies. Then, through an act of drunken foolishness, Uncle Dub had almost taken her life. Here she was, trying to do right, trying to prove what good citizens they were, and some fool wanted to ruin it all for her. She wasn't ready to allow a perfect stranger to take from her what a family friend could not. She wrenched her head away and tried to claw with her nails at any exposed flesh. She didn't remember screaming, but she must have. She thought she heard someone call her name. The sound of someone calling her name was the last impression to reach her before she saw the gloved hand swing toward her with incredible force. Blissful darkness settled over her before she sank to the floor.

TWELVE

Tarrant paced the floor, waiting for Jack to return with his last paycheck. He didn't even know why he was going through the formality. He'd quit in the middle of a pay period. Even though he had been doing well, he simply hadn't worked enough hours to make coming back here worth his time. The check was so tiny, pitiful, almost laughable. Jack had not been kidding when he said the pay would not be worth his time and effort. Up until the moment he'd pulled into the parking lot of Papa Jack's, he was still debating whether or not he should come back for it.

He told himself that he was coming back for closure—so that he could say that he'd never left a job undone. He had adopted that motto the moment he decided that he would go into the car and truck restoration business. He didn't want to become one of those car restoration wannabes that had more pieces and parts rusting in their front yards than a pick-a-part shop. If he was going to do this, he was going to do it first class all the way. He would do what he set out to do. That went for every phase of his life. He'd taken this job to get closure on Amber's accident. Now he had it. It was time for him to go. He had one final thing to do before he could call the job done. He had a few unsaid things he wanted to say to his boss lady.

Because he was working at the party, that didn't leave much of an opportunity for him to talk to her. "Yes, ma'am" and "Let me refresh that for you" were the limits of his conversation with her. But there was more he wanted to say to her. So much more. At one moment, when he watched her interacting with the guests from across the pool, he'd come so close to just breaking down and telling her what his family was urging him to do. He couldn't do that without admitting that was his ulterior motive all along. If he thought of exploring his feelings for her, would she see that as another ploy to gain her confidence? Would she look back on their shared kiss in the pool room and think of that as a trick to break through her defenses? Once he'd kissed her, all thoughts of planning any kind of revenge just flew out of his head. At that moment, all he wanted was Meleah.

Tarrant closed his eyes to brace himself against the uncontrollable surge of desire he felt each time the thought of making love to Meleah crossed his mind. He thought he could get those feelings under control. As long as he could think of her as the enemy, that is, partially responsible for his sister's accident, he could almost convince himself that he could never want Meleah. *Almost.*

Yesterday, when he saw her with her cool, confident barriers torn down, he knew he could never look at her as his enemy again. When she'd confessed her doubts about Jack's love for her mother, she'd given Tarrant a tiny glimpse into the young child everyone carried inside of them. At that moment, she'd reminded him of Alexa. For all intents and purposes, they were both struggling with the absence of a mother. Both were vulnerable, needing someone to help fill that void.

Tarrant didn't want to overanalyze the situation. He

didn't want to excuse all of Meleah's toughness and bravado as a cover for feeling abandoned. She was too smart, too confident for that. It was just that she'd shared a part of herself that he was sure she seldom shared with anyone. It was as if she'd shared with him a secret treasure. She'd trusted him enough to break down and cry in front of him. He would not betray that trust. No matter how much his father threatened to disown him if he didn't help sue Papa Jack's, he would not. He could not. That's why he was quitting. That's why he had to leave. But before he did that, he was going to make sure that she knew why he was doing it. No job left undone.

When he'd walked through the doors of Papa Jack's presumably for the last time, he had done so with resolve to say his good-byes to the boss lady. He nearly cursed aloud when Jack told him that he would be conducting the exit interview alone. Meleah would not be there. He would not get his chance. Tarrant's jaw clenched. Whatever headway he thought he'd made with her while they were alone in Jack's library, sometime during the night, he'd lost it. She would not come to him again. Maybe revealing that tender part of herself was too much for her. He had to know. He couldn't walk out of that door feeling like he should have said something, and didn't. When Jack retreated to the office to pick up Tarrant's check, Tarrant resolved himself to force a confrontation.

That's when he heard her call out his name.

"Boss lady?" He turned around, not sure which direction her voice came from.

When he heard a crash of boxes, and another cry more urgent than the first, he started toward the hall. Even as he picked up his pace, he could see the door swinging rapidly to a close. "Wait a minute! Meleah? Are you in there? Are you all right?" He pounded on the door. No one answered, but Tarrant was certain he heard someone stirring inside.

"What's all of the commotion about?" Charlotte came up fast behind him.

"Charlotte, who's in the storage room?" Tarrant said. "Who's in there?"

His expression startled her. Her mind went blank for a moment, trying to account for everyone at Papa Jack's this afternoon. "I'm not sure . . . Meleah said something about looking for something or other. Why?"

"Somebody slammed the door on me," Tarrant said. "I thought I heard Meleah call out."

"I'll get the keys," Charlotte said over her shoulder as she spun around and headed back the way she'd come. "Jack! Jack, get out here now and bring me the master keys."

It seemed an eternity to Tarrant. He continued to bang on the door, calling out to Meleah. "Hurry up, Charlotte!" he entreated.

Charlotte and Jack met in the middle of the hall. Jack's fingers were shaking so badly with anxiety that he could barely flip through the ring of keys.

"Give me those!" Charlotte snatched the keys from him. She fit the key into the lock with Tarrant and Jack breathing down her neck. As soon as Tarrant heard the lock click, he reached past Charlotte and shoved against the door.

"Meleah! Where are you?" He knocked aside a crate that blocked his path.

"Le-Le, sugar, are you in here?"

"Baby, answer me."

Their voices mingled and stumbled over each other.

"I'm over here." Meleah half rose, and called out weakly. Her hands clasped her aching jaw.

"Oh, my Lord! Meleah, sugar, what happened?!"

Charlotte gasped. She fell to her knees on one side of her, Tarrant knelt on the other side.

"Someone . . . in the storeroom," Meleah managed to say over their concerned questions. "Did you see him? Did you see him? He couldn't have gone far. Couldn't have . . . he—"

"No. We didn't see anyone," Charlotte said, smoothing her hand over Meleah's forehead. "Take it easy, sugar. We'll find him."

Tarrant leaped up and started to search immediately. "How many ways in and out of this place? He didn't come out the front. I would have seen him."

"Check the back door." Jack pointed toward the rear of the storeroom. "I'll look around in here."

Meleah tried to stand, then fell dizzily back again. "You let me get my hands on the son of—"

"Don't you move now. You could be seriously hurt," Charlotte cautioned.

"I just have a little headache. Nothing wrong with my hands. I can still choke the life out of the sneaky creep."

"And maybe a concussion. Don't you dare move again, sugar."

Tarrant came back, shaking his head. "No sign of him. I swear, Meleah, if I find out who did this to you . . ." His voice trailed off when Charlotte shook her head slightly and indicated that he might upset Meleah more.

"Yo, kinfolks. What's the haps?" Elliot walked into the storeroom. His gaze swept over the room, from the overturned boxes to Charlotte and Meleah and Tarrant standing protectively over them. "You carrying on the party from last night to here?"

Jack pushed past him and snapped, "We ain't got no time for any of your foolishness, Elliot." He directed his next sentence to the trio. "I'm going to call the police. Maybe they can figure some of this out."

"Police? What happened? What's going on?" Elliot searched their faces when no one answered.

"What are you doing here?" Tarrant said suspiciously.

"Who do you think you're talking to, big guy?" Elliot bristled. "Who do you think you are? These are my people. My kinfolk. You think you're gonna disrespect me in front of them?"

"I asked you a question, boy." Tarrant thought he sounded very much like his father at that moment. Scornful, intimidating, not taking any guff. Maybe he was overstepping his bounds by interrogating one of Jack's relatives. But he wasn't going to back down. Meleah had been attacked and within moments this clown shows up. He didn't trust him. There was no love lost. What did he have to lose by asking the boy a few questions?

Elliot walked up to Tarrant and bumped him with his shoulder. Tarrant shoved back.

"Whoa! Time out. Cut the testosterone fest," Charlotte interrupted. "I think we have more important matters to deal with, don't you? The police should be here any minute. You feel like talking to them, Le-Le?"

Meleah nodded. "I'd feel a little more dignified if I didn't have to do it on the floor of the storeroom."

"Here, let me help you. Lean on me," Charlotte offered. She helped Meleah rise to her feet.

Meleah stood up too quickly. She gagged as a wave of nausea washed over her. Her knees buckled. Tarrant was suddenly behind her, lifting her in his arms.

"Take it easy now," he murmured against her hair. She was too disoriented to protest. And it felt so nice just to lie there, cradled in his arms. She leaned her head against Tarrant's shoulder.

"Why don't I just take it easy," she echoed, her voice sounding distant to her.

Tarrant carried Meleah to her office, and laid her gently on the plush sofa. Tenderly he brushed her hair away from her eyes. When he saw the raw scrape on her cheek and the large, fresh bruise mottling her chin and jaw, he felt a surge of anger within him. As he caressed her hand, she stirred again.

"Tarrant . . ." she murmured, one hand lifting to touch the throbbing pain in her head.

"I'm here, Meleah. Just lie still."

"Did anyone get the license of the truck that hit me?" she moaned.

"I'll get you some aspirin, sugar. You just lie still," Charlotte said.

"What is going on around here?" Elliot demanded.

"That's what I'm hoping the police will find out." Tarrant made an effort to sound civil. Charlotte had been right. This wasn't the time to stir things up. Whatever issues he had with Elliot would have to wait. "Do you feel up to talking to them, Meleah?"

"I won't be able to tell them much. Whoever it was grabbed me from behind."

"Somebody grabbed you?" Elliot interjected. "My God, Meleah! Are you all right?"

"I'm fine. I'm fine," she said, waving aside his gesture of concern. "I'm just a little ticked, that's all. What I want to know is how in the world someone could just waltz right in here and nobody saw a thing. What good is a security system if a person can't feel secure"

"Do you think it was part of that same crew that attacked you a while back?" Elliot asked.

"No," Tarrant said, without hesitation.

"I was talking to Meleah," Elliot said pointedly.

"I told you, I don't know who it was. One minute I was looking for some old files and the next, I'm being shoved against a wall. That's all I know. Certainly not enough to give the police any help."

"Do the best you can. It'll be a start," Tarrant encouraged.

"Here you go, sugar," Charlotte announced as she brought a glass of water, and a couple of aspirin.

"Where's Pops?" Meleah asked.

"Jack's outside waiting to flag down the police."

"I told you," Meleah said, her voice strained, "I didn't see who it was."

"Was there anything distinguishing about your attacker at all, Ms. Harmon?" the officer who'd responded to the call addressed her, holding his notebook ready. "A distinctive voice or way of moving?"

"He talked in a raspy voice. It was kind of a whisper," she said immediately. "I guess he didn't want anyone to hear him."

"Or to be recognized," Tarrant offered.

"Any smells come to mind? Aftershave or cologne, or something that may have struck you as out of place."

"No, no, no," she said, shaking her head. She placed her hands to her head to stop the pounding.

"Maybe we should continue this at a later time," Tarrant suggested. "Ms. Harmon has been through a lot the last couple of days."

"If you can continue, ma'am, I'd suggest that you do. The fresher the incident is in your mind, the better. First impressions are usually lasting ones."

"I'm okay," Meleah said, pressing her lips together. "I'll tell you everything that I know, but I know it's not much."

"Try to remember," the officer encouraged gently. "Anything at all will help."

"He . . . he had on gloves . . . cloth, not leather. He placed them over my mouth and nose so I couldn't scream."

"And then?"

"I was . . . scared. And mad! I remember fighting back. I scratched him. I know I did. I'm just not sure where."

"May I?" The officer grasped her hands and turned them over. "There are still skin fragments under the nails," he addressed his partner.

"Ugh," Meleah said, with a barely repressed shudder.

"No, that's wonderful! We can analyze the samples and determine more about the person who attacked you. Whatever you do, Ms. Harmon, don't wash those hands! I'll call the lab and see if I can get someone out here to take some samples from you."

"I took a look around the storeroom," Tarrant volunteered. "Charlotte compared the contents to last week's listing. As far as we know, nothing else was taken. Nothing in this office has been disturbed, and no one got near the safe. Charlotte would have seen them if they did."

"Then maybe this wasn't a simple robbery attempt," Meleah mused. "It crossed my mind that it might have been. We've been attracting a strange crowd lately."

"You'd be surprised what kind of cockroaches four million will flush out," Elliot interjected.

"We won't know of any of the intruder's motives until we find out more about them," the officer said. "If I can use your phone, I'll see about getting some of our lab technicians out here."

"Go right ahead." Meleah waved him toward the

phone. She looked down at her hands, and shuddered again.

"You sure you're going to be all right?" Tarrant said softly.

She nodded wordlessly. When Charlotte, followed by Jack, poked her head in the door, Meleah smiled and invited them in.

"How're you feeling, sugar?"

"How's my baby feeling?" Jack echoed.

"I'm fine." Meleah plastered a weak smile on her face.

"You little liar. You don't have to put on the brave little soldier act for me. You ought to tell them to let you go home. Jack, make her go home."

"I can't just yet. They're sending more people over."

"Goodness! Whatever for?"

"What people?" Charlotte wanted to know.

"Meleah may have a bit of evidence that will lead them to the attacker," Tarrant spoke up.

"Disgusting," Elliot said and shuddered. "They're going to do some scraping under her fingernails and pull out some dead skin. Absolutely disgusting." He made a comic show of pinching the collar of his shirt together and shivering. "Grosses me out just thinking about what you might have grabbed and kept with you."

"What kind of evidence would that be?" Charlotte asked.

"I scratched him; the officer found bits of flesh under my nails. I guess they'll do a little genetic detective work and see what happens from there." Meleah splayed her fingers out in front of her and stared at them as if she'd suddenly sprouted hooves. She made a mental note to herself to never bite her nails again.

"You mean from an itty-bitty piece of skin they can

find out who it was without an eyewitness description of the creep?" She sounded awed.

"The officer seems pretty confident," Tarrant said.

"Whoever thought our little island task force would be so sophisticated," Charlotte murmured. "I guess I never gave them much credit. I thought all they were good for were stopping folks from throwing beer cans on the beach."

At Charlotte's admission, the officer placed the phone back in the cradle and said, "I am sorry for the wait and the inconvenience, folks. They promised me they'll have somebody here within the hour."

"In the meantime, Officer, can I get you anything?" Charlotte sounded a little embarrassed to have been caught trashing the police department. "A sandwich or something?"

"How about one of your special clubs?" the officer suggested. "If it wouldn't be too much trouble."

"Coming right up!" Charlotte peered at the officer's name tag. "Follow me, Officer Croft, is it?"

"Yes, ma'am."

After he closed the door behind him, Tarrant turned to Meleah and said, "Maybe you should see about getting the locks changed. And your security system isn't worth a damn." He threw a meaningful glance at Elliot.

"Don't think I haven't thought about it," Meleah admitted.

"Was the system turned on? It doesn't do anybody any good if it isn't turned on. My boy told you that when he set it up." Elliot defended his reputation as the hook-up man.

"I wish I knew what he wanted," Jack muttered. "What was he doing?"

Meleah shook her head. "We may never know."

"We'll find out all right," Tarrant said. His voice was

low and full of determination. No job left undone. He wasn't going anywhere. Not now.

Tarrant held the door open for Meleah and held out his hand to help her from his car. The car must have been one of his latest projects, still in its infancy. It had a black leather interior, almost fully restored. The exterior, however, was a different story. The car was covered with splotchy gray primer paint. His excuse for helping her out was that the door handles still weren't working quite right.

As he escorted her from the horseshoe-shaped drive up the front steps, Meleah noted the odd mixture of strength and tenderness in his grasp. His hands, though well-tended, showed telltale signs of hard work. A callus here, a small scar there. His hands were no stranger to hard work. Yet, as he helped her, he seemed overly concerned with not harming her own delicate hands. When he grasped her firmly, she felt the warmth of his hand course through hers. An unfamiliar feeling, but not unpleasant, spread through her. When she climbed up the first step leading to the front door, she didn't pull away immediately. Instead, she looked up into his face for any indication that he'd felt the same current.

His expression was enigmatic, almost brooding. As quickly as the warmth spread through her, it dissipated. She pulled her hand away.

"You didn't have to drive me home," she said, quickly climbing the rest of the stairs. She stood on the wrap-around porch, arms folded across her chest, regarding him uneasily.

"You're welcome," Tarrant responded.

"Let me rephrase that," she said, with a slight smile of embarrassment. "Thanks for driving me home."

"My pleasure." He then bowed slightly.

She paused, not ready to see him leave yet but having no real excuse to keep him there other than the fact that she wanted him to stay.

Tarrant felt the same reluctance. He couldn't just walk away. He'd proven that much when he couldn't quit Papa Jack's without saying good-bye. Tarrant reached up, and wound one of Meleah's curls around his finger. As he drew his finger downward, he traced the delicate outline of her jaw.

"I don't know if I feel comfortable leaving you here like this, Meleah. Are you sure you're going to be all right?"

"I'll be fine, Tarrant. Really I will. Thanks for asking. I'm sure Pops will be here soon to take care of me. He's just going to get things rolling at the restaurant and then he'll be here. He'll be here." Her voice trailed off, as if she were trying to convince herself of that fact.

"I don't mind staying until he arrives," Tarrant insisted.

Meleah considered his offer. Every cell in her body wanted him to stay. Every cell in her body was wanting, period. If she invited him inside, if she asked him to stay, she knew what would happen. It was as inevitable as the tide. She would wind up in his arms. Maybe it wasn't such a bad place to be. She had not minded being there when he'd kissed her that day in the pool room. She had not minded when he had comforted her after Dub had thrown her into the pool. But not now. Not when she was this vulnerable. Twice Tarrant had come to her rescue. He'd saved her from drowning and he'd come to her aid when someone had attacked her in the storage room. If and when she did go to him, she wanted the emotion to be pure. Not tainted with gratitude for what he had done for her. She was having a hard enough time separating lust from love. If she allowed him to follow her through that door, complicated emotions would intertwine even more, so that there was no untangling.

"Thank you, but no thank you." She placed her hand against his cheek to soothe away the worried frown. "If it makes you feel any better, I'll make sure to check all the doors and windows before I do anything else."

"Just be careful, Meleah. We don't know if that incident at Papa Jack's was an isolated one or not. Until we find the person who did it, I want you to be extra careful."

"I will be," she promised. "Good-bye, Tarrant."

"Meleah," he said, backing away. He watched until she'd opened the door, closed it, and he heard the distinctive *click* of the lock sliding into place. Not satisfied, but resigned to respect her wishes, he turned away, and started for his car.

Meleah watched him from the window until he drove from sight. Only then did she allow herself the luxury of falling apart. She grasped her arms, suddenly taken with an uncontrollable shivering. Fear as intense as the moment she was first attacked washed over her. She clamped her teeth together to keep from sobbing aloud.

She knew she would be all right eventually. But for now, she was afraid. Very afraid. She would even welcome *him* back to keep her company. She would welcome anyone who could calm her, take her mind from her fear. She clamped her hand over her mouth, and turned around. The house, so different from the one she'd grown up in, was a stranger to her. It was home, but it was no comfort to her. It was too quiet—almost sinister. How could it offer her shelter when behind any door could lie more danger.

"Come home, Pops," she pleaded aloud. "I don't want to be alone!"

Tarrant drove to the edge of the block, stopped in a squeal of brakes and tires, then performed a tight U-turn in the middle of the road.

"For heaven's sake, Meleah," he muttered aloud. "Why do you have to be so stubborn?" He hurried back to the Harmon house, and pressed the doorbell. He pressed it once, twice. When he received no answer on the third ring, he began to pound. Out of the corner of his eye, he caught a flutter at the window. A second later, Meleah opened the door.

"Tarrant," she said, her voice calm. Tarrant looked into her eyes. She'd been crying. He could see it in the reddened rims of her eyes. A wadded tissue peeked through her tightly clenched hand. "What do you want?"

"I'm not leaving you, Meleah."

"I told you—" she began sharply.

"I know what you told me. And I know what I have to do. I didn't come back to baby-sit you. I just don't think you should be alone right now."

She pulled the door open, and stepped aside.

"Come in, if you have to," she responded.

"You have the damnedest way of giving the most *unthankful* thanks I've ever seen," Tarrant commented.

"You're welcome," she responded, with a small smile. "If you insist on staying, make yourself comfortable. Snacks are in the fridge and I'm sure you'll find something on TV. The wide-screen one is in the family room. You should know your way around the place by now. Have a go at it. I'm going upstairs to crash. I need a very long nap."

"Sweet dreams," he called. As she passed from hearing, he added, "My Meleah."

THIRTEEN

Meleah lay curled under her covers for an hour with her eyes squeezed tight. She willed herself to relax but couldn't. Every sound, real or imagined, jarred her back to full wakefulness. She tossed back her blanket, paced the floor for a moment, grabbed a few magazines but couldn't relax.

When an unexpected rap sounded at her door, she cried out, then clamped her hand over her mouth.

"Who is it?" she called out, her voice nervous and high-pitched. She felt a little foolish. If someone was going to go after her again, they weren't going to knock.

"It's Tarrant," he answered. He opened the door a crack, and stuck his hand inside. In it, he carried a glass of milk.

"It's warm," he said. "I thought it might help you relax."

"Warm milk?" Meleah laughed a little as she climbed out of bed. "What is this? The kiddie hour?"

"You're welcome," Tarrant responded, without cracking a smile.

Meleah opened the door a little wider and took the glass from him. "Thank you," she said gratefully. "I guess that sounded a little harsh. You're going to have to overlook my being rude, Tarrant. I'm more shook up than I thought."

"I could hear you pacing," he said. "Do you want to talk about it? I know I'm not behind a bar anymore so I don't fit the stereotype of the sympathetic bartender. But I can still listen."

"What's there to talk about?" she asked, sipping at the milk. "Somebody jumped me, and now I'm *this* close to having a nervous breakdown." She pinched her fingers together to demonstrate how close.

"You might consider going to a support group."

"I'd feel foolish going to one of those. I mean, I wasn't really hurt and—"

"Somebody out there tried to hurt you. Whether he smashed your arm or your peace of mind, it's still the same. Talking about it helps work through some of the anger and the fear."

"You sound like you know what you're talking about."

"I do," he answered, though it seemed to Meleah a little reluctantly.

"You've been to one before?"

"Too many times to count," Tarrant said tightly, and glanced away.

"Because of your sister Amber?" Meleah asked softly.

"She's got so many problems. We've tried everything we could to help her. Even her own daughter is starting to call her queen of the support groups. You name them, she's been to them."

"But they didn't seem to help?"

He shook his head no.

"Maybe that's her problem," Meleah mused aloud.

"What do you mean?"

"Too many people trying to support her. Nobody is letting her stand on her own. I couldn't understand why everything that happened to her was my fault. Now I think I do."

"You don't understand." Tarrant bristled. He caught himself, seeing an equally tough wall building up in Meleah's eyes. It was an old argument—he-said she-said. As long as he worked behind the bar, no one was willing to tell him the whole story. Now that he had finally pieced it together, he wondered if it was too late to undo the damage he'd done by building such a wall of distrust between he and Meleah.

She broke the awkward silence by quickly finishing her milk and setting the glass on the table. "Thank you, Tarrant," she said softly. "There, is that gracious enough?"

"You're getting the idea, boss lady." He grinned at her and Meleah smiled back.

She wasn't completely oblivious to his dilemma. Amber was his sister. He loved her unconditionally. Amber would always be a sore point between them. As long as she could joke with him, she figured they were doing the best they could to get past his stumbling block of a family.

For a moment, he reminded Meleah of the Tarrant who showed himself at closing time—easy, eager to help, and quick with the wit. It was one of the rare smiles she might give him from across the room while they were both on duty. Sometimes, on odd occasions, something would strike them both as funny or interesting at the same time. As if coordinated by a choreographer, they would look up at the same time and catch each other's gaze. Both were willing to hold it as long as they could. Mere seconds seemed like an eternity. They were content to watch each other, willing to hold the connection. Then Papa Jack's business would interrupt them. And they would move on, break apart, as if nothing had passed between them.

Meleah's mind raced as fast as her heart. This was one of those connecting moments if ever she experienced one. Only this one was magnified by the power of ten. Instead of across the room, he was within arm's reach. There were no customers, no orders, no games to come between them. There was nothing to break the connection. She had to do something. She could feel herself reaching that place in her emotions where she definitely didn't need to be. It was too perfect a setup. She and Tarrant were alone. No one was expected back for hours and hours. They were even in her bedroom. She thought ruefully that all she needed were some candles and soft music and the mood would be complete. It was the most romantic setting she could ever imagine. And she was scared to death.

"Well, I'd . . . uh . . . better let you get some sleep," Tarrant said softly.

"But I'm not sleepy," she objected. "Not yet."

Tarrant mentally steeled himself. Meleah was looking at him again with those liquid eyes, making him want to forget the promise he'd made to himself when she'd reluctantly allowed him into the house. He was no fool. He wasn't blind. From the way she'd reacted to his kiss and the coolness he'd received following it, he figured she was afraid of another encounter. He wasn't sure why she'd be afraid of him. The fact remained that she was. Until he could help her set aside those fears, he wasn't going to push. He was going to apply the same determination that he'd used to prove Meleah and Papa Jack's guilty to gradually prove himself to her.

Tarrant didn't think he was being noble by reigning in his desire. It was no secret that he wanted her. Everyone, from his family to folks at Papa Jack's, had noted it if not remarked on it. When he'd kissed her, he'd done it out of pure selfishness. For weeks she'd teased him; Whether it was intentional or not, he hadn't considered. She'd tantalized him. She'd visited him in his dreams so that each morning he'd woken up aching. Needing. Wanting. He'd faced the day with a sense of anticipation and anxiety, knowing that he would have to work all night with her without having her. At the close of business he would go home alone, and start the entire frustrating process all over again.

When he had kissed her, it had been the culmination of weeks of suppressed need. When he'd looked at her across the pool room, he had the distinct impression that he wasn't the only one holding back. He'd kissed her because he thought that she wanted to, as well. Tarrant didn't think it was ego giving him that impression. He'd heard enough talk from the brothas and their real or imagined luck with ladies. They'd boasted of their conquests, convincing themselves that they'd gotten so far because the women they were with "wanted it." Tarrant had teased them in return, saying that the only reason those women gave in was that they were trying to get rid of them. He had once teased Jackie D, saying that he could probably time his lovemaking stamina within two seconds on a stopwatch. The last thing he wanted to bring to those conversations was his own version of how much his lady "wanted it." He didn't want to conquer her, he wanted to caress her. He didn't want Meleah to give in to him. He wanted her to give to him. The look she was giving him now, so full of mixed feelings, told him that she wasn't ready.

"Come on, boss lady." He grasped her arm and propelled her toward her bed. When he sensed, rather than heard her breath catch, he placed his palm over her face and gently pushed her head back into her pillow. "Get some sleep." When she tried to rise up again, he said, "I mean it."

Meleah pulled the blanket up to her chin and closed her eyes. "I'm going to sleep now," she said. "Happy?"

"Not yet, but I will be. I'll be right outside that door until I'm completely satisfied." He couldn't help but notice the irony in his words. When would he ever get the chance to say again that not sleeping with someone would leave him satisfied?

Tarrant shut the door behind him and sat on the floor across from her door. He listened intently. Of course she would be upset at his handling of the situation. He could hear her softly fuming to herself. But as the warm milk, and her own fatigue, began to take over, it grew quieter and quieter in her room.

Tarrant checked his watch. One hour had passed since he'd practically ordered her back to bed. All was quiet. Maybe too quiet. He poked his head in the door to peek in on her. She'd kicked her covers onto the floor. Smiling with tender amusement, he crept into the room, and picked them up.

Meleah lay on her side, with one hand resting across her stomach, her head lying on her other arm. She was breathing deeply and easily. He peered closely but didn't think she was faking just to avoid another near-miss-kiss. Her face was too reposed, her breathing was too rhythmic, to be a trick. He laid the blanket across her. As he stood over her, he constantly reminded himself not to reach out and touch her—no matter how much he ached to do so. His fingers clenched convulsively.

"Don't you do it, Tarrant," he murmured aloud. But even as he warned himself away from her, he could feel himself bending toward her. A simple kiss—that's all he wanted. It couldn't hurt, could it? Just a light peck to comfort her while she dreamt? He moved closer. He could almost feel the soft brush of her breath against his face as she sighed softly in her sleep.

A smile played across her lips. He wondered what she might be dreaming of. Him? Even in sleep, could she sense his presence? Was the smile encouragement to proceed?

He shook his head. He had to be out of his mind! What if she woke up and caught him staring at her? Would she be comforted? Or would he trigger her fear. He had invaded her bedroom. He didn't want to take the risk. Tarrant backed away and closed the door behind him as he left.

He was halfway down the hall when he heard her call out. It wasn't just a cry, she called out his name.

"Tarrant!"

In what seemed like only two steps, Tarrant had traversed the hall and was at her bedside. She sat bolt upright, her face frozen in a look of terror. Her arms were flailing in front of her, fighting an unseen attacker.

"Meleah!" Tarrant called out sharply, grasping her hands.

"No!" she sobbed. "Let me go! Let me go!" She tried to ball up her fists to fend him off.

"Meleah, it's me. It's Tarrant! You're having a bad dream!"

"Let me go!" She gulped for air.

"Meleah!" he said, shaking her, gently at first, then with growing intensity. "You're all right. You're safe now. I'm here."

He clasped her to him, rocking her as a small child as her sobs subsided. He heard her muffle a question in his shoulder.

"Tarrant?"

"That's right, Meleah. It's me. I'm here. I'm not going to leave you."

It seemed to Meleah as if a floodgate had suddenly

been released. She didn't know how long she sat there, allowing him to rock her as her tears flowed.

"I'm sorry," she said repeatedly. "I'm so sorry."

He reached for a tissue on her night stand, and started to dab at her face. "What are you apologizing for?"

"I feel so silly!" she wailed.

"Don't!" he said sternly. He grasped her face between his hands and said, "You have every right to feel scared. It's going to take time to work through it. I'll help you, if you want me to."

"I can't go through the rest of my life expecting you to rush to my rescue," she said.

"Why not? You don't think I'm up to the job?"

"I don't want to rely on anyone to make me feel safe," she said with a hint of warning.

"Everyone needs someone, Meleah."

"Why? So they can set themselves up to be hurt? I don't have to leave myself vulnerable like that, Tarrant."

"You think relying on a friend makes you vulnerable?"

"A friend?" she asked. "Tarrant, we're not . . . we're not friends," she said.

Instead of being put off by her denial, he was encouraged. "If we're not at least friends, then what are we, boss lady?"

"I don't know what we are. I can't figure out what we are because I can't quite figure you out."

"What's there to figure out? I'm just a man, Meleah, like any other."

"There's something about you," she said, peering closely at him. "I'm not quite sure what it is . . . but . . . maybe it's because you always seem to say and do the right thing at exactly the right time. Like . . . like it's all been rehearsed somehow."

"That's impossible." Tarrant felt a twinge of guilt. He had approached this job as if he were auditioning for a part. He had to convince Jack and Meleah that he was there on the behalf of his sister. Some of it was true. But he had to allay their suspicions that he had ulterior motives for hanging around. As he held her, he wondered if she would have calmed down knowing that he had plans of suing them to their last dime?

"I know it is, but everything seems to be so easy for you. You breeze into my father's business asking for a job, yet you're confident enough to know that he wouldn't turn you down. You've gained in confidence in areas where I obviously haven't. You're always there with all the right answers. You're almost too perfect."

"I'm far from it, Meleah." He shook his head, laughing slightly.

She brushed at his shirt where evidence of her tears still lingered.

"Why were you working at Papa Jack's?" she asked.

"Excuse me?"

"It's obvious you don't need the money. This shirt alone costs more than a week's salary." She tugged at the material.

"And don't forget tips," he added flippantly, reminding her of the time she'd beat him out of his when she shot the lights out the night of the free-throw contest. "Like I told your father, Amber wasn't covered by my parents' medical insurance. Do you know how much it is for one night in a hospital? More than what I was getting cleaning up after those armchair athletes, I guarantee you."

"You do have one character flaw," she said, frowning slightly.

"And that is?"

"That mouth of yours is too smart for your own good."

"Oh, I don't know," Tarrant said in a deceptively casual voice. "Some people think my mouth is my best feature."

Meleah meant to look away in derision of his leading comment, but instead she found herself focusing on the object of discussion. He had a wide, expressive mouth. It was quick to smile with his own brand of dry humor. When it came to working the crowd at Papa Jack's, she rarely saw him frown, not even when dealing with the most ungracious customers. And she'd seen what happened to the women patrons when he turned that smile on them. Tips! He received lots of tips spilling over from the brandy snifter he kept at the end of the bar. The end, she noted with a tiny hint of irritation, that she liked to perch at when she wasn't in her office working.

As she sat regarding him, another thought crept into her mind. She liked his mouth best when it was calling her name or using his own nickname. Everyone at Papa Jack's called her Le-Le. It was the name Jack had given her when she was a little girl and it had stuck. She didn't mind when Jack or Charlotte or Elliot used it as an endearment. But she was a grown woman now. She was trying to run a business. Who could take a woman named Le-Le seriously? Tarrant had started calling her boss lady. Boss. Lady. His boss. His lady.

Sometimes when he called her, his voice was pitched low—meant for her ears only. He used that voice during closing time. She would sit at the end of the bar. He would busy himself doing odd jobs behind the bar while she finished her paperwork. Anyone passing by might think that he kept his voice low to keep from disturbing her. Meleah knew differently. He spoke softly to get her attention. It forced her to look up at him. The smile of pleasure in his eyes when he'd succeeded in getting it was enough to let Meleah know that he was doing it for her.

"Meleah."

The quality of his voice grabbed her rapt attention. It was filled with the same intensity that could pull her from deep within the bowels of never-ending paperwork to focus entirely on him. She glanced up into his eyes. Usually his hazel eyes glittered with complex emotion. Not all of them could she discern. He was a private man, a man of many facets not visible to the naked eye. He let you see what he wanted you to see. She had always suspected that he was hiding something from her. But in his dealings with her, he'd always been courteous, respectful. He'd sometimes openly teased her like the rest of her friends and family at Papa Jack's, but it had been a mutual teasing.

Now, his hazel eyes were darkening. They were darkening with the one emotion she knew was always lurking beneath the surface. Like the embers of a well-tended campfire, the emotion waited for a single action to re-stoke the flame. All it would take was one movement, one sign from her.

She lifted her head ever so slightly. Her eyes were partially shielded by the sweep of her long lashes. "Yes, Tarrant?" she whispered. Her throat and mouth felt dry. She reached out with a tentative pink tongue and moistened her lips.

He leaned forward, too close. She could feel the warmth of his breath brush against her lips.

"Fire me," he said.

"What did you say?"

Tarrant shook his head. His voice was strained as he explained. "I said you'd better fire me. Tell me to leave. Tell me to go. I can't do it by myself. I can't quit—Lord knows I've tried, Meleah. I've tried to leave you. But I couldn't. I can't. I won't. You've got to fire me. If I stay, you and I both know what's going to happen."

"You're fired," she said, without a trace of a real intention to do so. "You are no longer an employee of Papa Jack's." She paused, then took his hand. Placing it deliberately against her breast, she said, "Now that you're no longer an employee, Tarrant, you are welcome to do this."

Tarrant bit his lip and moaned. "Woman, do you know what you're doing to me?" He hoped that she was fully aware of how she affected him. If she wasn't, if she had any doubts, she could end this torture right now.

There was still time. He could still walk away. Yet the longer he stayed, the more he realized that he had made a decision. He had made a choice. No more skulking. No more lying. He had deliberated between Amber and Meleah and had not chosen his sister.

"Do I know?" Meleah echoed. "I know it goes something like this." She slid her palms up and down his shirt. She massaged up to his shoulders, over his arms.

"And this?" he said huskily, massaging her in slow, concentric circles. He could feel her heartbeat quicken under his sensitive fingertips.

"Umm-hmm." Meleah nodded, closing her eyes.

"And this," he continued, rubbing his thumb against her swollen nipple.

"Yes!" Her voice came out on a sigh. She arched her back, offering more of herself to him.

"And what about this?" He opened her blouse and peeled the two layers aside. Opening the front clasp of her brassiere was a mere flick of the fingers.

When he bent his head down to capture her breast in his mouth, she became speechless. She could only nod her encouragement. Meleah rested her hand behind his head and caressed—encouraging, inflaming.

By the time he moved to her right breast, to pay it the same homage as the left, she was squirming under the covers. Her legs drifted apart, a welcoming invitation to him.

Tarrant placed his hands on the bed, one on either side of her. He moved from his perch on the edge of the bed to kneel in front of her. He grasped her hands and pulled her into a kneeling position as well. Then he cupped her face between his hands, searching her eyes.

"Meleah, are you sure you want to do this?" He wasn't sure why he'd asked, a feeling maybe. It was a nagging voice in the back of his mind that warned him to give her every opportunity to back out. Maybe it was something in her expression, so open and trusting. It was in complete contrast to the woman he'd kissed before. Before, Meleah had been guarded, cautious. It was more than protecting herself against a man she didn't completely trust. Somehow Tarrant felt that she had been protecting herself against all men. Night after night, he'd seen her in action. Closer to the truth, he'd seen her in inaction. She'd fended off the advances of the male patrons of Papa Jack's as if her life depended on it.

The more he thought about it, the more it made sense to him. Meleah wasn't being a bitch when she emphatically turned aside their proposals. She was waiting for the right one. She had been waiting to save herself for that first one. He felt his throat close up. No wonder Amber's friends had scared her so much. No wonder she hadn't wanted to talk about it. She'd held on to her virginity as a secret treasure. The thought that some lowlifes might plunder her was enough to send her into defend-or-destroy mode. She wasn't going to casually give away what she'd guarded all of this time. Now she was offering herself to him freely.

"I don't want to do *this,*" she echoed. "I want *you.*" No hesitation. No shame. Hastily, frantically, Meleah began to reach for his polo-style shirt. She grabbed handfuls of his shirt at his waist and pulled it out of the waistband of his pants. Tarrant raised his hands over his head, allowing her to pull off the shirt. His torso gleamed before her. Already a thin sheen of perspiration covered him. Dry mouthed, she ran her hands over his broad chest. She closed her eyes, making herself familiar with him by the sense of touch and smell. She already had a good idea of what he looked like unclothed. She'd imagined it enough times in her mind to know. She wanted to know him in every sense of the word, on all levels. Her tongue darted forward and tasted of him, too. She traced a line from his sternum to his navel, then back up.

Tarrant sucked in a deep breath, tightening his stomach. He lifted his gaze toward the ceiling, saying a small prayer of patience. He'd waited too long for this moment to rush now. But he could feel his will weakening. When curious fingers reached for his belt, he tried slowing himself down by putting his mind on other matters. He was not going to let her first time be one filled with haste and ultimate regret. With a single tug, she'd pulled belt from its loops and tossed it onto the floor. The sound of the metal buckle hitting the hardwood floor snapped him back to where he was and what he was doing. By the time Meleah's hands found their way to the silver buttons of his jeans, he was past the point of no return. Tarrant thought his knees would buckle. He wrapped his arms around her, as much for closeness as for support.

Meleah could feel him throbbing, straining toward her. She mirrored his stance by wrapping her arms around his waist. When she pressed her chest against his, she could hear as well as feel his breathing. He had gulped, trying to slow down his rapid, shallow fight for air.

"That's right, big guy," she murmured into his ear. She was laughing softly, feeling feminine and powerful in her ability to affect him this way. "Take deep breaths. In. Out. In. Out." As she directed his breathing, she punctuated each instruction with a slight thrust of her pelvis. The motion was subtle. Insidious. He started to move in sync with her, slowly, rhythmically.

Greedily he sought out her lips. In his own way, he meant to give her some of the same treatment. She had used her mouth to goad him, to taunt him, and to drive him to this point when he no longer trusted his ability to control the situation. As he kissed her, he allowed his tongue to slip in and out of her mouth in the same rhythm that she had set for them. In. Out. In. Out. Their entire bodies rocked in the same motion. Together, yet not completely merged, they continued to test the boundaries of their passion. It was a continuation of the teasing they had inflicted on each other since he had come to Papa Jack's.

Again the unseen choreographer that had orchestrated their stolen glances, their ritualistic mating dance around each other at the sports bar, guided their movements now in her bedroom. Unspoken permission took their teenager-like petting to the next level. Tarrant flexed his arms, communicating his next move. Meleah arched her back. She placed his hands at the waistband of her skirt and jerked downward. Skirt and dainty lace panties wound up in a heap next to Tarrant's belt and shirt. He swept his hands behind her knees, causing her to fall back onto the bed. Their lips, still sealed in a frenzied yet focused kiss, gave a preview of what their hips would strive to do.

His warm palms stroked the insides of her thighs, gripping and releasing. When he reached the juncture of her thighs to test her readiness for him, he was greeted with a rush of warmth and wetness.

Meleah felt in that instant all of the tables had turned. She was no longer in control. If she had any power to command while she was boss lady of Papa Jack's, she had none while in her own bedroom. She had certainly lost control of the responses of her own body. There was a time when she could issue herself a command, and it would be granted. She could say, Stop thinking about him and *poof!* All thoughts were out of her head. She could say, Don't worry about it— and magically, all doubts were out of her heart. Not here. Not now. No command she could bring to her lips could stop her from wanting him. She would not be able to get him out of her heart, not without help.

"Fire me," Meleah entreated, lifting up to meet him. "You're the boss."

Meleah closed her eyes, preparing herself to receive the answer to all of the mysteries between men and women. For so long, she had guarded her questions. She had never asked, never expecting to find a man who would hold the answer for her. This man holding her now had her answers. He could satisfy her curiosity. Judging from her response to his touch, that curiosity could very well turn out to be insatiable. The more he asked of her, the more she answered. Her responses became more confident. Each time she touched him, it was a quest for more knowledge. He didn't seem to mind her seeking. Her encouraged her exploration. Something as simple as a hum in the back of his throat, a moan in her ear, or a sigh settling across her skin let her know that she was on the right path. She was well on her way to total understanding.

Tarrant caressed her along both sides of her spinal column. He moved down along her back in pulses. The lower his hands traveled, the greater the tension in the front of his thighs. Carefully, deliberately, he telegraphed his destination to her as if to mentally prepare her.

Though foreseeable, Meleah found nothing in his method boring or predictable. The fact that he was taking his time was all the more exciting to her. He was building passion and expectation at the same time. By the time his palms came to rest against her bottom, she was gasping with pure, unadulterated need.

He squeezed her derriere, lifting her slightly from the mattress. Meleah moaned, pressing her head back into the pillows. Tarrant murmured something to her, but her thoughts were too incoherent to process something as logical as speech. She turned a questioning gaze to him.

"Relax, darlin'." His voice was soothing. "We don't have to go through with this. Not until you're ready."

"I'm ready!" she insisted. "I've never wanted anything . . . anyone . . . as much as I want you now, Tarrant." She closed her eyes, feeling a vestige of shame for sounding so needy. Part of her mind wondered if this was where it started. The women who were afraid of getting "played," was this how they fell into that endless pattern? Once they admitted their weakness, their inability to say no to the man touching them, is this how they wound up in their predicament?

"Look at me, Meleah," he urged her. "Keep your eyes on me." When he was sure he had her attention, he continued. "You know that I want you just as much. I swear, sometimes I thought I was going to go out of my mind with wanting. You don't know how badly I wanted to take you away from Papa Jack's and make love to you. Now we're here. We're at that place we've both been thinking about. Our bodies are telling us to go. You touch me once more and I'm likely to go off like a Fourth of July bottle rocket. But if you're not ready here, then it will all be for nothing." He touched his fingertip to her heart and her head to emphasize his point. "You tell me what you want. Tell me what I should do. If you say so, I'll leave."

Meleah felt her throat constrict with unshed tears. Why did she ever doubt him? He wasn't here with her for a quick Ladies' Night fix. He was here because he wanted her. "You can have me, Tarrant. Heart, mind, and soul," she confessed to him. She trembled, not because she had doubts or fears. She trembled with long-repressed passion.

Tarrant continued to move against her. She could feel the length of him press against her stomach. He squeezed her bottom once again. Meleah tensed, expecting to feel him surge forward. Instead he distracted her with a kiss. Tender at her first, he drew out her reservations. Gradually, hardly noticeable at first, he increased the tempo. She followed until she became impatient. She wanted more. Taking over the lead, she set the pace. Meleah was determined that if she could not control the response of her own body, she could try to bring Tarrant to the same level. Her tongue darted forward and retreated over and over, forcing him to chase after her. She heard him growl with muted frustration. Finally, unable to stand her teasing, with a muttered oath, he literally took matters into his own hands. He grabbed the base of his manhood stopping only to slide on a condom before he eased it toward the open, waiting center of her desire.

Again Meleah closed her eyes in silent expectation. "Look at me," Tarrant repeated, his voice almost harsh with intensity. He wanted her full attention, her full awareness. "There's no turning back, Meleah. I can't hold back now. Do you understand what I'm trying to say to you, boss lady?" His words were punctuated with staccato bursts of his rapid, ragged breathing.

"You know what, big guy? You talk too much," she goaded him. The compassionate man who had taken her feelings into consideration had been transformed into a man whose reason had been forsaken for pure emotion in just a matter of minutes. She pursed her lips to continue her teasing but didn't get the chance to finish. Tarrant responded to her taunt by a quick, almost defiant thrust of his hips. The effect was instantaneous. Pain and pleasure shot through her. Meleah gasped, surprised that so simple an act could make her complex senses go haywire. She hardly had time to process what had happened to her before Tarrant's continual rocking motion brought new sensations to bear.

He withdrew and surged forward. Each thrust became more intense. The hesitation between each one grew less and less. As he watched her expression change from apprehension, to understanding, to anticipation, he marveled how she seemed to be a mass of paradoxes. He knew that he had hurt her, unintentionally so. There was no way to avoid that. He suspected that she knew there would be some pain. Yet she had encouraged him. Even as he moved inside of her, she expanded to accommodate him. At the same time, she kept him tightly sheathed so that movement in either direction continued to give him pleasure.

When she moaned his name, it was his undoing. Tarrant stopped being a curious observer. He wanted to be a willing participant. As her expression of pleasure became more vocal, he found that he was the one having the difficult time remaining focused. He wanted to close his eyes. Let her feelings wash over him. Let them carry him away as she drifted. His eyes narrowed as his gaze became cloudy. Meleah's face swam before him as kind of dizziness swept over him.

Though part of his mind knew where he was and what he was doing, a part of him had moved beyond him. Something from deep inside of him was controlling him, driving to a point beyond the physical. Focused, powerful, and completely primal, that part of himself was seeking its companion spirit. That spirit, he sensed, was hidden within Meleah. The spirit within him would not be satisfied, would not be contained, until he had drawn it from within her, too.

Meleah grasped his forearms. Something was happening to her, something unexpected. She wished she could describe it. It began as a faint tingling sensation. She'd assumed it was an aftereffect of having the virginal barrier broken. But it was more than that. This sensation was spiritual as well as physical. It involved her entire being.

"Tarrant!" she cried out in desperation, clutching him. She was afraid. She had never experienced this sensation before. It was taking over, moving her limbs of their own accord.

"Shh . . ." he soothed. "It's all right, Meleah. Let go, baby. Don't be afraid." He felt her trembling but he continued to drive into her. "Stay with me, Meleah. Stay with me," he chanted. Faster. Deeper. Each thrust was more intense than the last.

Meleah's nails dug into his back, hanging on for dear life. She scored long trails of red streaks as she clutched at him. She moaned and gyrated, matching him thrust for thrust. Yet never once did she break eye contact. Their gaze was their lifeline, keeping them anchored when everything around them threatened to wash them away.

Now! The unseen choreographer brought their dance of ages to a crescendo ending.

"Please, now!" she echoed the words she'd heard in her head.

"Now!" Tarrant repeated. The spirit within him burst free, filling Meleah with its power. It flowed into her and through her, infusing her with its strength while sapping Tarrant of his. With a groan that was part fulfillment, part disappointment, Tarrant rested his head on the pillow of her breasts even as the tremors subsided from her body.

FOURTEEN

"Meleah? Are you awake?"

Meleah sat up to the sound of her father's voice. She experienced a moment of disorientation. She blinked rapidly, trying to force the fog from her brain. Disorientation quickly made way for panic as the events of the evening came back to her. She and Tarrant had spent the night together in her room. She looked around. Now he was gone, and with him any evidence that he'd been here. Part of her was relieved. The other part of her was confused, then irritated. Where was he? Why did he leave her like that? She looked down at herself. A correction. He hadn't just left her. Somehow, though she didn't quite remember when, she'd been dressed in pajamas. A single aromatic candle was sputtering on her chest of drawers across the room. It must have been burning for some time. The tiny votive candle, smelling exotically of jasmine, had almost burned down to the quick.

"Pops?" she called out.

He peeked into her room, and called softly to her. "How're you feeling, little girl?"

"I'm all right," she said, and patted the bed next to her. "How did it go tonight?"

"Busy as usual."

"Did anybody miss me?" Meleah drew up her knees

and hugged them. It was the first time in years she had taken an unscheduled night off.

"The usual suspects asked about you. But I don't want to talk about the restaurant tonight. I mean today," he said, glancing at the clock. It was nearly four o'clock in the morning.

"I suppose things would have been a little easier for you if Tarrant had been there to help out." Meleah felt a twinge of guilt—not because of what she and Tarrant had done. There were no regrets there. By both of them being absent, Jack had to do without his top bartender and her to take over as hostess and do the accounting duties.

"Oh, we made out all right," Jack said, dismissing her concern.

So did we, Meleah thought with a wistful sigh. She wished that she could remember at what point she'd fallen asleep. She wouldn't have minded a few minutes more of basking in the afterglow of Tarrant's attention.

"I told Tarrant to stay here with you. This is where I needed him to be," Jack said. "Don't you worry about me being shorthanded at Papa Jack's. He was only doing what I told him to do."

Meleah ran her fingers through her tousled hair. "I guess I've been asleep for a while. I'm not exactly sure what time he left."

"He didn't leave," Jack said. "That's what I'm trying to tell you. When I got in, he was crashed downstairs on the couch in front of my wide-screen. I left him there. I didn't have the heart to make him drive all the way home at this hour."

"Oh," Meleah said softly. Part of her wished that Pops had awakened him. Even after the intimacy they'd shared, she felt awkward and unsure. She didn't want to reveal that awkwardness to her father. He would be able to read through whatever bland pleasantries they managed to eke out for his benefit. He would see through the charade and would know what had happened the night before. The other part of her wished that Tarrant had not left her. Desire to wake up with him by her side competed with her fear of discovery. The sense of loss she'd felt when she first woke up and found him gone washed over her again. She put on the mask of boss lady to combat the sudden swell of loneliness.

"I still feel guilty for having him baby-sit me. I asked him to go back. He'd coddled me long enough. He wouldn't leave."

Jack laughed softly. "Good to see the man can still follow instructions to the letter. Even after he quit."

"He didn't quit. I fired him." Meleah couldn't help interjecting a reference to her and Tarrant's private joke.

Jack looked curiously at her, then shook his head. He contributed her obvious confusion of the facts to the strain of the last few days. He kissed her tenderly on the forehead. "Good night, sweetheart."

"Good night, Pops. I'll see you in the morning."

It seemed as though her head had just hit the pillow when Jack came knocking on her door once again.

"What!" Meleah said, barely disguising the irritation in her voice. "What is it, Pops?" She jammed a pillow over her ears.

"Telephone, Le-Le." Jack dropped the cordless phone into her lap.

"I'm not home," she said through a deep yawn. "Tell them I've run away to join the circus or the French Foreign Legion. Tell them I've been kidnapped by aliens."

"You'll want to take this one," he said quietly.

"Tarrant?" she asked hopefully. This late in the morning, he wouldn't still be downstairs? Would he? If he was calling her, then maybe he was prudent enough not to be there when she woke up.

"No. It's Officer Croft," Jack corrected. He didn't miss the way her expression brightened then darkened all in a split second.

"Hello? Yes, this is Meleah Harmon. Yes, of course. I can be there within the hour. Thank you, Officer. Good-bye."

Meleah turned back to her father. Her expression went from irritated to concerned.

"That was the police. Officer Croft," Meleah said unnecessarily.

"Yes, I know." He reminded her that he'd answered the phone. "They have news about your attacker?"

"He said he has some more information that I might be interested in. He didn't want to discuss it over the phone. I told him I'd come down. Would you . . . uh, Pops, could you . . ."

"You know you don't have to ask, Le-Le. I'm going with you. Just let me throw on some more clothes. Why don't you call Charlotte and tell her we'll be a bit late opening the place."

"All right. I'll grab a quick shower then meet you downstairs."

"Have a seat, Ms. Harmon, Mr. Harmon. Officer Croft will be with you in just a moment."

"We'll be right here." Meleah forced herself to smile. But as she sat down, she fumbled nervously with her keys. Jack placed his arm around her and squeezed her shoulder in sympathy.

"It's all right, Le-Le," he said in comfort. "It's going to be all right."

"I know. I just wish that I could put the past two months behind me. Between Amber and Dub and the creep who jumped me, I'm a nervous wreck."

By burying herself in her work she was able to push the horrible memories of Durell's attack to the back of her mind. She hadn't completely forgotten. Sometimes, when the conditions were just right, she would remember. It could happen at any time. Sitting at her desk as she worked on the books, lying in her bed at night, or in midbite as she grabbed a quick meal with Charlotte or Pops or Tarrant. No time was too obscure for those memories to force their way into her mind. No hard details. Everything seemed to be blurring together. All of the incidents combined were creating one giant knot of fear in the pit of her stomach.

The thought that there was someone out there roaming the streets free to attack again terrified her. Fear ate at her constantly. Though she tried to bluff her way through the attack, the fact remained that she was scared—and angry. Tarrant was the only one she'd allowed to see how deeply she was affected. She was angry for having her sense of security in her own place ripped from her. Most of all, she was angry at herself for her inability to push the incident out of her mind. Why couldn't she let it go?

"Sorry to keep you waiting, Ms. Harmon, but we've discovered something about your attacker that I think you should know."

"What is it?"

"First of all, let me apologize. The lab report of the tissue samples we took from your fingernails was tainted."

"Tainted?"

Officer Croft nodded gravely. "Some sort of screw up at the lab, pardon my language. At least, I think there's been a mistake. To be certain, we may have to take more samples from you."

"Oh! Oh, no," Meleah said, shaking her head. "I'm afraid that won't be possible." The events of last night with Tarrant might not be completely clear to her. Yet certain facts did remain fixed in her mind. She'd responded very passionately to Tarrant. All of her inhibitions were striped as naked as her body. She remembered holding on to him, gouging him uncontrollably when she'd reached a pinnacle of pleasure. Any skin samples from her now would not do them any good. It would only complicate matters.

"I've showered since yesterday, Officer Croft. I'm sure your samples wouldn't do you any good anyway."

"What was your lab report able to tell you, screwed up that it may be?" Jack pressed.

"We found traces of skin and blood underneath your nails, Ms. Harmon," Officer Croft continued. "But one other thing—we found something else, too."

"What did you find?"

"Ms. Harmon, were you aware that you were a carrier of the sickle cell trait?"

Meleah shrugged. "You call me down here to tell me that? Officer Croft, I've known since I was a little girl. Along with my mother's brown eyes, I inherited her blood. The sickle cell trait runs on my mother's side."

Officer Croft passed a manila file folder over to Jack, then to Meleah. He'd circled the area of interest in red ink. "Apparently this trait runs in your attacker's family, too. I don't have up-to-date statistics of what percentage of African Americans carry the sickle cell trait. But I can tell you this, Ms. Harmon. The odds that your attacker is also a carrier makes me very, very suspicious. Ms. Harmon, can you think of anyone who would want to hurt you? Any enemies of the business?"

"I manage a sports bar, for heaven's sake!" Meleah snapped. "That's nowhere near the world of big-business movers and shakers."

"It's that cursed lottery money," Jack moaned. "It has to be. Someone is probably trying to get to me through you. I guess I should have taken those notes more seriously."

"What notes?" Officer Croft and Meleah said simultaneously.

"What's this about a note, Pops? You never said anything to me about any notes."

"Nothing. A crank," Jack said uneasily. "I didn't want to worry you. You had so much on your mind already."

"You should have told me," Meleah gritted.

"Do you still have it?" Officer Croft asked.

"Them," Jack admitted, lowering his eyes. He couldn't bear to meet Meleah's look of incredulity. "No, I don't. I think I threw them all away."

"Them?" Meleah said, enunciating the word so that her lips hummed when she pressed them together. "Just how many were there, old man?"

"What did the notes say, Mr. Harmon?" Officer Croft interjected. If he didn't do something quickly, this follow-up investigation would turn quickly into a report for a domestic dispute.

Jack closed his eyes to think. "They weren't very creative. They came on different days and in different forms. Mostly ordinary sheets of white paper."

"What exactly did they say, Pops?" Meleah pressed. "With so many notes flying around like confetti, it's a wonder you didn't have one or two memorized."

"Something about me not deserving the blessings the good Lord gave me and . . . then it went on to say that sooner or later everything I cherish will be taken away from me."

"Did it mention your daughter specifically?"

"No. I'm sure of that. The note was very vague. I just assumed it was talking about Meleah. Everyone knows she means more to me than all the money in the world. I'd give everything I own to keep her safe."

"Officer Croft, do you think the notes and my attack are related?" Meleah asked.

"I don't know, Ms. Harmon. But if we had at least one of those notes, we could send it to the lab."

"This may be pointless if Pops didn't keep any of the notes."

"If I still have some, they will be in my office. I'll tear the place apart looking."

"Let me know when you find the notes."

"Don't you mean if?" Jack asked.

"I'm thinking positively. Sooner or later, all of the pieces will fit together."

"Good-bye, Officer. And thank you again." Jack also shook hands. He then placed his hand in the small of Meleah's back to guide her outside. As they stepped outside, Jack muttered, "That flatfoot couldn't put together a two-piece jigsaw puzzle."

"Pops! That's an ugly thing to say."

"I don't trust all of this technology mumbo-jumbo. He was quick to call in his computer geeks to find out who attacked you. I say there's no substitute for some old-fashioned legwork. I would have felt a lot better if they spent more time going over the storeroom where that animal was hiding."

"We went over this before, Pops. Too many people come and go out of that storeroom. It's like Grand Central Station. Folks are in and out of there all of the time. You know how many people we've tried to hire since you won that lottery. There's no way of getting proof positive from a half-smudged fingerprint. Let the officer do his job. He's doing his best, Pops."

"And that's supposed to fill me with confidence?" Jack sneered. "Meleah, we may have to figure this out on our own."

"Who would want to hurt me? Or you, for that matter? Do you really think it was the money? Do you think it was a kidnapping attempt?"

"If that's the case, we're dealing with a moron. Why would he tip his hand weeks before the kidnapping? To wear us down? To give us a false sense of security?"

Meleah shook her head. Too many questions, and obviously not enough answers.

"C'mon, Pops. Let's get back to the bar. Officer Croft didn't give us very much to go on. Do you think we should tell the others what we found out?"

"I think so. Maybe they can help us keep an eye out for men who are acting more stupid than usual."

Elliot folded his arms across his chest, leaned against the hood of his car, and glared at Tarrant from across the parking lot. Tarrant adopted a similar stance, but he didn't lean. He was one day away from delivering the antique-white, 1969 Chevy, and he wasn't about to let a stray scratch or nick ruin its value. He wouldn't have driven it out today except that the last time he started it up, he thought he'd heard a hint of a sputter. One last run up the cause-way and back, with a well-trained ear listening to the precisely tuned engine, and he figured he could get the timing right to make his baby purr like a kitten. Right now he was glaring with tiger eyes at that idiotic cousin of Meleah's.

Tarrant watched Elliot stand there and made a small noise of disgust in the back of his throat. The preening little peacock was dressed in fine clothes he'd probably mooched from someone else. Here it was, almost ninety degrees, and he was dressed to the nines. Silk shirt, buttoned all the way up to the collar, fancy tie, Italian leather shoes. What did he think he was doing? Dressing for a fashion show? He didn't see why the Harmons kept that goldbrick around. He had little inclination to do any real work and even less inclination to pay for the things people gave to him—things that other folks got by the sweat of their brow. As far as Tarrant was concerned, the boy was worthless. Worse than worthless. Something about that boy set Tarrant's teeth on edge from the moment they met. He'd tried to dismiss it before. Meleah's choice of companions had not been his concern. He had been more concerned with getting evidence against Jack and Meleah than becoming chummy with their relatives.

Things were different now. Meleah was his ultimate concern. After what they'd shared, he felt he could openly voice his misgivings to her. The plain truth was, he didn't like Elliot. He had never liked him. There was something about that boy that just didn't sit right with him. Maybe, Tarrant thought, it was the way he thought of Elliot as a boy even though he had to be close to thirty years old. He acted so childish. Another trait that bothered Tarrant. No one should act so. He couldn't be for real. The way Elliot had bucked up against him the other day reminded him eerily of the way his mother Hannah had behaved. One moment she was all grins, the next . . . well . . . a little alcohol and the woman's true colors shone through. No ray of sunshine. There was something dark and twisted behind that woman's smile. Elliot had the same clownish quality. That family was a family of masks.

Tarrant sighed. He supposed he shouldn't point fingers. For almost two months, he'd worn a mask. He'd been deceitful. He'd pretended to be something he was not—a friend of the family.

He shifted uncomfortably, breaking eye contact with Elliot first. No. He wasn't like them. When he'd made love to Meleah, he'd shown her all that he was. There was nothing hidden or covert about his motives. Whatever happened with Amber from that point forward, it would not involve Meleah. That much had become apparent to him.

He was glad when Charlotte drove up into the parking lot. He needed something to take his mind off of his brooding. Not long after, Leon pulled up, then Trae.

"All right, all right. Let's break this party up. We've got a lot of work to do before tonight. There's a pennant race game on tonight. And I, for one, don't want to be caught with our peanuts down." Charlotte hailed them, jingling a set of keys. She opened the front doors of the restaurant, then reached for the security panel to key in the code before the intruder alarm went off. Elliot followed closely behind her, saying, "Hurry up, Charlotte. Move your buns behind that bar. I need a drink."

"Boy, you'd better get away from me," she replied, shooing him away. "You ain't getting a thing until the boss says you can."

"What time are they supposed to get here?"

Charlotte shrugged. "They didn't say. All they said was they were going to be late so I should open up."

"We can see you rushed right over," Elliot grumbled, checking his watch. "I've been standing outside for an hour."

"Like that's my fault. It was my vacation day. I'm doing Jack a favor by being here."

"Aw, quit your whining, woman. It's not as if he isn't going to return the favor," Elliot grumbled. "You'll get what you deserve for all of your effort, Charlie." He plopped down at the end of the bar to wait. If he'd known that it would be a full two hours before Jack and Meleah showed up, he wouldn't have wasted his time. It wasn't if as he didn't have other things to do. There were people to see, deals to make, freebies to freeload. Why he was sitting around here waiting for those Harmons, he never knew. Any other time, he wouldn't have minded the wait. Not this time. As he sat with his elbows leaning on the bar, his fingers absently stirring the shells in his bowl of peanuts, he bemoaned with each passing moment his decision to stay. Charlotte refused to serve him any drinks. That kid Trae was off trying to find a hiding place for that cat of his. Leon had chased him out of the kitchen with a meat cleaver. And the big guy . . . well . . . he could have done without the open glares from him as he went about checking the bar's inventory. Elliot shrugged fatalistically.

He supposed the big guy was still carrying a grudge. Things hadn't been the same between them since yesterday when they almost came to blows. He supposed he shouldn't be too surprised. They were all a little upset about Meleah. Who wouldn't be. And Tarrant must be feeling a little protective and possessive about her. Everyone knew by now that he'd spent the night out at Jack's house. Without a chaperone, it didn't take a genius to figure out what must have happened between the two of them. So the big guy must be feeling pretty smug and pleased with himself. He'd finally succeeded where no one else had before.

Elliot glared back. That didn't give him the right to strut around here like he owned things. Who was he? A nobody. Some Joe Blow off the street. So what if he drove flashy cars. So what if all of the women flocked after him like flies around a dung heap. He wasn't so much.

When Tarrant passed by Elliot for the third time without speaking or even filling up his bowl of peanuts, Elliot bristled.

"What's the matter with you, big guy? You've got a problem?"

"Who? Me?" Tarrant said, pointing to himself.

"Yeah, you."

"Naw . . . *I'm* not the one with the problem," Tarrant responded, indicating by his tone of voice and direct gaze that Elliot was the one with the problem.

"A little more service and a lot less attitude and you'll probably get somewhere in this world, big guy," Elliot said. He pushed his peanut bowl across the bar and pointed to it.

Tarrant reached for the bowl, having every intention of shoving back. Or worse—crashing it down over Elliot's head. He would have liked to think that it was restraint that kept him from doing it. He would have even accepted self-control in deference to Meleah's feelings. He didn't think she'd respond too warmly if she knew that her lover had sent her favorite cousin to the hospital with a skull full of peanut shells and glass fragments. No, that wouldn't have gone over well at all. Somehow he had to come to grips. If he wanted Meleah in his life—and heaven knew that he did—he would have to accept the entire package. Quirky family and all.

The smile that spread over his face went from evil satisfaction at the image of Elliot wrapped from head to toe in bandages, to evoking sincere anticipation at the image of Meleah undressing before him. It hadn't been a full twenty-four hours, and already he was missing her terribly. He ached to hold her again. Tactile memories stimulated the nerves in his fingertips, coursed through his hands. Convulsively, he gripped the bowl of peanuts, spilling the contents over the bar. When Elliot gave him a strange look and clucked his tongue, Tarrant turned his back. He wished Meleah would could back. He didn't know how long he could walk this tightrope between wanting to drag her into the nearest room and making love to her again, and dragging Elliot out and tossing him into the nearest Dumpster.

When the front doors opened once again and Jack and Meleah walked through the door, both Elliot and Tarrant let out vocal sighs of relief. They exchanged glares once again before competing for Jack and Meleah's attention.

Elliot jumped up and pointed at Charlotte as she came from the rear of the restaurant, carrying a tray of glasses. "Tell her to get me a drink, Uncle J!"

"Somebody had better tell this wannabe Foster Brooks to get off my case," Charlotte shot back. "What do I look like? His personal maid?"

"Can it, you two," Jack snapped. "I'm not in the mood." He ducked behind the bar and poured two cups of strong black coffee. He took a swig from one cup, then handed Meleah the other. Wordlessly she sat down next to Elliot. She propped her chin on her fists and stared down into the coffee mug.

Tarrant kept working, but moved closer to try to catch her eye. She seemed to be lost in thought. Or maybe she was avoiding him. He tried not to feel rejected by her reaction. After all, a lot had happened to her the last few days. Maybe she was having trouble accepting what had happened between them. He wondered whether or not she had discussed it with her father or Charlotte. He couldn't tell by Jack's expression exactly what was bothering him. And Charlotte had been too busy grumbling about having to come in on her off day to give him any indication that she knew anything. The only one who was acting like the cat that had stolen the canary was that Elliot. That didn't tell him anything concrete. Elliot always had that expression on his face. He hung back, not forcing the issue when her family gathered around her.

"Le-Le, sugar? Is everything all right?" Charlotte asked, resting her hand on Meleah's shoulder. "What did the police say? Any more news on who attacked you?"

"Nothing really concrete," she said and shrugged. "They messed up the lab report."

"You mean, they didn't find out anything at all?"

"I didn't say that," Meleah said, then took a sip of coffee. "They think my attack and those notes may be connected."

"Oh," Charlotte said.

"So you knew about those, Charlie?" Meleah sounded incredulous and angry at the same time. "I guess I don't know as much as I think I know. How could you hide something like that from me?"

"We weren't doing it to be mean, sugar," Charlotte insisted. "You had so much on your mind with school and trying to manage this place. We did what we thought was best."

"Like hiring that goon to watch out for her," Elliot said knowingly. "That went over like a pit bull fight at an SPCA convention. I could have told you that you couldn't trust a man who wears his hormones on his sleeve. The man had sleazebag written all over him." Elliot shot a meaningful glance at Tarrant.

"Ell, you knew about those notes, too?" Meleah whirled on him.

"Only what I heard from talk around here," Elliot said, raising his hands. "Take it easy, Le-Le. You know

I wouldn't keep anything from you. I've got your back!" He smiled and patted Meleah on the back.

"We all do, my dear," Jack said, planting a huge kiss on her cheek. "I promise you, I'm going to find one of those stupid notes and give it to Officer Croft. But before I do that, I'm going to make sure that you never have to feel unsafe here again. I'm going to put a better security system in here. I don't care what it takes or what it costs. I'm going completely high-tech. Video cameras, motion sensors, those laser beam things that you can see only when you spray hairspray over them."

Her shoulders slumped forward as some of the resentment seeped from her. "Sorry I'm being such a witch, guys. I know you all meant well. It's just . . . I don't know—everything's been so weird lately. All of this talk about super-duper security is only making me nervous. I guess I want my life back the way it was."

"You mean before the money?" Elliot asked. "Did that creep who jumped you knock all of the sense out of your head, cuz?"

"I meant before all of this—" She stopped herself. She had started to say before she had ever met Amber Cole. When that woman had walked into their restaurant, she'd brought with her a dark cloud that no amount of money could dispel. But if she had not met Amber, she might not have ever known Tarrant like she knew him now.

This time she searched out his face. He was leaning against the counter, watching her as intently as he had the nights he had staked out the place. Quiet, disapproving, yet still so incredibly sexy. She hadn't been fair to him, ignoring him like that. As soon as things quieted down around there, they would have to talk. He had no way of knowing how she had struggled with herself, trying to decide if making love with him had been the best thing for them. Since it was her first time, after he had gone, she wasn't sure if her response to him was purely physical. She had nothing to compare her experience to. While she was dressing to get ready to go to the police department, each time her hands grazed her skin, she felt a rush of warmth and remembrance. Quickly she took a sip of coffee to keep from chewing on her lower lip in consternation. They definitely had to talk.

But it would not happen soon. Charlotte had predicted another killer night, and so it had been. Meleah didn't have the opportunity to say more to Tarrant than to respond to his orders to restock the bar. Though each time she handed him back a signed requisition form, his hand grazed hers. His expression spoke volumes when his voice could not.

By closing time, Meleah was both exhausted and expectant. She could barely wait for Charlotte to ring the closing bell. She hovered around the bar, mentally shoving each customer out the door. The slower each couple moved, the more intense her thoughts became. When each of the bartenders brought their cash receipts for the night and clocked out, Meleah hoped that Tarrant would be able to read what was on her mind. She wanted him to hang back. She wanted him to be the last one out. When she finally had a chance to talk to him, she didn't want an audience.

"I'm not going to be leaving you, Meleah. You might as well get that fact through your head," Tarrant said stubbornly. He watched as Meleah gathered the cash receipts from the day's transactions, and carried them to her office.

"Tarrant, it's late. I'm sure you want to go home and rest. By the look of these receipts, you've had a very busy day."

"I don't care if I served a thousand customers, boss lady. I'm not leaving you. There's a maniac running loose trying to hurt you. I can't rest knowing you insist on tempting him to attack you again."

Meleah lowered her lashes and murmured, "I'm sorry, I don't mean to be so defensive. I guess knowing why you're hanging around is just a constant reminder that everything isn't what it's supposed to be. I keep trying to tell myself to pretend that this isn't happening."

He gave her one of his lopsided smiles. "Who's to say that I wouldn't want to be here with you even if you weren't in trouble?" He held her office door open for her, and gestured for her to precede him.

"Tarrant Cole! Are you flirting with the boss's daughter?" Meleah said in a mock, astonished whisper.

"Maybe," he said cautiously. "Are you flirting back?" He wanted to be sure. Ever since she came in to work today, she had been all business. If it weren't for an occasional heated glance in his direction, he would never have believed that this was the same woman who had given of herself so freely to him. He hadn't wanted to push the issue. Tarrant didn't want to put her on the spot in front of her family and friends. But this not knowing was driving him a little batty. Now that they were alone, he felt emboldened, if not encouraged, to try to talk to her.

"Maybe," she returned in the same tone.

He settled himself in a chair facing the desk while Meleah turned on her computer and began to enter the night's receipts into her accounting files. She didn't glance up until an hour later when she noted Tarrant nodding sleepily in the chair. Without realizing that she was, she found herself smiling tenderly at him. There was something sweet, almost vulnerable about his unguarded expression. His chin was tucked into his chest, which rose and fell with his breathing. His hands were crossed, and tucked under his elbows.

He'd pushed the chair back to stretch out his long legs. When his head tipped backward, Meleah resisted the urge to grasp his face in her hands and brush a soft kiss on his lips. It was an urge that she had resisted all evening. Despite the attitude she'd adopted to cope with the evening crowd, she wasn't completely impervious to him. Each time a female patron had gone up to him, she'd felt a wild, jealous urge to drag the skeezer away from *her man.*

But she couldn't do that. If she'd suddenly broken out into a cat fight over a little flirting, everyone would suspect something was wrong. If they had any suspicions about Tarrant staying all night with her last night, they'd know for certain if she behaved out of character. She was still too unsure of how she felt about what had happened between them to listen to everyone else's opinion of her sexuality. So, as always, she played it cool. But that didn't mean she didn't get a little hot under the collar each time Tarrant appeared to be enjoying someone else's attention too much for her liking. Now that she was alone with him, she could explore these new feelings of passion and possession. When she raised her hands high over her head to stretch, the movement startled Tarrant out of his light doze.

"I'm sorry, Tarrant. I didn't mean to wake you up," Meleah said, though she was secretly glad that he was awake now.

"Don't worry about it. I shouldn't have been sleeping, anyway. I should have been watching you. How's it going?" he said, indicating Meleah's work.

"Almost done." Meleah sighed. "It's a little slow going. I'm not exactly sharp as a tack tonight. My mind is all over the place." She reached behind her, and tried to reach between her shoulder blades.

"Stiff neck?" he asked.

"I've been sitting in one place for too long."

Tarrant stood, and circled the desk. Without waiting for permission, he placed his hands on her shoulders, and began to massage gently.

"How's that, boss lady? Better?"

"Ummm," Meleah said in response. She rolled her head in slow circular motions. "That feels good, Tarrant."

Tarrant knelt close to her ear and whispered. "Do you know that I've been thinking about you all day, Meleah? I haven't been able to get you out of my mind."

"Tarrant—" Meleah began.

He felt his throat constrict at the tone of her voice, slightly disapproving. "Please don't tell me that you've had regrets about giving yourself to me, Meleah."

"I . . . I wasn't going to," she confessed. Meleah realized that as soon as she'd said the words, she knew they were true. She wanted Tarrant. She needed him.

As he massaged, Tarrant trailed his fingers along the front of her blouse. He plucked at one small pearl button, then another until he'd revealed the wispy lace of her camisole. With trembling fingers, he slid her blouse from her shoulders. Meleah caught her lower lip between her teeth. "I was just going to say—"

When Tarrant leaned toward her, kissing the tip of her nose, then moved possessively to capture her lips, the words flew from her mind. She could only manage a soft mewl of pleasure. He then brushed two butterfly kisses over her eyelids, her cheeks, then back to her lips. He nudged her mouth until she forget what she wanted to say. It didn't matter; she shrugged off the last voices of her doubts. Nothing mattered at that moment, only his touch.

"Meleah," he whispered. "Wait here. I'll be right back."

"Where are you going?" she cried out in dismay. When he pulled away, she suddenly felt desolate.

"To the men's room," he replied.

"The men's room? What for?"

"Trust me, boss lady. I won't be gone a second longer than I have to be."

While Tarrant was away, Meleah took a moment to alter the ambiance of her office. She lowered the lighting, piped in what she thought was the appropriate mood music. When Tarrant returned, he found her fluffing a pillow on the couch. He cleared his throat softly to get her attention. When she didn't turn around, he knew that she was still a little self-conscious. It was amazing to him. The same woman who had run the restaurant with all of the precision of a drill sergeant suddenly became shy and unsure around him.

Tarrant walked behind her, and wrapped his arms around her waist.

"Are you all right?" he whispered.

She nodded wordlessly, not trusting her voice to speak. "I'm still a little nervous," she finally admitted. "I guess that's why I've been avoiding you all night."

"You don't have to be nervous. I wouldn't do anything to hurt you, Meleah."

"I know," she said, and believed him. "I trust you, Tarrant."

Tarrant felt his heart skip, but he didn't speak. Did that mean she wanted him as her life partner? Did that mean she had chosen him? God knows that he wanted her—not just for now, but for the rest of their natural lives. Maybe she didn't believe that now. He didn't know if she would ever accept it. But they were together now. He simply held her, reveling in the feel of her warm body against his. When his arms closed around her, she settled her head against his shoulder with an audible sigh.

"Feeling better?" he asked.

"I feel fine," she said.

"You certainly do, boss lady," Tarrant teased. He led her purposefully toward the couch, lay down, then held out his hand for her to join him. She came to him, but he could see her beginning to doubt her conviction again. He warned himself not to rush her. He inched back, and lay on his side. She mirrored him, never losing eye contact with him. As long as she could see his eyes, read what she thought were the true intentions of his heart, she wouldn't be afraid.

Tarrant leaned forward, and placed the lightest of kisses on her forehead. He kept the gesture simple and unthreatening.

"So what now?" she asked.

"I know you still aren't sure, Meleah," he said. "I'm going to let you set the limits. You're the boss lady, so call the shots."

"I . . . I want to see you," she began hesitantly. She then cleared her throat, and said with confidence, "All of you."

"Yes, ma'am." He reached up to undo the buttons of his shirt, but Meleah stopped him.

"Let me." She loosened the first button, then the second, then third. As she worked her way toward the waistband of his pants, Tarrant forced himself to remain absolutely still. He hardly dared to breathe. Her touch was as soft, and as fleeting, as a butterfly. He didn't want a sudden movement to startle her and scare her away.

Instead of pulling his shirt tails from his pants, Meleah slid her hand inside of the waistband. Tarrant's sharp, sudden inrush of breath didn't unnerve her. It made her bolder, eager to learn what else she could do to make the hunger flare in his eyes. She probed deeper, losing interest in the last few buttons of her shirt. The further she explored, the weaker his resolve grew. He couldn't hold still. Not now! He had to move against her, to ease the almost painful strain of his groin against her hand.

With her free hand, she unzipped his pants to allow herself more access. Tarrant moaned aloud, and instinctively threw his leg over Meleah's. When he flexed his calf to draw her closer, only her hand separated them. She felt him growing firmer against her hand— leaping, pulsing, throbbing. Knowing that she had that effect on him made her feel strong and powerful.

"I didn't know it would be like this," Meleah said in awe.

"Like what?"

"Promise you won't laugh if I tell you."

"Now you know me better than that."

"No, I don't," she said seriously. "Not really, Tarrant. Isn't this what it's all about? Getting to know each other?"

"You're getting way too philosophical for me, boss lady. Too much thinking going on. Stop thinking so much and tell me what you're feeling."

"I feel like . . . like I . . ." She paused, struggling to find just the right words. "I feel like I hold the key to all the mysteries of the universe in the palm of my hand."

Tarrant chuckled, despite his promise not to laugh at her. She'd sounded so awed. "Mysteries? Is that what they're calling the male anatomy these days?"

"That's not what I'm talking about!" she protested, giving him a little chastising tweak.

"Do you want to explain what mystery you're talking about then?"

"I feel larger than life, powerful . . . like I could do anything."

"Keep touching me like that, and I'll do anything

for you," Tarrant murmured. "God, Meleah, that feels wonderful. Please don't stop!"

She grasped his slacks, and pulled steadily downward. Tarrant helped her to slide them over his feet. He then helped her remove her skirt and slip. She stretched her hands over her head when he took off the camisole. When he propped up on one elbow to stare down at her, Meleah self-consciously tried to cover her nakedness.

"Don't," he said, grasping her hand and placing it against his manhood again. "Don't run away from me, Meleah."

"Where am I going to go dressed like this? Or maybe I should say undressed?" She tried to joke, but her voice quivered. Goose pimples raised along her arms and legs. Tarrant stroked her leisurely—letting her get used to the feel of his hands on her bare skin.

"I can't get enough of touching you, Meleah. I'm not going to lie to you. When you walk around here in those jeans, it gives a man ideas. When I found you playing pool, I thought, I could lose my job for trying to put the moves on the boss's daughter. But I had to."

"Was it worth the risk?" she asked.

"Now why would you ask a question like that? You don't think you're worth a losing a job? Meleah, it's just a job we're talking about. I found this one. I could find another. But where was I going to find another you? Trust me, boss lady. It wasn't a hard decision to make."

Meleah grinned. Maybe Tarrant was laying it on a little thick. But she was enjoying every minute of it. That, alone, surprised her. The men who came to Papa Jack's all had a thousand lines, just like the one Tarrant just gave her. Each one varied on a single theme. They would do anything for one night with her.

The difference between those lines and Tarrant's declaration was the level of sincerity. He'd proven again and again that he cared for her—not just the temporary pleasure her body would bring him. If it were just about sex, she was sure that any one of those women hovering around him would do. It had to be about something more. She'd considered the idea that maybe it was about money. Yet that didn't ring completely true either. She'd felt this connection to him the moment he walked into Papa Jack's, long before Pops had won that lottery money. She couldn't get out of her mind the look that had passed between them the night he and his friends had come to celebrate. As much as she'd dismissed the group, he had stood out. He had remained in her thoughts.

"I can almost hear you thinking," Tarrant said. "What are you thinking about now?"

"I want to believe that you care," she whispered.

"I do," he insisted.

"Enough to say those very same words when and where it counts?" she questioned. It was a big gamble that she'd taken, to approach him so soon with thoughts of long-term commitment.

Tarrant paused, looking down at her. A slow smile spread across his face. "Are you asking me to marry you, boss lady?" He sounded shocked and pleased at the same time.

"You know, big guy, I think I am."

"You'd better be sure, Meleah. I don't take my commitments lightly."

"I am," she said, and laughed out loud. "I'm asking you to become Mr. Tarrant . . . uh . . . that is, I will be Mrs. Tarrant Cole. So what do you say?"

Tarrant grasped her face between the palms of his hands and replied, "I do."

"Then I will," she said solemnly. She took his hands and smoothed them over her—lower and lower.

Tarrant closed his eyes, allowing himself a moment to enjoy in reality what he had dreamed of all day. When she moaned aloud, it told him that she, too, was full of anticipation. Tarrant grasped her hips and pulled her to him. He needed to end the torturous wait that had kept him on edge all evening. He wanted nothing more than to plunge into her, and sheath himself in that warmth.

"Say that you want me, Meleah." Tarrant's voice was hoarse with desire.

"I do want you, Tarrant," she echoed. "All of you. I need to feel you. Please!" The urgency in her voice frightened her. She'd never needed anything so badly. Meleah had always prided herself that she'd never had to beg for anything in her life. The idea occurred to her that maybe she should feel ashamed for such a wanton display. Yet she couldn't help herself. She would do and say anything to have him quench the flame roaring inside of her. Greedily grasping with both hands, she guided him toward the source of her inner fire.

"Wait, sweetheart, wait!" Tarrant fought through the fog of passion to remember the reason why he'd made the trip to the men's room. She heard him fumbling for the thin, foil packet that he'd put into his pants pocket.

"Your timing leaves a lot to be desired," she teased him.

"Then let me see what I can do to get some of that old rhythm back," Tarrant returned. His back was to her for only a second before he took her into his arms again.

Meleah caught her lip between her teeth to still the

moans that rose from her throat. She clutched his shoulders, digging her nails into the firm, dark flesh.

"Please, Tarrant. Please!"

Meleah's plea for his touch filled his ears, and touched his heart.

"I love you, Meleah," he murmured as he came to her as eagerly as she accepted him.

FIFTEEN

"Ready to go?" Tarrant asked.

Meleah yawned and stretched languidly. "Do we have to?" she complained.

"No. We don't have to. We can stay here all night. You'll get no complaints from me. But you will have some explaining to do as to why you wore the same things two days in a row."

"What about you?" she asked, tossing his shirt back to him.

Tarrant grinned at her. "This is my uniform. No one is going to think twice."

"Well . . . maybe not about the clothes," she conceded. "But the lipstick stains from your mouth all the way down to your—" She emphasized her point by stroking a trail where the trail of kisses led.

"I get the point," he said, grasping her wrist to stop her from teasing him. He'd responded instantaneously to her touch. If he didn't do something, he imagined that Jack would send a search party after them. He buttoned his shirt, then placed his arm around her shoulder to guide her toward the door. Meleah entered the code that allowed them time to leave the building. In a few seconds, the motion sensors would activate.

"See you tomorrow?" he asked, brushing his lips

against the top of her hair as he walked her to her car.

"For someone who turned in his resignation notice, you sure are hanging around Papa Jack's a lot," she teased him.

Tarrant recognized that statement as her way of questioning just how long he intended to stay around. *Forever, Lord willing!* He raised his eyes to the star-filled sky to send up his wish. "I've got just as much right to hang around you as that cousin of yours," Tarrant said petulantly.

"Elliot? Now what made you bring him up?"

"No reason," Tarrant said quickly. He wished that he hadn't. As much as he wanted to share his feelings about that goldbrick with her, now wasn't the time. He was too filled with pleasant thoughts of her. Why ruin it with thoughts of Elliot? He didn't even know why the boy had come to his mind.

"What's going on between you two, Tarrant? Why all of the sudden animosity," Meleah wanted to know.

"Nothing sudden about it," Tarrant said, then shrugged his shoulders. "It's just not as hidden as before. I don't like the way he hangs around here all of the time."

"Tarrant!" Meleah laughed. "Are you jealous of my cousin?" It served him right, after he flirted with anything and everything moderately female all night long!

"Oh, come on. Give me a break. I'm not that petty . . . am I?"

"It sounds that way to me. When did you get so possessive?"

"Since I made you mine," Tarrant said seriously, squeezing her to him. "I can't help it if I'm a little jealous. I can't get a word in edgewise when he's around you."

"He wasn't around tonight," Meleah reminded him.

"And you see what we can accomplish when he's not around?"

"Accomplish? Like a task? Like something on a to-do list? Is that what you call what we did tonight?" She put on a mock expression of hurt.

"But you're on the top on my list, sweetheart. Or almost the top. When it comes to my closing duties at Papa Jack's, you fall somewhere in between emptying the ashtrays and checking the bathroom stalls for vagrants."

"I'm touched," she responded with a wry twist of her lips. When Tarrant leaned forward to kiss her, she twisted her head to the side, causing him to graze her ear instead.

"Okay, so I'll move you a little higher on the list if you kiss me again," he promised.

"No, that's not it." She sounded distracted, taking a step back toward the restaurant.

"What is it?" Tarrant turned in the direction of her gaze.

"I'm . . . I'm not sure. I think I saw someone inside."

"Inside the bar?"

"Yes. I thought I saw movement. It was just an impression. I can't be certain. Maybe it's my mind playing tricks on me. I'm still spooked about yesterday."

"There couldn't be anyone inside. The alarm would have gone off."

"Maybe I didn't set it right." Meleah was unsure of herself. "I was a little distracted at the time, you know. Some overzealous employee kept touching me. I guess he was trying to get himself fired again."

Tarrant gave her a half smile, though he wasn't entirely convinced. He'd seen Meleah enter that code several times. She didn't make mistakes like that, no matter how preoccupied she was.

"There it goes again," she said, trying to peer into the building. "I know I saw someone, Tarrant." She took another step away from him, her curiosity churning into fury. Pops had barely begun calling for security system estimates again when some lowlife decided to take advantage of the weakness of their current system. Well, she'd had enough. No more being a victim. This was her place! She was going to fight for it harder than she'd ever fought for anything in her life.

"Wait a minute!" Tarrant snapped, grasping her by the shoulder. "Where do you think you're going?"

"Inside," Meleah said, without a moment's hesitation.

"No, you aren't. You wait here, boss lady. I'll go."

"We'll both go," she countered.

Tarrant opened his mouth to argue, when something inside of Meleah's car caught his attention. "Neither of us will have to go." He gestured toward her cellular phone. "We'll call the police, and let them investigate."

"Whoever it is could be long gone by the time they get here," she complained.

"Good! Then no one will get hurt," he said, stabbing at the numbers 9-1-1.

"Tarrant, there's no time for this. There's no telling what the person's doing in there! What if the intruder's an arsonist? I won't stand here and let our dream go up in smoke."

"You can buy another dream, Meleah. You're rich enough."

"That's not the point! Pops put his entire adult life into this place. While we're standing here arguing, the intruder could be getting away!"

"Then let him go, Meleah! Damn it, woman! Who's going to replace you if you go in there and get yourself killed? I know you hate losing, boss lady. But geez, you're not backing out on this one."

"What do you mean, on this one? I'm not talking about a game."

"Neither am I. You said you'd marry me, Meleah Harmon. I'm not letting you out of this one. No last-minute clutch free throws. No playing with words about your salary. You're staying out here, safe with me, until the police get here. Let them handle it."

Meleah clenched her jaw stubbornly, then gave him a reluctant smile. "All right then. But you move around there where you can watch the back alley entrance. I'll stay up here."

"In the car, with the doors locked, and your fingers poised over the cell phone redial button," he insisted. He relayed their location and his suspicions to the operator and within ten minutes, a squad car pulled into the parking lot beside her.

"I think someone is still in there," Meleah said excitedly, leaping out of the car. "No one's left the building that we could see." She handed the officer the set of keys to Papa Jack's locks and gave her the security code to disarm the alarm.

As Tarrant joined her, Meleah murmured aloud, "I don't understand it."

"You don't understand what?" Tarrant asked.

"How anyone could be inside. We set the alarm. I locked the doors. How did they get in without triggering the alarm?"

"Could they have been inside when we left?"

"Then you didn't check the bathroom for vagrants?" She raised her eyebrows at him.

"I guess I had other things on my mind when I went into the rest room," he replied. He sobered, then asked, "Meleah, tell me again how many ways there are to get into the restaurant."

"Front and back door," she counted aloud. "Six emergency escape exits."

"And the windows?" he prompted.

Meleah shrugged. "Two large bay windows in the front. At least seven sets of two on either side of the building. I'm sure there are several windows in the kitchen and a few very high up in the rest rooms. Why do you ask?"

"Is it possible that not all of the entryways were hooked up to the alarm system when your cousin brought that guy through?"

Meleah shook her head. "Elliot assured me that his friend did a thorough job."

"Elliot again," Tarrant grumbled. "I know he's your cousin and all. But I don't think the boy knows what a real job is."

"Sure he does. He has to know how to recognize one because he has to know what to look for when he's avoiding them."

"That's not funny, Meleah," he said grimly.

She blew out a comic breath and when he didn't smile, she caressed his cheek. "Tarrant, I know my cousin isn't exactly an upstanding pillar of the community. He's lazy and shallow and when there's good gossip going around, he can get just as messy as the next person. But he's my family. He wouldn't do anything that would hurt me. Like he told us today, he's got my back."

When Tarrant didn't respond, she went on to say, "We've all got people in our family that are a little on the light side when it comes to morals."

"You don't have to rub it in," he said gruffly. "Amber's my cross to bear."

"So you know what I'm talking about."

"That still doesn't mean I have to like him."

"And I can't imagine Amber standing up at our wedding."

"She would probably balk at any bridesmaid dress that wasn't made of leather, anyway," Tarrant teased in turn.

When the officer returned, she found Tarrant and Meleah trying, without much success, to stifle their giggles.

"Anything, Officer?" Meleah cleared her throat and quickly composed her features.

"No sign of a break-in, ma'am. When I checked it out, everything seemed quiet."

Meleah didn't know whether to be relieved, annoyed, or embarrassed. "But I was sure I saw something moving around."

"Do you own a pet? I found a fresh traces of . . . well . . . pet waste in a corner of the pool room."

Tarrant and Meleah exchanged glances. "Whiskers," they said in unison.

"An old Manx cat," Meleah supplied. "It belongs to one of my employees." She muttered out of the corner of her mouth to Tarrant, "Remind me to have another heart-to-heart with Trae about that big stinky cat!" She directed her next comments to the police officer. "You think that's what I saw? Officer, the shadow I saw was much larger than a cat!"

"If there was someone in there, they're gone now. I could pass by a few more times on our patrol tonight to make sure that everything is all right."

"Thank you," Tarrant offered. "We'd appreciate that."

"Yes, thank you for stopping by. We're sorry to have bothered you," Meleah added. She waited until the patrol car was out of sight before letting out a cry of exasperation. "I know I saw something! And it wasn't Trae's cat either."

"But she didn't find anything," Tarrant insisted.

"That doesn't mean that there wasn't anything there. Tarrant, I want to go back in there. I want to see for myself."

"Meleah, why are you doing this? Why are you putting yourself in harm's way like this?"

"Ah-hah!" She stabbed a finger into his chest. "So you think there is someone there, too?"

"If you think you saw something, then maybe you did."

"I'm going in there, Tarrant. You can go home if you want. But I'm not leaving until I've satisfied myself."

Muttering under his breath, Tarrant grudgingly agreed to follow her. Meleah unlocked the door again and reached to deactivate the alarm. When she saw it had already been turned off, she turned flashing eyes to Tarrant. "Will you look at this?"

"What's the matter now?"

"I thought that patrolwoman told me she reactivated the alarm after she left. Evidently not. It's off again."

"Meleah," Tarrant whispered, his voice tight. "Did it ever occur to you that whoever has been roaming around in here knows the code?"

"But there's only three of us. Pops, me, and—"

"And who?" Tarrant pressed.

"And . . . and Charlotte," Meleah said, her voice quivering. "But I thought she left for the night. She and Pops left together. Pops! Charlotte? Are you still here?" Meleah called out.

Silence. Meleah and Tarrant exchanged glances. "They're not here," Meleah said confidently. "If they were, they would have shown themselves to the police."

"Unless they didn't want to be seen."

"Exactly what are you trying to say, Tarrant? Spit it out."

"I'm not accusing them of anything, boss lady." Tarrant noticed that he always called her that when Meleah was at her most demanding. "Maybe they didn't want to be found."

"Maybe you weren't the only one checking the bathroom for vagrants." Meleah chuckled and elbowed Tarrant. She tried to picture Jack and Charlotte scrambling for cover when they heard strange voices in the restaurant. As amusing as the idea was, it didn't satisfy her. Even if they had been caught in a compromising position, Jack wouldn't have stayed quiet—not in his place. He would have covered his embarrassment by becoming loud and boisterous, demanding to know why his tax dollars were spent harassing innocent civilians. Charlotte would have raised her voice to calm him down. If those two had remained in the restaurant when everyone else believed they were gone, Meleah would have known by now.

"You check the pool room. I'll sweep the kitchen." She headed for the kitchen.

"I don't think we should split up, boss lady."

"It's late, Tarrant. I don't want to argue with you. You want to get out of here sooner, don't you? We'll cover more ground this way."

"You're beginning to sound like those stupid kids in those slasher movies," Tarrant scoffed. "Strange noises in a dark place, police have gone and with them any weapons we could use against those things that go bump in the night, and the only two survivors split up. Yep. Definitely a script for a teen-scream movie."

"It was a dark and stormy night on the island," Meleah began in an ominous voice as she moved in exaggerated tiptoes away from him. Despite Tarrant's

misgivings, she was starting to feel better. With all of
the activity of the police and now them giving the restaurant a second check, an intruder would have been
long gone by now. She checked in the storeroom and,
as a last resort, her father's office.

Tarrant was opening the door to Meleah's office
when he heard her call out, "Tarrant!"

"Meleah? Are you all right?"

"I'm fine. Could you come here a moment, please?"

Tarrant found her standing in the doorway of Jack's
office. He peered over her shoulder. "What happened
here?"

"I wish I knew," Meleah returned. She stepped into
the office carefully, trying not to disturb any of the
scattered papers, books, and manila folders that had
been tossed around the room.

"Who could have done this, Tarrant? What on earth
is going on around here?"

"I don't know. But until we find out, don't touch
anything. I'm calling the police again. This time I want
them to do a more thorough search. Why didn't that
patrolwoman catch this before?"

"Because the door was locked. I only gave her the
key to the front doors. I had to use my master key to
open Pop's office. Don't call 9-1-1. I have Officer
Croft's number in my files somewhere. He's taken a
direct interest in this case. I think we should call him
instead."

"Come on." Tarrant took Meleah's arm and guided
her out of the room again.

"When I get my hands on the person who trashed
this room," Meleah said in warning. "I know they're
in here somewhere. You check the storeroom again
and I'll check upstairs."

"I really think we should let your police buddy handle this, Meleah." Tarrant's voice held a definite edge. This was not the time for her to play superwoman.

"If you think I'm going to sit by and let someone destroy our business piece by piece, you're out of your mind," Meleah snapped. "We've worked too hard and sacrificed too much to let some maniac take it away from us. Now the person who did this can't have gotten far. Are you going to help me or not?"

"I'm not leaving you alone," Tarrant said as he took her hand in his.

"I don't need a baby-sitter!" Meleah snapped, jerking away from him.

"What's the matter with you? I'm only trying to help."

"Your help could be costing us precious moments, Tarrant."

"So is your pigheaded, she-woman act, Meleah. Now come on!"

Meleah strode away from him. Her mouth was set in a rigid line of barely suppressed anger. She moved from room to room—flinging open doors and muttering curses as the search continued to turn up nothing.

"There's got to be a better way," she gritted. "Think, Meleah, think."

"Meleah, whoever it was is probably long gone by now."

"This alarm thing is driving me nuts. I would feel better if I knew for certain whether we had a faulty system instead of someone deliberately turning it on and off whenever it suited them. You still think it's someone we know?"

"The lure of money does strange things to people, Meleah. It could be anyone . . . anyone who has constant access to your family."

"Even you?" she challenged.

"Even me," he said, steadily meeting her hard gaze.

"I just want you to keep an open mind about the possibilities."

"I don't want to hear another word about it." Meleah's head then snapped up. Her gaze was focused on a far wall. "Come on!" she suddenly ordered.

"What the—" Tarrant began.

"Someone is trying to get out," Meleah said. "Someone who shouldn't be here." She dashed back to her office, took one look at the control security control panel on the wall, then shouted, "Upstairs, Tarrant! They're upstairs!"

"Meleah, wait! Where are you going?"

"I'm not letting them get away!" She dashed around him and headed for the stairs. Tarrant muttered a brief curse then followed after her.

"Will you wait up?" he bellowed.

Meleah didn't listen. She didn't want to hear him. All she knew was that someone causing trouble for her and Pops was probably still in the restaurant. She couldn't let them get away. She wouldn't!

The flashing light on the alarm control panel told her that a window upstairs had been opened. There was a balcony running along the top front of Papa Jack's. Maybe the intruder was hoping to shimmy down one of the support columns to get away.

When Meleah got to the head of the stairs, she gestured for Tarrant to take the billiards room at one end of the hall and she would take the other. If they were lucky, maybe they'd squeezed the intruder in between them.

"Meleah!" Tarrant protested. He didn't want to split up. If anything happened to her while they were separated, he would never forgive himself for letting her literally run over him.

"Go on!" Meleah urged. "I'll be all right. They're

trying to get out of one of the windows and out onto the balcony."

He nodded tightly and disappeared into one of the darkened rooms. Moving quickly, Meleah headed for the other room. She flung open the door and turned on the light switch. The room was empty. All the windows were closed. She tiptoed to one of the windows and checked the lock. There were only a few windows in the room. The third one she tried brought a cry of triumph from her. It was closed, but unlocked. She couldn't imagine that one of Papa Jack's staff would have simply forgotten to lock this one. She grasped the window sash and started to lift. On impulse, she grasped one of the cue sticks, then opened the window. The window was tall enough for her to step through without ducking too far. Meleah looked right, then left. Tarrant had already climbed out onto the balcony and was gesturing to her.

"Anything?" she called out. "Did you see anyone?"

"Nothing," Tarrant said.

"I didn't find much either, except this window was unlocked. They're here somewhere."

"The roof, maybe?"

She glanced up. The top of Papa Jack's was still several feet up. If someone did manage to climb up there, they must have had wings.

"This is ridiculous, Meleah. We need help. I'm going back in to call the police."

"Maybe you're right," Meleah said reluctantly. She turned to climb back through the way she'd come. Tarrant followed her lead. Being taller than Meleah, he had to duck to get back inside. He'd just poked his head inside when a movement out of the corner of his eye caught his attention. His brain was able to register only a slight, dark form moving toward him be-

fore an explosion of light and pain blocked out everything else.

He remembered thinking, *found our intruder,* before
the object of his thoughts grasped him by his arm and
pulled him inside.

Meleah was disgusted. She was sure she had the intruder this time. How could her hastily conceived plan
have gone wrong? The moment she realized that Pop's
office had been vandalized, she immediately changed
the code on the alarm system. No one was getting out
of Papa Jack's unless she gave the code to deactivate
the system. The more she thought about it, the more
she was sure that they should have caught the person
by now.

She didn't want to believe Tarrant's assertion that
the intruder was already gone. The alarm was activated
while she and Tarrant sat in her office. No one could
have gotten out. That meant . . .

"Oh no! Please, God, no!" Meleah prayed aloud.
That meant that the intruder had been here all along.
There was no telling when they got in—during the
normal business hours, probably. They hung around
until everyone left to make their move. Maybe they
didn't count on her and Tarrant staying as late as they
did. Maybe they didn't count on her thinking to
change the code so quickly.

"Tarrant?" she called from the hall. "I'm going to
make that call to the police now." She didn't wait for
a response from him. He would catch up to her as
soon as he'd finished with his search.

"Don't make that call, Meleah. If you do, it'll be the
last call you ever make."

Meleah spun around, surprised by the threat.

"If I don't call, the area will be swarming with po-lice."

"I don't think so. One false alarm is enough. They won't be so quick to answer a second time."

"I think you're wrong."

"We're not going to stick around here long enough to find out. Come on, Le-Le. Let's go."

"I'm not going anywhere with you," Meleah said raggedly.

"Don't make this harder than it is. I said, let's go."

"I won't go until I get some answers."

"Who do you think you're talking to, cuz? One of your restaurant flunkies? Or even lover-boy over there?" Elliot snapped. "I said move it!" His gaze flick-ered to his hand where he held a snub-nosed revolver. The butt of the gun was bloodied from the blow he'd delivered to Tarrant.

Meleah continued down the stairs, but threw a fur-tive glance back.

"If you're looking for lover-boy, don't bother. He's out like a light."

"What did you do to him?" Meleah gritted.

"Aw, cuz. Don't worry about the big guy. He's not dead. He's got a head like a rock. But you already know that, don't you? Seems like that's the way you like your heads. Nice and hard. Is that why you let him do you, cuz?"

"You've got a dirty mouth, Elliot," Meleah snapped.

"I'm just telling it like it is." Elliot shrugged.

"What I want to know is, why are you doing this? Why?"

"You should have listened to your lover-boy. Money is a powerful motivater."

"That doesn't make any sense. You have everything you ever wanted. You never had to want for anything, Ell."

"Wrong, sweet cousin. I want it all. I should have had it, too. All of this should have been mine."

"All of what?"

"Your life. Your respect. Your money. If Uncle Jack had only stayed with my mama, I could have been you. You don't know how many times I've sat and listened to Mama tell the stories about how it used to be between her and good ol' Uncle J. You know something, Le-Le? He hasn't changed a bit. He's still a randy old goat. I'll bet you a week's salary that what he's giving to Charlotte is just as much as he gave to my mother and yours."

"Don't you talk about my pops that way, Elliot. You shut your filthy mouth."

Elliot laughed harshly. "I'll bet you another week's salary that your mother jumped off that boat just to keep from having to do it again with Jack. The old man just doesn't know when to quit."

"I said shut up!" Meleah screeched at him.

"Sweet little Marian just couldn't handle it. But my mother could. She did. In fact, you were probably too young to notice how that long black hearse kept on a-rockin' long after the engine was turned off. That was good ol' Uncle Jack, being as generous with his lovin' as he is stingy with his money. Who knows, cuz. I could just as well be calling you sis. One little DNA test will prove it. You don't know how disappointed I was to learn that the lab screwed up those test results." He pulled aside his collar and showed her the scabbed-over claw marks.

Meleah clamped her hand over her mouth. Her stomach churned and threatened to come up through her mouth and nose. With eyes wide and haunted, she vigorously shook her head in denial. It was Elliot. All this time, he had sat next to her, laughed with her, listened to her secrets. He had been the one who'd hurt her the most. He'd attacked her in the storeroom.

"I . . . I don't understand." Meleah's voice faltered.

"No, I don't suppose you would, being a virgin and all. Oh . . . I forgot. You aren't a virgin anymore. You and the big guy had quite a time in there tonight. Maybe there's more Jack in you than I thought there was. Way to go, cuz!" Elliot gave her the thumbs-up sign.

Meleah felt an ocean of shame wash over her—not because of what she'd shared with Tarrant. She felt ashamed that someone she'd considered family and friend had turned what was beautiful into something cheap and meaningless.

"Why are doing this, Elliot? What do you want?"

"I'll tell you on the way."

"Where are we going?"

"In about six hours, the banks will be open. I want you to go to the bank and withdraw every cent your father owns."

"I can't do that!"

"You'd better find a way or I'll make sure that your precious pops never sees the light of day."

"Elliot, don't do this," Meleah pleaded.

"Shut up and get moving!" He shoved Meleah toward her office. "Get your keys. We're going for a drive."

"Where are we going?"

"Geez, you're a nosy heifer! I'll tell you everything you need to know in my own good time."

"Just tell me one thing, Ell," Meleah began.

"Move it! Quit stalling!"

Meleah glanced back upstairs. Elliot read the look as easily as if she'd spoken aloud.

"I cleaned big guy's clock too well. He won't be waking up soon to rush to your rescue."

"Was it you I saw that triggered the alarm the first time? Were you the one sending those threats to Pops?" Meleah asked over her shoulder.

"Nice touch, don't you think?"

"If you're looking for praises here, you're wasting your breath."

"Right now, Meleah, I don't care what you think about me."

"How did you get past the security alarms?"

"Simple. I disarmed them."

"How?" Meleah insisted.

"For all of your college education, you really are stupid. Why do you think they call me the hook-up man? You think I'd put up the rest of the fee for a security system and *not* find out how to disarm the thing? Why do you think it came so cheap for you? I put up the rest of the money." He laughed and gestured with the gun for Meleah to open the passenger side for him.

"Where did you get the money from, Ell? You don't work."

"I work very hard at convincing people I either have the money or know how to get it. That's where you come in, cuz. You're going to get my share, the security man's share, and hell . . . everybody's else share, too!"

After he climbed in, he gestured for Meleah to take the wheel. "Head for the marina."

Meleah gasped aloud. Were they going to hide out on a boat? She couldn't! She'd rather face her chances with a bullet than go out on the water!

Clenching the steering wheel as tightly as she clenched her teeth, Meleah pleaded, "Elliot, don't make me do this. Please, don't."

"I know. I know. You don't like the water. It can't be helped, Le-Le. It's the perfect holding place. Once

I've got you on the water, I know you'll be too terrified to try anything."

"Don't make me do this, Elliot. Nobody's been seriously hurt. We can still salvage something sane out of this, but only if you give up now."

"I'm not giving up! Do you hear me? I'm not. Now start driving."

With trembling fingers, Meleah tried to put the key in the ignition. It took three tries before she could hold her hands steady enough. As she pulled out of the parking lot, Meleah glanced up through the windshield. She thought she saw a silhouette in one of the windows. It was Tarrant!

Help me, Tarrant, she pleaded silently. *Help me!*

She tried to drive slowly, to give Tarrant a chance to get as much information about their direction as possible.

"I said, quit stalling!" Elliot delivered a stinging, backhanded slap to Meleah's face.

Tears of frustration and anger welled up in Meleah's eyes. "Touch me again, and I swear—"

"You'll do what?" he sneered. "You won't do a thing, little girl. I'm holding all the cards."

"Why?" she managed to choke out.

"Why?" Elliot mimicked her, twisting his face into a cruel rendition of the smiles he'd often given to her. "I told you why. I want to get what rightfully belongs to me. I'm taking back what should have been given freely to my mother."

"Pops didn't take anything from Aunt Hannah."

"Didn't he? How do you think he managed to get Papa Jack's off the ground, Meleah?"

"The same way he ever got anything—through faith and hard work."

"You stupid little slut. Jack never earned anything a

day in his life. It was Marian's money that started that pitiful grease pit you call a restaurant."

"My mother's money?"

"Blood money. Insurance money. Jack collected big time on the insurance policy on her."

"Are you trying to say that Pops killed my mother for the money?"

"I wish it were as simple as that. My mother would have had him put away a long time ago. But if she'd had him locked him up, I wouldn't be here today . . . or maybe I would have been with conjugal visits. It doesn't matter. I'm here now. What my family couldn't get out of the insurance money, we'll get out of the lottery money. It's a long time coming, but money, un-like former virgins, keeps its freshness. No, your father didn't kill her, not directly. But Mama told me that Marian loved you both so much. She didn't want to see you poor and struggling all of your days. So she went out on that boat knowing that it would capsize."

"You don't know that. Is that what Aunt Hannah told you? Are those the lies she's been cramming in your pointy little head?"

"They aren't lies!" Elliot said raggedly. "You don't remember what kind of mother Marian was, but my mother did. They were sisters, for God's sake. It's not too hard to believe that she would take her own life. That's the kind of woman Marian was, so loving, so unselfish. The night before she died, she was desper-ate. Your father was broke. He'd sunk every dime they had into a rundown money pit. She couldn't see her way clear, Meleah. Before she died, she called my mother, frantic with worry. There were so many bills. To hear my mother talk, if you'd heard Marian, you'd know that by the time she'd hung up the phone, she'd made up her mind. She didn't say it out loud and she didn't leave a note, but she took her own life just the same."

"You must think I'm stupid," Meleah sneered. "I don't believe that. And you know what, Elliot? I don't think you believe that either. You're just looking for a convenient excuse to take something you didn't work for. Same ol' Elliot."

Elliot started to laugh—an eerie, disturbed laugh that chilled Meleah to her very soul. "Okay, so I made some of it up. How much? It doesn't matter. The only truth you need to know is Marian was my mother's sister. Jack didn't deserve to do what he did to either one of them. Just like he didn't deserve to win that lottery."

"Just who in the hell are you to decide who deserves what?" Meleah flared.

"Why, my dear trash-mouth Meleah, I'm the one with the gun."

Meleah's mouth clamped shut. Elliot was right on that count. As long as he had the gun, he made all the rules.

"What happens when you get your money, Ell? Will you let me go?"

"You don't have to be afraid of me, Meleah. I won't hurt you. Remember, I got your back."

"Then put away that gun."

"Nice try, but I don't think I will. As long as I have it, you'll be less inclined to try something stupid."

"I won't try to run away."

"I'd like to believe you, Meleah. Really, I would. But I've gone to far too stop now. We'll just keep on like this. Before you know it, it will all be over and you can go back to your life as if nothing had ever happened."

"I wouldn't call robbery, assault, and kidnapping nothing."

"It's all a matter of perspective, cuz. Now keep your eyes on the road. We're coming up on our turn-off."

Again Meleah's hands clenched. Elliot intended to take her out on the water. She could hear the surf pounding against the rocky piers as she took the turn Elliot indicated.

The pounding in Tarrant's head wouldn't go away. He rubbed the back of his neck where the intruder had struck him and cursed his own clumsiness. He should have paid closer attention to what he was doing. Meleah told him that the intruder couldn't have gotten out. He should have trusted her instincts.

"I'm sorry, Meleah," he muttered. Suddenly her memory came crashing back to him, driving out the dull ache in his head. The pain in his heart, however, was harder to push aside.

Meleah! Where was she?

"Meleah?" He stumbled to his feet and headed for the hall. The sound of a car engine from Papa Jack's parking lot pulled him away from the door. He lurched toward the window. He peered out just in time to see Meleah's car pulling away. "No! Meleah, no!"

He couldn't see much, but he could see that she wasn't alone. She wouldn't have left him if she knew he'd been hurt. Whoever it was that hit him must have made her go.

"You hurt her and I swear I'll hunt you down!" Tarrant vowed. "You hear me? Don't you hurt her!" He pounded on the glass, making it rattle beneath his fist. He watched the car pull from sight. What could he have done to prevent this? If anything happened to her, it would be his fault!

"Go after her, you numbskull!" he then berated himself. Why was he standing there? He spun around, with every intention of getting into his truck and chasing them down. With the new set of tires and the engine literally ready to spit fire, he could catch up to them. But as he turned, the room seemed to spin out of control before his eyes. He felt a sudden wave of nausea grip him. Tarrant gritted his teeth, trying to fight the sensation. Disoriented, he wondered if there was another intruder in the room. The next, sudden blow to his face took up where the first intruder left off. Tarrant saw the floor rushing up to greet him as he slammed into it face first.

"Tarrant, wake up, son. Wake up!"

Tarrant opened his eyes just in time to see a river of water gushing toward him. He grunted, and tried to roll away.

"Take it easy, son. Take it easy now." Jack was kneeling beside him, helping him to sit up. "Are you all right?"

"I'm fine, I'm fine! Don't worry about me. Where's Meleah?"

"She's not here," Jack told him. "I was hoping you could tell me."

"Someone took her! We've got to go after them."

"I can put out an APB, an all-points bulletin alert for her, Mr. Cole. But we need you to tell us everything that happened last night when you were attacked."

Tarrant tried to focus his eyes. The blur before him that was asking him questions was Officer Croft.

"How long have I been out?" Tarrant looked around frantically. Pale sunlight was now streaming through the windows.

"I don't know. It's seven in the morning now," Jack told him. "What on earth happened here, Tarrant?"

"I wish I knew. One moment, I was waiting for Meleah to finish her paperwork, and the next we were chasing after someone who triggered the alarm. Meleah thought they might try to leave by one of the upstairs windows. She went one way and I went the other."

When Croft made a derisive comment, Tarrant became defensive. "I told her we shouldn't split up. She wouldn't listen to me."

"That sounds like Meleah, all right. Once she gets it in her head to do something, there's no stopping her," Jack agreed. "I swear, I think that girl is part mule."

"We searched the upstairs, but we didn't find anything. Meleah thought they might try to shinny down the balcony, so we looked out there. I was on my way back inside when someone clubbed me. The next thing I know, Meleah is driving off in her car. Someone was with her. I'm sure of it. I tried to go after them, but—" Tarrant grabbed his head again. The throbbing was making it difficult to think. Every sound reverberated in his brain.

"Don't worry, Mr. Cole. We can get every available unit out looking for her. Is there anything you can tell me about your attacker?"

"I told you, someone hit me from behind. They got me when I stuck my head in the window and . . . and . . . cologne."

"What?" Jack said in confusion. Maybe Tarrant's brains were scrambled more than he cared to admit.

"I thought I smelled cologne," Tarrant explained. "Cheap. It stank like yesterday's fish haul."

"Maybe it was the same person who attacked Ms. Harmon," Croft suggested.

"Why would he come back here?"

"If we knew what the motive was in the first place, we'd know why."

"Have you seen your office, Jack? It's been ransacked. Someone was looking for something."

"If I had to make a guess, I'd say it was that note, Mr. Harmon," Officer Croft offered. "When you left my office, did you tell anyone about the note?"

"Just everybody in the whole freakin' world," Jack muttered. "All of my employees know about those notes by now. But they wouldn't be involved in this."

"That's what Meleah thought. But someone knew the access codes to get in and out of Papa Jack's," Tarrant insisted.

"I know Charlotte didn't have anything to do with this. I can vouch for her."

"Until I know what happened to Meleah, I'm not trusting anybody!" Tarrant retorted.

"I'm telling you that Charlotte wouldn't hurt Meleah. You have to take my word for that."

"What makes you so certain, Mr. Harmon," Croft wanted to know.

Jack squirmed uncomfortably and said in chagrin, "I was with Charlotte until about four in the morning. Then I drove home."

"You didn't get worried when Ms. Harmon didn't show up at home?"

"No . . . not exactly," Jack admitted slowly. "I knew that she and Tarrant were . . . uh . . . working late at the restaurant, so I didn't think much about it. When she didn't show up by six, I thought I'd better swing by here. If she wasn't here, I was going to call your house, Tarrant."

"Someone took her. I'm not sure what time. It was late. Really late. When we were heading out, we thought we saw someone so we called the police. The time should be on the incident report. I'm surprised that her abductor hasn't tried to contact us. Not even a ransom note. If this was a kidnapping for money, wouldn't we have heard something by now?"

"I'll call in a team to have your lines monitored. If they do try to contact you, we may be able to get to them before we have to go through the rigamarole of a ransom drop."

Jack began to pace. "All of this money has brought us nothing but misery. I wish I'd never won that cursed money. Do what you have to, Officer Croft. Take every cent I own. I don't care about the money. I just want my daughter back."

"If they haven't asked for a ransom, Jack, maybe this isn't about money," Tarrant began.

"Of course it's about money. Isn't it always?"

"Not always. Sometimes it's about something more complicated."

"Do you even know what you're talking about?" Jack demanded.

Tarrant took a deep breath. He stood up, a little wobbly at first, then with growing confidence as he headed for the door.

"Where are you going?" Jack started to follow.

"Wait here," Tarrant indicated. "Maybe someone will call."

"I asked you where you are going, Tarrant."

"To check out a complication," Tarrant said, over his shoulder, and left Jack with the officer.

Croft waited until Tarrant was out of the room before saying, "Do you want me to put a tail on him, Mr. Harmon?"

Jack considered the option. He liked Tarrant. He had liked him from the very beginning—enough to give him a job without really checking out his references. He had invited him to his home, and encouraged him to stay close to Meleah—all because he was certain that Meleah like him, too. With Meleah's safety at stake, however, the question Jack really wrestled with was how much did he *trust* Tarrant?

Tarrant jumped into his truck and gunned the engine. He wasn't thinking about fine tuning or sputtering or making sure he didn't blow a gasket when he peeled out of the parking lot. The only thing he had on his mind was finding Meleah. As he drove, more on autopilot than with actual concentration, his mind raced ahead of his engine. He ate up the roads, wondering what more he could have done to stop Meleah's abduction. The closer he got to his destination, the deeper he felt a pang of conscience stab him. He was playing on a hunch now. If it panned out, he knew exactly what he could have done to stop this.

When he first realized that he had feelings for Meleah, he should have come clean about his reasons for hiring on at Papa Jack's. He should have told his family that he couldn't go through with it. He had told himself—but even then he had been playing both ends against each other. As long as no one knew exactly what he was doing, he could play it safe. And now, because he had played his cards so close to his chest, the one dearest to his heart was in danger.

So many "should have's" and "if only he hads." They kept roaring through his brain, pointing out at every opportunity how he had failed Meleah. He should have listened to his instincts. He should have stayed with her, no matter how much she protested. What could he have been thinking?

His fingers clenched on the steering wheel. "Hang on, Meleah," he muttered aloud. He glanced toward the sky and prayed to the powers that be. *Please! Please let her be all right.*

Tarrant peeled into the visitors' parking lot and shut

off the engine before he'd come to a full stop. The engine groaned and sputtered in protest, but he didn't care. He strode through the front doors, unmindful of the strange looks that the occupants of the intensive care ward gave him as he headed for his sister's room. As he approached Amber's door, he thought he heard voices—female voices.

Tarrant's heart froze. Could it be? Was she here? Part of him hoped that she was here. He knew then that she would be safe. But that hope was tainted with regret. If she was here, that meant that his hunch had played out. That meant that Amber had gotten tired of waiting for results from him, and had acted on her own. Maybe she suspected that he didn't intend to go through with their plan of vengeance. If that were so, he imagined that she would be mad enough to try something.

When Tarrant flung open the door, he found Amber lying propped up in bed. The television was blaring because the remote control had slipped under her head. Her cheek was pressed against the volume button.

"Amber," Tarrant said loudly, over the television. "Amber, wake up! Wake up right now."

"Hey, big bro," Amber said through a yawn. "What's goin' on? What are you doing here? It's not visiting hours."

"Stuff your visiting hours," Tarrant said curtly, not quite willing to believe that she didn't know what was going on.

"What's wrong?" Amber picked up on the strain in his voice immediately. She then saw the thin line of dried blood that ran from his scalp to his collar. "Oh, my God, Tarrant! What happened?"

"You'd better not be playing stupid with me, Amber."

"What are you talking about? Tarrant, what happened to you? Were you robbed?"

"You could say that."

"Are you just going to stand there, or are you going to tell me what happened?"

"Somebody took her, Amber."

"Took her? Took who? Who are you talking about?"

"You know who I'm talking about! Who have we been talking about since your accident! Who have we been trying to get to?" Tarrant said sarcastically.

"You mean Meleah Harmon? Somebody snatched her?"

"Yeah," Tarrant said again.

"Did you call the police?"

"They're out looking for her now."

"Then what are you doing here? Why aren't you out looking for her, too?"

When Tarrant said nothing, the light of understanding and indignation flared in Amber's eyes. "Now hold on a minute, Rant. You think I had something to do with that girl's disappearing?"

"Did you?" he asked tightly.

"No! Of course not! How could you ask me something like that? I can't believe you'd turn on me like that, Rant. Not your own sister."

"I'm running out of ideas, Amber."

"So you turn on your sister?"

"It's not too much of a stretch, Amber. You hate Meleah, don't you?"

"I don't care for the woman. You know that. But I want the money, big brother, not her."

Tarrant couldn't get out of his mind the thought of his sister calling on her lowlife friends to snatch Meleah. As soon as she mentioned money, it wouldn't take much to make more of them crawl out of the woodwork. Jack was worth millions now. All she had to do was promise them a couple of thousand. "Maybe you thought this was the best way to get it."

"You make another crack like that again, and I'll bust you over the head myself!" Amber threatened.

Tarrant sank wearily into the guest chair next to her bed.

"I wish to God you did have her, Amber. I don't know where else to look."

"This island isn't that big, Tarrant. If she's here, the police will find her."

"What if they've already done something to her? What if they've dumped her body in the Gulf? What if they've already left the island with her? They knocked me out. I don't know how much of a head start they have on me."

"Will you get ahold of yourself? Nothing is going to happen to her. She'll be all right."

"What makes you so certain?" Tarrant demanded. Again his suspicions rose to the surface. "Amber, that woman means more to me than—"

"Than your own sister?" Amber whispered painfully.

Tarrant shook his head. "Don't make me choose between the two of you."

"You've already chosen, big brother. I think I lost you a long time ago." Her eyes filled with genuine tears.

Tarrant's heart hardened against her. "Don't play me, Amber. I've had enough of your hysterics. You've had more than enough time to set this up. I swear, if you know something, and you aren't telling me—"

"I don't know where she is. I don't know what happened to her," Amber said through clenched teeth. "But I have to have faith that she'll be okay. Just like you've got to have faith."

Tarrant looked at her in surprise. "Faith? When did you get so spiritual?"

"When my own little girl wouldn't look at me. My own flesh and blood hates me."

"Squeak doesn't hate you," Tarrant said in exasperation.

"Don't give me that. She wishes I were dead."

"How can you say that?"

"Because she told me, Rant. Don't you see. She doesn't love me. She doesn't trust me. She's blaming me for her misery just like you're blaming me. But you know what? I don't blame you. And I don't blame her. Meleah, I mean. Just because I wanted the girl's money, doesn't mean that I wanted something to happen to her. How could I? She's the first woman I believed made you think about settling down. You do love her, don't you, Tarrant?"

Wordlessly he nodded once.

"That's all I need to know. Now tell me everything. From the time you went to work, to the time you realized she was missing."

Tarrant went through each detail as much as he could remember. He had to restrain himself more than once, to keep from bolting to the door. He felt so frustrated, so helpless. Again and again, he reproached himself for letting her get away.

"Oh, man, you've got it bad," Amber commiserated. "But I guess I already knew that. I knew it from day one."

"How could you know, when I didn't?"

"I knew then that you probably wouldn't go through with it. You couldn't do anything to hurt her. You were already falling in love with her."

"Amber, you know I wanted to get restitution as much as you did."

"Maybe at first you did. Then you kept doing things to show me that you were backing out. You kept changing your work schedule so that you'd be there while she was there."

"But she's always there."

"And you weren't? Tarrant, you were there morning and night. And don't try to tell me it was because Papa Jack's was getting so much business. Nobody works that hard. You were there for her sake. Admit it.' "'

"I wasn't there when she needed me."

"Yeah, you are, big brother. You're with her, even if she doesn't know it."

"That's not enough, Amber," Tarrant said, slamming his fist into his palm. The sudden, explosive declaration startled Amber.

"So what are you going to do about it?" Amber challenged.

Tarrant stood up. His face was dark and resolute. "What am I going to do about it?" he asked in a voice so chilling that Amber feared for the abductor. "I'll tell you what I'm going to do about it. I'm going to find her."

SIXTEEN

"I hope you find everything to your liking," Elliot said, bending over Meleah to tighten her restraints.

Meleah looked up at him, her eyes blazing. "If you untie me now, Elliot, I promise I'll knock you out before skinning you alive. You'll hardly feel a thing."

"That's very gracious of you, Le-Le, but I think I'll just keep you tied up a little while longer. In another couple of hours, the bank will be open. You make the withdrawal for me, and I'll be on my way. No harm, no foul. Isn't that what you sports people say to each other to make up for hurting someone?"

Meleah shook her head uncomprehendingly. Had her cousin lost his mind?

"It'll never work, Elliot. The police will be all over the bank. What makes you think that they'll let us waltz in there and waltz out with all of that money."

"I'm not going anywhere. You are."

"You're letting me go in by myself?"

"Don't get your hopes up. You're not going to get away before you do what I want."

"What makes you think I won't try to run? I know you don't expect me to cross my heart and promise to behave."

"The threat of death is a powerful motivater, Meleah. The very thought of it can make a person change their ways."

"What are you talking about?"

"I'm talking about your father, Meleah. Or Charlotte. Or even Tarrant. Or all of your customers."

Meleah remained silent, waiting for him to go on. "Then what?"

"What do you think this is? A low-budget movie or a children's cartoon? I'm not telling you everything. I've already said too much."

"What are you going to do to them?" Meleah pressed. "Get one of your hook-up friends to torch Papa Jack's? A drive-by?"

"None of your business. Now you be a good little tramp. Do as you're told and everything will be co-pacetic."

"What do you want me to do?" Meleah said, trying to sound subdued.

"That's better, cuz!" Elliot said brightly. "I don't believe you for one minute, but at least it's a start. See this piece of paper, Meleah?" He then waved a small slip of paper in front of her.

"So?"

"This is the number to a nice, little nest-egg account that I've set up. All you have to do is transfer a few of your funds into my account. No worrying about messy bags of marked paper money or exploding dye packs. That's so old and cliché. We wouldn't want your little arms to get tired before you've had a chance to hug your dear old daddy. The good robberies are all done online now."

"I'm telling you that it won't work. They'll freeze your account quicker than you can think, Ell. Can't you see that it won't work?"

"Give a little credit to the information superhighway. I've got so many accounts buried within accounts, shielded by encrypted accounts that it'll take a super-hacker to figure out where the money has gone. Before they get a clue, I'll be long gone."

Meleah shook her head. "It's not that simple. That same information superhighway can turn this planet into the closeness of a backyard barbecue. They'll find you. As soon as I make a transfer that huge, bank computer security—"

"Don't bother telling me about security programs. My hacker friends write and rewrite the books on computer security programs. Hell, forget the computer books. They crank out lines of code that run the banking systems in their sleep."

"What kind of sicko would agree to helping you steal someone's hard-earned money?"

"Jack didn't earn that money, Meleah. He won the lottery. He gambled, and that's what put him on easy street."

"My father paid his dues, Elliot. Every penny he spent trying to make a better life for us, he earned. He won because he deserved to win. And now you're trying to take it away from him. You make me sick."

"You think I care what you think about me? I don't. All I care about is the money, Meleah. If you were smart, you'd realize that's what anybody cares about. All of your sudden popularity with men has got absolutely nothing to do with you. Green is your color, little girl."

Meleah shook her head, trying to deny Elliot's statement. Yet in the back of her mind, she started to doubt herself. Tarrant was so attentive, so caring. Was it because of the money?

Elliot glanced at his Rolex. "Not long now, little girl. I've got a few more things to check on before we head out. You just sit tight, and be a good little millionairess, and I promise not to gag you. Promise me you won't scream? Because if you do, I'll have to knock you senseless."

"And risk me not waking up in time to go to the bank?" Meleah challenged.

"I can keep you here as long as I need to, cuz. If I knock you into next week, that means that much interest to collect."

"They're going to find you, Elliot."

"Maybe they will. But if you want them to find you alive and well, and not floating in the Gulf as food for the jellyfish, then behave yourself."

He checked Meleah's bonds once more. Satisfied that they would hold, he closed the door behind him, and headed for the upper deck.

Meleah strained against her ropes, trying to take advantage of any weaknesses. The bonds cut into her wrists, making her wince with pain. "I can't believe this is happening to me," she muttered. "This can't be happening to me. This is a bad dream. Come on, Meleah! Wake up!" She strained against the ropes once more, then settled back against the pole. There was nothing more she could do.

"Is that all you're going to do?" Amber said, staring meaningfully at Tarrant.

"What do you mean, is that all?"

"When you find her, are you going to sweep her off of her feet and declare your undying love?"

"Don't play with me, Amber. I'm not in the mood for it," Tarrant warned.

"I'm sorry. I didn't mean it. How are you going to find her? You don't even know who took her."

"First, I'm going back to Papa Jack's. Whoever was there was there for a while. Maybe they left something behind. A clue or something. Anything!"

"You used to be that passionate, that committed to me, Rant. What happened? What did I do to lose you?"

"You didn't lose me, Amber. You're my sister. I'll always love you."

"Maybe I didn't put that the way I meant to. What I wanted to say was, when this entire mess started, you would have moved heaven and earth to get the evidence I needed to use against the Harmons. And now . . . now . . ." Amber's voice cracked, but she went on. "Now you'll move heaven and earth to find her. Don't get me wrong, Tarrant. If she's the one that you want, then that's the way it should be. And because you're my brother, and I want the best for you. I can't undo everything that I've done to you. But I can support you now. You've got to keep the faith, big brother."

"How can I have faith? I don't deserve to expect that my prayers will be answered. I've broken almost every commandment there is. I've lied, lusted, coveted, and threatened to kill."

"Give yourself a break, Tarrant. You were only trying to help me."

"And look where that got Meleah."

"If you won't give yourself a break, give me one. I mean, I know you and the girl had a thing going, but—"

"You don't get it, do you, Amber? I love Meleah. I love her. And as soon as I get her back, I'm going to tell her. I'm going to take her away from here."

"You mean away from me."

"I didn't say that," Tarrant said defensively. "Stop putting words in my mouth."

"You stop trying to put one over on me. You're blaming me for what happened to Meleah. I had nothing to do with that, Tarrant. Nothing!"

"I believe you, Amber."

"Yeah, you believe me now. Or do you? You were

quick to think that maybe if I couldn't get my revenge one way, I'd get it another. I'm not like that, Tarrant. I'm your sister, for God's sake! You should know that."

"All I know is that I want her back, and I want her back safe. I'm not blaming you for anything. I'm blaming myself. I've handled this all wrong from the start."

"Maybe the idea wasn't such a good one, after all. Maybe we should have just taken our chances, and taken them to court from the start. But think. If it's any consolation to you, if I hadn't pushed you into trying to keep that bartender's job, you would have never gotten to know Meleah Harmon like you know her now."

Tarrant smiled despite himself. "Yeah, you're right."

"All right then. Go find that girl so you can stop being so grouchy. Man, you're getting on my nerves." Amber had smiled when she said it, but inside, her nerves were stretched tight. She'd been completely honest with Tarrant when she said she had nothing to do with Meleah's disappearance. But that didn't stop her from secretly gloating that something *had* happened to her.

How she hated Meleah Harmon! She had all of the breaks—good looks, wealth, friends. Most of all, Amber hated her because she had taken her only true friend away from her. Tarrant was her confidant, her consoler. Even after the accident, Tarrant had stuck by her. He had believed in her. To help her gather proof against that greedy, irresponsible Jack Harmon, and his entire establishment, Tarrant had given up his job, his true love. He had given up his car restoration business. He had set it aside to work for a pittance at the bar. Amber had wanted help, but she didn't think he'd go that far! Amber knew that he did it for her. He would do anything for his baby sister.

That is, he used to do anything for her. She was

used to being first in his thoughts. Not anymore. She knew that Meleah Harmon was the first name on his lips in the morning, and in his prayers at night, she was the last name on his lips in the evening.

"Go to her, Rant," Amber insisted. "Go find your woman."

Tarrant didn't bother saying good bye before leaving. For the first time since he was a young boy, his mind wasn't on pleasing his sister. He was out of his mind with worry. As he drove back to Papa Jack's, his hands clenched the steering wheel so tightly, his nails cut into the palms of his flesh. The muscles in his shoulders were bunched tight. A nervous tic appeared in his cheek. His jaws were clenched so tight, his teeth ground in frustration.

"Come on, come on! Get out of the way!" Tarrant blew his horn to clear the road in front of him.

When he nearly blew through a red light, Tarrant slammed his foot on the brakes, causing the cars behind him to come to an abrupt halt.

"Sorry," Tarrant muttered, and glanced up in the rearview mirror to check for any damage to the vehicles behind him. Suddenly his eyes narrowed suspiciously. It seemed to him that this same car had nearly slammed into him the last time he braked abruptly. Was it a coincidence that this same car would be trailing him for several miles? He wasn't sure, but he thought he recognized the driver. It looked like the officer who was supposed to be investigating Meleah's attack.

He waved to the car to show that he knew who it was, and what he was doing. By the time he pulled into the parking lot, Officer Croft was making no attempt to hide himself. He pulled alongside Tarrant.

"Find out what you wanted to know?" Tarrant demanded as Croft pulled up alongside him. The man didn't even have the decency to pretend that he had been following him, instead of following up on any leads about Meleah's disappearance.

"I think you can drop the attitude, Mr. Cole. If you care about Ms. Harmon like you seem to, you'd think that I'd get some gratitude for doing my job."

Tarrant did think about it, and realized that the officer was doing his best to be thorough. The fact remained that Meleah was out there.

"Any word?" Tarrant asked.

"No, sir. Not yet."

When Tarrant cursed in frustration, Croft asked, "Have you had that head looked at? That's a nasty bump you took."

"I'll be all right."

"Come on inside, Mr. Cole. You need that bump looked at. It'll do you no good to pass out from blood loss. I need you with your full wits about you."

Once they were inside, they were set on by an anxious Jack and Charlotte.

"Anything?"

"Is there any word?"

"What did you find out?"

Questions flew from every direction. When Tarrant's voice cracked with negative responses, Charlotte went straight into Tarrant's arms, and gave him a comforting hug.

"You poor sugar!" she murmured. "Are you all right?"

"I'm all right, Charlotte. How can you think about me when Meleah's out there somewhere?"

Charlotte took his face between her warm hands, and smoothed over his face. "She is going to all right, Tarrant. We have to have faith."

"You sound like my sister, Amber."

"Then maybe you should listen to her."

Tarrant made a derisive sound. If he hadn't listened to her, maybe Meleah wouldn't be in this mess.

"I guess Jack told you everything that happened."

"Uh-huh," Charlotte said with a nod. "You must be exhausted. Come on over here, sugar. Let me fix you something to eat."

"Nothing for me, Charlotte. I don't think I can keep anything down."

"A little ginger ale will settle your stomach." She squeezed him close to her again, before pulling away.

Again Tarrant felt a pang of conscience. He didn't think he deserved to be treated so kindly. If they only knew what he'd tried to do! He wanted to scream, *Stop being so nice to me! I don't want you to be nice to me.* Instead he hung his head and mumbled, "Thanks, Charlotte."

"Don't mention it, sugar. Just park your buns on that stool over there, and don't you move until you're feeling better."

She returned moments later, carrying a large glass of ginger ale. "There now, drink it all down," Charlotte soothed, handing Tarrant a glass.

He took it, and raised his glass to her in a toast. In doing so, he caught her reflection in the glass. Tarrant froze, not quite sure why he hadn't started his drink.

"Tarrant?" Charlotte noted his hesitation, and touched him briefly on the arm. "Are you all right? Why are you just standing there?"

"I don't know." His voice trailed off. "I thought I . . ."

"Maybe that knock on your head is making you loopy, sugar," Charlotte suggested.

"Maybe so," Tarrant said wryly. "For a moment, I almost thought I remembered something."

"Something? You mean about who attacked you and Ms. Harmon last night?"

Jack's ears perked up.

"Maybe," Tarrant said, then shook his head. "It's gone now." In frustration, he slammed the glass down on the counter.

"Don't push it, Tarrant. You'll only make it worse," Charlotte soothed.

"Why can't I remember?"

"Because your brains were scrambled, sugar!" Charlotte said. "Nobody expects you to remember anything after a blow like that."

"I've had my head twisted around worse than this before," Tarrant said wryly. It was hard trying to please so many people at once. For the past several weeks, he'd tried to be investigator, bartender, and lover. He had been doing a pretty good job of keeping his duties clear, his mission focused. The night of Jack's pool party, however, was where he seemed to lose his composure. Trying to watch Meleah all night, gather evidence for his sister, and be a bartender for one of the wildest parties he had ever attended had his head literally spinning in circles.

Tarrant swore to himself again as Charlotte refilled his ginger ale. "You're going to tie your stomach in knots again. Now stop talking, and drink."

In mock submission, Tarrant raised his glass to his lips. This time a memory did come back to him. It came back sharp and strong! A long, slow smile lit up his face.

"I've got you," he said aloud.

"What did you say?" Charlotte asked.

Carefully, deliberately, Tarrant set his glass on the counter again. He walked over to Jack and Officer Croft.

"Jack, can I speak with you for a moment?" His tone clearly said that he didn't want a third party involved.

"I'll see if there's any news about Ms. Harmon, sir," the officer said, moving away.

Jack ushered Tarrant into his office and said, "What's on your mind, son?"

"Maybe Charlotte is right about my brains being scrambled, but I think I know who might have Meleah."

"Are you remembering something about last night?"

"Not so much about last night, but at your pool party."

"What has that got to do with tonight?"

"I don't know. Maybe you can tell me."

"You'd better start making some sense, Tarrant. I'm in no mood for games."

Tarrant paused, took a deep breath. "And I'm not the type to play them, Jack."

"If you've got something on your mind, say it."

"Don't take offense at what I'm about to say, Jack, but how well do you know Hannah Caudle?"

"Hannah Caudle? She's been my friend for over twenty years. She's my wife's sister. I guess I know her as well as anyone."

"I don't think you know her as well as you think you do. I think she's got Meleah."

"Boy, now you really are grasping at thin air. She wouldn't hurt Meleah."

"You wife's been dead for a long time. But you kept up the friendship with her?"

"It would be closer to the truth to say that I kept the friendship with her husband Bill. But that didn't mean I barred the door if she ever came by."

"How often did she come by your home? Your restaurant?"

"Why are you asking these questions, Tarrant? What are you getting at?"

"The night of the party, Hannah, like everybody else, had a little too much to drink. She said some things."

"What kind of things?" Jack asked suspiciously.

"Mostly about Meleah, and how much she was like your wife."

"And?"

"And how much she missed Mrs. Harmon," Tarrant continued.

"And?!" Jack was getting impatient.

"Jack, don't get me wrong, but from the conversation we had, it seemed more like a gripe session. I'd be willing to swear that Hannah hated you."

Jack sat down weakly in his seat. "But why? What did I ever do to her? I've never been anything but a good friend to her and her husband. I know she was a little ticked when I chose Marian over her, but after all of this time, she should be over that. Tell me what she said. Tell me exactly, Tarrant. Don't sugar coat it."

"She said you were a lucky bastard," Tarrant began uneasily.

Jack gave a snort of derision. "Is that all? I've been called worse than that, son. I've called myself worse."

"It's not so much what she said, as much as how she said it," Tarrant insisted. "If you'd seen the look on her face, Jack, you wouldn't be so quick to laugh it off."

"I'm not laughing at anything. You obviously think there's something to this, otherwise you wouldn't have come to me about it. What else makes you think that Hannah may have taken Meleah?"

Tarrant rubbed his aching head. "I don't know," he said in frustration. "Everything is so fuzzy."

"Take your time, son, just tell me what you were thinking when you had this brainstorm about Hannah."

"One minute I was standing there, drinking one of Charlotte's concoctions. I was just thinking to myself . . . thinking . . . and then this memory came back to me. It was of Hannah at the pool party. Maybe it was the tone of her voice, or the look on her face, or a combination of both of those things, but while she was sitting at the bar, she followed you with her eyes. They were so full of hate, Jack. She blamed you for your wife's death.''

"That's ridiculous!" Jack shouted. "Hannah has never said a word to me about blaming me for Marian's death. Never! She's like family to me. If she had something against me, I would have known it."

"You trust her?" Tarrant asked softly.

"What kind of question is that?"

"A reasonable one," Tarrant answered flatly.

"Of course I trust her."

"Like you trust me?"

"Yes."

"Why?"

"Why what?"

"Why do you trust me."

"Because you've never given me a reason not to trust you."

"Is that why you sent the officer to follow me? Is that the kind of trust you have in me?"

It was Jack's turn to be uneasy. "There was nothing personal in that, son. The officer was only doing his job."

"I know that. But that didn't make it any easier to take."

"I know you'd never do anything to hurt Meleah, Tarrant. I know you care about her."

"I love her," Tarrant said stoutly. "I asked her to marry me."

"I kind of figured that you might get around to it. I didn't figure it would happen so fast. So what did she say? Did she say yes?"

Tarrant nodded tightly.

Jack whooped once, slapping his thigh. "I knew she would! I had a feeling about you, Tarrant. I just knew you were the one."

"Is that why you hired me without checking out my references?"

"Sure is."

"And why you pushed me toward Meleah?"

"Uh-huh," Jack said, grinning broadly.

"You trust me," Tarrant repeated.

"Son, I trusted you with my daughter's life."

"Well, you shouldn't have!" Tarrant snarled. His tone broke through Jack's celebration like a sledgehammer.

"What do you mean?"

"You're not as good a judge of character as you think you are, Jack." Tarrant's tone was filled with so much venom that Jack's face went from beaming to belligerent in a flash.

"Something on your mind, son?"

"Stop calling me that! Stop treating me like I'm part of your family. I'm not. And I don't deserve to be—not after what I almost did to you." Tarrant started talking. He talked as if his life depended on it. It did. If he didn't confess to someone what he and Amber had planned to do, his guilt would gradually eat him up from the inside out.

"You tried to break me," Jack said, his voice flat and cold. "I took you in, gave you a job, treated you like a son . . . and you tried to ruin me? Why? Why! Was it the money?"

"No, Jack. It was for my sister. It was for my family. For revenge."

"So why are you telling me all of this now? You could have gone on with your plan. But then, you would have lost Meleah."

"If we don't find her soon, we may still lose her. I'm

telling you this because you trusted me, and I almost ruined you. Hannah may pretend to be your friend, but she isn't. She has Meleah. I can't prove it; but my gut tells me that it's true. If I'm wrong, then you can have me thrown in jail, or in a nut house. I don't care."

"Don't get all maudlin on me, Tarrant. Don't you dare stand there and tell me that without Meleah, you wouldn't want to go on with your life."

"I don't have to tell you. You know that it's true."

"So," Jack said, after a long, expelled breath. "Do we tell Officer Croft what you think you know?"

"For the last time, Elliot, think about what you're doing!" Meleah cried out, trying to make her cousin see reason. "Just think about it. If you think you can just rob a bank and get away with it, you're out of your mind!"

"I'm not crazy!" Elliot snarled. "Stop saying that. I'm not crazy. You're the one who's crazy . . . thinking that you could shut us out, treat us like dirt, because you've got money now. You know what really galls me? You showed that thick-necked, earring-wearing grease monkey more real affection than you showed me. You treated me like one of your low-wage flunkies. I'm not going to forget that, cuz. Not ever. Now shut up, and get moving!"

Meleah closed her mouth with an audible click. Elliot meant what he'd said. If he couldn't get Meleah to make the transfer, he'd just as soon kill her, and try again with Jack.

Rubbing her wrists to restore circulation, Meleah started for the upper deck. As she stuck her head through the door, she thought she saw a movement out of the corner of her eye. She hardly dared to hope.

She kept moving. Maybe it was her imagination, maybe it wasn't. If it wasn't, she didn't want Elliot to have an inkling of what was going on. Because if it wasn't her imagination, if she had actually seen someone, she knew that they were there to help her. There was no doubt that the stealthy movement she thought she saw was there for her. A friend of Elliot's would have made themselves known. Wouldn't they?

"So what happens after I make the transfer?" Meleah asked.

"I let you go."

"Just like that? No more guns, no more ropes, no more hostage?"

"Just like that."

"Why don't I believe you?"

"You don't have to, Meleah. I don't expect you to buy in to what I'm telling you. You're too cynical for that."

"You mean smart." Meleah kept talking. She wanted to keep Elliot occupied so her would-be rescuer would have time to complete whatever preparations they were making to get her out of there. "No matter how many brains you have lined up ready to help you hide Pop's money, there will be someone smarter to come along, and find out what you did with it. No wrong goes unpunished, Ell."

"I am so sick of your moralizing! No one is going to punish me anymore. I've had all of the punishment I can stomach."

"You're wrong, son."

Both Elliot and Meleah spun around.

"Pops!"

"Jack!"

They hailed simultaneously.

"Pops, how did you—" Meleah began, moving toward her father.

Elliot grabbed her arm, jerking her back. "Oh, no, you don't, little missy. Get away from me, Uncle Jack."

"Let her go, Elliot," Jack warned. "There's nowhere for you to run. I've got the police waiting at all the exits."

"You're a liar. There's nobody here, or they would have moved in by now."

"I asked them to stay back. I told them I could talk you out of here before anyone gets hurt."

"No one is going to get hurt, as long as you let me do what I've set out to do." He squeezed Meleah's arm, and jammed the gun into her side. "See this, dear old Uncle Jack? If you don't move back, I'll kill her. I swear, I will!"

"What do you want, Elliot?" Jack tried to keep his voice calm and controlled. Inside he was starting to panic. Tarrant was right, sort of! It wasn't Hannah who'd taken Meleah. But she was indirectly responsible. When they'd gone to her house looking for her, she hadn't seemed surprised that Meleah was missing. She was almost gloating. When they pressed her for information, she only laughed. That wasn't the Hannah he'd known over the years. The woman gloating over his daughter's predicament was some insane, madwoman bent on revenge for slights—real or imagined. She had passed on that poison to her son. It took Bill Caudle, her husband, to calm her down and force her to tell what she knew about Meleah. Only then could they piece together Elliot's strange bond with his mother and his twisted plan to get revenge for her.

"He wants the money, Pops," Meleah answered for him. "He wants me to transfer it into some account."

"Is that all?" Jack laughed. "Is that all you want is money? Son, you can have it. Take it all! I don't give a damn about that. You can have every red cent, if you just let Meleah go."

"It's not just about the money, Jack. Don't get me wrong. I want that, too. But what I really want is to see you suffer like you made my mother suffer when you cut her loose."

Jack moved toward Elliot as he spoke.

"Stay back!" he screeched, waving the gun.

"Listen to me very carefully, Meleah." Jack spoke slowly and deliberately. "We're going to walk out of here, you and me."

"I'm warning you, Uncle Jack." Elliot pointed the gun directly at him this time.

"Pops, I can't. He's out of his mind. He'll kill you. Don't push him, Pops."

"He won't hurt us, Meleah. Just do what I tell you, when I tell you to do it."

Meleah took a step toward him.

"You bitch! Don't you move!" Elliot tried to pull Meleah back, and maintained his aim at Jack at the same time.

"Come to me, Meleah. Come on!" Jack urged. "Move, girl!"

"No!" Elliot screamed. He raised the pistol, and fired once into the air

Another shot rang out. And another! And another! They seemed to be coming from all around her. Meleah screamed, and brought her hands up over her ears. She tried to duck down, to scramble to get out of the way from the barrage of bullets. Suddenly someone clasped her around her waist, and dumped her over the boat railing. She fell head first, flailing her arms, into the choppy waters of the Gulf. She didn't have time to scream before water rushed into her nose and mouth. She kicked and clawed, trying to reorient herself for a dive to the surface.

Seconds later another body plunged into the water next to her. Tarrant! It was Tarrant! He reached out to her, grabbing her wrist. Meleah clung to him as he pulled her toward the surface. As they broke free, Meleah flung her arms around his neck, sobbing and trembling uncontrollably.

"It's all right, Meleah. It's all right," he soothed. "You're safe now."

"Oh, my God, Tarrant! How did you find me?"

"It's a long story," Tarrant said, treading water. "I'll explain it all when I get you back on dry land."

"Pops!" she called out suddenly. "Is he all right? Pops!"

Jack leaned over the railing. "I'm here, Meleah. Hold on. I'm throwing out a line to you."

"Oh, thank God!" she breathed. "Thank God you're all right. Where's Elliot? What happened to him?"

"Nothing's happened that a good hundred years in prison won't cure," Jack muttered.

Tarrant boosted Meleah by the waist to help her grab on to the ladder. She had barely reached the top before Jack pulled her over the edge, and hugged her close to him.

"I was so scared for you, Meleah girl," he said, desperately squeezing her. "I don't know what I would have done if anything had happened to you."

Several police officers tried to converge around them, but Tarrant waved them back. "Just give her a moment, please!"

"Tarrant." Meleah held out her hand to him. She moved from Jack's arms to Tarrant's.

"You're going to be all right, Meleah," he murmured, drawing her closer to him.

"No, Tarrant," she said into his shoulder. "No, I don't think I am."

Tarrant caught her as she suddenly went limp, and slumped to the deck.

Meleah awoke to muted sunlight streaming into the room, as it slanted across the bed. She stretched languorously, listening to the sound of pounding surf and crying gulls easing her back to wakefulness. She couldn't remember the last time she awoke to the sound of the Gulf waters against the rocky piers. She sat up abruptly, rubbing her eyes, and staring at the unfamiliar sights around her. This wasn't her room! She couldn't hear the Gulf from her own room. Where was she? The huge canopy bed she rested in was draped in white eyelet lace. The room was filled with pieces of French Provincial furniture, from the bed, to the chest of drawers, to the vanity mirror across the room.

She threw back the lace covers, and stepped onto plush carpet. She looked down at her feet, wiggling her toes, and reveling in the luxuriant feel of the carpet. That's when she noticed the clothes she wore. No more sopping wet T-shirt and jeans she'd worn the night Elliot abducted her. Instead she wore a nightgown of gossamer-thin cotton, trimmed in cobalt blue ribbon. So dainty, so romantic—the feelings evoked by the clothes she wore were a far cry from the harsh, terror-stricken hours she'd spent.

The events of the past few days suddenly swept over her. Despite the warmth of the room, Meleah felt a deep chill settle into her bones that made her teeth rattle. She reached for a matching robe that was draped across the bed. She then ran her fingers over the finely crafted wood of the bed posts. Where was she?

Another cry from a seagull caught her attention.

Her room overlooked the Gulf. The sound of crashing waves, and the smell of the salty spray, came through double doors that led to a circular balcony. She walked through the double bay doors. When Meleah pushed them open, she found that she was on the second floor of a three-story house. The smell of the Gulf waters was thick in her nostrils. She shaded her eyes against the sun's glare, and looked below her. From the edge of the house to almost a half-mile beyond stretched the beach. She looked up one end of the beach, and down the other. It had to be a private beach. There were no lifeguards on duty, no gaudy, rented shade umbrellas, no tourists. The nearest house was at least a mile away.

"I've lost my mind," she murmured. "Either that, or I actually drowned when I fell overboard, and now I'm in heaven." She returned to her room, at a loss for what to do next.

Meleah made up her mind to explore further when she heard soft knock at the door.

"Who is it?" she called out. For a moment, her heart pounded in her chest. She looked around for something to defend herself, if it came to that. Her eyes widened when Tarrant stuck his head in the door. "I didn't know if you were awake yet. I didn't want to disturb you."

"You're not disturbing me," she said cautiously.

"How did you sleep?"

"Obviously like a log. I don't even remember your bringing me here."

"I had my doctor give you a mild sedative."

"You drugged me."

"It was either that or watch your rip yourself to shreds with nightmares."

"I guess I was a little out of my mind."

"You had a right to be. But you're all right now," Tarrant insisted. "You're safe."

"Is this a safe house, then?" Meleah thought that maybe the police might have brought her here until she could testify against Elliot.

"You might call it that. But I prefer to call it home. It's my family's beach house."

"Home?"

"This is where I go when I want to get away for a while."

"Your home? You've got to be kidding. You can't afford a place like this on a bartender's salary!"

"Does this mean you're considering giving me a raise?" he teased her.

"Not likely." She snorted, again marveling at the luxurious room. "Anything I could offer you would insult you."

"Not everything," Tarrant said huskily. He wondered if she knew what effect seeing her like this had on him. As she stood in the doorway, with the sun streaming behind her, her body was perfectly revealed to him.

"How did I get here?"

"I brought you here."

"Why?"

"To keep an eye on you. You've been through a lot the past few days."

"Where is Pops?" Meleah suddenly said in alarm.

"He and Charlotte are . . ." Tarrant paused dramatically.

"Are what?" Were they dead? Had Elliot somehow hurt them?

"Don't get yourself upset again, Meleah. They're fine. They're better than fine."

"Where are they?"

"Your father and Charlotte are sharing a suite of rooms in another part of the house."

"I might have known," Meleah said, putting her hands on her hips. "Not even a kidnapping can pry those two apart."

Tarrant smiled. Now that was the spirited woman he'd grown to love! He'd been so worried about her. It had been two days since they rescued her from the boat. Two days! Most of that time she was lightly sedated to help her rest. "Are you hungry, Meleah? I can have something brought up to you."

"What time is it?"

"Almost noon."

"Just a muffin and coffee."

"Orange marmalade?" he offered, knowing it was her favorite. Meleah broke into a smile.

"Okay, make it two muffins."

"That's my girl. Be right back." When he returned, Tarrant pushed the door open with his shoulder. His hands were filled with a tray of several muffins, raisin toast, juice, and coffee.

"Mind if I join you?"

"Go right ahead," she said. The only place for them both to sit was the bed, so she gestured toward the patio. "Outside?"

He set the tray on the patio table, and gestured for to her take a seat. For half an hour, they sat in relative silence, eating breakfast and enjoying the sounds of the Gulf waters. Finally, curiosity made her break the silence.

"How, Tarrant?"

"How what?"

"How can you afford all of this?" She swept her arm to indicate the house, the private beach, everything. "And don't give me any line about tips and overtime either."

"I worked hard for everything I have, Meleah. I want to set you straight about that from the beginning."

"You mean you haven't done anything illegal to be so successful."

"That's right."

"So how did you do it? Did you win the lottery, too?"

"My family isn't hurting for money, Meleah."

Meleah didn't know how to react to that statement. All of this time, she'd known that there was something about him that she couldn't put her finger on. He was too smooth, too polished. But he worked hard, and he'd saved her life more than once. So she'd put aside her doubts, and in the interim, had given him her heart.

"What were you doing at Papa Jack's?" she said quietly.

It was time to tell the truth. "I came to get evidence against your family. For Amber. As soon as I did, we were going to have a battery of lawyers at our disposal to clear her of the accident and . . . for something else." He didn't want to say. After all they had been through, he couldn't lose her now by showing her the ugly truth.

"You said evidence . . . for what? For a lawsuit? You blamed Pops for what happened to your sister?"

"What would you have done it if was your family lying in a hospital bed—barely holding on to life? Wouldn't you want revenge? The police report said that their blood alcohol level was twice the legal limit. When Amber regained consciousness I found out where she'd been that night. I swore to her that I would prove that your father was negligent in serving alcohol to people who'd obviously reached their limit. That's why I took the job, Meleah."

"You wanted to sue us," Meleah said, clamping down tightly with every word.

"Yes."

"You lying, conniving, thieving bastard!" She picked up her plate, and threw it at him. "You tried to ruin us! When Pops won that lottery, you couldn't wait to swoop in like some kind of buzzard and take it away from us." She paused for breath as her anger and humiliation at being duped by him sank in. "And was going to bed with me part of the plan? Did you think I'd let a little pillow talk give you the evidence you needed against Pops? And your marriage proposal! God, how could I have been so stupid! You're worse than Elliot!"

"You proposed to me, remember?" he said calmly, in the wake of her outrage. "When I accepted you, I meant it, Meleah! You have to believe that. I had no idea that things would go between us the way they did. When I realized that I'd fallen in love with you, I told Amber that I couldn't go through with it. I couldn't hurt you. Not for all of the money in the world."

"Why should I believe you? You've lied to me for so long!"

"No matter how good or bad of a liar I was, Meleah, there are some things a man can't fake."

Meleah saw the raw, unfiltered truth in his eyes. His eyes, usually warm and teasing in regard to her, had suddenly darkened with long-suppressed desire. She should have been repulsed, disgusted by the naked desire she read in his face. How could he think she'd still want him after learning what he tried to do?

Tarrant grasped her hand, and raised it to his own lips. One by one, he drew her fingers into his mouth and laved them with a warm, wet tongue. With his other hand, he drew himself to her.

Meleah sat immobile in her chair as Tarrant knelt in front of her, trailing kisses up her arm. He paused at the juncture between her neck and shoulder and nipped softly. Meleah moaned audibly.

"No! Don't touch me! You liar! You used us. You used me!"

"Meleah, you know how much family means to you. It doesn't mean any less for me. I love my sister as much, or more than you love your father. But when she asked me to destroy your father by planting evidence against him, I couldn't."

"Afraid of going to jail?" Meleah sneered.

"Afraid of losing you," he contradicted. "I wouldn't risk that for anything in the world. Not money, not revenge, not anything!"

Meleah was hurt that he'd deceived her. But outweighing the hurt was the knowledge that he'd come to her aid time and time again. If he were out only to get her money, would he even bother caring for her?

"You do believe me, Meleah, don't you?" he insisted. "You know that I love you . . . and that is a bond that not even family can break?"

"I don't even know who you are!" she began.

Tarrant's eager mouth covered hers and cut off her protests.

"I'm a man who loves you, Meleah," he whispered hoarsely. "I'm the man who needs you, who wants you, and will always cherish you. When I asked you to marry me, I meant it then, and I mean it now."

Meleah turned her face away, exposing her throat to his slow, languorous kisses. Each one became more intense than the last. She was still so unsure. So much doubt clouded her mind. Doubt—and desire. There was no denying that. Even as she thought she should push him away, she was hoping that he would continue to touch her.

Tarrant grasped her shoulders, and with a force fueled with impatience, pulled her robe and gown aside.

She leaned away from him, trying to free herself; but he quickly closed the distance between them, and buried his face in the billowy softness of her breasts.

"Tarrant!" She clasped the back of his head, and pressed him closer. Tarrant's hands slid to her knees, and parted them. He pulled her to the edge of the chair so that the core of her desire collided with his hardening groin. Meleah felt him tense, every muscle in his body suddenly taut.

"Let's go inside, Meleah," he said. "I don't want to put on a show for the world."

She rose from her chair, and walked back into the bedroom. She didn't say a word as he took her hand. There were no words, no eloquent phrases that could describe what she saw in his expression. It was enough to know that he wanted her like no man had—no man ever could.

Tarrant turned to her. "Say that you'll marry me, Meleah. Tell me that you and I will always be together."

"We will be, Tarrant," she said with absolute certainty. "We will be."

Tarrant placed his fingers softly against Meleah's lips and whispered, "Shh! Hear that? They're playing our song."

Meleah's ears strained to hear. All she could hear was the piercing, poignant cry of a lone seagull circling the sky. A moment later, another seagull answered its call. Meleah smiled. Its mate, perhaps, separated by land and by sea, had come through who-knew-what adversities to find the other again.

"Care to dance?" Tarrant asked, taking her in his arms again.

The pounding of the waves beyond the bay doors was no match for the pounding of Meleah's heart, as she settled into the arms of the man whose love brought sweet harmony to the song of her soul.

EPILOGUE

One Year Later

"Come on in, Mama! The water's fine!"

"No, I think I'll stay right here, thank you. In fact, why don't you come on out and eat a little something, Alexa."

"Aw, man! Do I have to?"

"Do like your mother said, Squeak, and come out of the water." Tarrant pointed to his niece, then indicated a spot next to him on the beach blanket.

Alexa bobbed up from water. Her bright orange and white polka dot bathing suit contrasted with the fluorescent pink floats encircling her arms and waist. As she trudged up the beach, she bent down for a moment to examine something of interest to her in the warm sand.

"Oooo-wheee! Look what I found, Uncle Rant! Lookee! Lookee! Lookee!" She ran toward the huge, striped umbrella where her uncle and mother sat as they sipped lemonade and watched her play in the bluish gray waters of the Gulf of Mexico.

"Incoming!" Tarrant called out as Alexa barreled toward them, churning up sand as she plopped next to him. He covered their drinks with his hands to avoid getting a mouth full of grit the next time they drank.

"I found a tan and white striped one this time. See, Mama?"

Alexa stuck a pointed shell under her mother's nose. "Yes, it's quite lovely, baby. How many does that make now?"

"Six," Alexa said proudly. She opened her beach bag and dropped the treasured find into it.

"Maybe you ought to make sure that there isn't something still living in that shell this time," Tarrant warned.

Alexa giggled and nudged her mother. "Maybe you shouldn't be stuffing shells in your pocket before checking to make sure there's nothin' still living in them, huh, Uncle Rant?"

Mother and daughter collapsed into a fit of laughter at the memory of Tarrant clawing at his swim trunks when he realized that the pretty shell he'd picked up for Alexa still had an occupant.

Tarrant screwed up his face and mimicked Alexa's tone. "Maybe you ought to make sure there's nothing still living in them. Ha. Ha. Very funny."

"Don't be mad, Uncle Rant. It's not as if you're allergic to hermit crabs."

"Trust me, Squeak," Tarrant said, rolling his eyes comically. "No man wants to be told that he has crabs in his pants."

Alexa laughed again. "You know, Uncle Rant, that's sounds exactly like something that skeezer Miss Julie would say."

"Watch your language," Tarrant responded automatically. He tugged affectionately on Alexa's pigtail. "So when are you going to start calling me dad, too? Don't you think it's time?" He glanced at over Alexa's mother—her new mother. Meleah Harmon Cole.

Meleah swatted Tarrant with a towel. "Now, big guy. Don't go sounding all jealous on us. Give Alexa some time. There are a lot of changes she has to get used to."

"It didn't take her any time at all to get used to calling you 'mama,' " he grumbled. Yet he was pleased that Alexa had come to love Meleah as deeply as he had—and so quickly.

"You'll always be my uncle Rant," Alexa said, flinging her arms around her uncle and giving him a tight squeeze. "My favorite uncle. It just sounds too weird calling you my dad. But don't worry, Uncle—I mean, Dad. I'll get used to it."

Tarrant gathered Meleah in his arms, as well, as he shouted, "I feel a Kodak moment coming on. Everybody, group hug!"

Meleah burst out laughing as Tarrant used the opportunity to tickle her as she and Alexa pretended to try to wriggle free from his grasp. "Stop! Stop that!" she gasped.

"Tickle him, Mama!" Alexa pointed to a spot on Tarrant's bare torso. "He's really ticklish there."

Tarrant threw Meleah a look that said: *as if you didn't know.* Meleah read the look perfectly. Her shy, yet incredibly seductive smile in return made Tarrant want to jump up, fold up their beach picnic gear, and head back to the house. But he knew if he tried to end their picnic early—the first full day of summer, the first full day with Alexa legally adopted as their daughter—he would never hear the end of it. Alexa would never give him a moment's peace. And he needed more than a moment to show Meleah exactly what he was feeling right now. He would just have to put a lid on his passion. Besides, there would be plenty of time to demonstrate his feelings for Meleah later.

His parents, Ashton and Beryl, and the other newlyweds, Charlotte and Jack, were taking Alexa to dinner for a special grandparents only dinner. After that, they would spend the rest of the evening trying to figure out who would get Alexa first—since she'd promised to split her entire weekend between both sets of grandparents. Tarrant shook his head, grinning to himself. The arguing between the grandparents alone would give them more than enough time to make up for whatever he thought he was missing now.

For a brief moment, his happiness dimmed. Speaking of missing, he wondered what his sister was doing now. After Amber had left the hospital, she'd left them all. The D.A. had to let her go. Though she had been driving the night of the accident, she had not been drunk. The only one they could charge with vehicular manslaughter was himself a victim of the accident. With nothing to hold her down, nothing to hold her responsible, Amber was on the loose again.

It was a couple of weeks before they had an idea of where she'd gone. She'd admitted herself into a substance abuse clinic somewhere in Houston for a while—claiming that the hospital painkillers had her hooked on drugs again. For a while, Tarrant thought the lessons she'd learned during her ordeal would be lasting ones. But even that didn't last long. She was in and out of clinics, in and out of trouble. Same old Amber. Nothing learned.

A few more months of her runaway mentality and a brief petition to the courts were all they needed to transfer custodial rights to Tarrant. At that moment, he'd made up his mind. He was Amber's brother. He was not her keeper. He couldn't help her if she didn't want or need his help. But he could do something for Alexa. He would do something for her. He would love her and keep her. He would cherish her, knowing that those sentiments would be returned tenfold.

Meleah clasped his hand and squeezed, sensing his mental withdrawal. She leaned over and whispered seductively in his ear, "Last one in the water buys the next round at Papa Jack's."

With that challenge issued, she jumped up and raced for the water's edge. Tarrant let her pull ahead of him—content to watch the way her body moved. It didn't matter that she beat him. She was so much happier whenever she did. Not that he made it easy for her. He knew she didn't like to lose. She liked being handled with kid gloves even less. Her competitive spirit matched him move for move—whether they were shooting out the lights at Papa Jack's or turning out the lights to make their own moves in the privacy of their bedroom.

Meleah turned around, crooked her finger at him, and dove into the water. She welcomed the rush of the water around her as easily as she would welcome Tarrant's embrace. Now, she was not afraid of the water. He had taught her to swim. He had taught her to love. Fear had been replaced with confidence. Caution had been replaced with caring. She knew in her heart that no matter how far she went, he would always be there—ever watchful, ever loving.

ABOUT THE AUTHOR

Geri Guillaume is the pseudonym for an author who lives in Texas. A technical writer, she is also the mother of two children and raises horses.

Coming in July from Arabesque Books . . .

__ISLAND MAGIC by Bette Ford
1-58314-113-8 $5.99US/$7.99CAN

When Cassandra Mosely needs a break from her work—and from her relationship with Gordan Kramer—she vacations in Martinique and finds herself in a new romance. But Gordan is determined to win her back and with a little island magic, the two just may rediscover their love . . .

__IMAGES OF ECSTASY by Louré Bussey
1-58314-115-4 $5.99US/$7.99CAN

Shay Hilton is shocked when her ex-fiancé is murdered in her apartment, but when she comes face to face with her prosecutor, Braxton Steele, she is overcome with desire. When a storm traps the unlikely couple together, it's the beginning of a passion that will change both of their lives forever . . .

__FAMILY TIES by Jacquelin Thomas
1-58314-114-6 $5.99US/$7.99CAN

When Dr. McKenzie Ashford discovers that her new boss, Marc Chandler, may be responsible for her mother's death, she is determined to obtain justice. She never imagines that her quest might uncover long-hidden family secrets . . . or that her heart might be overcome with love for Marc.

__SNOWBOUND WITH LOVE by Alice Wootson
1-58314-148-0 $5.99US/$7.99CAN

After a car accident, Charlotte Thompson develops a case of amnesia and seeks comfort in the arms of her handsome rescuer, Tyler Fleming. But as they fall in love, Tyler realizes her true identity as the person he holds responsible for the tragedy that nearly destroyed his life. Will he be able to give his heart to this woman that he has hated for so long?

Call toll free **1-888-345-BOOK** to order by phone or use this coupon to order by mail. *ALL BOOKS AVAILABLE JULY 1, 2000.*

Name _____

Address _____

City_____ State _____ Zip _____

Please send me the books I have checked above.

I am enclosing	$_____
Plus postage and handling*	$_____
Sales tax (in NY, TN, and DC)	$_____
Total amount enclosed	$_____

*Add $2.50 for the first book and $.50 for each additional book.
Send check or money order (no cash or CODs) to: **Arabesque Books, Dept. C.O., 850 Third Avenue, 16th Floor, New York, NY 10022**
Prices and numbers subject to change without notice.
All orders subject to availability.

Visit our website at **www.arabesquebooks.com**